THE
Lost
EVACUEE

Cathy loves writing because it gives pleasure to others. She finds writing an extension of herself and it gives her great satisfaction. Cathy says, 'There is nothing like seeing your book in print, because so much loving care has been given to bringing that book into being.' Cathy lives in Cambridgeshire.

CATHY SHARP

THE *Lost* EVACUEE

HarperCollins*Publishers*

HarperCollins*Publishers*
1 London Bridge Street
London SE1 9GF

www.harpercollins.co.uk

HarperCollins*Publishers*
Macken House, 39/40 Mayor Street Upper
Dublin 1, D01 C9W8, Ireland

Published by HarperCollins*Publishers* 2023
1

A catalogue record for this book
is available from the British Library

ISBN: 978-0-00-853124-9 (PB)
ISBN: 978-0-00-853125-6 (TPB)

Typeset in Sabon Lt Std by Palimpsest Book Production Ltd,
Falkirk, Stirlingshire

Printed and Bound in the UK using
100% Renewable Electricity at CPI Group (UK) Ltd

This book is produced from independently certified FSC™ paper
to ensure responsible forest management.

For more information visit: www.harpercollins.co.uk/green

CHAPTER 1

Everyone was crowding up on deck, preparing to disembark from the ship that had brought them from England to Halifax in Canada. Over the days and weeks of their voyage, Julie Miller had met and talked to several of the children who had, like her, been sent out by the British Government to Canada – to protect them from the war that was raging in Europe, Julie had been informed by the woman in charge of the evacuation. Her father had been killed in France, her mother was ill, dying in a hospice, and her grandparents were long dead. Still only fifteen, she had no one who was prepared to give her a home and so she had been sent to a new country for a new life. No one had asked her how she felt about this, it was just presented to her as a fact and so Julie felt that no one cared whether she wanted to go or not. Crying did no good, even though at times she felt close to despair, but she'd found some comfort in caring for the younger children.

Julie had been sent to an orphanage after her father's death, when her mother, who had suffered from

1

diabetes for years, overcome with grief and often unable to afford her medication, fell into a coma one day. She had been taken away to hospital before Julie got home from school so mother and daughter never even had the chance to say goodbye. Rebellious, and not truly understanding why she'd been banished from her home, Julie had run away from the orphanage and gone back to the grimy streets of London, hoping to find her mother, only to discover that the house she had lived in all her life had been taken over by a stranger and her mother was dying, so Martha Cole, a neighbour who had been kind to Julie in the past, had told her. Martha had gone to the council for help and they'd said the best thing was to send Julie to Canada through the Government's evacuee scheme, because she couldn't run home from there.

'Please let me live here with you,' Julie had begged Martha. 'I'll be good – I won't cause you any trouble,' she promised, her eyes filled with tears. 'Dad wanted me to stay on at school and get a good job but I'll leave and go to work in the biscuit factory, and then I'll look after you.'

For a moment she'd seen hesitation in Martha's face, but then she'd shaken her head. 'I'm sorry, Julie. I'm old, your mother is beyond help, and I'm not sure this country will survive this war – we suffered too much in the last one. Go to Canada, girl, and make the most of the opportunities there. I'm told it's the best for you and believe me, if they'd have me, I'd come too.' She'd given the girl a printed paper, outlining all the benefits she would get from being evacuated but Julie had thrust it aside. She didn't want to be sent to a place where she wouldn't know anyone. It wasn't fair and it wasn't right.

In vain, Julie had pleaded to be allowed to stay, clinging to the hand of the only woman who had shown her kindness since her mother took ill, but Martha couldn't keep her and so a man from the council had escorted her to the collection centre and left her there. Julie had held back her tears then and she wouldn't cry now, even though inside she was shaking. This new world, this big country that Martha had said was so wonderful, looked strange and alien with its crowded waterfront, the buildings so tall and imposing and different to the smoky familiarity of London and she was afraid of what her new life would be like. Would the people who claimed her be kind or uncaring? Life at the orphanage had been difficult, the guardians harsh, the rules strict. All Julie wanted was to have her father put his strong arms around her and hear his deep laugh, but she knew that would never happen again. He had died fighting for his country . . .

Julie's throat was tight with emotion as she fought to banish the panic inside her, telling herself that perhaps it wouldn't be too bad. Surely there were kind folk here? But she'd met with little kindness in the last few years so had little hope of it now.

She looked around for Davey Blake, the older of the two boys she'd travelled out from England with, but she couldn't see him in the crowd of children lining the ship's rails to get a better view of the shore and the city of Halifax as it came closer and closer. Some of the buildings were very tall; there were tall buildings in London too, but these seemed to scrape the sky and were newer and stark in her eyes. She had been told some of the history of the place she'd come to and knew that the first Europeans to settle there had been the French, in the early 1600s, followed by the British in 1749. She knew, too, that Halifax Harbour was one of the largest natural harbours in the world and that in 1917 a munitions ship had blown up in the world's largest man-made explosion, after a collision with another ship, killing almost 2,000 people and injuring about 9,000 others as well as destroying many buildings. Now, though, Halifax was a thriving port, a busy hub for seaborn trade.

But what did she care for such things? Julie sucked in her breath, fear making her tremble as she longed for a comforting hand to cling to or a strong arm to protect her. All she had ever hoped for was to be loved, for someone to comfort her when she was hurt, but with an ailing mother and a father too often away, her tears had been shed alone and in the dark. Her grief was carried deep inside.

On the voyage it hadn't been too bad, because she'd had two younger children to care for, Beth and Arthur – and Davy Blake to help her. Thrust into a frightening situation, they had bonded, the younger ones clinging to Julie for support. She'd cared for them, giving them the affection and love that had so often been denied her. Davy was nearer her age, a lively lad, always talking, busy exploring and finding out what they needed to know from friends he'd made amongst the crew. She wished he was here now but he'd said goodbye to her earlier and wished her luck in her new

4

life. Julie knew that Davey was determined to return to England and thought he might have hidden, hoping to stow away and go back to London on the same ship. Julie didn't want to go back to a place where no one cared about her and so she would manage by herself – but she was holding tightly to Beth's hand. Arthur, the youngest of them all, was clinging to her skirt as always and she knew he was terrified. She looked down at him and smiled warmly despite her own fears.

'You'll soon have a new home, Arthur, love,' she told him cheerfully. 'Lots of folk want a boy.'

Julie thought Arthur had the face of an angel. When she'd first met him, his hair had looked dark, but once she'd washed it, she'd seen it was fair and his face was young and innocent. He was almost too pretty for a boy of five and she hoped his new family would be kind. People weren't always kind and even when they were your own family they weren't always to be trusted.

A face flashed into Julie's mind and for a moment she trembled inside as she remembered the heavy tread up the stairs and then hot breath in her face, stinking of beer, as she kept her eyes closed tightly and pretended to sleep. She'd refused to open them even when the deep voice commanded her to wake up, but she'd felt his hands – her uncle's hands! – touching her, and the memory made her shudder. At least she was safe from him now! Had he not been away serving in the army she might have had to live with him – and that would have been worse than being sent here.

Pushing the disturbing memory from her mind, Julie looked around her once more as Arthur tugged at her skirt as if determined to hold onto her forever.

'I don't want a new family. I want to stay with Julie,' a small voice said and she glanced down at the child clinging to her hand.

Beth had cried a lot for her mother in the beginning and Julie had taken her on her lap and comforted her, telling her stories she'd made up in her head. Now Beth followed her wherever she went. The fear in her eyes touched Julie's heart, partly because it echoed her own, and she bent down to kiss her and reassure her that it would be all right, that her new mummy would love her but even as she spoke the words, Julie knew there were no guarantees.

She understood that they would all go to new homes. It had been explained to them on the ship by the purser, who was kind enough but wasn't familiar with the needs of small children.

Some children had been allotted to families who had made their wishes known in advance, mostly childless couples who wanted a family. If Arthur or Beth was taken by someone like that, they might be lucky enough to be loved and happy in their new homes, but Julie was older, sixteen in a few weeks and most folk wanted young children they could make their own, therefore she would be considered too old for adoption. She shivered in a chill wind as the sun went behind some clouds.

Overhead, the seagulls swirled and dipped, their harsh cries seeming to be a warning to Julie's ears. They had been told the weather could be very cold here in winter and the wind from the sea went through her thin coat. During the voyage she'd spent most of her time in their cabin, caring for the younger ones and avoiding having to look at the dark, restless waves or experience the vast emptiness of the ocean, when there was nothing to be seen but grey water as far as the eye could see.

'I wish we could be together,' Julie said now as Beth's eyes filled with tears, 'but—'

The sound of a booming voice cut across her speech of reassurance. The captain was telling them through his loudhailer that they were docking, to stay on board ship until they were claimed, and she saw that the vessel had come in close to a pier; they would soon be walking into a new life here – but would they be lucky enough to find good people? Julie knew she had to be calm for the sake of Beth and Arthur, but inside her stomach felt queasy with nerves. She clamped her teeth as the ship's engines stopped. It was only a short time now until they were claimed . . .

The crew had been busy as they manoeuvred into place, but now they were laughing and calling to each other, perhaps relieved that the voyage was over. Davey Blake had told Julie they could be attacked by enemy ships out in mid-ocean but nothing had happened, apart from a storm, and they'd all survived the voyage. At least, she and the two little ones had, but where was Davey? Surely nothing could have happened to him? No, he must be hiding. Now the purser was checking names and people had started to come on board, strangers who sounded very different to the folk she'd known in London's East End.

Suddenly, those dirty old streets with their familiar

back-to-back houses, where the kids ran riot in worn-out clothes and often went hungry, seemed safe and very desirable.

'Arthur Gibbs?' the purser said. He looked towards Julie and then nodded. 'Come here, Arthur. Your new parents are waiting for you, lad.'

Arthur clung harder to Julie's skirts. She bent down and took his hand, leading him to the man who had been as kind as he knew how on the voyage, making sure they had food and telling them something about their new country. The man and woman standing just behind him were young, the man not more than thirty, Julie thought, the woman slightly younger. Both had fair hair and nice faces so they might be kind.

'This is Mr and Mrs Henderson,' the purser said and Julie made a mental note of the name. 'They live right here in Halifax and own a store that sells candy and cakes.'

The woman had a sweet smile and, as she held out her hand to Arthur, Julie gave him a gentle push forward. His bottom lip was trembling and for a moment he refused to let go but then the woman bent down and took his arm gently, turning him towards her. 'My name is Emily,' she said and nodded to Julie. 'Thank you for looking after Arthur on the journey. If you need help at any time, let me know.'

Julie thanked her and watched as Emily Henderson led the small boy away. She thought Arthur had been lucky but determined that one day she would visit him at the Hendersons' store to make sure. In her own mind, Julie had decided that she was going to work hard and make something of her life, and when she had a good job and money, she would look for both Arthur and Beth. She would make sure they were well and happy – unless she could keep Beth with her now?

'Julie Miller – this lady has come for you.' The purser's voice interrupted Julie's thoughts and she felt a jolt of fear as she saw the thin-faced woman staring at her. Her eyes were chilly and grey, as was the hair she had dragged back into a tight bun at the back of her head, and she didn't smile as she studied Julie.

'I am Miss Phyllis Cotton,' she said and gave Beth a look of disapproval. 'That child's nose is running – wipe it and do the same for yourself, girl, and then come with me. I don't have time to waste.'

Julie held back, unwilling to follow her. 'What about Beth?' she asked. 'Are you taking her too?'

'Certainly not. Of what use would a child of that age be to me? I see enough of them during the day at my school. The purser will take care of her until her family come for her.'

'Come along, Beth,' the purser said and bent down to pick her up. Beth gave a cry of fright and tried to grab for Julie's hand but her arm had been taken by Miss Cotton and she was pushed roughly ahead of the woman who had claimed her. Beth screamed and cried, calling Julie's name. She turned to look at her, the child's fear and distress causing her own eyes to fill with tears. It was so unfair that this was happening to them and they had no choice but to do as they were told!

'I'll come and see you,' she called, not knowing if it would be possible but wanting to comfort Beth before Miss Cotton hustled her away, Beth's cries of distress following her from the ship.

Her eyes were blurred with tears and Julie was scarcely aware of anything around her other than the crowds of people arriving and leaving. Further down the dockside there were other ships unloading their cargoes and one was loading great bales of something wrapped in tarpaulin. The salty air was spiced with scents, some pleasant like flowers and others strong like fish. Julie stared at a ship preparing to leave, suddenly filled with an urgent desire to get on it and return to England – if that's where it was going – but the hand that held her arm was firm and she was forced to walk on until they had cleared the busy port and she was led to where a man in a brown suit was waiting. He was younger than the woman who held Julie's arm, his hair brown and slicked back from his forehead with oil that smelled of violets.

'This is my brother Joe Cotton,' her captor stated as the man stared but didn't speak. Julie noted that he was just as thin and hard-looking as his sister, despite being younger. 'Joe lives in Halifax and will see us onto the bus.' She looked down her thin nose. 'Is that small bag all you have? Joe thought you would have a trunk to carry, that's why he came.'

Julie squirmed as she saw the disapproval in Miss Cotton's eyes.

'I've only got a spare dress and some knickers,' she said defensively.

'What? Well, it was irresponsible of those who sent you out not to make sure you had sufficient clothes,' Miss Cotton grumbled. 'I daresay I can find a few bits and pieces for you when I get you home, but they won't be new.'

'Where do you live?' Julie asked, finally looking about her at what on further investigation seemed to be much like the industrial area around the docks at home in London. 'Is it far?'

'I live in Lower Sackville,' Miss Cotton replied. 'It is much quieter there than Halifax. Joe says I should set up school here in the heart of Halifax but I do very nicely where I am and I prefer it.'

'You've always liked to be independent and go your own way, Phyllis.' Her brother had seemingly decided her statement worthy of a response. He turned a steely look on Julie. 'I hope you appreciate how lucky you are to have secured a situation as a helper at my sister's school. Just remember your place and do as she tells you, and you'll be fine, girl.'

His voice was harsh but at least he wasn't looking at her the way someone else had – someone who should have loved and protected her but had instead tried to do bad things to her when she was only thirteen. Not that her uncle had succeeded. Julie had bitten his neck so hard it bled and the next day he'd worn a scarf to cover the wound. The look he'd given her was so threatening that she'd known he would make her sorry if she told on him and so she lied when her father had asked her if something was troubling her – and now her father was dead and she could never tell him. Never see his warm smile or feel his strong arms lift her in a bear hug. He was dead and she would never trust anyone again.

Although she didn't like this man and woman who had taken over her life, Julie knew that she had no choice but to go with Miss Cotton. She had no money, no clothes to speak of, and no way of earning a living – but if she was expected to work in a school she would be paid and, once she'd saved enough, she would leave. Julie set her face in what she hoped was an expression of acceptance, but inside she was seething with anger and pain and resentment.

Julie knew she must do as she was asked and work hard and she would – but she wouldn't let anyone take advantage of her ever again. As soon as she could she would leave Miss Cotton and find a place she could call home and then she would look for Beth and Arthur – though the people who had fetched him had looked nice and she felt sure that he would be looked after and loved. It was Beth she worried for. The little girl would be frightened and lonely – and she might not be as lucky in her new home as it seemed Arthur had been.

CHAPTER 2

'I am sure they'll come soon,' Malcolm Ridger said to the little girl with the pale face and big blue eyes. She'd screamed and wept for several minutes after that nice young Julie had been taken off by the harsh-faced woman. Malcolm didn't envy her the life she'd have with Miss Cotton. He knew she was a skinflint and maybe worse. His sister Veronica, who lived in Halifax, had told him as much. Vee lived alone now that their parents were dead and her husband Bill Bittern had been killed in an accident at their sawmill five years earlier. Vee had never married again and never would.

'No one could replace Bill in my heart,' she'd told her brother. 'Besides, I've got you – why do I need anyone else?'

Malcolm had just hugged her. He worried for her when he was away at sea, doing the job he loved as the purser, taking care of things and people who needed reassurance while Vee lived in that big house all by herself. True, it was situated in a nice area, well away from the busy port and she didn't go short of anything because Bill had left her the house, a sawmill and woodlands as well as various other properties and quite a bit of money, while their parents had left their store to Malcolm and Vee jointly. If they hadn't, he would have given her half, and she kept an eye on their manager, Selmer Connors, though he would rather have died than cheat her. Malcolm knew that the man, a widower with a daughter, admired Vee from a distance and sometimes wished he would do something about it, because he suspected she was lonely.

A whimper of despair made him look at the child he was still holding in his arms. All the other children had been claimed and it was just Beth waiting now. Her new family were very late and Malcolm began to wonder if they were coming. Sometimes people offered to take a child and then changed their minds; they were supposed to inform the authorities if that happened but they didn't always and it looked as if that was what had occurred here.

Having never married, Malcolm didn't have much experience of dealing with children and wasn't sure what to do or say to the child, but then he remembered the barley sugars in his uniform pocket and he gave her two. The look on her face as she popped them in her mouth was something to behold and he smiled, feeling pleased as she stopped weeping. She looked at him.

'Are you my new daddy?' she asked as she swallowed the last of her sweets, having sucked both until they melted away. 'Can we go home now?'

For a moment Malcolm didn't know what to say. He gave one last look around the deck and then sighed.

'I'm not your daddy,' he said, 'but I might be an uncle – and I know someone who will look after you . . .'

Approaching the captain, Malcolm gave him an awkward salute while balancing Beth in the crook of his right arm. 'The child's family hasn't turned up, sir,' he said. 'Do I have your permission to take her home to my sister – just until we find out what has happened?'

Captain Peterson looked at him for a moment and then nodded. 'She's your responsibility, Ridger. I've a missing boy to worry about and I know the girl will be all right with Mrs Bittern. Yes, do that, but report back no later than fifteen hundred hours tomorrow. We have to turn this ship around – we're headed for Malta next.'

'Not back to England then?' Malcolm said, surprised.

'Important shipment.' His captain told him what it would be, then said, 'Maybe next time it will be England. Any particular reason?'

'Nooo . . .' Malcolm's grandfather had emigrated to Canada at the start of the century and the purser had family in London – cousins he'd never met and a great-aunt he'd met once years before. They were in his thoughts now that Canada was starting to feel the effects of the war and he'd been thinking that perhaps he should join the Royal Canadian Navy. Captain Peterson, he knew, considered they were doing their bit, bringing the children to safety in Canada and taking cargoes where they were needed. As Canada stood with Britain, their ships could be attacked, though it hadn't happened to this ship yet.

'I'll see you tomorrow. Good of you to take the child off my hands.'

With that, Malcolm knew he'd been dismissed. He carried Beth and her small bundle of clothes off the ship. At least she'd stopped crying since he'd discovered the magic of barley sugars. She was now in possession of the rest of the paper screw of sweets and sucking happily. He only hoped that Vee would be as happy to be saddled with a child but he'd tell her it was only temporary. The family would either turn up or they would hand Beth over to the authorities. There were surely loads of childless families who would love to have her.

'Are you mad?' Vee demanded as they came downstairs after putting Beth to bed in one of the many spare rooms. She stood squarely on her hearthrug which was thick and fluffy and white, and behind a massive fire screen logs were set to send the flames of a warming fire out when the sun set. 'What do you think I'm going to do with a child at my age?'

Vee was in her early forties but still looked like a young woman. She had smooth pageboy hair, a good dress and snakeskin court shoes. On her left hand she wore the wedding ring and large diamond solitaire Bill had given her. She was clearly a woman of substance, in control of her lifestyle and her finances.

'You're not too old to have a child,' Malcolm said and grinned at the face she made. 'Just too lazy.'

'You are heading for a fall, big brother,' Vee said, the light of battle in her blue-grey eyes but Malcolm could see she wasn't angry. She was looking at the child as if Beth were an alien but there was interest there too. Malcolm smiled inwardly. He worried for his sister, not because she couldn't take care of herself and the clothing store they owned jointly – she could do all that fine – but because she was restless and refused to let go of her grief over Bill. 'If she falls down the stairs and breaks her neck, don't blame me.'

'I won't,' he said, 'but you won't let harm come to her, Vee – she's a nice little thing. Cries a bit but loves barley sugar.'

'We have that in common then, the barley sugar,' Vee said drily. 'You used to bring me some back wherever you went but I suppose you gave them to her?'

'Yes, I did, but I have more. I bought them in the States when we docked there on our outward journey. We took desperately needed supplies from America to England and brought the children back here. Now we're going to do the same for Malta – though we won't be bringing children back – but we'll be carrying Canadian goods this time, mostly food. The barley sugars were those old-fashioned twists that you love, Vee, so I bought the whole jar and then some for me.'

'You always were daft,' his sister said affectionately. 'Well, how long am I supposed to keep her?'

'I should wait a week. I'll report to the authorities where she is and if no one turns up by then you can speak to someone about the best thing to do.'

'Fine.' Vee took a cigarette from a carved jade box that Malcolm had brought back from one of his voyages and fitted it into a black holder with a little gold band. She lit it from an onyx and gold-plated table lighter and drew deeply. 'That's better . . .'

'You really shouldn't smoke too much. I'm sure it's what gives you a cough.'

Vee glared at him. 'You shouldn't drink brandy or rum but I know you do!'

'Nonsense! I don't drink to excess – and look, I was thinking I might join the Canadian navy and fight the Nazis.'

'Damned idiot!' Vee discouraged him with a searing glance. 'You do that, Malcolm, and I'll sell my half of the store to Harold Trevors.' The man she spoke of was one of the richest in the area but they knew him to be a bully because of things he'd done in the past.

'Empty threat,' her brother laughed. 'You hate him more than I do – you would fight to your dying breath to stop him getting his paws on it. Your words, not mine.'

'He's determined to have it,' Vee said. 'I saw him in town the other day and he said if I didn't sell, I'd end up with nothing.'

'The bastard!' Malcolm exclaimed and then apologised. 'Sorry about the bad language but he wants sorting, trying to bully you, because I'm away.'

Vee raised her plucked eyebrows. 'You believe that pig of a man could bully me?' She smiled. 'I thought you knew better, big brother. Whatever he says is like water off a duck's back.'

'I do know, but it's the thought that he tried. Be careful, Vee. He's a snake and a poisonous one at that.'

'I, on the other hand, am a mongoose. I eat snakes for breakfast.'

Malcolm laughed. 'Yes, you do, but if you ever need help go to Selmer. He would fetch the law in.'

Indeed he would. Selmer's son-in-law, Hank Wrangler, was a senior local police officer and fond of locking up drunks and bullies. He said he didn't like an empty jail and was afraid of no one, even the rich and powerful, including Mr Trevors.

'I know.' Vee smiled wickedly. 'He'd love the opportunity to make me grateful to him so that he could get his feet under my kitchen table.'

'Who could blame him?' Malcolm replied. 'You make good coffee and your muffins are delicious – when you get round to making any.'

'Why should I when I have Aggie and she is such a good cook?'

'Not as good as you,' he replied, feeling disappointed. 'You always used to make muffins for tea.'

Vee laughed, eyes alight with glee. 'You're so easy, brother. Of course I made your favourite muffins when I heard your ship was in – lemon and blueberry too.'

'Thanks.' He smiled at her. 'You can make a lot of nice things now that you have a small guest. It's the excuse you need to cook more.' She hadn't bothered much since Bill died, but she'd always loved to cook for her husband and perhaps she would for the child.

'Perhaps . . .' She arched her fine brows at him. 'You don't need to worry about me, Malcolm. I'm perfectly fine.'

He nodded but knew she wasn't, not deep inside. She hadn't been since her husband died. Really, it was a stroke of luck that Beth's new family hadn't turned up. If they didn't claim her, it might be possible for Vee to adopt the girl. After all, she was respectable and well off. No one could object, surely.

Malcolm smiled as Vee's housekeeper brought in the tea trolly, which was full of good things, including his muffins but also finger sandwiches and pastry shells filled with fruit and jam.

Vee had asked him to stay with her in her home when Bill died and he'd never bothered to move back to his rooms over the store. He was away most of the time and they got on well. Malcolm supposed that one day he would retire and they would settle down into old age together. Vee had known love, but Malcolm had never met a woman he wanted to marry, though he'd known a few girls in various ports – all the sailors did. Most had wives at home but it didn't stop some of them indulging their natural urges and Malcolm went along sometimes with friends. Some of the girls from the Philippines were really lovely and he'd met a nice girl in Spain once but he was set in his ways and happy the way he was . . . except that no one could be truly content with this awful war going on.

Because of Canada's ties with Britain, many Canadian people thought they should automatically fight, but Prime Minister King and his parliament had disagreed. They would go to war but only because the Canadian people wanted it and their forces would be mainly volunteers. They didn't want to use conscription because that did not suit Canada's minority French population. However, a small number of troops had been raised to fight with the British and Halifax was heavily garrisoned because of it. Many more Canadians had begun to join the air force and the navy in their own country, and some had gone to Britain to join up. Although at the beginning Canada had few fighting ships, they were growing in strength because the British needed help to protect the convoys in the Atlantic. However, everyone knew that the biggest contribution that Canada could make was through its rich resources of wheat and other foodstuffs and its ability to make goods needed for the struggle in Europe.

Malcolm's conscience pricked that he wasn't part of a fighting force, but perhaps Captain Peterson was right and he really was doing his bit; one day, though, he would find out if those cousins and his great-aunt were managing and help them out if he could. Vee was already doing her best, regularly contributing to the fund-raising efforts that were now a part of their lives, but perhaps they could do more.

CHAPTER 3

After they left the bus they walked for a long time. Julie felt cold and tired and wanted to ask how much longer it would be before they got to wherever they were going. She saw cars and trucks pass them, clearly going their way, and two of the drivers waved but they didn't stop to offer a lift.

'Is it much further?' she ventured at last, when they had long ago left the commercial area of Halifax far behind and came to what was more of a country setting, with lots of trees and fields and similar-looking houses. Most of them were constructed of wooden clapboard with steps up to a veranda and some were painted white or shades of grey and green. They all had large gardens and were set widely apart. Used to crowded streets where the houses were built in terraces and stained with soot, Julie felt the strangeness of it all but liked it too. 'Can't we get another bus or something?'

Miss Cotton's cool eyes flicked to Julie's face. 'I hope you won't be sickly. I asked for a healthy girl to help me in my work.' She must have seen something in

Julie's face, because she frowned. 'You're fifteen – it's quite legal for you to work. Did you expect to be given everything and do nothing in return?'

'No, Miss Cotton. I'll be glad to work,' Julie said truthfully. Her father had wanted more for his daughter, for her to have a good education and make something of herself, but that life was over. Julie knew she must do what she was told, at least until she could afford to look after herself – but it wasn't what her father had promised that her life would be.

'One day you'll be better off than us and live in a nice house and eat cake every day,' he'd teased her and she'd laughed, because she'd loved him. She'd loved her mother too but Sheila Miller seldom felt well enough to talk with or tease her daughter. She'd been sickly, plagued by her debilitating illness for as long as Julie could recall. Tears stung her eyes as she thought that her mother was probably dead by now.

'You'll be better than us, girl – have a decent life and education. I'll see to that,' her father had promised. Only he'd died and now Julie had no choice.

Miss Cotton's voice cut into her memories. 'I am glad to hear it. Teaching is a privilege and I shall instruct you in my methods. I run a school for girls. My pupils are taught to read and write and cook and sew. It is what they need to prepare them for life; some will have piano lessons, some drawing and a few will learn languages; many of them can speak a little French already because in parts of Canada French is spoken more than English – do you know the language, girl?'

'My name is Julie and it is only polite to call me by it,' Julie said raising her head to look at Miss Cotton defiantly. 'If you expect me to be polite and help you, then you should do the same, don't you think?'

Miss Cotton blinked hard and for a moment her cheeks flushed but then she gave Julie an angry stare. 'I will treat you as you deserve,' she said in a flat tone. 'As yet you have given me no reason to respect you, Miss Miller.'

Julie flared with mutinous rage inwardly but then inclined her head. 'Fair enough, Miss Cotton,' she replied, suppressing her feelings. 'I understand I need to prove myself. And no, I don't speak or understand French. I wasn't taught it at school. They thought reading, writing and cooking was enough – oh, and I can sew and embroider well because my mother taught me.' Before she'd become so ill, Julie had been shown how to sew and she'd carried on afterwards because she loved it. 'I can cook quite well, too.'

'I will be the judge of your talents,' Miss Cotton told her. She stopped in front of one of the houses. It was quite small, painted pale green and grey and it had heavy lace curtains at the windows. Most of the other houses in the wide, treelined avenue were larger. This one looked as if it had been squeezed in between the more imposing houses to either side, which had trees and lush bushes along the divide. However, it had wide lawns, a white picket fence and neat flower beds each side. Like their owner, the house and gardens were neat and mean and pale. 'I like to garden on my free days,' Miss Cotton remarked. 'You may help me if you wish or go for walks. I believe in fresh air and exercise.'

'Thank you,' Julie replied meekly. 'I thought I caught

sight of a lake as we walked. Am I allowed to walk there?'

'Provided you do not get in the way of the sawmill or flirt with the loggers,' Miss Cotton said and then, as Julie stared at her, continued, 'That is one of the industries we have here. There are a lot of trees further inland and the sawmill is set near the river, not far from the lake. It is half an hour's walk or more and you do not seem to enjoy walking that much.' She sniffed her disapproval.

'It just seemed we might have gone on a bus rather than walk . . .' Julie's words died away as she saw the look Miss Cotton gave her.

'I have no money to waste when it's perfectly walkable. I suppose you have got used to buses in London – that is where you came from, I've been told. I should have thought you would believe yourself in paradise here – clear air and the smell of flowers. This is a much better place to live than those filthy streets you all live in.'

'Ours wasn't dirty,' Julie said lifting her head proudly. 'Dad had a nice house he rented for five shillings a week and the street cleaner swept the gutters and paths regular.'

'Regular*ly*,' Miss Cotton corrected. 'You can speak properly so please do so. I cannot have you setting a bad example for my pupils.'

Julie wanted to protest that if she didn't want an East End girl, she shouldn't have taken her, but bit back the words. Arguing wasn't going to get her anywhere.

She looked about her as they went up to the veranda

and then in through the front door. It was painted white inside and the floors were polished wood. A neat doormat was just inside and Julie dutifully wiped her feet. She was led into a kitchen that was larger than she'd expected, fitted with tall dressers and a deep stone sink with draining boards to either side. The table was scrubbed pine and set with thick blue and white earthenware, similar to a service her mother had used and the sight of it made Julie's throat catch with grief, because for the first time she saw something familiar.

'I suppose you are hungry,' Miss Cotton said and Julie nodded. 'You may have bread and jam. You will find them in there . . .' she indicated a pantry door. 'Cut two slices for each of us and bring the pot of strawberry jam you see on the bottom shelf. If you are still hungry, you may have a slice of my seed cake.'

'Thank you. I haven't eaten since early this morning . . .' Julie's thoughts went to Beth and Arthur. She hoped they were having something nice to eat and felt a pang of loss, wishing that she'd been able to see Beth's new family so she could be sure she was all right.

Miss Cotton made a tutting sound but uttered no further remarks, merely watching as Julie moved towards the pantry. 'Wash your hands first, Miss Miller.'

Julie halted and turned towards the sink. There was a hard green soap in a dish and a cotton towel. The water was warm and she did as she was told before fetching the food. A little to her surprise the bread was fresh, studded with seeds and delicious when she bit into it and Miss Cotton only frowned at the amount of strawberry jam she used. Since she wasn't forbidden, Julie put the same large dollop on her second slice and devoured it, before returning to fetch the seed cake.

'Clearly, you need to be taught table manners,' Miss Cotton said, 'but I can see that you were very hungry. You may have a medium-sized slice of cake, girl, but not half of it.'

Julie moved the knife in and cut a smaller slice. 'Would you like the same, Miss Cotton?'

'Yes, but a little smaller,' she replied. 'I can see I shall need to bake more often now you are here but you're a growing girl so need your food and I daresay they didn't feed you much on the ship.'

'We had enough, but this morning everyone was too busy to think of feeding us after breakfast.'

'Well, you will eat plain fare here but behave and you will be given your fair share. And I have some old dresses that you can cut down for yourself. You told me you can sew?'

'Yes, Miss Cotton.' Julie hesitated and then carried the plates to the sink. 'Shall I wash them for you?'

'I'll see to them later,' Miss Cotton said. 'I will show you how another day but now I should take you to your room.'

After Miss Cotton had left her to settle in, Julie went to look out of the window. There were more houses behind the garden, which was long and became narrow at the bottom, as if the neighbours had moved their fences over. It was an odd-shaped plot and finished in a kind of rockery and then a fence at the back. Lots of trees and bushes obscured the view into the neighbouring gardens and she could only see the roofs of the houses beyond but she got the impression that it was open countryside then, and a bit wild-looking. She recalled that the purser, Mr Ridger, had told her there were still some parts of the area that were wilderness.

'One day, it will all get built on, I daresay,' he'd said with a slight sigh. 'But for now there're some pretty wild places to explore if you get the chance.'

Miss Cotton's house seemed a long way from the centre of Halifax, so although what she'd seen so far looked pretty and nice, it appeared a bit isolated to Julie, who was used to crowded London streets and she wasn't sure how she would feel living here.

The orphanage had been in the country and Julie hadn't liked that much – it had seemed like a prison – but it might be better here. At least she wouldn't starve just yet and she'd known what that felt like when she'd run away from the orphanage. It had taken ages to get home and she'd had no food . . .

Julie shook her head. There was no sense in dwelling on the past, because she couldn't go back until she'd earned a lot of money for her fare. Miss Cotton hadn't mentioned wages but she would surely pay her something, wouldn't she?

Julie's gaze went round the small bedroom. It was just big enough for a single bed, a wardrobe and a small chest of drawers, but it was comfortable enough. She would be all right here for a while and when she had the money to leave she would look for Beth first and then Arthur, because she was sure he would be safe with the Hendersons. Maybe she would be able to visit both of them, take them out to tea once she had some money . . . A little smile lit her grey eyes and, had she known it, her pretty face. Julie had no mirror to see herself and had never taken much notice of her looks when she had, but she was an attractive girl with a determined mouth, slanting brows and a nose that turned up slightly and had freckles in the summer, her hair brown but with a hint of red when lit by sunlight.

She sat down on the bed. If she'd had a book she would have read it, but there was nothing personal in this drab little room. She might as well return to the kitchen and see what she could do – though everything was neat, clean and soulless in there just as here. Miss Cotton's residence was a house but as yet Julie could not think of it as a home.

CHAPTER 4

'Am I home?' The child looked up at Vee with such uncertainty in her wide blue eyes and such anxiety that her heart caught. It was quite clear to her that the little girl had suffered neglect or a careless mother. She was just six and she'd been sent away from all she knew to live with strangers. She'd even been torn from the girl who had looked out for her on the ship, a girl named Julie. Malcolm hadn't said yesterday where Julie had gone or mentioned her surname and he would be away for at least two to three months now so she couldn't ask him, otherwise she might have made contact with the girl, asked her to visit.

'Yes, Beth, you are home. I am going to look after you . . .'

It was a reckless statement and Vee knew it almost as soon as she spoke the words but in the few hours she'd been with her, Vee had taken to the child. She'd been surprised, unprepared, when Malcolm brought Beth to her, but it was what she'd always wanted in her heart – wasn't it? She and Bill had hoped for a child but it had never happened and they'd accepted it as God's will. Now it seemed she had a chance to make good that lack.

She was lonely without Bill and knew there would never be anyone else to fill the void he'd left behind. She'd had plenty of offers, some unspoken, others spoken over and over and she'd turned them all down. Vee had loved Bill with all her heart just as he'd loved her. It would feel like a betrayal to love again romantically, but not to give the kind of love she could already feel for this child. No, Bill would have approved of that, she knew. She could hear him inside her head.

'That's right, Vee,' he seemed to say and laughed the way he always had. 'You've got someone to love and look after now. She's yours. Fight for her. Make her happy and strong the way you are.'

Vee felt warm, as if her beloved husband had put his arms around her and hugged her. She only had this feeling now and then, sometimes when she slipped on his dressing robe in the evenings, or strangely, when she was out walking alone and she felt that he was with her, talking to her, telling her about the trees and the flowers the way he always had when they were together.

Yes, Bill approved. Vee decided she would go to the authorities the next day and put in a claim for the child, sign the necessary papers and make it legal. She would adopt Beth, give her the Bittern name and a share of her wealth when she died. Malcolm would get the house for his lifetime and then it would go to this child who had stolen her heart, bringing her back from a cold, lonely place. He would understand. Malcolm always understood her. It was why he'd brought the child to her.

Vee smiled and bent down to pick Beth up. She kissed her cheek, which was a little sticky with the honey she'd had for breakfast. It was the first time she'd tasted it and the look on her face had been pure joy.

'I'm going to be your new mummy,' she told Beth as she carried her through to the big kitchen where Aggie, her housekeeper was preparing the vegetables for lunch. 'I think we need milk and cookies now, Aggie, and I shall bake later today. What do you think this little one would like?'

'Some of your honey cakes or jam tarts,' the house-keeper replied. 'She's a pretty child, Miss Vee.'

Aggie had worked for Vee's mother and still thought of Vee as a young girl so perhaps she was getting a little old for the extra work Beth would make.

'Will we need more help now we have Beth?' Vee asked, because it was always best to be straight with Aggie, who stood for no nonsense.

'So we're keeping her then?' Aggie nodded her satis-faction. 'Good. It's what this house needs – a child to laugh and play. Well, we could get someone to do the scrubbing and chop wood, but otherwise I can manage.'

'Do you know someone we could employ?' Vee looked at her. Aggie had spoken decisively so she'd had it on her mind before this. 'Someone we can trust?'

'There's a good many I wouldn't,' Aggie replied darkly. 'But yes – there's a lad and his mother could do with a bit of help. Saralee will scrub and maybe do a few more jobs and Rob will chop wood and run errands.'

'Ask them to come then,' Vee said and smiled as Aggie poured milk from a tall blue jug that was cold from the pantry into a blue and white mug that little hands could hold easily. Their pantry was big and deep and always cool with its stone floor and marble shelves. Food kept well there and Aggie refused all offers of what she called those new-fangled 'frigrators'.

'If I don't know how to manage food without it going off too soon then I ought,' she'd told Vee and, as far as Vee knew very little was ever wasted. Some of the leftover food may have made its way to one of Aggie's lame ducks but that was her privilege as a member of the family. It was one of the things Vee liked best about being comfortably off. She didn't have to question such things so she didn't.

'They'll want twenty dollars a month,' Aggie said. 'Sixteen for Saralee and four for Rob.'

'Make it twenty for Saralee,' Vee said, 'and ten for the lad.' She could afford it, so why not? She was always generous and looked after her employees. It was just the way she was, though she could be stubborn when she chose.

Aggie nodded and smiled, as though she'd expected her reaction. Aggie knew her too well, Vee thought with an amused smile as she turned away.

She left the child to Aggie as she went to prepare for her daily visit to the clothing store. It was a thriving business and sold outer clothing for men, women and children. The profits had increased since Vee started running it and she was considering expanding into silk underwear for the ladies of the town and perhaps a knitwear department too. The only reason she hadn't done it yet was because there was already a shop selling those items on the other side of town. It was run by a widow in her sixties and didn't sell the kind of quality that Vee wanted to stock. At the moment any lady needing silk or fine wool had to catch the bus into Halifax centre, where there were bigger shops and busy streets. There they could buy what was needed but why should they have to?

Maybe she would visit Mrs Haley's shop and have a word with her. It would be awful if Vee took her trade so she wouldn't do it unless Mrs Haley agreed it wouldn't affect her business. After all, Vee didn't need the extra money – it just made good financial sense. She wasn't one of those folk who thought money meant everything, but she would do what was necessary to make her businesses thrive.

Yes, she decided, she would drive over and speak to Mrs Haley and on the way back she would call in at the lumbermill. It was one of the businesses that Bill had left her. A man's world really, but Vee had kept it for sentimental reasons because it was the way Bill had started out, becoming just a part of his small empire but important to him. Vee couldn't have kept it if she hadn't had a good manager but she trusted Jago Marsh implicitly. Some men wouldn't have employed a manager who had Jago's disabilities, but Bill had and Jago was good at his work. Without him, she would have sold the lumbermill – which would've suited Trevors just fine.

A scowl turned her attractive face hard as she thought of the man she despised. Harold Trevors had come sniffing round before Bill was hardly buried, within days of the funeral. He'd offered to buy anything she didn't want but the way he'd looked her up and down had turned Vee's stomach. She'd never forgotten one night when she was young – before she met Bill – and she never would. Trevors might think she'd forgotten the way he'd mauled her when they'd met at a barn dance. He might even have had his drunken way if it hadn't been for one of her father's employees walking round the back of the barn and seeing her struggling.

Mr Jacks had hauled Trevors off her. 'He's just a daft lad, Miss Vee,' he'd said. 'No harm done but best to keep it quiet – don't want to upset your dad, miss.'

So Vee hadn't told anyone, not even Bill. He would have gone after Trevors and thrashed him so she'd kept the secret but sometimes she wondered if she ought to have told. Maybe he thought he'd got away with it once and he could again.

She hadn't liked the way he'd looked at her, as if she were fair game now she was a widow. Next time, if there was a next time, she would report him if she didn't kill him first. Vee carried a tiny pistol in her bag and she knew how to use it. Whether she ever would, was another matter, but surely Trevors wouldn't be mad enough to try violence on her?

'Well, I'm sure I don't care what you do, Mrs Bittern,' Widow Haley said. 'I'm selling this property next month. I find it a bit too much for me and I've been made an offer for the shop. I'm moving to Toronto to live with my brother and his wife.'

'You've been made an offer for the property?' Vee looked at her thoughtfully. It was a nice little shop and with some paint, new shelves and the right stock could do well. 'Do you mind if I ask how much you were offered?'

'Four hundred dollars,' the woman said looking triumphant. 'Mr Trevors said it was only worth three hundred but when I hesitated, he gave me the extra hundred dollars.'

'I'll give you six hundred for it,' Vee told her. 'If you haven't already signed?'

'Why?' Widow Haley looked bewildered. 'It can't be worth that much – there's a shop just up the road that's bigger and that's only four hundred dollars.'

'I like it,' Vee said and dismissed the niggling doubt that she was inviting trouble. 'Have you signed the contract?'

'It was to happen tomorrow and complete within the month.' Widow Haley looked uncertain. 'I don't know, Mrs Bittern. Mr Trevors is a bad man to upset and he was so insistent that I sell to him.' She shook her head but looked regretful. 'Someone told me to ask you if you wanted to buy, but . . . no, I can't go back on my word. He might not like it and he makes me nervous.'

'All right.' Vee smiled at her. 'I wish I'd known you wanted to sell, Mrs Haley. I am always interested in nice properties.' She stood and pulled on her leather gloves. 'I hope you enjoy your new life.'

'Thank you – and I'd have rather sold it to you. I just can't, because he might – he might do something nasty and I can't leave until it's all settled . . .'

'It doesn't matter,' Vee told her. 'Don't worry.'

'My brother will say I am a fool but he doesn't know Mr Trevors.' Widow Haley looked uneasy.

Vee nodded. She understood why someone like this elderly widow would be scared to say no to Trevors. 'Well, I'm sorry too, but perhaps it is for the best.'

Vee wondered why Trevors was so keen on buying all the property he could here. Lower Sackville was a quiet place and she couldn't see the property values changing as things stood . . . of course, if considerably more folk moved into the area, land for building could be scarce. To get to Upper Sackville you needed to cross the river and though there was both a ferry and a stone bridge, it had slowed down the expansion that had been so thrusting in Halifax itself. However, she mused, if it became easier to travel between the two locations, land could suddenly become more valuable. Halifax was crowded and the land in both Upper and Lower Sackville might look very tempting one day.

Vee shook her head. She didn't need to build her empire. She had all she wanted – and yet perhaps she might buy a few strategic properties when the chance arose. Not everyone would be afraid of Harold Trevors . . .

CHAPTER 5

Beth ran her hands over the smooth surface of the shining wood of the dressing table which was set with pretty things that she hardly dared to touch. Her bedroom was so dainty and fresh and she'd never had such lovely things. When she was younger and Daddy was home, Beth had been happy enough except for the terrible rows her parents had sometimes, but then her father went away and didn't come back and her mother had gone out to work all day because they needed money and then she'd been knocked down in the blackout. For a while Beth had lived with her granny, but Granny Barton was old and she'd been unable to look after Beth properly, though she'd cried when she didn't know Beth was listening to the man from the council, telling her what was best.

'You are too old to have the care of a young child, Mrs Barton. You will need care yourself in a few years and the best place for that is in a home. I'm afraid the decision has been made for her own good. Beth will travel to Canada on the next ship available.'

It hadn't been poor Granny's fault that Beth was sent

away and it sounded as though she would be put somewhere too, because there was no one left to care for her now. Beth hadn't even known where Canada was. It had all been so frightening, the journey to the ship and then the voyage itself. She'd felt sick a lot of the time. If Julie hadn't been there, she would have been terrified. Julie had soothed her tears and helped her when she was sick and Beth had learned to love her on the voyage – she was like the sister she'd never had – and she missed her even now although it was nice in this house. She had lovely things to eat and toys to play with and better clothes than she'd ever worn in her short life. Miss Vee, who'd said she would be her new mummy, was lovely and Aggie was too, reminding her a little of her granny, though Aggie wasn't as old as granny.

She hoped that these people loved her and would keep her always, but she wished that Julie was here, too, then it would be perfect. Beth had asked Miss Vee where Julie was, but she didn't know. Remembering the sour look the woman who had taken Julie away had given her, Beth said a little prayer that Julie would come to no harm. If only they knew where she was, Beth would ask Miss Vee to let her come and live with them.

Miss Cotton's school was just half an hour's walk away from her house. There was a bus, which she informed Julie she used occasionally in the winter when it was bitterly cold and dark at night. However, she got up early and made the journey each morning on foot.

'Well, are you ready, Miss Miller?' she asked Julie

after a breakfast of porridge with a little honey. 'I prepared sandwiches for lunch and a flask of soup. We can make tea on the stove in my kitchen at school; that will be one of your jobs because it is too far to come back for lunch and we shall be home by four or soon after. My girls leave at three thirty.'

Julie absorbed the information in silence. Her life was clearly to be regimented and filled with tasks that Miss Cotton thought right.

'It is good to work and be busy,' she'd told Julie the previous evening when she'd brought out a sewing machine. 'Can you use this?'

Julie looked at it for a few minutes and then nodded. 'Yes, Miss Cotton. I used a similar one at school and my neighbour had one, too. She showed me how to make myself a dress on it once, though mostly I sewed by hand. It was quicker on the machine.'

'That was sensible of your neighbour,' Miss Cotton replied. 'I'm glad you are a practical girl. Life isn't easy for any of us and we have to be prepared to work if we are to get through. You can make yourself whatever you like from the clothes I've given you, so it is up to you. When we've finished for the day, you will have the evening to do your own work after you've eaten and washed up. The housework is done for me so I do not require anything of that nature from you.'

Julie thanked her since she seemed to expect it. Perhaps she was being generous in her own way. At home, Julie would have done ironing, mending and various other small jobs. Sometimes she'd scrubbed the floors for her mother, though mostly Ma had done that herself until she became too ill and a neighbour did it for her. Julie didn't mind household tasks. She thought she might have been happier helping about the house but she was told to stay in her room and sew or go out for a walk if the evening was fine and light enough. Julie had wandered around the area but she hadn't gone as far as the river or the lake, or the lumbermill yet. She was hoping to do that on Sunday. Miss Cotton said it was the best day, because the mill would be closed.

'Mrs Bittern would never allow her men to work on a Sunday,' Miss Cotton told her. 'She is a real lady and sets an example to be followed. On Sundays we go to church and we walk. You will not sew on Sundays.'

Julie had never been to church much. Her parents didn't go except for funerals and weddings which they didn't take her to, but she'd been with the school at Christmases for carol services and they had been lovely so it would be something to do, something to keep her from going mad with boredom.

Sewing her new clothes was interesting. She was grateful for the chance to make her own things rather than being given a dress and told to wear it, though the colours of grey and dark blue were not her favourites. However, she could make them look nice and neat, which would surely win Miss Cotton's nod of approval. After all, it was only for a while, just until she could save enough to leave this place and try to find Beth and Arthur, though she was sure he would be happy because the people who had claimed him looked kind and caring. But Beth's distraught face lived in her mind and sometimes kept her awake at night. She wondered, too, how Davey Blake had got on. Had he returned to England or had someone found him on the ship? She would probably never know.

Julie's first day at school had gone better than she'd imagined. Now, on her fourth day, Julie had begun to enjoy her work. Until lunchtime, she sat with young girls of eight or nine and oversaw their sewing and their reading, then Miss Cotton took them for music, cooking and writing and simple maths. It was a routine that never wavered.

In the afternoons, Julie's pupils were ten-to-twelve-year-olds and she'd asked Miss Cotton where the older children went to school.

'They go to Halifax – if their parents send them,' Miss Cotton dismissed the question with a sniff. 'Here, my girls learn what they need to know to be good daughters and help their mothers. It is all most of them will ever need. They will be married young and have their own families although some may go on to higher school but that is not my concern.'

Julie thought that their pupils would struggle at the school she'd gone to at their age where she had learned to stand up for herself when the boys and sometimes older girls had pulled her hair and called her names. She'd once punched a boy in the face for jeering at her because her frock was dirty, and he'd had a black eye, but he hadn't told on her and they'd been friends afterwards.

The girls here were mostly quiet, well-behaved daughters of parents who could afford to pay a small weekly sum for their education. Julie wondered why they didn't go to a proper school, one that taught subjects like science and geography and history. Perhaps their parents didn't want them mixing with boys, she decided. Julie felt Miss Cotton's girls were wrapped up in fleece to protect them; they were mostly prissy little things who hardly ever dared to speak up, although she was encouraging them to ask about what they were reading. At the moment it was *Little Women*; Julie was supposed to hear them read and she did, but one of the little girls had asked her to read and so she decided to do that too – just a few pages, before they took up their own books and they all stared at her as she read to them.

The girls had to read a little history and so Julie learned from their lessons about the first settlers and the wars with the French and the Mi'kmaq who lived there long before the settlers. It was interesting to know that the British Army had garrisoned the Citadel until 1906, when it had been replaced by Canada's own forces, and it made the area come alive for her. Although she had seen hardly anything of Halifax on their way to Lower Sackville, she knew that it was a thriving port and now hosted a large number of Canadian military personnel. It was on alert for air raids and attacks, just as London had been and everyone feared havoc and destruction like that which had happened towards the end of the First World War when terrible damage had been caused by the explosion of the French munitions ship SS *Mont Blanc* when it collided with the Norwegian vessel, SS *Imo*.

She was able to help the girls with their sewing and would have liked to give them cooking lessons as well but Miss Cotton wouldn't let her do more. Instead, she sharpened pencils, collected up exercise books and placed them on Miss Cotton's desk. It wasn't really enough, but it was better than when she was sitting in her room alone in the evenings.

After church on the first Sunday, Julie asked permission and then set off in the direction of the lake nearest to Miss Cotton's home. She'd learned there were other lakes and a river in Lower Sackville and the surrounding districts but this one had the lumbermill that belonged to a Mrs Bittern. Once, Julie had been told, there were many such mills along the wide river but much of the timber had been ruthlessly cut down and not replanted so fewer existed these days. Mrs Bittern's was the largest in the area now and Miss Cotton clearly respected the wealthy Mrs Bittern, though Julie sensed she was also a little jealous of her.

The water was clean and sparkling as she approached the lake. She could hear it burbling and see it tumbling over rocks at the edges and could see the evidence of the work that went on here. Some huge tree trunks were in the water, lashed together by ropes, and she could see piles of other logs stacked everywhere, also the machinery that cut wood. There were various sheds and buildings to one side and she thought they spoiled the beauty of the place a little but it was a vast body of water and most of it was still free of the polluting touch of man.

Julie looked up as a bird that had been singing flew off with a squawk of dismay. What had disturbed it? As she stood stock still, her heart racing, she saw a young man emerge from the trees and walk towards the edge of the lake. He knelt down and looked at

44

the logs floating in the water, checking the ropes that held them, Julie thought. As he straightened up, he glanced her way and for a moment his gaze rested on her and then he walked away. She noticed that he dragged one foot and she thought he might have a club foot. One of the boys at her school in the East End had been hampered like that and Julie had always felt sympathy for him, because he couldn't play the way other boys did, but the man walking away from her carried himself proudly and his disability didn't seem to stop him doing as he wanted. She heard an engine start up and thought that he was driving away. He'd come in on a Sunday just to check that all was well, she thought, and she wondered who he was – he was very good-looking . . .

Shaking her head, Julie banished the thought. She was not interested in men and she was never going to marry. She'd loved her dad and he'd been kind and loving but her uncle . . . well, he was a very bad man. And then there was the man at the orphanage. No, men were definitely not to be trusted. In fact, she wasn't sure *who* she could trust anymore. For a moment her unhappiness swamped her. Her father had loved her. How much she wished she could see him again but she knew she wouldn't.

Julie had hoped her new family would care for her and she would be accepted and appreciated, but Miss Cotton was a cold woman who seemed to care for no one, at least it seemed that way to the girl who longed to be loved.

CHAPTER 6

'I made sure the logs were secure, Miss Vee,' Jago said and received a smile and a nod from his employer. At twenty-three he was young to be a manager but he'd worked for her family since he was thirteen. Bill had taken the strapping lad on, at first out of pity for his disability, but he'd proved himself a good worker, reliable and honest. Vee had made him manager when the man Bill had employed for years had finally retired at the age of sixty-seven. He'd told her she could rely on Jago and she could. 'I can't understand how that raft came loose last month,' he said now. 'They were secure, but I suppose the rope must have frayed underneath.'

'Or been cut by someone.' Vee shook her head. 'Still, we got the timber back . . . it just made more work for you.'

Jago looked thoughtful. 'It might have been deliberate. I don't trust that Harold Trevors. He's been sniffing around, asking questions about the business, but I've warned the men not to tell him anything.'

'Trust him and you're a fool,' Vee said harshly. 'But you aren't, Jago. You may have a physical disability

46

that some mock you for but you're a thinking man and you see folk for what they are.' She smiled. 'How is Maya today?'

'Ma is very well and she thanks you for the gifts you sent on her birthday. You're too generous, Miss Vee.'

'I like your mother and I like you,' Vee said and looked at him enquiringly. 'What did you think to my little Beth then?'

The child had been playing with a pretty porcelain-headed doll that Aggie had produced from somewhere, which had once been Vee's, and she'd laughed as Jago entered the room but out of happiness at what was her first toy. Her look of wonder and then her excitement, as she discovered it had pretty clothes and hair she could rearrange, had made both women smile. She'd shown Jago the doll, running to him and holding out her arms to be picked up. He'd smiled but he hadn't touched her or attempted to pick her up.

'You can be a friend to my daughter,' Vee told him now. 'I know why you didn't respond – you think folk would believe the worst. But we're not like those ignorant people who shout abuse at you, Jago, or think you evil just because you limp and I hope you know we are your friends.'

All his life, Vee knew, Jago had suffered from verbal and sometimes physical abuse, because of his disability. He had learned to keep his distance, to wait before giving a smile or reaching out to others. Jago grinned now, his face lighting up with good humour and something more – a kind of wry acceptance.

'I know you aren't – nor was Mr Bittern, and the men respected him – and Aggie has a sharp tongue but not a bitter one. Your brother, too, is a good man and he did a fine thing bringing the child here. I just didn't want to frighten her. Most children scream and run away if I try to talk to them.' Something flickered in his eyes momentarily and was gone.

Vee nodded her understanding. She could see the pain mirrored in those dark eyes despite his smile and it hurt her. He was a good-looking man if you didn't count the club foot and she felt sorry that he would probably never know the joy of being loved or of having his own children. She knew from experience that a life without children could be lonely and he would not always have his mother at home on the small farm they ran. Jago's mother looked after their two cows, using the butter and milk they produced at home while Jago grew most of their food and raised a few pigs, turkeys and hens for eggs, ducks now too, he'd told her proudly quite recently.

'I found a duck with a broken wing,' he'd said. 'She was wild but I fed her and looked after her, dug a pond for her too. When she took to swimming in it, her mate flew in and they nested, so I now have a whole family of ducklings as well as the parents and we hope to take a few of the eggs they produce in time – but for now we'll just let them bide.'

Despite his work on his small farm, which he'd inherited from his father, Jago was never late at the lumbermill and he was always the last to leave. Vee paid him generously and she believed he would work for her as long as she owned the mill, though she had an idea that he had an ambition to own it one day. If, as she suspected, he saved his wages and came to her one day asking to buy, she would sell to him – but for his sake he had to be well-prepared, because Harold Trevors would be the enemy of anyone who bought her mill. His determination to own as much land as he could would be frightening if she didn't feel equal to standing up to him.

Trevors wouldn't actually try to harm her. He dared not, because she was too influential and had too many friends. Had anything happened to her, and he'd been suspected, the good folk of the town might take revenge and he'd probably either find himself locked in prison or – in the old days – strung up from a lamppost. These days he might find his tyres slashed and rude remarks daubed on his front door which wouldn't kill him but it would shame him and destroy the position he was trying to build as a respectable and important man in the area.

Vee nodded to Jago. 'I appreciate you stopping by the mill just to check on your day off, Jago.'

'Maya wanted to go to church,' he said with simple honesty. 'She visits with a friend for a while after and then I take her home so it's no trouble to me.'

'You must have work at home?' she suggested but he laughed.

'Nothing an early rise can't cope with, Miss Vee.'

'What of your lunch? Maya cooks for you on Sundays, I know.'

'I grabbed a pastry before we left and we'll have supper when I get home.'

Vee shook her head and led the way into the kitchen

where she insisted he sat down and ate a plate of ham and eggs cooked by her before he left to fetch his mother. 'I value you,' she told him. 'I can't have you going hungry. You're a big lad.'

'And you're a good cook, Miss Vee.'

Beth came to his side as he drank the large cup of coffee Vee poured for him and he took her on his lap. She looked up at him with her wide, clear eyes.

'What's wrong with your foot?' she asked innocently.

'It's a thing that I was born with,' he said. 'It doesn't work as it should.'

'Does it hurt?' she inquired and he shook his head.

'Sometimes my leg aches a bit but since I had this special boot that Miss Vee got made for me it isn't much.'

'Good,' Beth said and patted his face with sticky hands. 'I like you, mister.'

'My name is Jago,' he told her and put her down. 'And now I have to leave. Thank you for the food and the coffee, Miss Vee.'

'You're always welcome. Come here, Beth. Jago has to fetch his mother.'

Beth sucked her thumb as he stood up, then, 'My mummy is dead – a car knocked her down in the blackout but I've got a new one now. Daddy went away a long time before that and my gran said he would never come back so will you be my daddy?'

Jago ruffled her hair and chuckled. 'I can't be your daddy but I'll be your uncle or your big brother if you like.'

Beth's face lit with a beaming smile. 'I never had a brother. I'd like you to be my brother, please.'

'Then I will,' he promised. 'Now you be a good girl

for Miss Vee and I'll bring you a candy cane next time I come.'

Vee reached for the child's hand; she was smiling as she said, 'Don't you go spoiling her, Jago. Aggie does enough of that already.'

'She's worth spoiling though,' he said and went off with a laugh. Jago had an awkward loping walk but she noticed that he moved swiftly to his truck once he was outside and didn't seem to be hampered too much. She'd heard about the special boots for clubbed feet and ordered one for him when he was younger. Jago had been overwhelmed and she made sure he got a new one whenever it was needed. He'd told her he could buy his own now but she still did it.

It was one of the best things about having money. She could actually help people she cared about rather than just feeling sorry for them.

'Two cents for your thoughts,' Aggie said interrupting them.

'Oh, they're worth a lot more than that,' Vee told her with a smile. 'I think I'll take a pot of tea through to the parlour.'

'Take the child and I'll make it and bring you some cake for her,' Aggie said. 'You always were one for taking in the waifs and strays, Miss Vee. I mind the time you brought home that stray mongrel dog and what a packet of trouble that caused.'

'Poor Roly,' Vee said with a smile. 'He would steal from the kitchen.'

Aggie shook her head. 'If I left sausages or meat and turned my back, he'd be off with them the instant he could.'

'Yes, he was very bad,' Vee agreed. She looked thoughtfully at Beth. 'Perhaps we should get a dog for the child – just a small one . . .'

'Perhaps,' Aggie agreed. 'But make sure the next dog you buy isn't a thief.'

'Aren't they all where food is concerned?' Vee asked, but since she was on her way through the hall Aggie didn't hear her. Just as well, because Vee was thinking she really might ask about a dog as a pet for Beth.

She'd informed the authorities that she was prepared to keep Beth and to adopt her if she was acceptable. Her request had been met with a smile of approval and a shake of the head when she suggested they might want to investigate her as a suitable foster mother.

'You have no need to prove yourself, Mrs Bittern,' the man in the administrative office had told her. 'That child needs a good home and there's none better to give her that than you.'

'Supposing the folk turn up who should have had her?' Vee asked.

'Then they may apply for another child on the next transport from England. They didn't collect her as arranged so as far as we're concerned, she's yours.'

Vee had accepted the man's judgement, but she'd still spoken to her lawyer about making it legal and he was looking into that aspect for her. Vee didn't believe in doing things by half and she wanted it signed and sealed. Beth was hers and she didn't want strangers turning up one day to claim her, for her own sake as well as the child's. If she let herself love Beth – and who could resist those eyes? – she wouldn't be able to bear losing her a few weeks or months down the road . . .

'He was a nice man,' Beth said, shattering her thoughts. 'I liked him. I'm glad he's going to be my brother.'

'Yes, you can trust Jago,' Vee told her, 'but you shouldn't always trust strangers. Only do so if I approve of them and *never* go off with a person you don't know, whether it's a man or a woman.'

'I'll remember,' Beth said looking at her solemnly. 'I'd like to see Julie again one day, Mummy. She's lovely too.'

'When Uncle Malcolm comes home we'll ask him if he knows where Julie was taken and then we'll see what we can do. Will that make you happy?'

'Yes, please,' Beth said and hugged her. 'I am so glad that I came to you but I do miss Julie. I hope she's all right.'

'Well, I hope so too, darling,' Vee told her. 'We will try and find her just as soon as we can.'

Jago was smiling as he picked his mother up from her friend's house. Maya didn't go out that much but she did enjoy singing in church and so he often brought her in to visit the place of worship, leaving her to walk home with her friend for a cold lunch while he checked the lumbermill or spent some time just sitting by the lake watching the birds.

'You look pleased with yourself?' Maya questioned. 'What have you been up to, my son?' She always knew his moods, seemed to anticipate what he would say or do and he believed she had the gift of second sight, though they never spoke of it.

'I looked in on the yard to make sure that timber was safe,' he told her as they drove off. 'I told Miss Vee it was fine and she cooked me ham and eggs.'

'You shouldn't have let her,' Maya scolded. 'She pays you good wages. You didn't ought to let her cook for you, Jago.'

'I said no but she insisted – you know what Miss Vee is, Maya. She goes her own way.'

Maya nodded and smiled at him. 'I know. I hear she has a young child living with her?'

'Yes. A girl named Beth, a pretty little thing. She calls Miss Vee her new mummy and she's going to be spoiled.'

'Well, you could've knocked me over with a feather,' Maya replied with her lopsided grin. Jago's mother was a native of Canada, one of the Mi'kmaq people though her grandfather had been a white man and Jago's father was also white. Maya's mother and grandmother, though, were of the Mi'kmaq people who had lived in the area for centuries before the arrival of the settlers, hunting for their food. These days some of her mother's people lived on land that was reserved for them, often in small tin-roofed shacks, but Jago and Maya lived in a good cabin built of logs and lined with solid wood that Jago whitewashed regularly. The floors were also of wood but covered in the main by colourful rugs that Jago's father had bought for her. In the bedroom there were some fur rugs that Maya had made from animal skins that she'd cured and dyed herself as a young woman. She'd brought them with

54

her as her dowry when she'd married Jago's father. They had a toilet out back that Jago had somehow rigged up a flushing system for, taking the waste to a drainage ditch and a deep sewer, and they had a well of fresh spring water that served all their needs. Away from the built-up area in country that was wilderness apart from their cultivated fields, there was no running water, though Jago planned on running pipes from the fast-flowing river one day when he could afford it. For the moment he fetched the water and filled up a covered tank out back of the house so that there was always fresh water available.

Like Jago, his father had worked his own land as well as labouring at the lumbermill. He'd died of a sudden and virulent fever when Jago was still at school and it had been hard for Maya to keep her son clothed and fed so buying him special boots or paying to see a specialist was beyond her. She'd been lucky enough to get a job working at the Ridgers' clothing store, just scrubbing floors and cleaning windows, but then Miss Vee had seen her with Jago and everything changed.

Mr Bittern had taken Jago on at the mill and Miss Vee had taken him to see the specialist and had the boot made. The lad's wages made it possible for Maya to stay home and look after their cows and other livestock as well as cooking. Miss Vee had given them their lives back and Maya thought she was second only to God.

'Well, I just hope that child appreciates how lucky she is to have Miss Vee take her on,' Maya said but Jago wasn't listening. He'd just seen a girl he'd noticed earlier walking down the wide avenue. She'd been at the lake but she'd been looking about her, lost in wonder and he thought she hadn't seen him. She was right pretty, seen close up. Jago liked the way she walked with her head up – she was determined and something told him life wasn't very happy for her right now. He understood that feeling all too well and, had he been alone, might have stopped and offered her a lift – though she would probably have been horrified if she'd seen his boot. Most girls either mocked him or looked terrified. Yet there was something about this girl that called to him.

'You dreaming again, Jago?' Maya asked and Jago laughed.

'You know me too well,' he said. 'You needn't cook me supper tonight, Ma. Some of those pastries will do just fine.'

CHAPTER 7

Miss Cotton looked at Julie in approval as she saw the grey dress she was wearing when she came out of her small bedroom. 'Yes, that is very suitable for school,' she said. 'You are quite good at sewing, Miss Miller. I wasn't sure you were telling me the truth but that is a creditable effort. I am pleased that you took so much trouble.'

Julie murmured something about it being good of Miss Cotton to supply her with the materials but she wasn't even listening, carrying on as if Julie hadn't spoken.

'Now I can leave you in charge of the sewing classes for the older girls as well,' Miss Cotton went on. 'You can actually teach them something instead of just watching as they do the work I set for them.'

'Yes, miss,' Julie said. If Miss Cotton imagined she just sat there with her mouth shut and watched, she was mistaken. She had already sorted out many small pieces of embroidering and plain sewing that the girls had got wrong but there was no sense in pointing that out as Miss Cotton never listened to a word Julie said – she was there to do as she was told and that was it. Her opinion was not required and her conversation was not welcomed and usually ignored. She was just the girl Miss Cotton needed to sit in with one class while she taught the other. It was made plain to her that she was an evacuee, a girl who received charity and was not worthy of being consulted.

However, Julie was determined to make herself heard that morning. 'May I ask you a question, Miss Cotton? It's important.'

'What? Oh, if you must. I don't want to be late for school.'

'How much will you pay me and when?' Julie said swiftly.

'Pay you?' Miss Cotton looked shocked. 'What nonsense is this, girl? I have you brought out from that slum you lived in to a decent home, I feed you and give you clothes – what more can you expect, you ungrateful girl? If I expected to pay, there are plenty of young women here already!'

Julie stared at her, horrified. So she was little more than a slave to this woman? True, she was given the freedom to walk where she liked when not at the school and her work was pleasant enough, but if she received no wages then she was tied to Miss Cotton for life. She had relaxed into a kind of defiant acceptance of her situation, believing that in a year or so she would have saved enough to move on, but now that hope had gone. She felt humiliated and close to tears. Was her work worth so little?

'Really! Did you imagine that I consider what you do worth more than your bed and board? I could let that room for a few dollars if I chose.'

Julie couldn't find an answer, even though she knew her silence had made her employer even more angry. Her eyes stung with tears she was trying not to shed as she struggled with her disappointment. She felt a hard knot inside her chest but she fought to control her expression. It wouldn't be wise to let Miss Cotton see the extent of her dissatisfaction.

'Well, don't sulk, girl,' Miss Cotton said. 'In time, when I consider you worth it, I may give you a few cents to spend in the holidays.'

Julie's head went up. She didn't want to be given a few cents when her employer decided she was worth it. Surely she was entitled to something each week even if the work she did wasn't skilled or difficult? How easy would it be to find work elsewhere? Wild thoughts of running off to look for work ran through Julie's mind but she had no training and the only things she was really good at were sewing and cooking. Perhaps she could find work as a seamstress? In London, she knew there were many workshops where the girls worked long hours for small wages that barely paid for food and lodging but at least it would have been a start while she looked for something else. She wasn't sure that it would be easy to secure the kind of work she wanted here. She hadn't yet found time to walk around the town, because Miss Cotton lived too far out but there must be shops and bars and restaurants there so she might find employment – and yet that would be the first place Miss Cotton would look and she had papers that made her Julie's guardian.

She felt trapped. A prisoner. She wasn't locked in

her room at night but she wouldn't put it past Miss Cotton to do it if Julie gave her any reason to doubt her.

Holding back the tears as she followed Miss Cotton to the school, Julie wondered what she could do to win her freedom. Would Miss Cotton let her go when she was older? Where would she go? What could she do if no one wanted a seamstress?

Clearly, she must stay with Miss Cotton until she was older and the woman no longer had the right to fetch her back from wherever she ran to. She gritted her teeth against the long, lonely road ahead, not knowing that things were about to get much worse.

It was as they walked home that evening that a few flakes of snow began to fall. It had been a cool autumn, colder than Julie was used to at home in London, but now she shivered despite the warm coat she was wearing. It was made of wool and Miss Cotton had produced it from a trunk in the attic, saying it had been hers as a young girl. Julie noticed the smell of mothballs but that soon wore off and it had kept her warm, but now she shivered despite the coat.

Miss Cotton looked at her sharply. 'I hope you're not coming down with something, Julie. I don't want an invalid on my hands, especially now that Ralph is coming to stay with us for a while.'

'Who is Ralph?' Julie asked as the back of her neck prickled.

'My brother's son,' Miss Cotton replied with a thin smile. 'My brother has important business in the States and while he is away, Ralph is to stay with us. His mother died some years ago and there has been some trouble at his boarding school. He was very unfairly blamed for it and has been expelled, so until his father returns and finds a new place for him, he will live with us. Ralph is seventeen, eighteen next spring. My brother wanted him to go on to college but now . . . well, perhaps he'll take him into the business.'

Julie wondered about Miss Cotton's nephew as they walked the remaining distance to her home. What would this Ralph Cotton be like? If he'd been expelled from school, he might be trouble so perhaps Miss Cotton would be so busy with him, she would forget Julie and it might be a chance for her to . . . what?

It would be dangerous to run away without somewhere to run to, Julie thought. She knew so very little of the area to which she'd been brought. She could find her way to the school and the lake and lumbermill and she knew there was a bus that would take her to the town, if she had the fare, but of course she didn't. It seemed as if she was stuck here whatever happened, because she had nowhere to go . . .

Ralph Cotton arrived that evening and from the moment that he looked at her, Julie knew she would have to leave as soon as she could. He was sly and malicious and she sensed that he was seething with anger inside. Julie had no idea why Miss Cotton's nephew was so angry inside but he was and she believed he would take it out on her if he could.

Miss Cotton was different with Ralph. She smiled and laughed, offered him cakes and iced lemonade for his tea and generally made a fuss of him. Julie thought she made herself look silly but perhaps that thought was generated by jealousy, because whenever Miss Cotton looked her way, the foolish smile vanished and her eyes became narrow and hard.

Why didn't Miss Cotton like her? She had tried her best to do everything her employer asked but it was never enough and the malicious teasing started that night when Miss Cotton went to the bathroom. Ralph sidled up to Julie and tugged at her hair hard.

'You're ugly, evacuee brat,' he said with a kind of glee. 'Your hair is badly cut and you have dirt in your ears.'

'No, I don't. I wash them every morning,' Julie said, flinching away. She'd met his sort in the school playground when she was younger and she'd given more than one bully a black eye. 'If you pull my hair again, I'll hit you. Don't you dare to touch me!'

'What will you do about it, ugly girl?' he said, leaning closer so that she could feel the warmth of his breath on her face. 'Run to my aunt with your tales? She won't believe you, because you are just an unwanted poverty-stricken brat sent out from England – a charity girl.'

Julie felt the smart of tears but held them back, determined that he shouldn't see how much his taunting hurt. It hurt because it was true. She was a charity girl that no one wanted or loved and she couldn't see a way out of the trap she was in. With no friends or family and no money she had no option but to stay here until she was allowed to leave – and when would that be?

Tipping her chin up, Julie glared at her tormentor. 'If I am ugly, I don't care,' she said defiantly. 'I shan't go to Miss Cotton because she's as mean and nasty as you – but if you come near me again, I'll make you sorry!'

For a moment his eyes gleamed with malice and she thought he meant to hit her but then his aunt called from her sitting room and he turned to answer the summons, but at the door of the kitchen, he looked back. 'I'll get you, charity girl, and I'll make you sorry . . .'

Julie turned back to the sink and got on with the dishes, her shoulders straight and her face drawn into a mask of indifference. Her stomach was churning with anger and humiliation, but pride made her carry on as if nothing had happened.

'Haven't you any sewing to do?' Miss Cotton asked a few minutes later. 'I am taking Ralph out to meet some friends of mine. If you have no sewing of your own, you can mend the blouse in the washing basket. It must have torn on the line somehow.'

'I'll be happy to mend it for you – and anything else,' Julie said, though inside she felt resentful and angry. Why was Miss Cotton so cold and uncaring to her when she doted on that horrid Ralph? Because she was just a charity girl no one wanted and he was her nephew. Life was so unfair!

'Just the blouse,' Miss Cotton said and nodded. 'We may be late back. Don't wait up for us.'

Julie couldn't bring herself to answer. She just nodded, feeling miserable. It was the unhappiest she had been since she was sent out here, even worse, somehow, than when she'd been told she would not receive wages. She blinked away angry tears as her employer and her nephew left, hardly noticing the malicious look Ralph threw at her.

How long would he stay with them? Julie wasn't sure she could bear his mockery for too long and she didn't imagine he was finished with her. He would make her pay for her show of defiance. Tears suddenly ran from her eyes and then she was sobbing hard. Life was so cruel! She felt so alone and empty that she thought it might be better to die than live this way . . .

Her tears lasted only a few minutes and then her head came up and she wiped her face. No, she wouldn't give in! She was worth more than all these people who scorned her and she would fight back. She wouldn't let that horrid Ralph win.

It was very late when something woke her and she heard the bedroom door handle turn. A shiver went down her spine, because she knew who was standing outside her door. She'd locked it and wedged it with a chair before she went to bed, convinced Ralph would take his spite out on her one way or another. Julie had no idea why he had it in for her. Perhaps he was angry because his school had expelled him or perhaps it was just his nasty nature, but he'd been intent on mischief from the moment he saw her.

She heard him tug at the handle and push against the door but it held against him and then she heard Miss Cotton's voice and sensed that he'd gone away. Julie felt sick for a moment, full of fear, her heart racing. It was like the time her uncle had come to her room and touched her. She'd bitten his neck hard to stop him in the end, despite his threats, and she would do the same to Ralph, perhaps worse. She'd been frightened to say or do too much to her uncle, because her father really liked him and despite loving her might not have believed her – but she didn't care about Miss Cotton or her nephew. Anger rose in her, banishing the fear and she made up her mind as she lay there that night, wondering when Ralph would try to punish her next: if Ralph Cotton tried to abuse her, she would stick her scissors in his flesh! And if things got too bad, she would run away. She could lie about her age, pretend to be older so that she could get a job and she would do anything rather than live here with people she was beginning to hate.

Julie would have gone on hoping that Miss Cotton would eventually think her worthy of a small wage had Ralph not arrived but if she was forced to defend herself against him, who would Miss Cotton believe? Her life was about to get even worse and she wasn't sure what to do. If she ran away, she had to have a plan. If she could get to Halifax, perhaps she could find work there and if it was big enough to get lost in they might not bother to look for her when she'd gone. And she might be able to find Beth. Arthur was surely all right with his new parents, but she needed to know Beth was safe.

Julie tossed and turned, unable to sleep. She didn't want to go on living here and yet she had nowhere to go . . .

CHAPTER 8

'Miss Vee, there's a person at the door says he's come for the child. I told him I didn't think you would be letting him take her – that's right, isn't it?' Aggie's outraged expression told Vee her feelings on the matter.

Vee's eyes narrowed and flashed with the light of battle. 'What sort of a person, Aggie? Is he respectable?'

'Looks the mean sort to me, close-set eyes,' Aggie said with a little sniff. 'Says the child belongs to him. Says he paid for her passage out here and wants what belongs to him.' Her eyes met Vee's. 'Shall I tell him to crawl back under the stone he came from?'

'Slimy toad, is he?' Vee laughed, because it was the way Aggie described her arch enemy, Harold Trevors. 'I'll see this person in the kitchen and you'll remain with me, Aggie. If he paid towards her passage then I will reimburse him but he can't have our Beth.'

'Over my dead body,' Aggie said and set her mouth hard. 'Do you want me to take my broom to him, Miss Vee?'

'Only if he refuses to leave,' Vee said with a hint of laughter in her voice. 'We'll see him off between us.'

66

The man waiting on the back porch was more like a weasel than a toad, Vee thought, with a thin nose and mouth and sly eyes that looked her up and down as if weighing up his chances.

'I've been told you've got the kid,' he said, launching into the attack like a cornered beast. 'She's mine, so hand her over. I paid ten dollars towards her passage.'

'Then you shall have your money returned,' Vee said. 'You were not at the ship to collect her and so she was given to me and this is where she is going to stay. Aggie, give this – this person, twelve dollars out of the housekeeping purse for his trouble in coming here.'

The man stared at her angrily. 'Now see here, Mrs Bittern, I want that child. My wife can't have none and she's expecting her.'

'Then you should have been at the ship when it docked,' Vee said coolly. She didn't believe the story of the childless wife for a moment. If this creature had a wife – and she doubted it – he wouldn't trouble himself to bring a child out from England to please her. 'I don't know who told you a child was here but whoever it was clearly did not know the position. The child is legally mine and you have forfeited your claim, if you ever had one. I am willing to give you the money you say you paid for her passage.' She nodded to Aggie, who placed the notes on the scrubbed pine table and stood back, looking as if she wanted to keep a distance because he smelled. 'Take it and go before I call on the law to remove you.'

The man looked at her through narrowed eyes and then made a dart into the kitchen, snatched the money and retreated to the door. 'It's like he said, you think you're above the law,' he snarled and then left hastily as Aggie reached for her broom, looking back to fling the words at them. 'You just wait. That kid belongs to me and I've got rights. That's what he said and you'll be hearing from my lawyer!'

'Who did he mean?' Aggie muttered, slamming the door after him and locking it as though she feared he might try to return.

'I'm not sure, but I think it could only have been one person . . .'

'You mean that toad Trevors?' Aggie demanded with a jut of her jaw. 'Why would he send a creature like that here, Miss Vee? He must know you wouldn't let him take the child.'

'Trevors doesn't want the child,' Vee said, thinking it through, 'it was just to upset me, make me think I could lose Beth, but I made sure legally that couldn't happen. It's an empty threat, Aggie, so I'm not going to lose sleep over it.'

'He looked like a nasty bit of work,' Aggie said and sniffed her disgust. 'I'd be careful, Miss Vee. It might be an empty threat, but what's the point of it? Why would they want to upset you?'

Vee shrugged. 'I really don't know. I offered for a property he'd arranged to buy but she wouldn't sell to me because she was afraid of him so I can't imagine what that was all about. Unless it was a warning.'

'Well, just you be careful,' Aggie gave her a dire look. 'I've never trusted that man. He wouldn't dare to harm you if Mr Malcolm was here but he might not be back for a long time.'

'I am a match for Trevors and his minions,' Vee said stoutly, but she couldn't help wondering why Harold Trevors should send someone to try and frighten her. If he had, of course. 'It was just a spiteful act,' she told Aggie. 'Nothing to worry about.'

'Let's hope you're right,' Aggie said and shook her head. 'If you like I could ask Selmer to send his son-in-law round?'

'I don't think we need the law involved just yet,' Vee said and smiled. 'But I shall keep my wits about me, Aggie. He's up to something but I have no idea what.'

Nothing sinister happened for two days and then Aggie came into the sitting room where Vee was reading a story to Beth that morning, her expression one of foreboding.

'He's here, asking to speak to you, Miss Vee – that toad Trevors. Do you want me to send him packing?'

'No, ask Mr Trevors to come in,' Vee said and, as her housekeeper went out with a darkling look at the child, she took Beth by the hand. 'Could you go upstairs and fetch a handkerchief from my drawer, darling?'

'Yes, Mummy,' Beth said and got up obediently.

'Then go to the kitchen and ask Aggie for a cookie and milk before you bring it back.'

The child smiled and ran off eagerly. Vee went to the window and looked out at her back garden. There was a light frosting of white over the lawns, flowerbeds and shrubs as the weather turned much cooler than of late. She was still looking out when she sensed that she was no longer alone. Turning, she looked at the tall, heavily-built man who stood there staring at her with what could only be dislike.

'Mr Trevors,' she said in a flat tone. 'What can I do for you?'

'Stop interfering in my business for a start!' he said rudely.

'I wasn't aware that I had.' Her fine brows arched in disbelief, giving him her haughtiest stare.

'You offered two hundred dollars above my price on that property across town.'

'Ah yes, I had forgotten. I considered it worth the price but she kept to her word to you and refused my offer.'

'She asked me for more and when I refused said she'd decided not to sell so I had to give her the extra. I call that interference.'

'Perhaps, but business is business, Mr Trevor. Well, you bought the property so why have you come?' Her gaze narrowed, eyes like flint as she met his angry look.

'Because you owe me,' he said and his eyes gleamed with sudden avarice. 'I want that lumbermill of yours – name your price and I'll pay.'

'The mill isn't for sale,' Vee replied meeting his fierce stare without flinching. 'I've told you so several times.'

'What does a woman of your age want with a mill?' he demanded, his voice becoming guttural and bullying. 'You've got no heirs except that brother and he isn't around most of the time, doesn't even look after what he has.'

'No, I do that with the help of my staff,' Vee said. 'Besides, I fail to see what difference it makes to you what we do with our property.'

'I want to be the main property owner in Sackville and I intend to get my way, so why not make it easy on yourself and sell to me?'

'Because I do not wish to sell and . . .' She paused for effect, letting her words sink in. 'I wouldn't sell to you if I did!'

'Blast you! Just because I got drunk once and made a pass at you—'

'It was more than that,' Vee said, 'but I do not let it influence me. I believe the property in Sackville may climb steeply in value one day – when they build more bridges, making it easier to get from Upper Sackville into Halifax. Though who knows how long it will be before folk move in to build? Land is becoming scarce, building land that is, because we have a lot that is of no commercial use, too rough and wild, but it is obvious that one day the need will be there and then land and property here will rise in value.' She smiled as she saw the expression in his eyes. 'Did you think you were the only one to work that out? I am sorry to disappoint you, Mr Trevors. I have no intention of selling my property and I may be buying more.' Let him make what he would of that! She rang the bell for Aggie. 'Good day to you . . .'

'You vixen! I'll—' Trevors moved towards her as if he would strike her but at that moment the parlour door opened and Aggie entered accompanied by a young man wearing a uniform.

'Selmer's son-in-law called round to see you, Miss Vee. Wants to know if you will open the bazaar this Christmas same as always.' Aggie's eyes were bright with the light of battle as she looked at the man she despised. Harold Trevors scowled at her but moved away from Vee.

The tall, powerful man with Aggie turned his dark eyes on Vee's visitor. 'Ah, Mr Trevors. Sorry to interrupt but Selmer asked me to call by and I happened to be near . . .'

Vee smiled inwardly. Aggie had clearly summoned him and he stood with his hand on the gun holster at his hip, looking crisp, clean and certain of his position and duty as an important member of the local police force.

'Thank you, Hank,' Vee said, smiling in welcome. 'Why don't you stay for coffee and some of Aggie's apple pie and we can discuss the bazaar. Mr Trevors was just leaving.'

Harold Trevors glared at her as he left, Aggie following him like a guard dog, all bristles and teeth, determined to see him off the premises. Hank lifted his thick dark brows at Vee.

'Was he causing you trouble, Miss Vee?'

'He would like to if I didn't have such good friends,' Vee said with a smile. 'I am too well protected.'

'Shall I arrest him for drunk driving and lock him up for a few days?' Hank offered.

'Not unless you catch him driving while under the influence,' Vee said and laughed. 'Thank you for suggesting it, though. I can manage Mr Trevors – and if the time comes when I can't, I'll let you know. Now, about this bazaar – which charity are we supporting this time?'

'It's food parcels for the British folk,' Hank said with his charming smile. He was a very handsome man, dark eyes and hair, and in the prime of life, big with broad shoulders and an air of authority that few challenged. 'They're suffering something awful, I've heard. We're going to send them tinned salmon and whatever else they need most.'

'That's worth supporting,' Vee told him. 'We have relations in Britain, you know – distant cousins we've not heard from for years. Malcolm was telling me he is going to try and trace them when he gets time. And my husband had a cousin there too – he left him some property but as yet my lawyer can't trace him. He and his family seem to have disappeared.'

'You should contact the Red Cross,' Hank told her. 'Give them the information you have and they may be able to trace the family for you through the British branch.'

'Yes, I might do that,' Vee agreed. 'I'd like to know if they're all right – but that's for us to sort out. I'll gladly help at the bazaar, Hank. What do you need most?'

He pulled out a list and handed it to her and they talked for a while over a pot of coffee and a plate of pie before he took his leave. 'I'll be seeing you,' he told her. 'Now you be sure to call me if you have any bother, Miss Vee.'

'I surely will,' Vee said and smiled as the younger man took his leave. His arrival had been helpful, but she wasn't afraid of the man that had threatened her. If Harold Trevors thought he could intimidate her with his nasty tricks he had another think coming.

She was thoughtful, though, as she sat down at her desk. Hank's visit had made her more aware of something that had been on her mind for a while now. She opened her address book and ran her finger down the page. Ah, there it was, Paul and Sheila Miller. She had an address in London, though a letter she'd sent a few years back had not been answered and a second one had been returned stamped 'addressee unknown'. In the first letter she'd told Paul that Bill was dead and had left a property to Paul, which would revert to Vee after fifteen years if not claimed. Now, she decided, she could pass what information she had to the Red Cross and they might be able to find the Millers. The least she could do would be to see what they needed and send them a parcel. It must surely be welcome at a time like this?

CHAPTER 9

The handsome man with the limp was up at the lake again. Julie, who came as often as she could, had found a place she liked to sit which was sheltered by rocks to either side and where the sun felt warm on her face, even though it was cold in the shade, bitterly cold.

Hearing a loud splash, she looked about her, startled. Had something or someone fallen in? As her gaze was drawn across the wide expanse of the lake, she saw a man swimming strongly and knew it was him, the man she'd seen here several times on her Sunday afternoon visits, although she wasn't sure if he'd seen her; if he had, he'd ignored her.

The water must be so cold and yet he swam as if he enjoyed it. His dip was brief, though, and then he was climbing out just a short distance from her . . . naked. She didn't turn her head as he stood, shaking the water from his hair, and she admired the lovely pale tan colour of his skin as he dried himself briskly before dressing. In the water his disability had not been apparent, but now, as he rubbed at his ankle, she saw what made him drag his foot when he walked, then he pulled on thick socks and slipped his misshapen foot inside a heavy boot, lacing it tightly.

Sympathy for his pain, which she understood was not just physical, swept over her. Julie understood what a disability like that must have cost him all his life. She'd suffered enough at school from cruel taunts, because her classmates believed her mother was a drunk. They hadn't understood that her mother had diabetes and when she had an attack in the street, as had happened on more than one occasion, she appeared drunk. It was a lack of sugar and an insulin reaction, but even Julie hadn't understood why it happened when she was young. She knew now her mother could have controlled her condition better but she had seemed incapable of doing so and many times couldn't afford to, therefore her health gradually became worse and worse, which meant that often Julie's clothes and hair went unwashed.

Brushing aside thoughts of her past, Julie watched as the man walked away. He hadn't noticed her or seen her watching him and she was glad. He might have felt she was spying on him and been angry or humiliated. In fact, she had thought how beautiful his body was as he emerged from the water, strong and full of life like the pictures of a young Greek god in the books Julie had loved to read at school, but, on dry land, he was once more a victim of his disability.

Julie wiped a stray tear from her cheek. Whoever he was, he would not want her to feel sorry for him.

She waited until she heard the sound of his truck

driving away and then got hurriedly to her feet. She would be late for tea and Miss Cotton would scold. Ralph would leer and mouth, 'Charity girl' at her. He was always giving her threatening looks and hissing things as she passed him and though he'd never tried to open her door again, Julie disliked him very much and wished he would go away. It seemed, though, that he would be with them for a long time since his father was in America on business to do with the war and would be away for months. Ralph's father was in manufacturing and building, which meant he must be quite wealthy. Perhaps that was why his son was so arrogant? He thought his father's wealth entitled him to take whatever he wanted.

How could she bear living close to him for so long? He made her skin crawl and her fear was icy at times. No matter how often she told herself not to be afraid, she was. Ralph was horrid and she was beginning to hate the sound of his voice. She wished he would go away and never come back.

Julie was hurrying to get home when the heel of her shoe caught and snapped off. She tried walking in one shoe but could only hobble and decided to remove them both. Sitting on the pavement, she was slipping the second shoe off when a truck went by. It stopped just down the road and then backed up to her. Julie tensed but then the driver got out and she saw it was the man from the lake. Her heart raced a little but he smiled and her apprehension vanished.

'Having trouble, miss?' he asked.

'I lost the heel of my shoe and I need to get back or Miss Cotton will be cross.'

A soft laugh broke from him. 'Can't have that,' he said. 'I'm Jago Marsh. I work up at the lake – will you allow me to give you a lift, miss?'

Julie hesitated momentarily and then inclined her head. 'Thank you,' she said, walking shoeless to the truck, which he had opened for her to get into the passenger seat. 'I'm Julie and I was up at the lake too.'

'Nice to meet you, Miss Julie,' Jago said and started the engine. It was an old truck and noisy so he didn't try to make conversation as they drove. Only when they stopped at the end of the street where Miss Cotton lived, did he look at her again. 'I hope you'll be all right now?'

'Yes, I shall. Thank you for being kind, Mr Marsh.'

'Most folks call me Jago,' he said gruffly. 'Mebbe we'll meet again at the lake?'

'I hope so,' she said and then, blushing ran off because he might think the worse of her if she lingered.

He was nice and she liked him, but if Miss Cotton saw her talking to him, she would tell her off and it was hard enough living there now since Ralph's arrival. She didn't look back and so didn't notice that Jago sat watching until she entered the house.

'She is pretty and her tits are great,' Ralph told his friend, Pete Trevors. They'd been at the same boarding school together and been expelled at the same time. Their fathers had forbidden them to meet but they ignored the rules, as they always did. 'I'm going to have her one of these days when my aunt is out.'

'Miss Cotton will throw you out if you do,' Pete drawled and lit a cigarette. He shared it with Ralph.

'Why not go into Halifax and find a girl who'll do it for a few drinks? There's bound to be one.'

'I want *her*,' Ralph said, his mouth twisting. 'I want to make her suffer, the little cat.'

Pete shrugged. 'I'm not interested in that kind of sport,' he said. 'I like girls who are willing. If you have money in your pocket a lot of them are.'

'Your father gives you money. Mine is a skinflint,' Ralph muttered sullenly. 'Once my allowance is gone, I've nothing left to last me the month – and he stopped it for two months because I was expelled. My aunt gave me a few dollars but not enough.'

'I have to earn anything I get,' Pete replied, a sour look on his face. Ralph knew Pete's father was rich but he'd never had much to do with him. 'My father gives me a small allowance and that's it. If I want more I've got to work. Mom gave me more but since she left . . .' Pete shook his head.

'When my father gets back, I'll have to work too, either in his new munitions factory which is really busy now because of this war, or maybe on a building site.' He made a face of disgust at the idea.

'I wouldn't mind that,' Pete said and shrugged. 'My father wants me to do his dirty work and I hate it.'

Ralph nodded indifferently. He had no idea what Pete meant. 'What shall we do now then?' he asked. 'I'm bored.'

'Let's drive into Halifax in my truck and get drunk,' Pete said. 'We can play pool in the bar or just look at the women – and maybe, you know . . .' He raised his eyebrows suggestively and Ralph grinned.

'OK,' Ralph agreed. He had nothing better to do,

spending most of his time just mooching around so he was free and bored. 'Let's see if we can find anyone to pick a fight with. I feel like a fight . . .'

Pete nodded and started up his truck. He zigzagged across the road, narrowly missing hitting the verges on either side, making Ralph laugh, especially when a lorry came round the corner and they had to swerve out of its way, causing the driver to honk at them. This was better. This was what he enjoyed. He grinned at Pete. 'I'm still going to teach that little cat a lesson, but she can wait a bit longer . . . I enjoy seeing the way her eyes spark when she tries to hide her anger but can't. Same with her fear – she can't hide that, either. It's too good to rush.'

CHAPTER 10

Julie knew she had to think of a way to leave Miss Cotton's house. Ralph was making her life unbearable, pinching her spitefully whenever he got the chance and hissing in her ear about what he would do to her when he got her alone. She'd given him some murderous looks but knew that if he was determined to attack her, he would find the opportunity. Her bedroom door was locked at night and she'd taken to locking it any time she left it, slipping the key inside her dress for safekeeping. If he found it, he would steal it and she would have no defence as she slept.

That Sunday morning Miss Cotton announced that she was taking her nephew to friends in Halifax. 'We shall be gone all day,' she said in the flat tone she used to address Julie. 'There is bread and cold meat in the pantry. You may have the day to yourself once you've been to church.'

Julie thanked her, feeling a wave of relief. For once she would not have to contend with Miss Cotton's objectionable nephew following her if she left the house. His threatening looks had made her afraid to go for walks alone and she'd pleaded a headache the previous Sunday, preferring to stay in and sew rather than venture out. Today, she would go for a long walk to the lake despite the cold. It had looked as if it would snow for a few days now, but though some had fallen overnight, it hadn't settled yet and the earth was sticky and muddy underfoot.

Walking on pavements or grass wherever she could, Julie made her way towards the lake where the lumbermill lay silent. No work was ever done on a Sunday in Mrs Bittern's mill, although the men sometimes worked on Saturdays and Julie had heard the noise of the saws from a distance, but she hadn't ventured near. Now, she walked briskly, enjoying the clean bite of the frosty air that was made pleasant by a wintry sun. It felt so good to be out and free of unwanted attentions.

Finding a log that had been left by the side of the burbling water, Julie sat for a few moments, watching birds flit down to drink from little pools and listening to their cries and the sounds of other small creatures moving about within the wood. She felt relaxed, even happy. It was a nice place to live – or it would be if Miss Cotton were kinder and her nephew would go away. Julie had begun to really enjoy her work now. The girls had been snooty towards her at first but she had managed to gain their respect, perhaps because she'd helped them without sarcasm or sharp words and they smiled at her now, so despite the cold manner of her employer, she could have been content were it not for Ralph.

Julie understood that he meant her harm. He was older than her and thought himself a man. She feared he would do something bad to her if she didn't get away, but how could she go with no money? She knew no one and had no idea what to do . . .

'Aren't you cold?' The man's voice startled and scared her and she looked up. It was Jago Marsh, the man with the foot that dragged on the ground a bit, the one she'd seen swimming in the lake who'd given her a lift home when her heel broke. Her slight panic receded but her cheeks felt warm as she saw him looking at her with interest.

'No, not at the moment,' she said and he stood a short distance away, seeming hesitant to approach. 'Mr Marsh, you work here, don't you? I'm not doing any harm, am I?'

'No, you're not doing any harm,' he said and smiled. Julie thought his smile was nice and the little flicker of apprehension inside her died away. She didn't feel threatened by this man. 'I just wondered if you were all right?'

Julie hesitated, tempted to tell him that she was afraid of Ralph and unhappy, but she didn't know him. How could she pour her troubles out to a stranger? Besides, she didn't imagine he could help her.

'I was sent out from England as an evacuee,' she said at last. 'I work for Miss Cotton at her school.'

'Yes, I've seen you with her,' he agreed and sat down opposite her. 'Did you get into trouble the other night?'

'She scolded me for ruining my shoes, but it didn't matter, they were her old ones she'd given me for work.'

Jago frowned, paused, then, 'If you wanted to go

83

into town on a Saturday afternoon to shop for a new pair, I take Ma sometimes and there is room for you.'

'That's kind . . .' Julie looked away, too embarrassed to tell him she had no money. 'When I can afford . . . one day, perhaps. That would be nice, thank you.'

He nodded and got to his feet. Julie noticed that he used the strength in his arms to push himself up. 'Well, I'd best get on – Maya will have finished her visit with her friends and be waiting. It was nice to meet you, Miss Julie.'

'Perhaps we can talk again?' Julie spoke the words and then blushed furiously in case she sounded too forward. She liked him and didn't want him to think her a forward girl. 'I-I don't have many friends here.'

He nodded as if he approved and then walked away, limping. Julie wanted to call him back, to beg him to stay – ask him if he could help her find work somewhere else, but she couldn't find the right words. Perhaps she was being ungrateful, just as Miss Cotton said. She'd been given a bed to sleep in, food and clothes, and that was perhaps as much as she ought to expect for the work she did. It wasn't hard work and she knew that girls who went into factories back home would need to work harder than she did. But she'd hoped for a new, loving family and instead she was just a charity girl to Miss Cotton and her nephew, there to do as she was told and say as little as possible.

Sighing, she got to her feet. Perhaps if she explained to Miss Cotton, told her what Ralph had whispered to her, she would make him stop. Her life wasn't so very bad when she could come to a lovely spot like this and enjoy it. Feeling braver, she decided that it was time she spoke out, stood up for herself . . .

'You wretched, ungrateful girl! Hold your hand out!'

'No, why should I?' Julie said, putting her hands behind her back. 'I've told you the truth.'

'Liar!' Miss Cotton grabbed her arm and then held her wrist with one hand while administering three sharp cuts with the ruler on the curled fingers of Julie's fist. She had refused to open it and so been hit across the knuckles, which hurt even more. 'Ralph would never say such filthy things. Wash your mouth out with salt water and then go to your room.'

'No, I won't!' Julie cried defiantly. She wasn't going to rinse her mouth with salt water for telling the truth, but she rushed for her room and went inside, slamming the door behind her. As she took out the key to lock herself in, her arm was caught and, although she struggled to retain it, Ralph wrenched it from her. 'Give that back to me!' she yelled.

'Here you are, Auntie,' Ralph said, looking innocent as Miss Cotton opened the door and he handed her the key. 'Lock her in or she might run away.'

'She is capable of anything,' Miss Cotton said. 'Thank you, Ralph. We'll see what a few days of bread and water will do for the ungrateful girl!'

'I told you the truth!' Julie said defiantly. 'He said bad things to me – and he's tried to get into my room at night—'

'Ridiculous! My nephew would never do such a thing.' The door was slammed in Julie's face and locked. 'When you apologise and learn your place, you may resume your work and eat with us again – until then you will stay in this room.'

'It's the truth!' Julie called but she knew Miss Cotton would never believe her. She was being punished for what Ralph had said to her – his filthy words attributed to her. She knew it was useless to protest further, even though anger and resentment boiled inside her. She wanted to pummel the door, kick it down and run from here, but the wood was solid and there was no escape until Miss Cotton let her out. In the meantime, she had nothing to do but sit here and stare at the wall. She had no materials left to make anything and she'd never been given a book to read since she came here. Even at the orphanage there had been books to read, and they had been her one escape.

Running to the window, she looked out into the street but although the lamps were lit no one was about. Her window was a casement and she could have opened it and climbed out, but there was a long drop to the ground and she was afraid of breaking a limb if she jumped. Returning to the bed, she sat down and crossed her arms over her chest but she refused to cry. Crying was for little children and never did any good.

Miss Cotton wouldn't let her starve. Even she wasn't that cruel. Julie would just sit here and make up stories in her head. Her father had done that when she was little, telling her his stories. Later, when she'd gone to school and learned to read, she'd discovered that Daddy's stories were often based on fairy tales from books, but he'd always given the princesses in the stories her name. So it was Princess Julie who was wakened by the prince with a kiss or let down her long hair to help her prince rescue her. If she had long hair like that, perhaps she could use it to escape.

Julie's feelings of despair and misery eased as she made herself think of happier times, when her mother had been well, showing her how to sew and cook, and her father had loved and spoiled her. Why did people have to die? A tear trickled down her cheek at the thought but she brushed it away. No matter how horrible things were, she wouldn't give in. She wasn't going to cry and if Ralph tried his tricks on her again, she would make him regret it!

Julie remembered how nice it had been by the lake. She made up her mind that the next time she saw Jago Marsh she would ask if he knew where she could find work. Somewhere away from this place – somewhere Miss Cotton and her nephew couldn't find her. She wished she'd talked to him more, but she hadn't liked to in case he thought her too forward. But perhaps he wouldn't want to help her. Despite herself, tears stung her eyes. Was there anyone she could trust – anyone that might care how she felt?

Brushing her tears away, she told herself to stop being silly. She'd learned the hard way that no one wanted her now. Julie had to stand on her own two feet. It was useless to ask for help.

CHAPTER 11

Pete's head was thumping when he got up. It was the result of too much drinking and he cursed, wishing he hadn't spent so much time in the bar the previous evening. He threw up into the toilet, hating the sour taste in his mouth, but then, he hated most things about his life these days. It was when he was with Ralph that he did stupid things, like getting drunk with him and making a nuisance of themselves. He wasn't sure why he went along with Ralph's ideas, unless it was because he needed a friend.

Life had been hard for Pete since his mother left them two years earlier. Until then, although aware of an atmosphere between his parents at times, things hadn't been so bad. When he was home from school his mother took him places and gave him anything he wanted, and she visited him at his expensive boarding school, bringing him hampers of wonderful food that made him popular with the other boys.

It hurt Pete that she had just run off and not even contacted him once since. He sometimes wondered if she'd an accident because, surely, she wouldn't just cut him out of her life – his father, yes, Pete knew she didn't love him, but she'd always loved Pete, hadn't she? Yet he hadn't even had one letter in two years and he didn't know why.

His father had told him she was a selfish bitch who had run away with a lover but was he telling the truth? Pete's mother might have been selfish and he'd heard his parents arguing often enough, but what had *he* done to make her hate him? And she surely must or she wouldn't have cut him out of her life.

It had changed Pete's life so much. Holidays were no longer something to look forward to and now he was living at home all the time, he hated it. His father made him do jobs he disliked, such as collecting money from folk who couldn't afford to pay and he'd been told that they had to pay, even if he needed to threaten them.

'People are keen to borrow when they need money and the banks won't lend it to them,' Pete's father grunted when he questioned his methods. 'They mostly don't want to repay it so we need to persuade them a little.'

'What if they haven't got the money?' Pete asked, squirming inside at what he was being forced to do.

'If they don't have money, they must give me something else as surety,' his father told him, adding angrily, 'Don't look like that! I'm just asking for my rights.'

'But if they can't pay and they've given you all they have, what do they do?' Pete had persisted and earned a clout on the side of the head.

'You're like your mother, always blaming me and playing the innocent,' his father accused. 'Where do you think the money to keep you at that school came from? If you want the things that being rich buys then you have to earn it, right?'

Pete had nodded, resentful that his father had hit him. It hadn't hurt that much but he didn't enjoy being treated as if he was some kind of skivvy, less than dirt beneath his father's feet. He wondered if it was legal to threaten folk and to make them give his father their goods as surety until they could repay, but he did not dare to ask more questions for fear of a more severe punishment. He knew his father had started with nothing and was a self-made man, richer than most around here, but it was only now that he'd begun to understand how he'd done it and to wonder just how close to breaking the law his father had come in his various dealings.

Was that why his mother had left? Because she didn't like the way her husband conducted his business? Pete could only wonder and wish she would write to him. If she asked him to go and live with her, he would jump at the chance. He wished he could live anywhere but here with the bad-tempered man who was his father. His deep distress over his mother's sudden departure was the reason he'd made friends with another boy who had lost his mother. Ralph Cotton wasn't popular at the school and he'd attached himself to Pete. Perhaps because he'd felt they shared something, Pete had accepted a friendship he might otherwise have rejected. He knew that Ralph was sometimes reckless and even vicious, but in his own mood of resentment and unhappiness, he'd gone along with Ralph's schemes and been expelled from school. It was the worst thing that could have happened. If he'd still been at school, he wouldn't have had to do the things his father expected of him. He was even more miserable now, living in this big house that seemed so empty without his mother.

Where was his mother and why didn't she want him anymore? The hurt was like a raw lump in his chest, threatening to choke him, but he fought it down. His father said she wasn't coming back and he had to get used to it.

Feeling disgruntled, Pete left the house and got into his truck. One of the things his father wanted him to do was cause as much trouble as he could up at the sawmill without doing real damage. His suggestion that he should start a fire had met with a sharp smack at the side of his head.

'I want to make bother for that woman and her foreman, not to destroy the place. It's a nice piece of property and I'd like that woodland she owns. It's no good to me if it catches fire, idiot!'

'Why don't you buy it?' Pete had asked and received another blow for his pains. So he'd loosed the logs from the raft and watched them float away and he'd pushed over a stack of wood in the store, but there wasn't much he could do unless he set fire to a pile of lumber.

Pete decided he would take a look round, see if he could interfere with the machinery, but he wasn't going to risk cutting himself and he had to be careful because Jago Marsh had taken to walking round checking on a Sunday since Pete had cut those logs free. He didn't particularly want to confront Jago. It was odd, but he sort of admired him for not giving in to his disability – and Pete could imagine what his father would say to that! If he got the chance he would cause some minor damage, but he wouldn't do anything that might cause anyone an injury or threaten their life, he decided. If his father wanted more, he could do it himself . . .

Jago saw the truck drive away as he pulled up outside the lumberyard and frowned. What had Pete Trevors been doing here? He'd discovered one or two small accidents to the piles of lumber recently – or he'd thought they were accidents, but perhaps they had been deliberate, just like Miss Vee had suggested?

Why would Pete want to cause trouble for them? Jago pondered the question and then decided that the youth wouldn't but might do it if his father put him up to it. He walked round the yard and saw that some logs had fallen over – or been pushed – but it was just a few minutes' work to stack them. The machinery shed was kept locked and the padlock hadn't been touched. If Pete was causing the trouble, he was only half-hearted about it.

Shaking his head, Jago walked down to the lake. Sometimes, he took a swim and the cold water seemed to help his foot when it was aching and he didn't mind the chill as he swam, but today it was too cold. He looked about him, half hoping that he might see the girl, but there was no sign of her. She hadn't come last Sunday either and he wondered if she was ill. He hoped not, half-tempted to go to Miss Cotton's house and ask after her, but then he thought better of it. She wouldn't want a man like him enquiring after her and it might get her into trouble with her employer.

Jago had tried to put the girl – Julie she'd said her name was – from his mind, but the memory of her wistful face kept popping up in his head. There was something about her that had touched a chord within him, but he knew he couldn't expect her to feel the same. She was beautiful and he was disabled, the nicer word for being crippled, but he'd been called 'cripple' often enough by cruel lads who wanted to taunt him. Once, that might have made him cry, inside if not outwardly, but Jago had learned to be at peace with what he was. He'd overcome much of the difficulty of his foot by becoming strong and fit. As a young lad he'd chopped piles of wood for his father and lifted heavy weights, forcing himself to go on even when his shoulders ached. Then, when his father died, Jago had taken on much of the work he had done on the farm. His determination showed in his face and the set of his shoulders and the men at the sawmill respected him, even liked him. Yes, they were friends, as was Hank, the friendly law officer who often called round to see if things were as they should be. Jago liked Hank's father-in-law, Selmer Connors, as well.

Jago stifled his disappointment that the girl wasn't here. Perhaps he'd frightened her away by speaking to her the last time he'd seen her. He'd been careful, not wanting to scare her, but he hadn't seen her since. Shrugging, he completed his inspection and returned to his truck. His mother would have had her time with her friends after church and be ready to go home now. Nothing had changed much. Julie was lovely but he might have known she wasn't for him . . .

It was harder than Julie could have imagined to remain shut up in that little room for more than a week and have nothing but bread and water. She was given one

93

slice of bread without butter and a glass of water in the morning, before Miss Cotton went to work and another when she returned in the evening. Nothing was said as the tray was thrust at her and, with Ralph standing there leering at her from behind his aunt's back, she made no attempt to escape.

On the fourth day her bread had a scraping of butter on it and Miss Cotton looked at her oddly. 'Are you ready to apologise?' she asked.

'I told you the truth,' Julie replied stubbornly, raising her head to look her squarely in the eyes. 'You called me a liar and punished me, but it's him you should punish.'

'You are a foolish, stubborn girl,' Miss Cotton sighed. 'Have it your own way. If you won't apologise, you may stay here – though it's inconvenient.'

'I'm not a liar and I won't say I am!'

Julie kept looking at her and saw a flicker of doubt in her eyes but she went out and locked the door behind her. Julie turned away, sitting down to eat her thin slice of bread. She was so hungry. Two slices of bread for the whole day just weren't enough and her stomach rumbled and protested. A loud sniff escaped her, but she swiped a hand over her face. She wasn't going to cry. She wouldn't let them break her; even though she felt dirty and cold and hungry, she wasn't going to give in.

Eight days had passed when she heard the key in the lock of her door once more in the middle of the morning. Julie stiffened, because it wasn't yet time for Miss Cotton to return from school – it couldn't be more than midday, surely? As the door opened, a feeling of fear swept through her as she saw Ralph standing there, a grin on his face.

'Surprised?' he asked. 'She keeps the key in her pocket but I knew she would have a spare and I found it.'

'Get out of here!' Julie shouted. Her eyes were moving around the room, looking for something she could use to hit him with but there was nothing – but there were her sewing scissors if she could just reach them! He was moving into the room, that mocking look in his eyes. If she could just grab her scissors . . . Making a sudden dash towards them where they lay on the top of the sewing machine, she managed to grab them, but Ralph had seen what she meant to do and he seized her wrist. He twisted it, forcing her to drop them. He was too strong for her to resist and now he was pushing her backwards. The backs of her knees were against the bed and she could feel the pressure as he thrust her downward, landing on top of her as her balance gave and she fell on the bed.

'No, you don't,' he muttered as she bucked and struggled beneath him, her hands going for his face. One hand grabbed her wrist, hurting her as he bent it back, making her wince with pain. He was strong and heavy too and she was gasping for breath, frightened and desperate. As he let go of her wrist to pull up her dress, Julie knew it was her one chance and she plunged her fingers into his eye. He gave a shriek of pain and rolled away from her with a curse.

'You little bitch!' he said and moved away from her, a hand over the eye she'd stabbed with her nails. 'I'll make you pay for that!'

His threats terrified her but as he turned away to

use water from her glass to rinse his eye Julie pounced on her sewing scissors and held them before her like a double-pronged knife.

'Try again and it will be these next time,' she declared, though inside she was shaking with fear.

For a moment she saw anger in his eyes but then they both heard the door open downstairs and a voice calling. It wasn't Miss Cotton but Ralph startled and went out immediately, leaving the door open behind him. Julie pulled it shut and used the key he'd abandoned to lock herself in. She leaned against it for a moment, catching her breath as she struggled to calm herself. What would have happened if the voice hadn't called him from downstairs, she wasn't sure – could she have carried out her promise to wound him with the scissors or would he have overpowered her again?

As her breathing returned to normal, she heard voices from the kitchen. Ralph was laughing. She heard the kitchen door shut with a bang and went to her window to look out. Ralph had left with another young man, more serious-looking than Ralph but still a teenager. Now she heard the sound of an engine starting up and knew that Ralph had gone in the other man's truck. His name was Pete and his mother had bought him a truck as soon as he'd passed his driving test. Julie had heard him telling Ralph about it one night when Pete called round to take him out. Miss Cotton hadn't seemed too pleased when they left but she hadn't tried to stop him.

Julie was alone in the house and she had the key to her door. After Ralph's latest attempt on her, she knew she had no choice but to escape while she had the chance because Ralph would find a way to pay her back for the pain she'd given him.

Julie went to the wardrobe and pulled out her clean dress and then stuffed it into the small bag she'd brought with her together with her underclothes. It was all she possessed. She had no money of her own, not a cent but she knew where there was a small amount of money in a pot in the pantry. Miss Cotton used it to pay for the milk she had delivered. It wasn't much and it didn't belong to Julie – but surely, she was entitled to something after several months of working at the school and she needed a little money, if only to pay for the bus to Halifax and then . . . well, Julie didn't know what she would do when she got to the busy maritime city, but perhaps she could find a job there. She would do almost anything rather than stay here.

CHAPTER 12

'It's a letter from Mr Malcolm,' Aggie said, bringing the envelope to Vee as she sat reading by the window that overlooked her garden. There was nothing much to see but the snow that had been falling softly overnight, covering trees, bushes and the ornamental fountain in a soft crisp blanket of white. She looked up with a smile and accepted the letter. 'Posted in Malta some weeks back – so they got there all right.'

'Yes, must have done,' Vee agreed feeling both pleasure and relief. 'I've never minded that he was gone for long periods before, Aggie – but I worry about him now.'

Aggie sniffed in agreement. 'Of course you do. Wouldn't be human if you didn't while this damn fool war is going on!' That raised a smile, because Aggie never minced her words and the names she called Hitler – well Vee sometimes wondered where she'd come by that sort of language. Not that it wasn't appropriate in the circumstances.

'Aggie,' Vee reproved, 'I hope you don't say things like that in front of the child?'

'Of course I don't,' Aggie retorted with a darkling look. 'You're moping because she started school today. You'd rather have kept her at home with you and taught her yourself – why didn't you?' Vee was perfectly capable of taking Beth through her tables and helping her read; she could have taught her book-keeping and house management too, all of which were more likely to be useful than book learning in Aggie's opinion.

'She needs to make friends,' Vee said, admitting to herself that Aggie was probably right. She glanced at the clock on the mantle. Only another hour and she could fetch Beth home. 'It has seemed a long day without her, though.'

'Bound to,' Aggie agreed. 'I miss her round my feet in the kitchen but I suppose you're right. Children do need to be with other little ones now and then.' She looked at Vee sharply. 'You won't send her to that Miss Cotton's school in Lower Sackville when she's older?'

'No, I shan't,' Vee assured her. 'I don't know why you don't like her, Aggie. Miss Cotton always seems perfectly nice when I see her. Not that she visits Halifax often.'

'Don't ask why, Miss Vee. Just stick to what you've just told me and I shan't tell tales – though I could.'

The glare that accompanied Aggie's words was enough to warn Vee that Aggie had good reason for not liking the school teacher. She did have thin lips and a smile that was more saccharine than sugar, so perhaps Aggie was right. Vee had no intention of sending Beth to her school. She thought the child intelligent and wanted her to learn more than just cooking and sewing. Vee's father had believed in educating girls and she'd gone to a good school that taught her to be curious about the world around her and it was what she wanted for her Beth.

Her Beth! A smile touched her mouth as she thought about the future. It was nice to have a daughter she could teach and bring up as a young lady. She would enjoy shopping for clothes for her and accompanying her to her first dances and parties – until she started courting.

Malcolm knew her so well! She'd been desperately lonely after Bill's death but now she had someone to love and fuss over – and she did love Beth. The child had touched her heart, bringing back warmth and a feeling of joy – something that had mostly been missing these past years. Opening her brother's letter, she read the few lines quickly and then more slowly.

His ship had been under fire on the voyage to Malta and it had sustained some damage, but they'd been luckier than other ships, which had been sunk within hailing distance of the beleaguered island. Some of the crew had been injured but he was fine – just a small cut and some bruises. The ship had needed substantial repairs, which was why he would be in Malta for some time. He'd written to let her know, because he'd understood she would worry if she heard the ship had been attacked.

Vee closed her eyes for a moment. Thank God he was all right! She worried for him always but he was a grown man and she couldn't prevail on him to stay safely at home in Canada when he knew what he did was necessary. He wouldn't have been the brother she loved if he had. He could quite easily have managed the store when their parents died, but he'd always wanted to be a sailor and the life suited him. Vee sighed. You couldn't keep the people you loved tied to you by a piece of cord, even if you wanted to. Aggie was correct. She would have preferred to teach Beth at home, but it was right that the child should make friends.

Glancing at the clock, she decided to get ready and walk to the school. She could call in at the store and have a word with Selmer on the way, thank him for sending his son-in-law to check on her every now and then. It was nice to be liked and her friends were good people. She'd always known they were there if she needed help.

'You know we're always here for you, Miss Vee.' Her manager at the store gave her a look that was half respect and half the kind of adoration she would only deserve if she were a saint, Vee thought, smiling inwardly. She knew the old fool was in love with her and had been for years, but she was past all that, though she liked and appreciated his loyalty. 'Anything, anytime for you.'

'I want some pretty clothes for Beth,' she told him. 'Something better than anything we have in stock. Will you try and source something for me, please? If we like them, we could try stocking them in the store, too.'

'I'll do my best,' he promised. 'It won't be easy because of the times – some of the prettiest stuff comes from France but I'll surely try and please you.'

'I know you will,' Vee said and smiled at him. 'I don't know what I'd have done without you all these years, Selmer. You won't retire and leave me just yet, will you?'

'They'll carry me out before I leave,' he assured her with a grin.

Vee laughed and took another look around. Everything was just as she liked it, fully stocked, the counters neat, the display bright but not ostentatious. They looked what they were – a well-established family firm and that was as it should be. There were more modern shops in Halifax that had huge displays in their windows but this shop spoke of quality the moment you walked in. She'd always sourced a lot of her stock from Britain – tweed, pure wool, and good leather shoes, but that wasn't as easy these days. Their American lines were more prominent at the moment and they were good, but she would go back to buying British goods when she could – nothing was nicer than those wonderful Scottish plaids and woollens.

Smiling, she left the store, aware that Selmer's gaze followed her. She resisted the temptation to turn and wave as she walked away. Sentimental old fool! She didn't know why she'd spoken that way – but perhaps it was time she let him know how much she'd always relied on him to just be there.

Vee collected Beth from school and despite the November chill they went to the ice-cream parlour for a dish of delicious creamy dessert that tasted of strawberries with a crispy wafer and a drizzle of maple syrup. Beth tucked into hers, her face a picture of wonder. She'd never tasted anything like this until recently and could hardly believe it when Vee told her every time that she could choose whatever she wanted.

Thinking about the kind of childhood she suspected Beth had endured, made Vee sad so she tried not to, preferring to give her treats that made her little face light up with joy.

'Did you enjoy school today?' she asked Beth when they'd finished their ice cream and were walking home through the leafy streets of the older part of the town. Here it was more peaceful away from Halifax's busy port, fresher and cleaner too and the bigger residences had been built years before and housed the wealthier of Halifax's residents. There was a faded charm about the area now, as many of the buildings were no longer as pristine as they once were, which made them more beautiful to Vee's eyes. She wouldn't have given you two cents for a modern apartment in one of those high-rise buildings that some folk preferred. She wanted a garden that bordered countryside at the back and a wide avenue at the front. Nothing would have persuaded her to move to a modern house, even if it was a mansion – the kind Trevors had built for himself and his wife and son before his wife had suddenly left him. Vee didn't blame her, though she knew it would have hurt the man's pride. Even disliking him as she did, she hadn't gloated at his misfortune. Vee didn't hold grudges and she wasn't vindictive. She wished the man no harm, providing he left her alone. She understood that his son was a chip off the old block in that he drove all over in the truck his mother had bought him on his seventeenth birthday, making a noise late at night and causing bother in the quiet streets. What made a young man do things like that? Was it wildness or was he unhappy? She'd only met his mother at the occasional function but she'd seemed pleasant enough.

Vee dismissed the thought and looked down at the child by her side. Beth was quieter than usual. 'Something wrong today?' she asked. Beth hesitated for a moment and then looked up at her, eyes wide and clear.

'The boys pulled my hair and the girls wouldn't sit with me because they said I was a vacuee . . . what is a vacuee?'

'An evacuee,' Vee said and smiled. 'It just means you came from another country because of the war.'

Beth nodded. 'My daddy went away and left us before the war because he and Mummy were always fighting and then Mummy was knocked down in the blackout and died. Granny said she couldn't keep me because the lady said she was too old and she cried.' Beth tipped her head to one side. 'One of the girls said you were too old to have a child like me – you aren't, are you?' There was fear in Beth's eyes and Vee realised what was upsetting her. Beth feared that she would be sent away again. She squeezed her hand reassuringly.

'I'm not old at all,' she told Beth. 'Young enough to see you become a grown-up with a family of your own one day.'

Beth's smile lit her eyes. 'Good. I said so and hit the other girl for saying it but the teacher smacked my leg and told me not to be a bully.'

'Did she now? Perhaps I should have a word with her?'

Beth shook her head. 'It didn't hurt. I've been smacked harder. Anyway, I don't care. I made friends with another girl who says Mabel is the bully, not me. She's afraid of her but I'm not.'

Vee thought it was the longest conversation they'd had since Beth's arrival and to her mind it showed that going to school was the right thing. Beth could stand up for herself and she needed to – Vee knew that only too well. She smiled approvingly. Beth might look little and vulnerable but she was tougher than she looked. It was probably a skill learned long before she came to Canada.

'Just remember I love you and so does Aggie,' Vee told her. 'If you need help at any time or something worries you, tell us and we'll help – but it's always best to stand up for yourself if you can.'

'I was afraid on the ship, because it was so strange and I didn't know what was happening,' Beth said. 'Julie told me I would have a new mummy but I wasn't sure it was true – but now it is.' She looked happily up at Vee. 'I like Julie. Can I see her one day please?'

'Did Julie work on the ship?' For a moment Vee struggled to remember. She'd forgotten about Julie. 'Oh, didn't she come out with you?'

'Yes. She came from London with us in the cabin – Arthur, Davey, Julie and me. Julie and Davey looked after us. Davey didn't say goodbye but Julie held my hand until . . .' Beth hesitated.

'Until what, darling?'

'A lady took her away. I don't think she wanted to go but the lady pushed her and it made me cry.'

'Ah, I see. That's when Uncle Malcolm picked you up and gave you barley sugar?'

'Yes.' Beth sighed contentedly. 'I liked it – but not as much as the ice cream today.'

'I'm glad you liked your ice cream. I'll take you for another one when I fetch you tomorrow.'

Beth nodded and skipped away as they approached the house. Aggie was standing at the kitchen door looking for them and drew Beth inside, chafing her hands to warm them and fussing over her. Vee watched indulgently. She wasn't sure which one of them spoiled Beth the most – Aggie with her cakes and special biscuits or Vee with her ice-cream treats, her new clothes and toys. Still, she was worth spoiling. The house had been quiet until she came, now it rang with laughter and life as Beth brought her joy to it. Vee wished Bill was still around to enjoy her – he would have loved her.

Aggie looked at her as she entered the kitchen. Beth was already sitting at the table drinking milk and a plate with one of Aggie's peanut butter cookies was on the table in front of her.

'That weasel was here while you were out,' she said. 'Left a note for you – it's in the parlour. I'll bring your coffee in a minute.'

Vee nodded and removed her thick coat, hanging it in the hall cupboard on her way to the front parlour. She went to the fire and warmed her hands. It was bitterly cold out and she didn't envy those with no home to go to on a day like this . . . the temperature would drop overnight and the ground would freeze.

Sitting in her favourite chair, she opened the letter Aggie had placed on her desk and sighed as she read it. A frown creased her forehead. It was another offer for the lumberyard – or more like a threat. It was Trevors' last offer and if she was wise, she would take it. What was that if it wasn't an ultimatum? She wondered if it was malicious enough to have a restraining order put on him but then decided not to bother. He would just find another way to annoy her. She had no intention of selling him the lumber-mill or the woodland that supplied much of their timber. Vee would simply ignore the letter as she always had his veiled threats in the past. She didn't think he would dare to try anything too drastic, because he was just a bully and she'd long ago learned that the only way was to ignore them – or give them a black eye.

Vee laughed softly. Beth had hit her tormentor at school. For Vee it wasn't that simple but there were things she could do to make life less comfortable for Harold Trevors. Did she want to put herself to the trouble or not?

Aggie brought in the tray then. Coffee and cake and her special biscuits.

'Jago was here. His friend has a pregnant dog and says they'll want to give away the pups when they arrive. They know who the father is so he reckons they'll be nice little things, if you fancied one for the child?'

'Will they be big dogs?' Vee asked, seeing the gleam in Aggie's eyes.

'About the size of a spaniel but a mongrel, according

107

to Jago. The girl might like a dog – and if she grows up with it, it will protect her.'

'Why not?' Vee said. 'I haven't had a dog for years but I like them.'

'Aye, I know,' Aggie said. 'You had a great big lout of a thing when you were a teen. Followed you everywhere – until Harold Trevors shot him in the woods and claimed he thought it was a wolf. Mmm, perhaps it's best we don't have one . . .'

'If he shoots my dog this time, I'll have the law on him,' Vee said. 'We know who killed Rufus, even though his father said it was him, not his son. He didn't want to admit his son took the rifle and shot my dog out of spite. He'd have been in trouble for leaving his gun lying around where the boy could get it.'

'Broke your heart over that dog,' Aggie sniffed. 'I'd shoot that Trevors given two pins and so would a few others.'

'We can't go round shooting folk even if we'd like to,' Vee said but smiled. 'Don't worry. He's all bluster and spite. If he did something really nasty, he knows I'd never rest until he was behind bars. We'll have the dog, Aggie – Trevors isn't going to control our lives, whatever he says or does . . .'

CHAPTER 13

It was snowing, the ground icy hard beneath her feet.
Julie shivered as she left the bus that had returned her
to Halifax. Dusk had fallen a while back and she felt
scared as she looked around at the dark shapes of the
buildings, although the snow made it lighter than it
might have been otherwise. She had no idea where to
go or what to do and wondered whether she'd made
her life worse by running away. It was just so cold!

Her flight had been impetuous and she had only a
few coins left after paying the bus fare, hardly enough
to buy her more than a bun or a cup of coffee and
her stomach rumbled with hunger. She almost wished
herself back in the safety of Miss Cotton's spare room
– except that it wasn't safe while Ralph was there.

She walked slowly, carrying all she possessed in her
small bag, the bag she'd brought out from England
and which was truly hers. How she wished she was
back in the dirty streets of the East End – even with
the bombs falling in London, as she knew they were
from headlines in a paper she'd seen lying around at
the bus station, she thought she would feel safer than

she did here. At least there she knew people and might have found work. Would someone employ her here?

Julie's sixteenth birthday had come and gone unmarked soon after she'd arrived in Canada four months ago. She was quite tall and well-developed for her age. People would be more inclined to employ her if they thought she was older and they might believe her if she said she was eighteen. It wouldn't hurt to tell a small lie surely? She decided that she would tell them she'd been a waitress in London before she came to Canada. It was no good lying about that part, because they would know her accent was different. She would say she'd come out as a minder, looking after the evacuee children – well, in a way it was true. She had looked after Beth and Arthur, and she still thought of them both with affection. Her accent would cause curiosity, and it was best to stick as closely to the truth as she could.

She walked down to the docks, shivering in the bitter weather. She needed to find work and somewhere to stay for the night. Her nose was cold, her hands were cold and her feet were like blocks of ice. She longed to be somewhere warm drinking hot coffee or chocolate. Mr Ridger, the purser on the ship, had given them mugs of hot cocoa on the night of the storm. He'd come to make sure they were all right and then made them delicious milky cocoa. He was a kind man. She remembered the way he'd tried to comfort Beth when Julie was forced to leave her.

Three ships were anchored at the docks but they were in darkness, all signs of loading or cleaning abandoned on this dreadful night. Julie shivered and hugged her coat tighter around her neck, turning back towards the town. There was nothing for her here and she didn't know why she'd come – there was no way home for her without money to pay her fare. She wasn't even sure she would be better off in London when she really thought about it.

Julie felt in her pocket. She had just three cents left. Julie knew that for certain it wouldn't even buy her a bun and a coffee. She'd been sent to buy buns once when Miss Cotton hadn't had time to bake and the cheapest had been more than she now possessed.

She passed warehouses and what looked like a factory – perhaps she ought to ask for work there in the morning – but what could she do? She could make tea and coffee, cook, wash up, and sew, nothing more useful. Factories and warehouses would want experienced staff.

In London everything would have been dark by now, because of the blackout that had been ordered at the start of the war. Here there were lights on in shop windows. Julie was fascinated. She'd seen nothing of this part of Halifax when she'd followed Miss Cotton. She realised that this must be the old town centre because the buildings looked softer, older and more familiar than those she'd seen on her arrival, almost like the prettier parts of London with trees lining the paths, and she felt easier somehow.

She could see a small café across the road and walked over to it, looking in the steamy window. It looked so warm and inviting with its bright red tablecloths. A girl not much older than her was serving a table with three men seated on the dark wood chairs, handing them plates of what looked like apple pie and cream and big mugs of coffee. Julie's stomach gurgled and she couldn't help herself as she entered and sat down at an empty table.

'What do you want?' the girl asked seeming bored.

'Apple pie and coffee,' she said. The girl looked at her oddly but went off and fetched it. Julie thanked her. She ate the pie slowly, savouring every mouthful. It was good, though she thought she could have made a better one. She drank her coffee, making it last.

The café was emptying. The three men had gone and now the girl who had served her was putting on her coat, leaving. Julie sat where she was, making out she was still drinking. Perhaps ten minutes passed and then the man behind the counter came over to her.

'Sorry to hurry you, miss,' he said in a pleasant manner. 'But it's time you paid and left. I'm ready to close.'

Julie looked at him steadily. 'I have three cents – but I'll wash up for you and I'll come tomorrow and wash up all day, if you'll feed me.'

'You ate my pie and couldn't pay?' he asked, frowning. Julie's stomach clenched with fear. Would he call the law and have her arrested? He hesitated for a moment and then nodded. 'You'll wash up until I tell you to stop and I'll pay you two dollars a week.'

Julie stared at him and then smiled and breathed again. 'Thank you,' she said. 'I should have asked for work first . . .'

'You were hungry,' he said and grinned. 'I'm Andy and I expect you to work hard. You might not thank me when you've been here a week.'

'Oh, I will if you pay me and feed me,' she said and got to her feet. 'I'll see you tomorrow.'

'And where will you sleep tonight?'

Julie hesitated, a cold shiver at her nape. She'd thought it too good to be true. 'I'll find somewhere . . .'

'My wife will let you sleep in the back room for now,' Andy said and she relaxed again. 'She'd have my hide if I let you sleep rough on a night like this – it's going to snow hard.' His eyes narrowed. 'You're from England – London if I'm not mistaken?'

'Yes. I came out to help with some children who were evacuated. I had a job for a while but I had to leave.'

'You can tell my wife your story – and don't think to lie. She'll throw you out on your ear if you do.'

Andy's wife gave her a hard look when he took her in, dark eyes narrowed and suspicious as she listened to his story. She was a big plump woman and wore a loose dress that was a bit dowdy. 'She's down on her luck, Cath,' he said. 'She comes from London too.'

Cath nodded, her expression still wary. 'What's your name, girl?' Her faint accent told Julie that she'd been a Londoner once.

'Julie – Julie Miller. I looked after some evacuee children on the ship coming out. I can cook, clean, wash up and sew.'

'Can you now?' Cath said looking thoughtful. Julie suddenly realised, as she crossed her arms over it, that her big stomach was because she was carrying a baby. She had blonde hair that might have been pretty had

113

it not been dragged back into a tight knot at the back of her head. She looked tired and pale, as if the effort of childbearing was almost too much. 'Can you knit too?'

'I can soon learn,' Julie offered. 'I'll do whatever you ask, Mrs . . . Andy didn't tell me his second name?'

'Cath will do,' she said. 'Right, you'll earn your keep, girl and any funny business and I'll send you packing – but you're welcome to stay in the back room. It isn't a palace but better than you'll get at a boarding house on what you'll earn.'

'Two dollars a week and her food and board?' Andy said and his wife nodded. Julie felt a sense of relief. Two dollars wasn't much but it was better than nothing. When she'd managed to save some money, she could look for work as a seamstress – unless she liked it here . . .

The back room was small and had obviously been used as a store. There was a camp bed that Andy put up for her, an armchair that had seen better days and a large pine chest, as well as some empty tea chests and a collection of bits and pieces piled up in one corner. Cath brought her a pillow and some blankets and told her she could have a wash in the kitchen when they'd gone up for the night.

'I told you it wasn't much of a room,' Cath said, glaring at her as if daring her to agree. 'If you stay, I'll sort those bits out and you can make it more homely.'

'Thank you! You and your husband are very kind . . .'

Cath gave a harsh laugh. 'Told you I was his wife, did he? We're not married. I came out looking for a better life a few years back. Worked in a canning factory for a while and then I met Andy. He invited me to move in with him – but he never put a ring on my finger . . .' Her eyes narrowed. 'He has an eye for the women. It's why he offered you the job – but just say no. Andy won't force you, but he will try it on and I'll have you out of here faster than you can blink if you think you can snuggle up with him. He's mine – understand?'

'Yes.' Julie lifted her eyes to Cath's. 'I just want to get on and I'll leave when I can afford it. I want to be a seamstress.'

'That's another reason you got the job. No one wants to wash up greasy dishes. They all leave when they can find a better job. He thought I'd be glad to do it for free and I did until I got pregnant the first time.'

Julie was surprised; she hadn't seen any signs of children.

Cath shook her head. 'I lost two before this so I told him I wasn't going to work all hours – least, not until the baby is born and then we'll see.'

'I'm sorry you lost your other babies,' Julie said. 'It happened to my mother but she had diabetes.' She saw that meant nothing to Cath; most folk didn't know much about it. 'It made her ill and I helped at home so I'll help you as much as I can.'

'You're an eager little thing,' Cath said and her expression softened for the first time. 'Maybe we'll get on all right, provided you remember what I told you about him . . .' She jerked her head towards the other room where Andy was listening to a weather forecast on the wireless.

'I will,' Julie promised. 'And I'm not interested in anything like that; I just want to be comfortable and work hard.'

'Good. I'll let you settle then and bring a cup of coffee later. You can tell me the truth then . . .'

Julie sat down on the bed, looking about her when Cath left her. She expected the work would be harder than it was at Miss Cotton's school but at least she'd got away from Ralph and she didn't believe Andy would come after her – he didn't seem the type. Cath was just warning her off and that was fair enough. Julie wouldn't give him any reason to think she was interested, because she wasn't. Her experience of male attention had mostly been unpleasant – apart from . . . but that had only happened twice. Once when he'd given her a lift and a few minutes' talk up at the lake. Jago, he'd said his name was, and she'd liked him, but she would probably never see him again and all she really wanted was to have the freedom to make her own life – but what did she tell Cath? If she told her the truth, would she send her straight back?

In the end, Julie gave Cath part of the truth. She'd looked after children on the way out and found work – but her employer's nephew had tried to molest her so she'd run away. Cath looked at her for a long time before she nodded.

'You're telling me the truth, if not the whole story,' she said. 'So you can stay for now and we'll see how

116

you like it.' Her gaze assessed Julie. 'I reckon you'll move on soon enough if he gives you trouble, but I've warned him you're still young so maybe he won't. Just how old are you?'

'Eighteen . . .' Julie ventured but Cath shook her head.

'Seventeen at the most I'd say,' she said and laughed as Julie hung her head. 'Well, more like sixteen, I reckon, which is just as well: he doesn't go for them that young.'

'I don't think he would,' Julie replied. 'I am sure Andy loves you – the way he spoke of you when he said you'd let me stay.'

'Is there anything more I ought to know?' Cath asked but her eyes gleamed at hearing Julie thought Andy cared for her. Maybe if Andy had married her, she might feel more settled.

'No, nothing,' Julie replied. She couldn't risk being sent back to Miss Cotton.

'Well, it's settled then,' Cath told her. 'Get to bed, because you'll be up early. I've some jobs need doing before you leave for the café. If you want the toilet there's one just out there. Take the torch.' She indicated a torch hanging from the wall near the back door. 'We've got one upstairs but you'll use the outside loo. I don't want you coming upstairs at night.'

Julie nodded. Cath seemed a bit paranoid over Andy and she wouldn't want to get on her wrong side . . .

'Whatever you say,' she agreed and Cath's eyes narrowed.

'You must have had a bad time, kid,' she said sounding sympathetic. 'I know what men are, see.

My old man was forever cheating on my mother, broke her heart he did. I make sure Andy can't do the same to me!' She winked at Julie and went out, leaving her to finish her hot drink alone.

Julie could hardly believe she'd fallen into a job so easily and, while her situation was far from perfect, she felt warm and at least she was safe for now. If she could just earn enough for her fare, she would move on to another town so that Miss Cotton and her horrid nephew could never find her.

Julie lay down on her bed, closing her eyes and smiled. She had been lucky to find somewhere she could stay as well as a job she could manage. The weather was very cold now, because there were only a few weeks or so until Christmas. It was a long time since Julie had celebrated Christmas and she didn't suppose she would this year, but there would be bright displays in shop windows when she had time to look and perhaps she could visit a church to hear the carols. That would be nice, she thought, relaxing into the warmth of her blankets. She was safe here for a while and if Miss Cotton did happen to find her, she would run away again, but before she did, she would try to discover where Beth had been taken. Arthur was all right, she was sure of that, and would have a lovely Christmas with presents and a tree, but Beth's tearful face was vivid in her mind. One day soon she must find her and make sure she was safe.

CHAPTER 14

Jago looked for the girl every day on his way to work at the lumbermill but he hadn't seen her now for weeks. He'd hoped he might come across her at the lake once the weather was slightly better, but she never came. More than a month had passed now since he'd spoken to her but she was often in his thoughts. He hoped he hadn't put her off coming to the lake when he sat and talked to her; maybe he should have known better than to speak to her . . . and yet she hadn't seemed to feel disgust when she looked at him. She had been unhappy, though, he knew that, and it played on his mind. He certainly wouldn't want to work for Phyllis Cotton – she had a reputation for being mean . . .

Just before Christmas he decided to linger outside the school late one afternoon. It would be closing for the holidays and perhaps the girl would look happier. Parking his truck across the road, he watched as the pupils left in little groups, laughing and chattering, excited about the festivities, and then Miss Cotton came out but she was alone. Where was the girl?

Jago waited for a few minutes longer, hoping the

girl with the pretty face and sad eyes would come, but she didn't. He wondered what had happened to her. Folk said she was one of the evacuee children from London and it was unlikely she would have relatives here – so where had she gone? He felt a shaft of worry for her. There was a lot of open countryside and woods, rocky terrain, places she could get lost if she didn't know the area, some of them more dangerous than others. Jago wouldn't want any harm to come to a girl like that and wished he'd spoken to her for longer, asked her if she needed help – but he hadn't wanted to push his company on her if she needed to be alone. He understood how that felt.

Jago gave up and went home. He had supplies under a tarpaulin in the truck, including a Christmas tree he'd cut himself for his mother. She liked to trim it on Christmas Eve and he liked to watch and to put the silver star on the top branch for her. He'd done that since he was a boy and his father had lifted him up so he could reach. He felt sad about the girl and decided to ask his mother if she knew anything when he got home.

'You hadn't heard?' Maya looked at him in surprise. 'Miss Cotton was very put out over it – the girl ran away and there's been no sign of her since.'

'She ran away – when?'

Maya frowned. 'I think it was the night of that terrible blizzard we had about six weeks ago. Miss Cotton told the authorities and they looked for her but she wasn't found.' Maya looked at him, clearly surprised by his interest. 'What do you know of her?'

'She was up at the lake on a Sunday a couple of times. I said hello once and gave her a lift when she broke the heel of her shoe.' He looked puzzled. 'She couldn't just disappear. Did they search the lakes and the woods?'

Maya shrugged. 'Someone said they thought they might have seen her get on the bus to Halifax but she didn't have much money so where she went after that no one knows.'

'Are they still looking for her?'

'If she was caught in that storm, she could be dead,' Maya told him. 'Her body may be lying in a ditch or something . . .' She caught his arm as he turned towards the door. 'It was weeks ago, Jago. If the rangers didn't find her, you won't after all this time.'

Jago hesitated and then nodded. His mother was right. Besides, he had no idea where to look for her but he felt an ache in his chest and knew that he would be looking in every ditch and under every bush on Miss Vee's land come the morning. Even if she was dead, she deserved a proper burial.

'Perhaps she found a new job in Halifax,' Maya suggested. 'I doubt she was happy at that woman's school.'

'I hope she is alive and well,' Jago said and turned away. His mother knew him inside out and she would think he was daft grieving for a girl he'd only met briefly.

Vee watched indulgently as Beth opened the pile of gifts waiting for her under the tree, her eyes wide with excitement. She'd been thrilled with the tree, exclaiming over all the glittering balls and the candles. Vee had let her have one of the strings of candy that also adorned the tree. However, this morning she had not believed all the parcels were for her.

'But Father Christmas only brought me one present and that was a long time ago,' she'd told Vee. 'Mummy said it was because we were too poor. Then Daddy left and Mummy had to work in the factory so I hardly ever saw her. Then – then she got knocked down and died too so Granny said Father Christmas wouldn't come to me.'

'Well, she was wrong,' Vee said feeling choked. Beth's short life had been hard and full of sadness. She was glad she had the chance to make it better and she wondered how her relations were faring in London . . . Bill's cousin too. Had they survived the bombing wherever they now were? Did they get enough to eat? She'd contacted the Red Cross through her solicitor but he'd told her there wasn't much chance of finding folk in London at this time.

'There are a lot of displaced and homeless families there at the moment – many killed in the air raids,' Mr Swanson had said looking troubled. 'I have relatives in London too and they've told me it is horrendous. However, we can try through the Red Cross – and it's worth contacting the Salvation Army as well. I'll write and ask them to make enquiries.'

'Thank you. I really want to contact them, not just because of the war. Bill left them that property, you know.'

'Well, it comes to you in time if they don't claim

it.' He looked at her oddly, as if thinking she would do better to keep it.

'But Bill wanted his cousin to have it and that's what matters,' Vee said, softening her words with a smile. 'You know I'm right.'

'You're a good woman, Vee Bittern. Most would send one letter to the last known address and hope nothing came of it.'

'I'm not most folk,' Vee said. 'If they're alive that property is theirs. So please, do what you can to contact them.' She wondered if Paul had been killed. The last letter they'd had before the war, before Bill died, had said he was joining the regular army. Paul had wanted to visit Canada one day, but his wife wasn't too keen. Perhaps she hadn't wanted to keep in touch?

Vee frowned. She believed there was a daughter who must be in her mid teens now. Vee ought to have offered to give her shelter for the duration of the war but she had been too wrapped up in her grief to think of it. Mother and daughter could have come out, the pair of them would have been safer here . . .

'Mummy!' Beth showed her the big doll with the porcelain head and blonde curls. It was dressed in a pretty blue and white gingham outfit that matched Beth's own dress and cardigan. 'Look, it's the same.' She tipped her head on one side knowingly. 'You bought it for me, didn't you? A girl at school told me there is no real Father Christmas and presents are bought by mummies and daddies . . . Is that true?'

Vee looked at her and decided on the truth. 'Yes, darling. Father Christmas is just a fairy story we tell to little children to make them happy and excited – but you're a big girl now. Are you disappointed?'

Beth shook her head. She approached Vee and then clung to her, putting her arms around her. 'I'm glad. I'd rather it was from you. I love you, Mummy.'

Vee felt the tears in her eyes and hugged her. 'I love you too, darling, and I'm glad you like your new doll – what will you call her?'

Beth thought for a moment and then smiled. 'I'll call her Julie after my friend on the ship.'

'That's a nice name,' Vee agreed. 'Now, you've got lots more presents to open. Some are from Aggie and one is from Jago. He brought it yesterday for you and put it under the tree. I think he made it for you himself. It's that big one over there . . .'

Beth skipped away from her and tore the brown paper from the large parcel, revealing a beautiful doll's cot. It was made of pine and the ends had been carved and polished. Inside was a pillow and a cover to match in a patchwork of different-coloured materials.

'Maya must have made those,' Vee said, admiring the lovingly worked quilt. 'We will thank them when they come to dinner this evening.'

Beth sat her new doll in the cot and then returned to open the rest of her parcels, which included sweets, puzzles and a colouring book as well as a pretty bead necklace.

'Selmer and Hank gave you the colouring book and crayons,' Vee said. 'You can thank them this evening, because they are coming for dinner too.' She smiled as Beth shyly brought her a parcel from under the tree. 'Thank you, darling. Selmer and Hank brought these for me. They always bring me a box of coffee-cream chocolates at Christmas, because they know I like them.'

'Will I be allowed to sit up for dinner tonight?' Beth asked and was rewarded with a smile.

'Of course you will. We're having a turkey with all the trimmings. You couldn't miss that, could you?'

Beth laughed in delight. She'd never had turkey before and usually she went to bed after her supper. Vee sometimes had friends to dinner at night, but this was the first time she had allowed Beth to stay up and eat with the guests. She was still young for such things – seven next birthday – but she was a good girl at the table and had soon leaned the proper manners.

'When is your birthday?' Vee had asked her. Because Malcolm had brought Beth to her, she didn't have the papers that had come out with her on the ship which would probably include a birth certificate. All she had were the adoption papers that made Beth hers. When he came home, she would ask Malcolm to get the original papers if he could; if not, she would send to England for them when the war was over. 'We'll have a party for the friends you've made at school then, if you like?'

Beth looked at her for a moment, then, 'I don't know. I never had a birthday party but I think it was in the summer. Once, Mummy made me a lovely cake for my birthday and the sun was shining.'

'Shall we say June the fifteenth?' Vee said. 'It's my birthday too so we'll celebrate together.'

'Yes, please!' Beth ran to her, clutching the doll

again. 'I'd like to share with you, Mummy.' She produced a small parcel from behind her back. 'Aggie helped me make these for you.'

'For me?' Vee smiled as she opened the parcel. Inside were some of Aggie's rum truffles and chunks of coconut ice in pink and white, not quite as neatly formed as usual. 'These look delicious,' Vee said and popped a truffe into her mouth. 'Would you like a piece of coconut ice?'

Beth nodded and chose a lump of the pink sweet, chewing it with evident delight as she sat on Vee's lap. 'I'm lucky, aren't I?' she said. 'I was afraid on the ship that someone nasty would take me – like the lady who took Julie. She had a hard face and looked angry. I was lucky Uncle Malcolm brought me home to you.'

'Oh no,' Vee said, her throat tight, tears hovering. 'I think I'm the lucky one.' Smiling as she kissed Beth's clean-smelling hair, she held back her emotion. 'Perhaps we might ask Julie to tea one day – if Miss Cotton will let her come.' She smiled at Beth's surprise. 'Oh yes, I think I may have discovered where your Julie is living. Selmer, who works for me at the store – remember we saw him when we got your new dress?' Beth nodded. 'Well, he said he thought there might be a girl called Julie with Miss Cotton. I'm going to ask her after Christmas if it is the nice girl who came out with you.'

Beth clapped her hands in delight. 'That's wonderful! Please ask her to come, Mummy. I love Julie too.'

'Then I shall too,' Vee said and hugged her tight. How lovely it was to feel her little warm body close to her heart. It was the best Christmas for years – the best since Bill died.

'Run away?' Vee looked at Jago in surprise when he told her that Julie had gone missing and then nodded. 'I can understand why she might do it – but where would she go?'

Beth had gone to bed after dinner, so tired she couldn't wait to go to sleep and Vee had been telling Jago about her plans to find her daughter's friend.

'She might have come to Halifax,' Jago said. 'I'm going to ask Hank to look out for a young girl of about sixteen who looks as if she's in trouble.'

'I'm sure he will if you ask,' Vee told him, feeling sad and frustrated. If only she'd tried harder to find Julie months ago, instead of waiting for Malcolm's return, this might not have happened. 'Can you give him a good description of her?'

'She has blue-grey eyes and straight dark hair that she ties back at her nape,' Jago replied. 'She's pretty but she looks sad and she's about five foot six tall. She has a London accent, so different from most folk round here.'

'Hank will keep an eye out for her,' Vee promised. 'I'll make sure of it.'

'Thanks, Miss Vee,' Jago said and smiled his slow smile. 'I've looked around the lake and the woods and she's not lying there dead – no sign that the animals have got her either, I'd have found evidence if they had but there's nothing. I spoke to the rangers – one of them told me they discovered that someone recalled seeing a girl carrying a small bag that night of the hard blizzard, getting on the Halifax bus but they didn't speak to her.'

'Then she may be here somewhere. I suppose it depends how much money she had saved.' Julie could have kept on going, travelling across country by bus or train.

'I don't think it would have been much,' Jago replied. 'I never saw her in the shops ever – and that Miss Cotton is mean. She might have thought it was enough to give her food and a bed.'

'Surely not?' Vee frowned. 'I'll have a word with her after Christmas. I'll write and ask her to call on me and then I'll ask her why the girl ran away.' She looked at him thoughtfully. 'Beth said her friend's name was Julie and if it *is* the same girl, it's a pity Malcolm didn't bring them both to me but I suppose he couldn't if she was claimed. Well, Julie can come and stay with us if Hank finds her – I've plenty of room.'

'Let's hope he finds her alive and well,' Jago said and then, changing the subject with a little nod, 'thank you for the coat you gave Ma, Miss Vee. It's so warm and she loves it.'

'Well, thank you for my tree – and that turkey you gave us was delicious. How many do you rear each year?'

'Only a dozen or so. I give them to friends,' Jago said and grinned. He looked thoughtful for a moment, then, 'I'd like to talk to you after Christmas, Miss Vee . . .'

'You can talk to me now,' she invited but he shook his head.

128

'It's business and this is Christmas,' he said. 'I'll come and see you next Sunday.'

'You do that,' she agreed. 'In the meantime, have a word with Hank about Julie.'

'Yes, I knew the girl was missing,' Hank told him later as they were having a game of pool in the billiard room. 'Miss Cotton reported it two days after she went off. She claims the girl stole some money from her but admitted it was only a few cents she'd kept for her milk money. She said it was all the girl had since she'd only given her bed and board and her clothes.'

Jago frowned. 'I suspected as much, so she can't have gone far with that. She must have found shelter or work in Halifax or one of you would have seen her sleeping rough on the streets.'

'In the weather we've had lately she would freeze to death,' Hank said. 'Maybe she got lucky and someone took her in, gave her work and somewhere to stay.'

'Where would you suggest I look?' Jago asked. He looked at the officer doubtfully. 'I don't get much time but I have a few days off now.'

'You'd need to search twenty-four hours a day,' Hank told him. 'She could be anywhere, Jago. It is an almost impossible task, especially if she doesn't want to be found. Leave it to us. We'll keep an eye out for her and if she is found, we'll inform Miss Vee. She's offered a place for the girl to live so that's probably best for her.'

'I just want her to be safe,' Jago replied. 'I reckon she's had a hard time of it one way and another.'

'A lot of the kids they bring out have,' Hank agreed. 'I'm not saying you shouldn't look in shops or cafés – if Miss Cotton was telling the truth she isn't trained for much so she might end up anywhere there was work.'

'That's helpful, thanks,' Jago said. 'It may be that she found something like that; I hope she did for her own sake.'

Hank potted the wining ball and looked at him with a grin of triumph. 'Mind not on the game, Jago? I know you've got a good heart, but just be careful. Miss Cotton swears she gave the girl no reason to run away. If anything has happened to her . . .'

'You think folks would blame me?' Jago shook his head. 'I would never harm her or anyone else, you know that, Hank.'

'I know it but if – and it is only if – something bad happened to her folks might remember you were very interested in a girl you don't know . . .' His gaze was curious, half warning him off.

Jago shook his head. All his life Jago had had to contend with people crossing the road to avoid him because of his deformity. It was as if they thought he might have horns and a forked tail, simply because he wasn't like other lads. Jago had cried over it when he was still at school, hurt by the bullying and ignorance of other boys.

'You're just different,' Maya had told him as she'd comforted him. 'It's just ignorance and fear of what they don't understand and some folk are real uncomfortable around someone who has a disablement. You have to be bigger than them, Jago. You have to understand they

130

can't help themselves and accept it. Crying or getting angry will make the bullies worse – and the others, well, they just don't know how to look at you, but you don't turn your head away in shame. Do you hear me? You're as good as anyone else and don't you forget it.'

So Jago had let the insults and the rude faces go by as if he hadn't heard or seen them and most of the boys, who were simply ignorant, grew out of it and learned to respect him as the boss of Miss Vee's lumbermill. One day, if she would allow it, he would own the mill himself. He didn't yet have enough saved but he would in time, if she would keep it for him. He knew others were looking at her land and the mill with envious eyes. Much of the timber locally had been cut down over the years without being replaced, but Miss Vee's land had been harvested judiciously, with new saplings being planted each year so that they would replace the trees taken as logs for the mill. It was a sustainable way of managing the land and Mr Bittern had been unusual in seeing that it had to be done for the future. Others had just cut down whole swathes of forest without making any provision and that would see an end to the lumber business if the process wasn't reversed. Jago understood the need for profit but he also understood that you had to be at home with nature, to nurture your land and environment if you didn't want to ruin it forever. He was at home in the woods and enjoyed living away from the busy port of Halifax . . . the wilderness was a place of wonder for Jago.

Hank was right in one thing he'd said. Jago didn't have the time to search the busy port and town centre as it needed to be searched for the missing girl. His free time was on a Sunday and many of the shops and factories would be closed then. He would take a walk around the port and the town but his hopes of finding Julie were not high. If she'd stayed in Lower Sackville, he might have found her living rough in the woods, but he wasn't a townie. Hank would be more likely to spot her in the course of his duties, but that wouldn't stop Jago from looking. He wasn't sure why Julie was so important to him. He just knew she was . . .

CHAPTER 15

Christmas was just a memory and she was back washing dirty plates and glasses. Her hands were so sore and red! Julie looked at them ruefully as yet another pile of plates was brought in by Sally-Anne, the girl who waited at tables in Andy's café. She dumped them down on the long pine table, giving Julie a sour look.

'That's it. I'm off home for the night. If he doesn't close now, he can wait tables himself.'

'Who will cook then?' Julie asked. She looked at the clock on the wall . . . it was only a quarter to six in the evening and they normally stayed open until half past six.

'You can do it,' Sally-Anne flung the words at her as she left. 'And if he doesn't like it, I'll quit. There are better jobs elsewhere.'

Julie watched as the girl stormed off, clearly in a mood. She complained every day that she was over-worked, and threatened to leave at least twice a week but still came in each morning. However, she seemed really annoyed that evening.

Andy came in from the bar. He looked at Julie as she stood with her arms in soapy water up to her elbows. 'Sally-Anne just stormed off,' he said. 'You'll have to serve, Julie. We've got half a dozen customers waiting.'

'I've got all these to do!' Julie indicated the pile of dirty plates.

'You can finish here when we're closed,' he said and gave her a winning smile. 'Help me, Julie. I'll give you extra in your wages.'

Julie nodded and wiped her hands on a towel hanging next to the deep sink. Andy and Cath had shared their Christmas meal with her and Cath had given her a small gift of a new pair of stockings so she couldn't refuse his request. She put on one of the spare aprons and went through the door into the café. Every table had customers seated and most of them looked impatient. She approached the first table and wrote down their order on a notepad she'd found in the apron pocket, taking it to the counter to Andy before making her way round the room.

Soon he had plates of ham and eggs, fries and steaks as well as bacon ready for her to deliver, along with cups of coffee or soft drinks. Julie no sooner delivered one order than another was ready. Customers got up when they'd eaten and paid at the counter, behind which Andy was cooking his meals. However, as soon as she had cleared one table, Julie returned to find someone else occupying the chairs. She looked at Andy but he just shook his head. While he had customers, he would continue to serve up food.

'It's nearly half past six,' Julie told him as she

collected a plate of apple pie and cream. 'Cath wanted us back early. She said she thought the baby might come soon.'

Andy batted away her concern. 'There's a couple of weeks to go yet.' He clearly wasn't about to close when they were this busy. No wonder Sally-Anne had stormed off. She'd been working flat out all day.

Julie's legs and back ached. She'd spent hours at the sink and now she was kept busy serving when she ought to have been nearly finished. She thought of all the dishes waiting to be washed. She would be lucky to get home for another hour even if they actually managed to shut the door!

At last, the flow of customers stopped and Andy turned the card to *Closed* on the door reluctantly. 'Well, that's it,' he told Julie. 'I'll finish up here – you get the dishes started and I'll give you a hand when I've done.'

Julie nodded but didn't believe him. As she returned to the kitchen, she heard the doorbell go again and groaned. Andy might have turned the card but he hadn't locked the door.

'Good evening, officer,' Andy said and sounded jocular. 'Come to arrest me for working overtime?'

'I will if you like,' a pleasant, deep voice answered. 'I'm looking for a young girl, about sixteen, dark hair, grey-blue eyes. She's been reported missing – Julie Miller. She worked for a Miss Cotton in Lower Sackville and ran off.'

Julie's blood ran cold. The police were looking for her! She hadn't taken much but it seemed Miss Cotton had reported her theft of a few cents and now she might be arrested.

'Any further details?' Andy asked him. 'Sixteen you say – is she pretty, tall – thin or what?'

'Miss Cotton was a bit vague, just the hair colour, brownish she thought – wasn't even sure about the eyes; said she was a plain, sullen girl. She paid for her to come here so she's miffed over the girl's disappearance. If you see her, let me know. We're on the lookout for her.'

'Right,' Andy replied cheerfully. 'I'll remember that. Is she in trouble?'

'Not much. Stole a few cents, Miss Cotton claimed, but she didn't pay her for months of work so it's a dubious point. Anyway, let me know if she comes asking for work – find out as much as you can about where she's living. She must be living rough unless someone has given her a home. Oh, and she's a Brit. Came out with the evacuees.'

Julie heard the bell jangle as people left the café. She felt sick and nervous as she carried on washing the pile of dirty dishes. They were all draining when Andy walked into the scullery. He stood looking at her in silence for a moment, then, 'I suppose you heard that? Not that it was a fair description of you.'

'Yes – why?' Julie tried to brazen it out but the look in his eyes told her that he knew. 'Cath knows about it, Andy. I didn't take much – just my fare back to Halifax. I wouldn't have taken it if she'd paid me.' She raised scared eyes to his. 'Are you going to tell on me?'

'Why should I?' he said but didn't smile. 'You're a good worker, Julie – but you realise you might get into trouble if you run off again? If I told the law that you'd stolen from me, they would arrest you and put you away for a couple of years.'

Julie was startled. 'You wouldn't do that? I haven't touched anything of yours.'

'No, and Cath would have my guts if I did,' Andy grinned at her then to show he hadn't meant it. 'I was just teasing you. Now, come on, leave the rest for the morning. We have to get back to Cath. She'll be screaming blue murder if we're any later.'

Julie nodded, wiping her hands before putting on her coat. It was still cold outside, though not as bitter as it had been just before Christmas. She'd hardly known it was Christmas. Andy had shut for one day and cooked a nice meal of roast pork for them but there were no gifts from him for Julie or for Cath. She'd wondered why he didn't give his wife anything but she'd said it was just his way.

'Andy works hard for his money. He has to pay off a debt to a man called Trevors,' Cath had told Julie. 'I don't know what happened or why but he owes him several hundred dollars and Trevors isn't the sort of man who allows a debt to go unpaid.'

Julie nodded. She hadn't expected a gift but she felt a bit sad for Cath that she'd not been given something nice at Christmas. However, she had sufficient money to buy clothes for herself and the baby and seemed to be content with that most of the time.

When they got in that evening, it was quiet at first, no sign of life downstairs – and then they heard the screams from above. Andy looked at Julie in alarm, swore softly and took the stairs two at a time. Julie stood at the bottom and listened. She wasn't allowed up there, though she would have liked to see what was going on. Cath was clearly in pain and perhaps she could help . . .

After several minutes, Andy came back down, his face was white and he was clearly shocked. 'Something's wrong,' he said. 'Go up and sit with her, Julie. I have to fetch a doctor.'

'Yes, I will,' Julie said and ran up the stairs to the landing, hesitating until she heard the next scream. She walked quickly towards the sound and then stopped at the open bedroom door, feeling horror as she saw the bright crimson stain spreading over the sheets beneath Cath. Surely childbirth wasn't supposed to be like this?

'Andy's gone for the doctor,' she told Cath and went to stand by the bed. 'Is there anything I can do?'

'Nooooo!' Cath wailed and writhed with agony. 'I had a fall down the stairs earlier. Got myself up here but – but it's coming too soon!' Her voice rose to a shriek. Julie moved closer and reached for her hand. Cath gripped it tightly and it hurt but she didn't flinch. 'Where the hell have you been?' Cath muttered between clenched teeth. 'I've been lying here for ages, waiting and waiting . . .'

'I'm sorry. The café was busy.' Julie let go of her hand and went to fetch a cloth from the washstand in the corner. She poured water from the pink jug into a matching basin and dipped the cloth in it, returning to wipe the sweat from Cath's brow. 'I wish we'd come sooner.'

'So do I!' Cath caught back a sob. 'If the baby dies

this time . . .' She gave a wail of despair, her body jerking with the pain.

Julie wanted to tell her it wouldn't die but she couldn't force the words out. Something was badly wrong and it would be a stupid lie. Her throat was tight with emotion. She didn't want anything to happen to Cath, who had been kind.

'The doctor will be here soon,' she soothed again and Cath looked at her in desperation. 'Just try to relax . . .'

'Andy isn't a bad man,' Cath said suddenly. 'What I said about him wasn't true . . . look after him for me . . .' Cath choked on her tears. 'I'm just a jealous cow. He's a real nice man and I love him.'

'I know,' Julie said and stroked her hair because it was all she could do. 'You'll look after him yourself – and he loves you, too.'

Julie wiped Cath's sweating forehead with the cool cloth and held her hand but felt useless in the face of her agony. The tears were building in her throat, because there was nothing she could do. This was all wrong. She knew it instinctively but didn't know what to do to ease her. Cath's body was wrenched with pain but despite all the signs of birth the baby wasn't coming as it should and all Julie could do was to pray the doctor would be in time. It seemed a long time before Andy returned with him and Julie was relieved to be sent back to the kitchen to boil lots of water and make tea to sustain them all.

It was hours later, and for the past several minutes everything had gone quiet. Then Andy came downstairs with the doctor, looking as white as a sheet. He went to the door with him and then returned, his eyes dark with grief.

'Both dead,' he said and seemed to choke on the words. 'Both gone . . . there was nothing he could do. It was too late . . .'

Julie felt the tears in her eyes. She sat down at the kitchen table and looked at him, shocked and disbelieving. It didn't seem possible that it could happen to a healthy young woman and yet she knew that it did – she'd heard her mother speak of women dying in childbed in the squalor of the East End of London, but she'd never seen the agony or heard the screams before.

'I am so sorry, Andy,' she said in a tiny voice that seemed to come from far away.

'It was my fault,' he said and jumped up looking furious. 'I stayed at the bloody café when she was dying and she needed me. If I'd come sooner . . .' His hands clenched in anger, the knuckles white, and his eyes were dark with pain.

Julie couldn't say anything. He would always blame himself. It was just bad luck but he would always believe that if he'd been home sooner, Cath might have got the help she needed in time. It was so shocking, so final, that it felt as though the world had suddenly gone dark and cold. Julie was shivering, freezing despite the warmth of the kitchen. She realised that for Andy the world probably had crashed around him; he'd loved Cath more than anyone had understood. Cath, in her insecurity, certainly hadn't realised how much she meant to him.

'Bugger him! It's his bloody fault I work so hard,' Andy swore, startling Julie and then rushed out of the house.

'Come back!' Julie called. Cath was lying upstairs. They would come to collect her and take her away soon but she needed to be cared for first . . . it couldn't be left to strangers.

Julie brushed the tears away from her face and went to the staircase. Cath had been good to her. The least she could do was to make her fresh and clean before they came to take her away.

Julie was in bed trying to sleep when she heard Andy come in. He was thrashing about, knocking things over and she heard him swear. She got up and went through to the kitchen. She hadn't undressed because she knew she couldn't sleep. As she saw Andy slumped at the table, his head in his hands, she could smell the strong odour of liquor on him. He looked up at her, a strange wildness in his eyes. Andy didn't normally drink but he was drunk now and out of his mind with grief.

'I never told her I loved her,' he said, his voice slurred and filled with self-pity and anger. 'I never told her that she was the one . . .'

'She knew,' Julie said, but she wasn't sure if Cath had really known.

'It's my fault she's dead – and that bugger is to blame. He'd been round earlier, demanding his money again and I thought an extra few dollars would help me get out of debt . . .' Andy shook his head. 'Now, she's gone and it's all for nothing. I'll kill the bugger if I swing for it!'

Julie was shocked. He didn't mean that, surely? It was just his grief talking. He'd loved Cath and now he was suffering.

Julie tried to comfort him. 'No, you won't kill anyone. She wouldn't have wanted that – you know she wouldn't,' Julie said, feeling helpless as he burst into noisy sobs. She'd never seen a man cry like this and it was hurtful. He was normally so sure and so cheerful but underneath he had needed Cath's steady hand.

Andy raised his head and looked at her. 'Did they come? Did they take her away?'

'Yes. I washed her first. Made her look nice.'

For a moment he just stared at her and then nodded. 'Thank you. She would have liked that – she liked you. Go to bed now, Julie. I'm not in a fit state for company.

Julie looked at him for a moment more, then inclined her head and left him. He would come to terms with his grief and until then he was best left to himself, though, oddly, she wasn't afraid of him.

As she lay down on her bed, Julie pondered her own future. What would happen to her now? Would Andy let her stay here now that Cath was dead or would he send her away? If he sent her away, she didn't know what she would do. Her wages wouldn't cover the cost of accommodation and allow her to save for the future so she hoped she could stay but wasn't sure he would want her in his house without Cath. Her own tears fell then, wetting her pillow. She had just begun to settle and she would miss the young woman who had been kind to her, especially if she had to move on.

For a week the café remained closed. Andy was drunk most of the time; it was the only way he could manage, because his grief and remorse tortured him day and night. Julie understood that he drank to forget his guilt at leaving Cath alone when she'd needed him and she stayed out of his way as much as she could, cooked food for them both and leaving his on the table. Sometimes he ate it, though whether it was hot or cold she didn't know. She heard him come and go and then, one night, he stood outside her door and told her the funeral was the next day.

'You'll come,' he said. 'Cath liked you. So you'll come with me.'

Julie got ready the next morning and he was waiting in the kitchen. Dressed in a navy-blue pinstriped suit she'd never seen before, he looked pale but he was sober and grim. Julie wore her grey dress under her coat but she only had a wool hat so that had to do.

They walked to the church, which was a few streets away. When they went in there were three or four others who nodded to Andy and stared at her as they took their seats near the front. Then the music played and some men carried in Cath's coffin. It was very plain but had a cross of white flowers on the top. Julie wished she had some flowers to offer Cath, because she'd been kind in her way and she'd liked her.

When it was over, they went outside and three men came up to Andy and told him how sorry they were.

He thanked them and then one of them asked when the café would open again.

He looked at Julie as if she knew the answer and then shrugged. 'Tomorrow, I suppose . . .' The men were looking at Julie. Andy frowned and then nodded. 'She's Cath's sister,' he lied and their faces looked uncertain, as if they didn't know whether to believe him. 'She brought her over because of the bombing.' They nodded then and Andy touched Julie on the arm. 'We'd best get on. We've work to do if we're opening tomorrow.'

Julie didn't answer. She'd thought for a moment he would give her up but he hadn't. He was silent as they walked home but then he looked round the kitchen, as if recognising that she'd kept it clean.

'You can cook,' he said looking at her. 'I'll get someone else to help with the washing-up as soon as I can. You can help me with the meals in future.'

'Yes, all right,' Julie said. 'As long as you don't expect me to do both.'

'I said, didn't I?' His tone was warning so she went to her own room and changed into her oldest dress, ready for work. 'You need an apron – but Cath has some.' He pointed to a drawer. Julie went to it and took out the white aprons inside, showing him them. 'They'll be too big but you can wrap them round you.'

'Thanks. Do you want me to clean the tables and tidy up for a start?'

'Yes.' He took a key from his pocket. 'You get started. I'll be along later.'

Julie took the key without a word. He had already had a glass of whiskey. It wouldn't surprise her if he

144

got drunk again. Cath's death had changed him and she suspected there was something else eating at him, but didn't know what. She left the house and walked to the café alone. Julie hadn't seen much of the city yet but she liked this part of it better than the very busy commercial areas around the docks. It was old-fashioned and reminded her a little of home.

She opened the café and boiled water so that she could wash the tables and then the floor. She was halfway through cleaning the kitchen stoves when Andy walked in carrying some large boxes.

'Supplies,' he said. 'Everything we left has to be thrown out or we might poison the customers.'

Julie nodded. She'd found some rotten food and put that out in the bins but Andy now emptied the big fridge completely and refilled it. He said you couldn't be too careful about food being fresh.

'What do you cook best?' he asked as she finished her cleaning. He'd made some coffee and pushed a cup towards her. 'Cath used to make cakes and apple pies. I did the breakfasts and steaks.'

'I can make apple pie and cakes,' Julie told him. 'I was taught at school and my gran taught me too, until she died. Mum didn't cook fancy food much but she made rock cakes and sponges so I can do all sorts if you want.'

'Make something we can sell tomorrow,' Andy invited, pointing to the pile of fresh foodstuffs he still hadn't put away.

'I'll make some Madeira cake, some buns and a big apple pie for a start,' Julie suggested. He nodded, crossed his arms and sat on a stool watching as she worked. Julie knew she was being tested so she tried her hardest to make the cake light and delicious, the buns tasty and crisp round the edges and the pie crust golden and delicious.

Andy nodded when she'd finished and tried one of the buns. 'Not bad,' he said. 'Not quite up to Cath's standard but you'll get there.'

Julie smothered her objections. She knew the buns were good. Better than Cath's if he were honest but she wouldn't expect him to admit it. Since Cath's death he'd put her on a pedestal.

'Put them all in the glass cases in the counter,' he said. 'You can make some more fresh in the morning. These won't last five minutes if we're busy. You'll need to make much bigger batches of the buns and at least six apple pies.'

Julie nodded. She knew how quickly the cakes and pastries sold out when folk just wanted a cup of coffee and a bite to eat. At lunchtime they asked for the meals that Andy cooked but, in the mornings and afternoons, the sweet treats were more popular.

'Did you find someone to wash up?' Julie asked and he glared at her.

'Give me a chance. You'll have to do a bit for a start. I'll give you a hand when I get a break.'

Julie sighed. That meant she'd be doing the cooking and the washing-up. Andy's little notice in the window for another waitress had gone unanswered for weeks. Sally-Anne sometimes didn't turn up and then Andy served the customers himself. It got him behind with the cooking, which caused complaints, and it would be even harder to find someone to wash up. It was because Andy didn't pay much. Julie had heard Sally-Anne grumbling about her pay enough times.

Julie knew that she herself might earn more elsewhere but was nervous about leaving because it would mean finding somewhere else to stay and giving a reference. She'd been lucky Andy had taken her on, she knew that, but he'd been in need of someone who would stand for hours at the sink and not demand a fair wage.

Cath had made her cakes at home, getting up early in the morning to bake before he left for work. The café opened at eight thirty for breakfast and closed at six thirty or so in the evening, but it was often later.

It was going to be a long hard day for Julie. She remembered her time at Miss Cotton's house, when she'd had free time at the weekends. Seen in retrospect it seemed pretty good now – if it hadn't been for Ralph. Remembering his taunts and the way he'd attacked her Julie smothered her regrets. Andy was all right most of the time. Even when he drank too much, he wasn't nasty, just morbid. He expected her to work hard and he didn't pay much but at least she had money saved now – twenty dollars and a few cents.

Julie smiled to herself. One day she would have enough money to set up a little business for herself, sewing, she thought, and perhaps cooking too. She didn't mind hard work if it led to something good. And at least Andy didn't try to get into her room at night. A little shudder went through her as she remembered Ralph and her uncle and the man at the orphanage. Those had been the worst times of her life and she would never forget them. At least here she was safe from Ralph, because he would never find her.

CHAPTER 16

'I can't buy it yet,' Jago told Vee that afternoon when he called to see her after work. 'I'm not sure what you'd want for it but I have a few hundred dollars saved. I don't mind waiting for a while yet but I just wanted to be sure you wouldn't sell to anyone else.'

'I have no intention of it,' Vee replied. 'Yes, I've had offers – more than one as it happens, but I wouldn't want to sell to the men who made them. When you're ready, it's yours, Jago. One offered fifteen hundred dollars, another two thousand. I think somewhere between the two might be fair – what do you think?'

'I think it is worth more,' Jago said honestly. 'I could pay you half of it now and the rest in a couple of years or we can wait until I have the rest of the money saved.'

'Why don't we settle on a figure in the middle and you can pay half and the rest later?' she suggested and smiled. 'I had an idea what you wanted, Jago, and I've decided to put the money I get from selling the mill into property. I'm going to buy shops, two of them. They're nice little properties and will be easy for me to let to people I can trust to pay their rents on time. It will be simpler for me to look after shops than a lumbermill – and I'd really like you to have it.'

'I'll pay you the two thousand dollars for the mill,' Jago replied firmly. 'The woodland isn't included in that offer, Miss Vee but I'd like to buy stretches of timber when and as I need it, if that is all right with you?'

'You're too honest for your own good,' she objected, smiling. 'I would have let you have the woodland in the deal.'

Jago shook his head. 'That lumber is worth a lot of money, Miss Vee. Why do you think others are sniffing round, offering for the mill? It's because we've managed our woods, replanted and looked after them, instead of just ploughing them up for farmland.'

'Bill always believed in that,' she agreed. 'I know you're the right man to have my mill, Jago, and I want you to have the woodlands too. They should be yours as surety for the future. I'll sell you all of it for two thousand dollars and no arguments. You can pay me when you pay me and there's no interest.' It was a generous offer – she knew it and so did he, but she was as stubborn as Jago, and after some hesitation he laughed and offered his hand.

'You're not a good businesswoman, Miss Vee,' Jago shook his head at her but he was grinning. 'I don't know how to thank you.'

'Don't. It's a waste of time.' She smiled at him. 'I shan't have a son to take over, Jago. Beth wouldn't have the first idea how to run a lumber business – but shops and property are always worth investing in. It will be a lot more valuable when they build more bridges to carry the increasing traffic.'

'If they ever do,' Jago warned and she smiled.

'A little bird tells me that it might not be as long as you imagine,' she said. 'And your lumber will be in even greater demand for more housing.'

'It isn't mine yet,' he replied.

'My lawyer already knows what I want and he'll have it done in no time,' Vee told him with a wicked grin. 'By next month you'll own your mill, Jago. And don't worry about rushing to pay. I'm in no hurry.'

'That's really good of you, Miss Vee.' He shook his head, unable to believe it was happening so fast.

Vee laughed in delight. 'I couldn't have planned it better,' she said. 'Malcolm isn't involved in the mill so I don't need to ask him, though I would have asked what he thought if he were home.'

Jago nodded. 'You'll be worried about him?'

'Yes,' Vee agreed. 'I had one letter from Malta but nothing more. I thought he would be back by now.'

'There's been no news of his ship going down?'

'No – so that's good news,' Vee agreed. 'I daresay I'm worrying for nothing.'

'I certainly hope so.' Jago hesitated, then, 'Did you speak to Miss Cotton about Julie?'

'Yes, I did. She wasn't helpful. Said Julie was an ungrateful girl and a thief, but when I asked why a young girl would run away in a blizzard if she had a good home and job, she looked a bit odd. Mumbled something about a disagreement between Julie and her nephew.' Vee frowned. 'I've heard he's a bit of a rogue. He was sent home from his school for climbing through the window of a girl's bedroom – a tutor's daughter – when she was in bed. Pete Trevors helped him get in, apparently, but didn't go in with him. Ralph Cotton and the girl were caught in a very embarrassing situation and she was sent to an aunt and he and the Trevors youth were expelled.'

'Then perhaps Julie ran away because of him,' Jago said with a stifled oath and a look of outrage. 'Hank hasn't heard anything at all?'

'Well, he says there is one lead he is going to follow up – a young girl looking for work.'

Jago nodded. 'She could be anywhere now, I suppose. Well, I'd best get home or Maya will worry. Let me know when you want me to sign the contract, Miss Vee.'

'I surely will – give Maya my love.'

Getting into his truck, Jago paused for a moment. This was a momentous day for him. He'd never been really certain he would ever own the mill and he could hardly believe it was his. Shaking his head over Miss Vee's generosity, he started up and drove off. He couldn't wait to tell Maya that his dream was about to come true.

Vee stood at the window and watched Jago drive away. She was glad that was done. She'd worried what might happen to the mill if the day came when she couldn't look after it or Jago left to work elsewhere. Not that he would have done so without seeing a new man in place, but Vee needed people she could trust to look after her businesses. The clothing shop was doing better than ever now she'd introduced the lines of fancy underwear. She'd sourced them eventually from a

151

French supplier in Montreal whose firm made the most beautiful lace negligees and underwear. It was a wonderful addition to her stock.

With the deposit Jago paid her, Vee could purchase two little shops. They were side by side, next to a busy little café in Halifax. She'd popped in and bought coffee and cakes when she was looking at the shops and all of them were very tasty. In time she might be able to purchase the café too, and she'd want to employ whoever made those delicious little cakes. The girl who was serving said they were new; apparently, they had a different cook. Vee had sent her compliments to the cook when she paid the man behind the counter and she'd thought he'd looked at her a bit oddly.

Dismissing the memory as unimportant, Vee turned as Beth came into the room carrying a book. She held it out. 'Will you help me read?' she asked, looking shy and yet pleased. 'Miss Black says my reading is getting better.'

'Of course I will,' Vee said and looked at the book she'd chosen. 'Ah, *Black Beauty*. Yes, I like this story. Where are you up to?'

'Let's start at the beginning,' Beth said. 'I finished it but I'd like to read it again with you so I understand it better.'

Vee smiled as they settled on the comfortable sofa together. It was much better to buy shops than own the mill, even though it had been Bill's and she might feel a few pangs when she signed it away, but she had to think of her little girl and the future. Trevors would never stop pestering her until he knew the mill was no longer hers. Once he understood it was sold he would give up – of course he would, because Jago was capable of standing up for himself.

Jago walked the woods, deciding which trees were ready for cutting and making a mental note of one that might have some sort of blight and would need to be culled and burned to stop it spreading. Trees could take disease and die just as easy as humans if they weren't properly cared for, but he would nourish and care for the woodlands he loved – soon to be his. A warm feeling spread through him as he envisaged his life, living on the farm and working at the mill. He loved the smell of fresh-cut wood but he also enjoyed the smell of the forest, the sweet smell of spring which brought carpets of flowers, and the darker scents of the undergrowth, wild garlic, fungi and mould and the small, furtive creatures that lived hidden amongst them.

It was usually only smaller mammals, as there were no thickets or ground shrubs for larger beasts to hide in because the woods were properly coppiced and tended every year and that was what Jago had come to do, armed with saws and choppers.

He could hear the whine of the saw at the mill and knew that an order for timber was being prepared. He'd discussed it with Ticker, his headman, and knew that it would be done well. Jago didn't need to be there to watch. It was better to leave the men to it and get on with some maintenance. If a small amount was cleared regularly, it kept things right and just as he liked them.

He took the dying tree out first and dragged it to a designated clearing where there was provision for burning dead wood, making sure to collect any fallen foliage or broken branches. It looked as if it had been attacked by some kind of beetle but was soon burning safely in the pit. Jago would check on the fire to make sure it was out when he finished for the day. He never left anything to chance, especially where fire was concerned. Carelessness could lead to a huge loss of timber and profits.

For the next few hours he worked at coppicing, taking useful wood for fires and carving home in his truck. By the time it was getting dusky his shoulders ached and he was tired, but he checked on the fire before he returned to the mill. It was still smouldering so he doused it with water and covered it with damp earth, watching the last flicker die out before driving to the mill. The men had mostly left for the day and Ticker was just locking up as he arrived.

Jago told him about the diseased tree and they decided to search the woodland the next day to make certain there were no more.

'The order got off on time,' Ticker said, chewing gum. 'We had another three come in not long after you left. All required for ship refurbishing so we'll need a good hardwood.'

'We can source it when we're looking for any further signs of disease,' Jago said, nodding.

They parted contentedly and Jago drove home. As he went past the school, he thought about the young girl who had worked there for a few months. If she was in Halifax she must have work, because Hank had had men out looking for a girl living rough and they hadn't found her. Maybe she was fine, Jago thought and put her from his mind. If she was in trouble he would help her, should she be found, but she was probably having a wonderful life now she'd left the tight-fisted Miss Cotton's establishment. He could only hope that was the case. He frowned at himself, knowing that he was a fool to dwell so much on a girl he didn't know and would probably never see again, but something about her had bothered him. The deep unhappiness and loneliness he'd sensed had touched a chord within him . . .

CHAPTER 17

Julie looked at the pile of greasy dishes in the sink. She'd been on her feet since six that morning, baking fresh cakes and pies to start them off. During the day she'd alternated her time between cooking and washing dishes and her back, feet and legs all ached something rotten. It was no good, she couldn't do it all. Andy had promised to help her with the washing-up when he wasn't cooking meals but he'd developed a habit of leaving the café to fetch supplies – and, more often than not when he got back, she could smell strong drink on his breath. He wasn't getting drunk as much now, but he certainly stopped for a drink. His cooking left something to be desired these days and people were asking more and more for her cakes and pastries.

'Still at it?' Andy said cheerfully as he came through. 'I'm off, Julie. You can lock up.'

'What about all this?' She pointed to the pile of dirty dishes. 'I could do with some help here.'

'Sorry. I have to go and see someone.' Andy's smile left his face. 'I don't know if Cath told you – I owe money on this place. If I don't meet the monthly

156

payment, he'll close us down and what I make these days hardly clears what I owe him each month by the time I've paid the bills.'

'But we're so busy. I don't understand it . . .' She looked at him uncertainly. 'Is it worth all the work and trouble if it doesn't pay?'

Andy shrugged. 'What else do I do? I've had this place years. It used to be profitable until, well . . .' He sighed. 'I was a damned fool. I gambled on a horse that was supposed to be a sure thing. It lost and I couldn't pay so I had to borrow the money and the bank don't lend money for gambling debts.'

'How much do you owe?' Julie asked.

'More than I did at the start,' Andy replied. 'He charges high interest and if I miss a payment, it doubles and trebles. I doubt I'll ever repay it, because he just keeps demanding more.'

'Then why don't you just give him the business and start over somewhere else? Or sell it and go away where he'll never find you. If he's charging you so much interest, he's a crook. I've heard of men like that – in the East End they called them loan sharks and that's what they are!'

Andy chuckled. 'You look pretty when you're angry, Julie. I've wondered myself why I don't just go off and leave him to take it – it's what he wants. He's a greedy, bad man and if I had the courage, I'd shoot him down like the cur he is!' For a moment anger flashed in his eyes. He was remembering the night he'd worked late and Cath had been dying.

'Don't talk daft,' Julie said, because she knew it was just wild talk. 'If you just went away and he took over you could start fresh but if you killed him, you would be punished.'

'I know – Cath said the same thing.' Andy grinned at her, his anger vanishing. 'Maybe I could sell the property to someone I know wants to buy and start over in another town far from here.' He hesitated and looked at her uncertainly. 'Would you come with me if I did that, Julie?'

'I might if I didn't have to do all this washing-up . . .'

'I'll get someone in,' he promised. 'I'd better go. If I'm late he'll add another fifty dollars to the bill.'

Julie sighed as he left and then turned back to the sink. The sooner she'd got this finished, the sooner she could go home and make herself some supper and then sit down with a book. She'd started borrowing books from a library and found she enjoyed reading stories these days, and if Andy kept his word and she didn't have to do all the washing-up she might try making some pretty clothes – examples that she could perhaps sell to a shop near the café that had started selling nice things.

Julie ate her supper alone and left sandwiches for Andy if he came in late, which he often did these days. He would probably go out and get drunk again because his mood had been dark when he'd left to pay his debts.

Julie went to bed when the kitchen clock struck nine. She had to be up early or the café couldn't open. She needed to bake and then, if Andy was still sleeping it off, she would have to open up and hope that he came in later.

Lying wakeful for a while, she listened but Andy didn't come in so she put out her light and went to sleep, pretty certain that he would be drunk when he got home.

In the morning there was still no sign of Andy, nor any that he'd come in that night. His sandwiches were still under the teacloth, untouched. Shrugging, she got on with the baking. While the cakes and pies were in the oven, she made herself another sandwich. An hour or so later she left for the café, carrying the tins of cakes and pies.

She had them set out under the glass domes when Sally-Anne came in, ten minutes late. She glanced round guiltily. 'Is he in?'

'No, you're lucky, he hasn't come yet,' Julie replied. She liked the older girl even though she could be sulky and sometimes had temper tantrums. She still threatened to leave at least once a day.

'You won't tell him I was late?'

Julie promised she wouldn't just as the first customers entered. One wanted coffee, apple pie and cream, the other wanted ham and eggs. Julie cooked them and then got on with more baking. What she'd done earlier wouldn't last all day. She was surprised when Sally-Anne came in with the greasy plates and handed her ten cents.

'The customer liked his ham and eggs so much he sent you the change.'

'That was kind of him,' Julie said. 'You should have half. You served him.'

Sally-Anne shook her head. 'He always gives me ten

159

cents anyway,' she said, 'but he said your cooking was much better than Andy's.'

Julie laughed. 'Don't tell him that or he'll have me doing the lot.'

They were both still laughing when they heard a voice calling from the counter. Sally-Anne huffed her displeasure but went out. Julie heard her give a little cry and went through quickly. She hesitated as she saw the law officer and Sally-Anne staring at him as though she'd seen a ghost. Her heart caught with fright.

'What's happened?' she asked, feeling breathless. She curled her hands at her sides, an icy chill at her nape now.

'I am afraid your employer has been killed,' the officer replied, looking grim. 'He was found lying in the gutter – probably knocked down by a vehicle but we don't know yet and we've been told that he'd been drinking heavily earlier yesterday evening.'

'That's a wicked thing to say!' Sally-Anne cried. 'Andy didn't drink much.'

'He's been drinking more since Cath's death,' Julie stated and both the officer and Sally-Anne looked at her. 'He and Cath let me sleep in their back room and since she died and the baby died too, he's been unhappy and drinking a lot more.'

'That fits with what we've been told,' the officer said, nodding. 'I'm sorry to give you such bad news, young ladies.'

'What should we do now?' Sally-Anne asked. 'Do we carry on working? Who owns this café now?'

'I can't help you there but if you keep working someone will be along soon enough to tell you.'

160

'Andy owed someone a lot of money,' Julie said thoughtfully. 'Perhaps whoever he is, he'll take the café to repay Andy's debt.'

The officer nodded. 'That may well be the case. In the meantime, you should carry on, unless you decide to shut up for a few days out of respect.' He looked from one to the other. 'You're both a mite young to have the responsibility so I'll look in again tomorrow to see if you're managing. And don't worry about the funeral. My boss will take care of that. He knew and liked Andy; you'll be informed so you can close and attend on the day.'

With that he left, leaving the girls staring at each other in dismay. For a moment neither of them said anything. Sally-Anne swiped at the tears on her cheeks.

'I liked him, even though he was mean with his money,' she said in a choked voice. 'I never knew he was in debt.'

'He owed a lot to a man who charged him high interest,' Julie said, feeling a churning in her stomach as she remembered Andy's mood before he left the previous evening. 'He thought he might lose the café because he couldn't pay it off, however hard we worked.'

'What are we going to do?' Sally-Anne asked, just as two customers came in.

'We'd better carry on until we see who owns it now,' Julie said. 'We can look for new jobs but you tried and couldn't find anything you liked, could you?'

Sally-Anne looked thoughtful. 'I was offered other jobs that paid more but I didn't want to leave, not really. I liked working here.'

'Me too,' Julie agreed. It was hard work but Andy had been pleasant to work for while Cath lived – and despite Cath's fears he'd never bothered either of the girls who worked for him. As they looked at each other for a moment before Sally-Anne moved away to serve the customers, they knew they were going to miss Andy. It was a strange and difficult situation to be in, because they had no idea what would happen next.

Julie went back to the kitchen. Andy was dead! It was a horrid shock because she'd liked him. He didn't keep his promises and was often thoughtless, expecting too much of her and Sally-Anne, but he'd given Julie a job when she needed it as well as a home. She would be doing all the cooking now and the washing-up until they could find someone to help. Now that they were in charge, perhaps they could offer more wages until whoever now owned the café came to claim it.

CHAPTER 18

Vee answered her telephone later that morning. It was her solicitor, Callum Jefferson, who gave her some disturbing news.

'That little café next to the two shops you recently purchased may be for sale sooner than we thought,' he said. 'The owner – Andy Machin – was knocked down and killed last night by a driver who apparently didn't stop. Certainly didn't inform anyone so there's some suspicion about how and why it happened.' He paused significantly.

'What do you mean?' Vee asked, shocked and disturbed by what he was telling her. 'They think it was deliberate?'

'I've been told in confidence that there is some doubt, that's all,' he confirmed. 'It all seems a bit of a mess. They don't know who owns his business now but whoever it is will come forward sooner or later and they may wish to sell. It would be nice if you were able to purchase it as you already have the other properties on that corner situation. If there is redevelopment in the future, it would put you in a good position owning a prime location.'

'Yes. We'll have to see what happens, though I like my shops as they are,' Vee said. 'I am sorry the café owner died like that and – well, it's disturbing that it may have been murder.' She shivered.

'I shouldn't let it upset you. A personal dispute no doubt – most murders are, I believe. People fear strangers but when murder happens it is often someone they know.'

'It's just so unpleasant. Bad enough that he should be killed – but if it was deliberate? I can't imagine why anyone would do such a thing.'

'There are some nasty types about, though we don't often get that kind of behaviour round here.'

'No, thank goodness. It was kind of you to ring me.'

'I daresay the police will sort it soon enough.'

'I certainly hope so!'

Vee was thoughtful as she replaced the receiver. She didn't like to think of anyone dying that way. Shaking her head, she went through to the kitchen to tell Aggie to be careful on her way home. She couldn't say why it had given her an uneasy feeling . . . it didn't bear thinking about.

Vee collected Beth from school that afternoon and they drove home after visiting a shop in Halifax to buy Beth some new shoes. Young girls grew so fast and Beth seemed to be shooting up, perhaps because of the good food she ate these days. The weather was beginning to pick up again, still cold but the sunshine warmed the streets making them feel better than when it was bitterly cold. As they passed the shops she had purchased, she saw a man entering the café next door. Now what was Harold Trevors doing there? Vee had thought about taking Beth there for a change, but she wouldn't now. She shook her head; even if he was interested in buying the property he surely wouldn't be there so soon after the owner's death?

'Aggie has made some nice buns for you and an iced sponge,' Vee told Beth as they passed the ice-cream parlour they often visited. 'We won't stop this evening but we'll come on Saturday.'

'I like Aggie's buns,' Beth said and clung to Vee's hand. 'I like everything about living with you, Mummy.'

'I'm glad, darling. Now tell me what you did in school today?'

'We started making cards for Mother's Day,' Beth told her. 'Teacher says it's a long way off but this way we can take time over them and make them very special with pictures and sewing and everything. I'm making one for you, of course.' She smiled happily up at Vee, sending all thoughts of the café and what Trevors was doing there from her head. 'And we did history – all about when the British soldiers were garrisoned here and the citadel . . . oh, lots of things.'

Vee nodded. 'The British kept a garrison here until about 1906, I think, but now we have our own soldiers and some of them are away fighting with our friends the British people.'

'Yes, I know.' Beth smiled at her. 'I didn't know anything about Canada before I came here, but I'm learning and I think it is a lovely place to live.'

'I'm glad,' Vee said and drew to a stop in front of the impressive house Bill had built when they married. 'Now let's go and show Aggie your new red shoes, shall we?'

Beth trotted off, happy, skipping in front of her up the path. Vee had forgotten all about Harold Trevors being at the café she'd thought she might buy. The child's innocent delight in her new life made everything else unimportant.

Sally-Anne entered the kitchen where Julie was working, her face white, eyes wide and scared. 'You'd better come,' she said. 'A man just came in and he says he'll be our new boss once it's all sorted. He wants to see you. I don't like him, Julie. He frightens me . . .'

Julie dried her hands and followed her back into the café. A man with dark hair, a square jaw and thick lips was drinking coffee, looking about him with interest. He turned his harsh gaze on the girls as they entered, giving them a long hard stare.

'This place could be worth having,' he said. 'I'm expecting hard work from you two while things get sorted so don't let me down – and I'll know if you cheat me.'

'How do we know this place belongs to you?' Julie asked, something rebelling inside her. He turned his slate-grey eyes on her then and fixed her with a piercing look that made her spine tingle. 'We don't know you. We don't even know your name.'

'I'm Mr Trevors to you,' he said. 'Just watch it, girl. I'm a fair employer but a bad enemy.'

Julie raised her head and looked at him. She could

believe that he would be a bad man to cross and knew at once that she wouldn't want to work for a man like this – he was frightening. Besides, she would never forget that look of desperation in Andy's eyes when he'd spoken of owing more money than he had at the start. She was sure this was the man who'd had the hold over him and instinctively disliked and distrusted him.

'I shan't be working for you,' she said in a clear voice that hid the trembling inside. 'I'll clear up but when I leave this evening, I'll put the keys back through the door.'

The man leaned over the counter and grabbed Julie by her apron halter. She could smell stale tobacco on him and something else unpleasant, his breath hot on her face as he glared at her. 'You'll do nothing of the sort! I want this place kept going until I'm ready to take it over – so that's both of you. If I find it closed, you'll be sorry.'

Julie didn't answer. She was too frightened of him to say more, but she wouldn't be bullied into working for this man.

The doorbell clanged behind him and he let go of her immediately as customers entered the café. 'Thanks for the coffee, I'll be back,' he said in a normal voice and walked out just as if he hadn't threatened them with violence.

The two girls gazed at each other in silence. Sally-Anne looked as scared as Julie felt. 'You'd better serve,' Julie whispered as she saw two regular customers sit down. 'We'll talk later.'

She went back to the kitchen and took some cakes

and pies out of the oven. Her hands were trembling but she drew a deep breath and told herself not to be silly. Mr Trevors was a bully but he couldn't force them to work for him and Julie decided she wouldn't stay a minute longer than she had to – but it was frightening, because she didn't know what to do or where to go.

Sally-Anne came in and sat down at the kitchen table about half an hour later. 'I've put the closed notice up,' she told Julie. 'I can't stay here. I'm scared that man will come back.'

'He's a nasty piece of work,' Julie agreed. 'Well, I'm not going to work for him. I'll do what I said. When we've finished for the day, we'll take our wages and leave the rest of the money in the till – and we won't come back.'

Sally-Anne's eyes filled with tears. 'I'm frightened,' she said. 'I'm going to tell my gran when I get home but I think I'll leave Halifax. I have a cousin lives down the coast who owns a grocery store. He said I could come work for him so I will, at least for a while, though it won't be much fun as it's a really small town, but I can't stay here.' She looked at Julie. 'What will you do? If you stay in Andy's house, he'll come after you.'

'I can't stay there for long,' Julie agreed, feeling anxious. 'I don't know what I'll do. I have a little money saved, not much but enough to pay for food for a while. Andy didn't own his house. Cath said the café was his but the house was just rented and I couldn't afford it so I'll have to find a room or something.'

Sally-Anne hesitated, then, 'You could come with me. I'm not sure if my cousin would give you a job but . . .' She faltered and Julie knew it was a half-hearted offer.

'It's all right. I'll think about what I want to do. I know I've got a week or so before the rent is due so I'll take a little time to decide.'

'Well, I'm going now,' Sally-Anne said. 'I'm due three days' pay but I'm taking a week's money. If I were you, I'd do the same. I didn't ring up the last few meals so he'll never know. We could take it all if we liked.'

'You do what you want. I'll take what I'm due,' Julie said. She looked round the kitchen. 'I'm going to clear up and then I'll take this food. There's no sense in letting it waste. Do you want any of it?'

'I'll take that apple pie for my gran if you like.' Sally-Anne looked regretful. 'She liked your cooking. I'm sorry I shan't see you again, Julie. I wasn't very friendly when you first came, but I like you.'

'I like you too and I'll miss you,' Julie said and they hugged each other. 'I hope you enjoy working for your cousin.'

'Anything would be better than staying here and working for that bully,' Sally-Anne told her. 'Andy didn't pay me much but I liked him and that man scares me.'

'Me too,' Julie said. 'I liked Andy but I don't like that man.'

She started the washing-up the second Sally-Anne left the kitchen and then cleaned all the surfaces. Perhaps she was a fool but she felt a sort of duty to Andy to leave the café right. When she'd finished, she packed the leftover food into a paper bag and put her coat on, stopping to take the two dollars she was owed from the till. There was at least twenty dollars and some cents left so Sally-Anne hadn't taken more than she ought.

Julie locked the door and put the keys back through the letterbox and then walked slowly through the streets. It felt strange to be walking about in the middle of the day and she looked about her at the shops. The two shops next door were closed for renovations, so a notice in the window told her, and would reopen soon. It also stated that staff would be needed – but they were too close to the café. If Julie worked in either Mr Trevors might come after her. He couldn't force her to work for him but he might make life difficult – and Julie knew she had to be careful. Miss Cotton had reported her for leaving and that meant the police might still be looking for her.

None of the other shops she passed had notices that staff were needed and she sighed, wondering where she could go and what she could do now.

Back at Andy's house, Julie sat and ate some of the food from the café with a cup of coffee she'd brewed. Did everything here belong to that man too? Was he the one Andy had owed so much money to? She suspected that he was and that unless a relative came forward to claim Andy and Cath's possessions, he would take them all as his right to recover the debt.

She kept thinking about Andy's death following so close after Cath's. He had still been drinking a lot, but not so much these past couple of days. It was strange that he'd been knocked down – he must have been drunk not to notice a vehicle coming, she supposed.

It was cold and there was no wood or coal in to make a fire. Andy had always looked after the big pot-bellied stove. Julie shivered. She knew Cath had some more blankets stored upstairs and she wasn't supposed to go up there, but no one was there now to mind.

Deciding that Cath would probably say it was all right now Andy wasn't around, Julie went up to the bedroom above the kitchen. It was a large room because it had once been two rooms but Cath had joined them together. She liked space to move and breathe, she'd told Julie once.

The bed was unmade and smelled as if it hadn't been changed for a long time. Julie had taken away the bloodied sheets after Cath's death but Andy hadn't made it properly and it was just a mess of blankets. He probably hadn't slept there since Cath died. Julie pulled a blanket from the bed and then looked round the room. There wasn't really much of Cath's to show she'd ever lived here, just a few clothes hanging on a rail and some shoes. She didn't have jewellery or fancy bags, nothing much really except for a little music box.

Julie picked the box up and opened it. Inside was a lace handkerchief. She pressed it to her nose. It smelled of lavender, the only perfume Cath ever wore, and she'd used lavender bags for her sheets and her clothes. The box was just a cheap one, not worth much, but suddenly Julie was determined it wouldn't fall into the hands of that man – why should he have Cath's box? *She* didn't owe him anything.

Julie looked for anything else she might take. There was a comb and some soap that smelled of lavender.

Cath's shoes were too big for Julie but there was a pretty flowered dress in cotton. If she found somewhere to live, she might be able to make it into something for herself.

Retreating to the ground floor with her blanket and the few of Cath's treasures she'd rescued, Julie went through to her bedroom and sat down on the bed. She had to make a plan but wasn't sure what to do and there was no one she could ask for help, no one she could even talk to about her problems.

As she mulled over her options, she thought of something and smiled. It was so pretty up by the lake in Lower Sackville. Maybe Miss Cotton wouldn't bother looking for her after all this time and she might see the man with the nice face. Perhaps, if Julie asked him, he would tell her of a place she could find a home and work. She had a little money saved, but it wouldn't last long . . .

Julie left Andy's house the next morning, carrying all she possessed in her bag and a paper carrier bag that she'd found in the kitchen store. She had enough food for a while, a few dollars tucked inside her bodice – and she'd made up her mind. She wasn't frightened of Miss Cotton now; she could return the few cents she'd taken when she ran away – and surely her horrible nephew Ralph would have gone home by now? She had nothing to fear from returning to Lower Sackville, might even find a job there . . .

She paid her fare on the bus, which took her into a quiet street in Lower Sackville not far from the church. She passed the school where she'd worked, heading away from the small town, through leafy avenues and on towards the rows of neat houses where Miss Cotton lived, then turned and walked up to the lake, carrying her bags. A few times she sat on a fence to rest for a moment and munched a piece of cake that she'd baked for the café.

It was only when she reached the lake and realised the sawmill wasn't working that she remembered it was a Sunday and the mill closed on Sundays. She might have to wait until the following Monday to see the man she hoped to see – but then, again, he might come later, to check that everything was all right. If he didn't, she would have to find somewhere to sleep, because it would turn cold later. She looked about her nervously. Perhaps one of the sheds would be open . . .

Making her way to one of her favourite spots by the lake, Julie sat on a rock and watched the water. Jewel-like birds flitted down to drink and search for food, seeming not to notice her sitting quietly. She ate some of her sandwiches, throwing crumbs to them. It was cold but pleasant and she realised she had missed this place. Her life with Cath and Andy had been busy and she'd found it pleasant enough, but here it was so peaceful and she hoped she could find somewhere to live and work nearby so she could visit in her spare time. She hadn't had much time to herself while working at the café and for a while she relished the feeling of freedom – for once in her life she could do whatever she pleased.

As dusk fell, however, and no one came near the lake, she started to feel cold and was glad she'd brought a blanket with her, just wished she'd brought all of them, but they would have been too difficult to carry. Where could she stay? Julie considered trying to find a room somewhere but that would have eaten up her small store of money too quickly. It was only for one night. Surely she would be all right here for one night? She looked about her, unease prickling her as the light faded and the cold deepened, suddenly realising it could be a lonely cold night. The saws were silenced until the next day and there was no one here. As her gaze lighted on a wood store, she nodded to herself. There was a roof and a back wall to protect her if it either rained or, more likely on this now-bitter night, snowed. She had Cath's dress. It was big enough that she could put it on over her own, then her coat, to keep her warm. It couldn't hurt for one night and she was starting to feel very cold.

Perhaps there was a brazier in one of the buildings the timber workers used but she thought they would be locked. She peered into the office and saw a black, fat-bellied stove in there. If she could get in it would be warmer there but the door and windows were locked safely. It would have to be the wood store, which was half open to the elements, but at least she would be sheltered there and, in the morning, she would look for somewhere better. Someone would come then and she could ask advice. She crawled behind a pile of wood and discovered it was warmer away from the wind, settling down with her clothes either pulled on or covering her and the remains of her food in the paper bag beside her. She'd drunk water from the lake, because it had looked clear and clean in the shallows and she wasn't hungry. She could manage here, until the sawmill was open and she could ask for help . . .

Julie woke, shivering. It was pitch black and for a moment she wondered where she was, then she remembered she was in the wood store at the sawmill. A snuffling noise warned her that she was not alone and she smelled a strong odour close by. The sound of grunting and the rattle of paper told her that it was some creature after the food in her carrier bag. She gave a cry and sat up, terrified that it would attack her. All she could see was a large dark shape, which she thought might be a bear. She'd been told by the girls at school that both bears and coyotes were sometimes seen in the woods but Miss Cotton had maintained that they were long gone, only to be found further away in the more mountainous areas, saying it was just a tale that they sometimes went after people's food stores.

The creature, whatever it was, looked at her with eyes that seemed to glow in the dark and made a growling sound in its throat, looming towards her through the gloom. Julie screamed, jumped to her feet and ran. Terrified, she ran as fast as she could into the shelter of the woods, where it was even darker but it seemed a little warmer under the canopy of overhanging branches. She fancied the creature was pursuing her and went on running, her fear lending her speed she'd not known she had. Her feet flew over the debris that had accumulated on the floor of the woods and she was breathing heavily, her fear telling her that whatever had been after her food was now after her.

It was so dark that she couldn't see where she was going, and her chest hurt as breathing became more difficult. She was panting, fighting both her terror as the panic possessed her and for air. All sensible thought had gone out of her head – she just wanted to get away from whatever was following her. Then, quite suddenly, she caught her foot in the twisted root of an ancient tree and went headlong into its massive trunk, hitting her forehead on a knobbly bit, aware only of her terror as everything went black. She was unaware that the snow had begun to fall softly, or that the creature had long ago given up its slight interest in her. Above her the thick canopy of overhanging branches kept most of the snow which had begun falling from penetrating through to where she lay, unconscious. Yet her body felt the cold as the frost thickened and deepened all around her and she sank into a state of floating, hovering between life and death.

CHAPTER 19

On that Monday afternoon, Vee arrived at the school gates a few minutes later than usual. A telephone call just as she was leaving the house had delayed her but she'd hurried all the way and she looked eagerly for Beth at the gates. There was no sign of her, however, and most of the children had already gone, only a few of the older girls and boys lingering as they talked and laughed. Feeling a bit anxious, Vee went up to a teacher who was speaking with an older pupil.

'I'm looking for Beth,' she told him. 'Is she still in school? Has she been detained?'

'No, she wouldn't have been detained on an afternoon like this,' he replied. 'It's going to be a cold night, Mrs Bittern. Isn't she around?' He turned and called to the group of girls. 'Has anyone seen Beth – Mrs Bittern's girl?'

A chorus of denials and shakes of the head greeted his enquiry and then one of the girls said, 'I think she went with her uncle. I'm sure I saw a man holding her hand – at least, I think it was her.'

'When was that?' Vee said sharply, fear clutching at

her heart. 'Because it wasn't her uncle. My brother is still away.'

'The man was waiting outside the gates. I was just coming out,' the girl said staring at the teacher. 'I only saw their backs as they walked away. She was pulling at his hand as if she didn't want to go but I thought . . . I didn't know it wasn't her uncle . . .' She looked anxious and guilty. 'I should have called out to her and asked if she was all right . . .'

'That would have been a good thing to do.' The teacher looked at Vee in sudden concern. 'You wait here in case she just went to the toilets, Mrs Bittern. I'll go and look – Tom, you come with me.' He summoned one of the older boys to go with him.

Vee wanted to join in the search but she knew she had to wait. She shivered in the cold, feeling the ice on her face despite being well wrapped up against the weather. It had turned frosty over the weekend and in recent days they'd had more snow intermittently, but it hadn't laid as it did earlier in the winter. Fear for Beth was beginning to grip her. Was that girl mistaken and Beth had wandered off, thinking to make her own way home? She hoped that was the case – or had someone really taken her? It was a nightmare every mother feared when a child was missing.

But surely, she wouldn't wander off alone on an already dark afternoon like this? Vee had told Beth to wait in the playground if she was ever late and she'd warned her not to go off with strangers. Who would want to take her? Vee couldn't imagine why anyone would do it and yet it did happen – children were taken away by those who wished them harm. Yet that was something you read of rarely in the paper, something that happened far away, not here in this suburb where almost everyone knew each other and a stranger would be noticed.

When the teacher and pupil returned looking anxious some minutes later, a sick fear took hold of Vee's heart and mind. She loved that child and if anything had happened to Beth, she would never forgive herself.

'Beth isn't in school, Mrs Bittern,' the teacher told her. 'She isn't the sort to hide so she must either have gone home or someone has taken her. You should check at home and if she isn't there ring the police. It's going to be a bad night for a child to be lost.'

'I know that!' Vee said more sharply than she should have, because he had tried to help. 'Beth has been told to wait for me, so I don't think she would have wandered off. If she isn't home, I certainly will phone the police.'

'She wouldn't have gone to a friend's house for tea?' he questioned, still unwilling to think the worst.

'Not without asking me,' Vee said firmly. The girl who had thought she might have seen Beth leave with a man had gone now. 'That girl – the one who thought Beth left with her uncle. Do you know her name?'

'Yes, of course. Shireen Blane. I could phone and ask her parents if she remembers what he looked like, though if you recall she only caught a glimpse of their backs. It might not even have been Beth she saw.'

Swallowing her fear and a growing panic, Vee nodded. He was trying to help, but making it worse.

'Yes, th-thank you . . . Please do ask her to tell you all she knows. The police will want to know . . .'

Vee turned and hurried to her car, driving straight home. Her throat was tight with emotion and she had an awful feeling that Beth *had* been taken – and that it had been done to punish her for some reason. Because surely no one could mean that lovely child harm? Why would they? She was innocent and sweet. Tears burned behind her eyes as she fought the panic inside her. Beth would be found. She might even be there when Vee got home.

Aggie looked at Vee as she walked in, her eyes narrowing as she sensed her fear. 'What's wrong? Where's Beth?'

'I don't know. She wasn't waiting for me at the school gates and a teacher searched the school and couldn't find her. One of the girls thought she might have gone with her uncle . . .'

'But Mr Malcolm isn't home and if he was he wouldn't do that without telling you first,' Aggie said. 'She wouldn't wander off or go with a friend, would she?' Aggie looked as upset as Vee felt.

'I don't think so,' Vee said, her voice a gasp of fear. She felt so shaky that she had to sit down suddenly. 'Who would take her? Why would anyone do something so wicked?' It was unimaginable! She couldn't bear to think of her little girl at risk of harm – or even death. Yet her mind took flight and terrible thoughts crowded in on her. 'She's so young and innocent!'

'She's a little angel. A childless woman might covet

her . . . or . . .' Aggie shook her head. 'No, we mustn't start thinking bad things, Miss Vee. Why don't you ring Mr Hank right now and tell him? He'll organise a search for her. She can't have gone far and he'll find her if anyone can.'

'Yes, I'll call him now . . .' Vee's heart was racing. Supposing something terrible had already happened to Beth? It didn't bear thinking of! Tears stung her eyes but she fought them. She had to stay strong. She would get Beth back! She would, because she had to.

'I'll bring you coffee and maybe a drop of something stronger,' Aggie called after her. 'We could both do with it!'

Vee was lucky enough to catch Hank before he left his office for the night. He listened to her fears, asked for a description, though he'd spent time with Beth at Christmas. 'I need accurate details to circulate, Miss Vee, and you know her better than anyone,' he told her in his strong voice that was deep and somehow comforting. 'We'll send it to our colleagues in all the surrounding districts and tell them to be on the alert for anything that seems odd – a man with a little girl who seems reluctant to be with him – we'll leave nothing to chance.' He hesitated. 'She might have wandered off but even that's dangerous for a child that young. I heard there was a bear around – although that's probably just a rumour. No doubt she'll turn up safe and sound.'

'Thank you . . .' Her voice shook as she tried to hold back the tears. 'A man did try to claim her once – said he'd paid for her passage out but I gave him the money and he went . . .' She hesitated, afraid to voice what she feared.

'Go on, tell me,' Hank encouraged. 'You know you can say anything to me, Miss Vee.'

'The man who claimed that Beth should have been his – he said Harold Trevors had put him up to it. Well, I *thought* that was who he meant from what he said. I think this might be a warning to me because I refused to sell the sawmill and the woodland to him . . .'

For a moment there was silence, then, 'That's a serious allegation, Miss Vee and I'd need proof before I could arrest him, but I'll set things in motion for the search and then I'll pay Trevors a visit.' He was silent again for a moment. 'Didn't I hear you were selling the sawmill to Jago?'

'Yes, I am. He wanted it and I like him. Do you think Trevors could have heard about it too? It wasn't supposed to be common knowledge yet but these things get out.'

'It might explain why he— But that's speculation,' Hank said firmly, checking himself. 'Let's not jump to conclusions – and don't panic, Miss Vee. If she's out there, we'll find her.'

Vee caught back a sob of fear. 'You'll let me know?'

'As soon as I know something positive,' Hank promised and replaced his receiver.

Vee sat down, her legs feelings as if they'd give way if she didn't. She looked up as Aggie entered with a tray of coffee, the brandy decanter and some cakes and little sandwiches. 'I couldn't eat anything,' she protested.

'We'll both have something to warm us up and maybe a bite to eat,' Aggie said firmly. 'I'll be here with you through the night, Miss Vee, or however long it takes, and we have to keep ourselves going.' She pressed a cup of coffee laced with cream and brandy into Vee's hands. 'No arguments. If anyone can find her, Hank will, so just you sit there and let him do his job.'

'Supposing they harm her?' Vee looked at her. 'What am I going to do if they hurt my little girl, Aggie? I can't bear to think of what might happen to her.'

'It won't happen. Stop upsetting yourself, Miss Vee,' Aggie said but the worry in her face told Vee that she too was gripped by the same fear that Beth would be hurt – or perhaps just disappear forever . . .

Beth knew she shouldn't have gone to the man, but he wasn't horrid-looking or strange; he was quite young and nice-looking and the way he'd held his hand out to her had made her take it. He'd said that her mother had told him to look after her because she couldn't come. So she'd gone with him and he'd given her a sweet and promised to take her home, but when she'd asked where Mummy was, he hadn't answered and then, when they were in the truck he'd parked round the corner from the school, she'd suddenly remembered the warnings she'd been given not to go with strangers.

Beth had tried to pull away from him then but he'd locked the door and told her to behave. 'I won't hurt you, but if you make a fuss or start screaming, you'll never go home again,' he'd said sharply and his nice smile had disappeared. He'd looked angry and strange and she'd been frightened but she hadn't screamed. Perhaps if she had someone would have rescued her. Now she was alone in the dark and she was terrified.

Beth had no idea where she was. Before the man left her in this dark place that smelled musty, he said she must do as she was told and keep quiet or he would just leave her locked up forever. She'd cried then and tried to cling to him, begging him to take her to her mummy, but he'd just pushed her away.

'I'm just doing as I'm told,' he'd hissed as he went out and left her locked in the dark place. It was big and empty apart from a few wooden crates. He'd told her to sit and wait for him. 'Behave and maybe I'll come back and get you . . .'

Beth had retreated from the door, terrified of the cold dark place she'd been imprisoned in. What would happen to her and why had she been taken like this? Why was she being punished? What had she done wrong to deserve this? Her heart was beating fast and she was trembling, tears close as she tried to look around her in the gloom. Had Mummy told the man to do this? No! Her mother would never do something like this to her. Even in the midst of her panic, Beth knew that was true, knew without doubt that her mother would be worried, would be looking for her. Perhaps she would tell Hank, the nice police officer who had come at Christmas, and he would look for her . . .

She tripped against something on the floor and found it was a pile of old sacks. They were softer than the crates and she sank down on to them, shivering and shaking as the tears started. If the man didn't come back, she might die here – but why had he taken her and what would he do when he returned? She just didn't understand any of it.

Weeping, she wrapped her arms about herself and gave in to her grief. Life here in Canada with her new mother had been so wonderful and she didn't want to die. A spurt of anger rushed through her, overcoming the fear. Suddenly, her head went up and she jumped to her feet and ran to where she believed the door was. She found it but it wouldn't open so she beat against it with her fists, shouting and screaming. The man had told her to stay silent but she would *not* do that. She wanted to be heard and found, because she knew her mummy would be searching for her. All she had to do was to make so much noise that some-one came!

CHAPTER 20

Jago knew it was unlikely that Miss Vee's little girl would have got this far by herself, but Hank had phoned the sawmill office and told him what was happening, how they had a big search going on for the child.

'I'd appreciate it if you and your men would join the search,' Hank told him. 'I don't think she'll be in Lower Sackville. She's either miles away, dead, or she'll just turn up. We have to pray that it's the third option . . .' He hesitated, then, 'We've never found that girl that Miss Cotton reported missing . . .' The anxiety was there in his voice. A girl who went missing on purpose was one thing but a second, much younger one – that could mean bad things were happening . . . the stuff of nightmares.

'No, and I searched myself for weeks,' Jago told him regretfully. 'Hank, we'll do our bit here, search all the sheds and the woodland.'

'Thanks. My colleagues in Halifax and both Upper and Lower Sackville will have enough to do looking in outbuildings and knocking on doors, but if you can search your land, it will be a big help.'

'Not quite mine yet but it will be,' Jago said confidently. 'Thanks for letting me help out. If we find anything we'll let you know . . .'

Jago caught the men as they were about to leave for the night. When he explained the problem, none of them refused to help.

'We'll take the storm lanterns as well as our torches,' Jago said, 'and we've got three guns on the premises. Each group will take one with them and if you find anything just shoot into the air then we'll meet up. That way, if anything is found we'll all know.'

'It's odd,' one of the men said. 'I found a bag in the wood store this morning – the one with the logs we're keeping for that special order. Nothing in it but there was a bit of food scattered. Looked as if an animal might have got in there.'

'You didn't mention it, Bob.'

'Didn't think it was important,' Bob said regretfully. 'But the child only went missing this evening and I found the bag this morning.'

Jago frowned. He'd checked the locked sheds on Sunday and seen nothing but he hadn't been to the wood store. 'No, it couldn't have been her. She wasn't carrying a bag. She's just a small girl and she'd been in school . . .' He gave them an impression of Beth's height with his hand. 'Hank doesn't expect us to find anything, this is just to tick our area off his list of places to search.'

The men nodded their understanding and split into three groups. One would search all the sheds and outbuildings and the perimeter of the lake. The other two groups would search the woods, dividing and then meeting back at the sawmill unless a gun was fired and then they would seek out the group that had put up the warning.

They knew it would be a long, cold night. If there was any chance that a child was out there, they had to find her before she froze to death . . .

The shot was fired about half an hour after they'd started the search. Jago was startled. He hadn't believed for a moment that they would find the child. How was it possible that she have got here to these woods? It was too far for her to walk – unless someone had brought her here and abandoned her.

He made his way to the spot where the sound of a second shot told him it was urgent and saw his men grouped around something on the ground. One of them was kneeling by what looked like a pile of rags. His heart caught. Surely it couldn't be the child? The shape was too big.

'What have you found?' he demanded, his voice sharp with anxiety.

'It's a girl – not a child,' a voice said. 'She'd crawled inside that old redwood that has a hollow trunk, the one we keep meaning to fell but is no good for timber. I think she may still be alive . . .'

'Let me see, Jem.' Jago knelt beside the still figure, turning her onto her back and feeling for a pulse in her throat. For a moment he thought Jem was wrong, because she was so cold, then he felt the slight pulse. She was alive – and as he looked closer, he knew that it was Julie – the girl he'd been searching for all these weeks here in his woods! Emotion rushed through him, threatening tears of relief but he choked them back – this was no time for personal feelings.

Stripping off his warm coat, Jago wrapped it around the girl and bent to lift her in his arms. Jem put a hand on his shoulder.

'Let me help you, boss,' he said and picked her up effortlessly. 'She's lucky to be alive in this weather.'

'I'll take her home to Maya,' Jago said and looked at the others. 'Have you searched all your area?'

'Most of it. But we'll keep searching, boss – just in case.'

'When you have finished, go home. We'll ring Hank and tell him what we found and if you should find the child, someone come and let me and Hank know . . . both of us.'

'Sure thing, boss.'

Jem carried Julie to Jago's truck and they settled her in the front seat, covering her with more jackets to try and warm her up.

'Give Dr Barlow a ring and tell him what I've done,' Jago said, 'and ask him to come out to me if he can. She'll need to be seriously warmed up and watched and Maya will do that. If he decides she needs hospital then I'll take her in but I think she'd be better with someone to care just for her rather than a hospital bed and busy nurses.'

'Yeah, will do; and I'll make a call to Hank, too, and let him know about the girl. She must be the one went missing a while back, I reckon. I'm glad we found her. She's been there a day at most, I'd say, so it's lucky we spotted her – a night like tonight, she probably wouldn't have survived.'

'You're right,' Jago said grimly. 'I just hope she will now – and the little girl. I can't imagine what Miss Vee will do if she loses her . . .'

Jago's grim expression didn't change as he drove home. Julie had been close to death when they found her, but he'd seen no sign of injury apart from what looked like a bruise on her forehead. That might be the reason she'd lost consciousness or possibly she'd recovered enough from that to crawl inside the tree but then passed out again, her concussion made worse by the bitter cold. Once that took hold folk could just become too numbed in body and mind to fight it. So it was possibly just the bitter cold that had made her fall into this state. She looked to be wearing several layers of clothes and by crawling into the warmth of the hollow tree, she had probably improved her chances of survival. He prayed that it wasn't too late for her.

Jago prayed for the missing child too. She was a sweet little thing and it made him angry that anyone would want to harm her. If he knew who had abducted her, he would take his rifle and shoot the devil – and there were a lot more who would do the same thing if they got the chance, too. It was the worst thing ever to harm an innocent child.

His anger got him through the drive home and then Maya took over. His mother was out of the door and waiting for him when he drew up. It didn't surprise Jago. She always knew when he was troubled and he nodded towards her, letting her know she was right as she came to the door of the truck.

'We were looking for a lost child,' he told her, 'and we found the girl – the girl I told you about.'

'I know,' she said and Jago didn't question her. Maya often knew his thoughts. He never asked how. It was a gift she had, just as she had her gift for healing. It was the reason he'd brought the girl home instead of taking her straight to the hospital which would have taken far longer. Maya would nurse her back to health. She would do it for him as well as the girl and he trusted her more than unknown doctors and nurses who couldn't possibly know her importance to him.

'I have a bed warmed,' Maya told him. 'She'll have your room and you will sleep on the couch.'

Jago nodded. Maya was the boss when it came to things like this and he was content that it should be so. Warmth hit him as they entered the kitchen of his home. Maya would have built up the fires throughout the home so that it was welcoming when he got back. He could smell one of her broths cooking and felt the tension leave his body. If anyone could bring Julie back to life it would be Maya.

He wondered if Hank would be lucky enough to find Miss Vee's little girl. He prayed that would happen and he knew miracles did happen. He'd thought he would never see Julie again and now here she was in his home. Maya was watching as he carried her through to his room and as he placed her tenderly in the clean bedding that his mother had prepared, he heard a little cry leave Julie's lips. She was alive but in distress and it hurt him to hear her whimpers and see her face drained of colour.

'She will heal, Jago, it's nothing I can't manage,' Maya told him. 'Go eat your soup and leave her to me. When I call, you come, and not before, you hear?'

Her look was gentle and loving, taking the sting from her words. Jago obeyed without question, just as he always did. His leg ached a bit. The cold weather always made it worse and all the extra walking hadn't helped – but he was so glad he and his men had joined the search for the missing child. If they hadn't, Julie might have died and he would never have known she was there until it was too late.

And Hank would find Miss Vee's little girl, Jago suddenly felt sure of it.

As he sat down to eat the delicious ham and pea soup with chunks of fresh crusty bread and butter that his mother had prepared, a warm feeling crept over him. He had a feeling that it would turn out well. Perhaps he had some of his mother's special sight because somehow he knew everything would be all right.

CHAPTER 21

The phone ringing woke Vee from an uneasy sleep as she sat dozing in her chair. Before she could move, Aggie had snatched it up and was answering. Her cry of 'Thank God!' made tears start to Vee's eyes as her friend looked at her and nodded. 'She's been found safe and well in a deserted shed down on the docks. Hank took her to the hospital and they are keeping her in for the night and in the morning, if she's well, he'll bring her home . . .' Aggie relayed as Vee got up and gestured for the phone.

'Hank,' she said as she placed the receiver to her ear, 'is she really all right? What happened?'

'She's fine now,' he told her. 'She was frightened and screaming when one of my men found her but as soon as she saw me, she calmed down enough to tell me what happened. She was abducted, Vee, but he didn't touch her or harm her, just locked her in the shed and told her she would go home when he was ready, made a few threats to keep her quiet but didn't hurt her.'

'Oh, my God,' Vee said feeling sick. 'I can't believe anyone would do that to an innocent child! And for what reason? It's so wicked!' Yet relief was seeping through her. Beth was alive. She'd feared she would never see her again, never know the truth of what had happened.

'Yes, it is – and if I get him, whoever he is, he'll learn the error of his ways. Beth gave me a description, Miss Vee and it wasn't Trevors, not personally, but . . .' His silence said it all. He thought the same as she did but had no proof. 'I shan't be leaving it here. I've set a guard on her room at the hospital and I'll be paying Mr Trevors a friendly visit, just to see his reaction. If this was meant as a warning to you, he'll think twice about doing it again.'

'Thank you,' Vee whispered, feeling faint. 'Thank you all so much . . .'

'One other bit of news – that girl of Miss Cotton's has been found in the woods in Lower Sackville. Jago took her home to Maya – she was barely alive.'

'I suppose he joined the search for Beth. I am lucky to have such good friends. I can't thank you enough, Hank.'

'It's my job,' he said. 'I'll see you tomorrow. You get some sleep now; your little girl will be fine.'

'I should go to the hospital and make sure she's all right,' Vee said when she replaced the receiver but Aggie shook her head.

'You are not going anywhere tonight,' she said. 'Go to bed and he'll bring her home in the morning like he promised. She'll be sleeping and it'll only upset her if you wake her.'

Vee hesitated and then nodded. Aggie was right. If Beth's life was in the balance she would have been told. She must wait until the morning, though she didn't think she could sleep.

'What kind of a man would do that?' she asked Aggie who just shook her head.

'There are nasty types about, you know that. Always has been and always will. Never thought we'd come up against it but we'll just have to be more careful in future until they catch whoever it was.'

'I'll make sure her school knows that no one but you or I will fetch her unless we phone and tell them differently.' Vee smiled at her. 'Now go to bed yourself, Aggie. Thank you for sitting up with me, but I'm all right now.'

Aggie nodded. 'I reckon we both know who did this, Miss Vee – if it had been a real abduction by a child molester she wouldn't have been found alive. No, this was meant as a warning. You see if I'm not right.'

'He can't think he can get away with this,' Vee said giving Aggie an angry look. Her nails curled into the palms of her hands as fury built inside her. She was so relieved Beth was alive but outraged it had happened at all. 'Abduction is a serious crime.'

'It ought to be a capital offence,' Aggie said darkly. 'I'd take a gun and shoot him myself if I knew for certain. And don't think I couldn't – my pa taught me to shoot as a girl.'

'Yes,' Vee chuckled. 'I believe you would – and I might too. Hank has promised to do what he can but if it *is* Trevors, he'll have covered his tracks . . .'

'Let it be known that you'll pay for information leading to the arrest of the person responsible,'

Aggie said. 'I don't reckon whoever did this could resist earning a few dollars for giving information. Anonymously, of course.'

'I'll see what Hank says about it,' Vee replied. She yawned. 'I'm going to bed, Aggie. I feel drained.'

Beth was a little quiet when Hank brought her home the next day. She ran to Vee and hugged her and then cried, but her tears dried as she was taken on her mother's lap and given chocolate cake to eat.

'Can you tell me what happened?' Vee asked her as she stroked her hair. 'What did the man look like?'

'Nice. He wasn't as tall as my friend Hank,' Beth said, 'and he wasn't old. I believed him when he said you'd sent him. It was only later when he told me he'd hurt me if I didn't go with him that I knew he was a bad man – like you told me about.'

'Just remember, Mummy will never send anyone you don't know to fetch you,' Vee told her, gently stroking her cheek. 'It will be me or Aggie or someone you know well like Hank or Jago. Anyone else tells you they've come to collect you, run back to a teacher and tell them or just scream.'

Beth nodded solemnly. 'He shut me in that shed and I was hungry. I told him it was time for my tea before we got there but he just laughed and said, "Too bad, kid." He said I would stay there until he was ready to let me go home.'

'But he didn't hurt you?'

'Just where he grabbed my wrist,' Beth said and held out her arm. Vee could see a dark bruise and knew that some force had been used to stop Beth

196

breaking away. She felt coldness at her nape, because she knew it could have been so much worse and her throat tightened with emotion and anger too. Bending her head, Vee kissed the dark mark and Beth smiled. 'It feels better now.'

Vee sent her off to the kitchen to find Aggie then looked at Hank. 'Have you any idea who did it?'

'Well, it sounds as if it was a youth rather than a man – which is interesting.' He nodded thoughtfully. 'There are a few rich kids who drive around in the trucks their parents give them and cause trouble, break a few windows, scratch cars and throw a few empty beer bottles around. It's mostly just boredom, I reckon, and I wouldn't have thought abduction was in their heads.'

'Unless someone put the idea there?' Vee suggested. 'Is Harold Trevors' son one of those lads that are causing trouble?'

Hank nodded. 'They mostly get up to mischief on Saturday nights, drinking and stuff. This doesn't fit with the usual behaviour but I might just pull some of them in and see what happens. I've had occasion to get heavy once or twice – and don't ask, Miss Vee. It's official business so I can't tell you but I'll be investigating.'

She nodded. 'Thank you for finding her as quickly as you did, Hank. It does seem a little odd, though. I wonder if you were meant to find her easily?'

'Yes, that occurred to me too. It begs the question of motive and I can't see what that might be, unless it was simply to upset you.'

'Yes.' Vee looked at him grimly. 'I think we know who planned this, Hank. But it's a matter of proving it.'

'It is a long road with no turning point,' Hank said obscurely. 'And there's more than one way of skinning a cat . . . I'll find out,' he told her. 'You can rest easy on that, Miss Vee. When I do, I'll have him locked up for a long, long time. Abduction is a very serious offence, even when no physical harm has been done.'

'Good,' she said. 'I'll sleep more soundly when you do. But I doubt he would do the same thing twice.'

'Next time it may be directed at you,' Hank agreed. 'I don't need to warn you to be careful.' He frowned. 'It's a pity Malcolm isn't around. Have you heard from him recently?'

'Not for months,' Vee said. 'I'm worried, of course, but I think if his ship had been sunk, we would have heard something by now.'

'They say there's times when no news is good news,' he agreed. 'Let me know if you're worried about anything or see anyone loitering near the house and I'll send a man to investigate.'

'Thank you, but I can't believe anyone would really harm me. I can't see him risking his own neck to murder me.'

Hank nodded but she could see he was doubtful. 'I must get back to the office,' he told her. 'You keep safe and remember you can phone me at home if need be.'

Vee nodded. A chill slid down her back as she thought about his words. Hank obviously agreed with her that she had an enemy – but would Harold Trevors really go so far as to arrange for her to lose her life? Surely Vee's death couldn't benefit him, because everything she had would go to those she loved – unless he just wanted revenge. Yet if he'd wanted to really hurt her, he'd had his chance with Beth. She hadn't been harmed and she'd been left in a place that was bound to be searched – it could have been otherwise. There were wild, rocky areas where she could have been abandoned and perhaps never found.

No, it had just been a little warning, Vee decided. And she'd turned down several offers for the sawmill and woodlands before she sold to Jago, not just the one from Harold Trevors, so any one of those men could have felt annoyed and slighted by her. Yet she knew instinctively that only one really hated her.

It was the following afternoon when Vee and Beth returned from school that Aggie told Vee that a woman had come to the house to see her. 'She says she's been left a property – a café next to some shops you own and she wondered if you would be interested in buying it.'

'Well, yes, I might,' Vee said and smiled as Beth picked up one of Aggie's honey cakes after a nod from Aggie and started to eat it. 'It was a thriving little place but I saw it was closed the other day. I was told the owner had been killed by a speeding car and no one knew who it belonged to now.'

'She claims it was left to her by a cousin,' Aggie said. 'She seems a nice quiet lady, not the sort to lie, says she couldn't believe it when her cousin was killed that way. He'd made a will, years ago, and never got round to changing it so the property came to her.'

'Did she leave a phone number?'

'No, she said she'd come again in the morning.' Aggie looked at her oddly. 'What would you be wanting with a café, Miss Vee?'

199

'I'm not going to run it myself,' Vee said with a smile. 'I should find someone to run it for me, of course.'

'I still don't see the point in it,' Aggie said shaking her head at her. 'You don't need another piece of property. Why do it now? You were never interested before.'

'I've sold the lumbermill or I'm in the process of doing so,' Vee said. 'There's hardly any spare land around here now and the value of land and property is bound to rise in Halifax over the years. It will ease the congestion if they getter better links to Upper Sackville in time but it may be years before they build more substantial bridges.'

'For my part I hope they never do,' Aggie grumbled. 'If that happens it will spread everywhere and there will be nothing beautiful left – too many folk and too much building.'

Vee nodded in agreement. 'That's possibly true,' she agreed, 'but it's bound to happen one day and I can't let Trevors have it all his own way. If I don't buy it, he will.'

'Then let him,' Aggie said. 'That man is a nasty piece of work, Miss Vee, and there's no telling what he might do if you seriously anger him.'

'So everyone is supposed to just let him rule the roost?' Vee replied with a flash of annoyance. 'The richer he becomes the more powerful he will be and someone needs to stand up to him. Besides, he is a bully and a coward.'

'So he might be, but he knows your vulnerable spot. If I were you, I'd just keep my head down for a while and don't do anything to annoy him.'

'I think my just being alive annoys him,' Vee said. 'Besides, that café is right next to my shops and it makes a nice corner block. I can't see why he'd want to buy it when I own the properties next door. I'm sure there are other properties he can buy if he wants.'

'Have it your own way – but don't say I didn't warn you. You were lucky to get Beth back this time, next time you might not be as lucky . . .' Aggie gave her a darkling look. 'It might be easier to let him win.'

Vee shook her head stubbornly. She couldn't be cowed by what had happened to Beth – that was what whoever had planned it wanted. It had been a threat to her, a warning of what could happen if she stepped out of line. Yet Vee didn't believe Beth had ever been in real danger. The man whom she believed was behind it had too much to lose, to risk murdering an innocent child. There were folk round here who were not above stringing a man up for a crime like that and he wouldn't risk it. No, it had just been meant to scare and upset her and it had succeeded, but now she was angry and her stubborn nature refused to be cowed. She would make sure Beth was safe but she wouldn't just give in and let that man win.

CHAPTER 22

Jago looked at the girl lying in his bed. She looked flushed and her hair was damp with sweat. His throat tightened and he swallowed, fear and regret swiping at him. She was too young to die!

'Shouldn't you be on your way to the lumberyard?' Maya asked entering the room behind him with an armful of towels and clean linen.

'Will she live?' Jago asked. It was a question he'd asked his mother many times since bringing the girl home and she gave him a straight look.

'I've told you she will,' Maya said patiently. 'Have faith, Jago. She's very ill but she's young and strong and I promise she is getting better. You won't see an improvement until the fever breaks.'

'I know . . .' He smiled at his mother. 'Thank you for looking after her. I could have taken her to the hospital but I thought she would be safer here and it means a lot of work for you.'

'When have I ever minded work?' his mother asked. 'You have a sawmill to run, Jago. Get off and do your work and leave mine to me.'

'Yes, Ma,' he said, laughing. 'You know where I am if you need me . . .'

'If you don't go, I'll take my broom to you,' she threatened but with a smile in her eyes.

Jago grinned and left. He was thoughtful as he drove in to work. The heavy snow of a few nights ago had cleared as if by magic and at last it looked as if the better weather might be on its way. Spring, summer and autumn were busy for Jago and his workers. The woodland had to be looked after if it was to go on producing for future generations. That was the thing about trees, you didn't plant new saplings for your own gain but for those that followed – sons and grandsons or daughters.

Jago wasn't sure that he would ever have a son or daughter to take over the woodland and care for it as he did. What girl would ever want to marry him? He knew better than to expect it, even though he suspected that he had already given his heart to a girl who hardly knew he existed . . . but provided she lived and had a chance to be happy, Jago would be content. Her death would devastate him but he believed in his mother's power to heal and although he knew Julie was very ill he was whistling as he drew his truck into the yard.

His half-smile disappeared as he saw the truck parked there. It belonged to Pete Trevors, the son of a man he disliked. Pete gave the impression of being as arrogant as his father and ran with a gang of youths who often caused trouble in Halifax. He turned to look at Jago as he approached, his gaze disdainful as it lingered on the heavy boot that enabled Jago to walk more easily than he could without it.

'My father wants to see you,' he announced as if it were a royal command. 'This afternoon, after you finish up for the day.'

'I may not have time,' Jago said. 'I have to get home early. Tell your father it isn't convenient – another day, perhaps.'

'If you don't come you could be sorry!' Pete snarled, his eyes flashing with temper.

'Are you threatening me?' Jago asked, meeting the youth's gaze with one that was equally determined. 'I don't take kindly to threats.'

Pete stared at him belligerently for a moment and then his gaze dropped. 'My father has a proposition for you. It's to your advantage to come.'

'Thank your father but I'm still too busy,' Jago replied. 'If he's too busy to come here, please tell him to telephone or put the proposition in writing and I'll consider it.'

'Mighty cocky these days, aren't you?' Pete said angrily. 'I remember you years ago before I went to boarding school – all the kids laughed at you and you just turned away and didn't answer. You acted as if their words didn't hurt you.'

'After a while they didn't,' Jago said honestly.

'Well, my father knows how to hurt and he doesn't just use words,' Pete told him with a sneer. 'Ignore him and you may wish you hadn't.'

'Any more threats and I'll fetch my shotgun,' Jago told him grimly. 'I'm not afraid of you or your father, Pete Trevors – tell your father that and remember it yourself.'

Pete stared at him for a moment and a shudder

went through him. 'If you're not afraid of him, I am. I wouldn't be in your shoes.' At that he turned and walked away, leaving Jago staring after him. He watched as the truck disappeared from view and then shook his head, walking towards his office where he could hear the telephone ringing.

'Hi, Jago Marsh speaking,' he said and heard a laugh he knew well at the other end. 'What is it, Ma?' Why would she telephone him? She never did. His heart caught with sudden fright. Had something bad happened at home?

'I just wanted to let you know her fever has broken,' Maya said. 'She was awake and took a cup of hot milk with honey and now she is sleeping – but it's a healing sleep, Jago. She'll get stronger each day and you'll be able to speak to her this evening when she is rested.'

He closed his eyes in thankfulness for a moment. 'Thank you, Ma,' he said and she laughed again.

'Thank God, too, Jago. It was touch and go for a while but I never thought she was meant to die. She is still weak but she will recover over time.'

'With you to look after her,' he agreed. 'You saved her life, Ma.'

'No, not all by myself,' Maya said. 'You did that by bringing her home when she was found. She needed love and care and she still does – this girl is suffering from more than spending a night or two in freezing temperatures. Her spirit needs to heal as well as her body.'

'I know, that's why I brought her to you instead of the hospital,' Jago agreed. 'They could have healed her body but not her spirit. You'll do that, Ma.'

'With your help,' Maya replied. 'Don't be late home, Jago.'

'I won't,' he promised, smiling as he replaced the receiver.

'Boss?' The voice of one of his men recalled his thoughts to work. 'Would you come and check this order for fencing timber?'

'Coming right now,' Jago replied and followed in the other man's footsteps. He was hard put to it not to grin like a fool, all thoughts of the incident with Trevors' son vanishing like morning mist in the sunlight. Julie's fever had broken. She would heal now and that thought warmed and pleased him.

Julie looked into the face of the woman bending over her and started. She was a stranger. Who was she? Where was she? For a moment she was afraid and then the woman's rather harsh features settled into a smile and her fear was gone.

'You've been looking after me,' she said uncertainly, her throat dry. 'You gave me a drink earlier. Please, tell me, where am I and who are you?'

'I am Maya, Jago's mother. He found you up in the woods by the lake. You were slowly freezing to death and you've had a nasty fever but you will be better now.'

'Thank you,' Julie said and a little sigh left her lips. There was something nagging at the back of her mind but it was difficult to think properly. 'Who is Jago?'

'He works up at the woods, looking after the lumber business and the sawmill.'

Julie felt puzzled for a moment as she struggled to

focus her thoughts and then she remembered sitting by the lake on a beautiful afternoon and a man coming towards her, smiling at her. Slowly, her mind came out of the fog that had held it. She gave a little moan as she felt the aching in every part of her body, but tried to keep herself from falling straight back to sleep as the weariness swept through her.

'Does he . . . is his foot not quite as it should be?' she asked and Maya nodded.

'My son has a club foot. He was born with it and has suffered because of it, but he conquered the disability when he got the right boot and he doesn't let it ruin his life – or he tries not to.'

'It's sad for him and for you,' Julie said. 'He has a lovely smile, though. I noticed his eyes . . . they smile and not just his mouth.'

'You really do remember him,' Maya spoke thoughtfully. 'He wasn't sure you would – you only saw him a couple of times . . .'

'Oh, no, I've seen him more than that,' Julie corrected. 'At least three times at the lake, though only once close to – and he gave me a lift in his truck once and told me his name was . . . Jago!' she finished triumphantly and almost immediately put a hand to her head. 'Oh, my head hurts and my eyes feel so tired and heavy . . .' Her body ached as if she had been beaten all over and she was so weak it was a struggle to keep her eyes open. Her tongue moved over her lips. 'Thirsty . . .'

'You should sleep again,' Maya said. 'But first drink this – it will help you regain your strength.'

'Is it milk and honey like last time?' Julie recalled

the taste of it though not drinking it, just that something nice had been on her tongue.

'No, this is different, something I brew myself,' Maya said. 'Are you hungry yet?'

Julie shook her head and gave a little shiver as she suddenly remembered. 'A creature – I think it was a bear – ate my food . . .'

'They get hungry too,' Maya told her. 'It probably woke up in the spell of milder weather we had before and wandered down from the mountains, then when the snow came unexpectedly it needed to eat before it could sleep again. If you hadn't run away, it might just have taken the food and gone again.'

'I was frightened,' Julie replied. 'I was asleep in a wood store and the noise and the smell of it woke me.'

'Bears do smell mighty strong,' Maya agreed and laughed. 'Most folk would do the same as you did, but it was lucky you were found in time.'

'I hit my head when I tripped,' Julie said, remembering it all as the fear came back to her. 'When I woke it was dark and I crawled into what looked a warm place inside a tree trunk. I was cold and a kind of numbness gradually came over me and then . . . then I don't remember.'

Maya nodded, 'That's where they found you, inside the tree, luckily for you. They were searching for Miss Vee's little girl and found you. I doubt you would have survived another cold night if they hadn't . . .'

'Then I was lucky,' Julie said looking at her in wonder. 'Did they find the little girl too?'

'She was found, but not by my son,' Maya said.

'But tell me, why were you there? Folk thought you'd gone to Halifax and you were looked for there.'

'I did go to Halifax and was there for a while,' Julie explained. 'I found a job with a man called Andy and his . . . his Cath. She was having a baby but she died and Andy started to drink.'

'Did he attack you?' Maya frowned. 'Is that why you ran away again?'

Julie shook her head. 'He was just sad and so he drank too much and then he was knocked down by a car or something and died. A horrid man came and said the café would be his soon and that Sally-Anne and me had to keep working there, but we didn't like him so we both left after he'd gone.'

'So you came back to Lower Sackville – but why the wood store up at the lake?'

'I had nowhere to go and . . .' Julie faltered. 'I like the lake when the sun shines but it was cold in the snow so I thought I'd shelter for the night and then ask for work in the morning.'

Maya looked at her in silence for a while and then a smile crept into her eyes. 'It was meant,' she said simply. 'You will stay here with us and help me until you are strong enough to find the life you want – whatever and whenever that may be.'

'You'll let me stay here?' Julie said looking at her in wonder. 'You don't even know me!'

'I know a good heart,' Maya replied and her eyes smiled though her face might have been carved of some hard stone. 'And you will help me – can you cook and sew?'

'Yes, I can,' Julie said quickly. 'I love to do both

those things. I thought one day I might earn my living sewing for other people.'

'Time enough for that,' Maya told her. 'I have more than enough to do on the farm. When you're well enough, you can cook and mend – Jago is always tearing his clothes. It's his work that does it and I mend as best I can but you can do it for him now.'

'Oh, thank you! Thank you so much. I cooked at the café and folk liked my food – and I've always loved to sew . . .' She faltered looking at Maya anxiously. 'Will Jago mind me staying here?'

'God bless you, child,' Maya said. 'He brought you to me. He can hardly complain if I keep you for a while. I daresay he won't mind too much . . .'

'Good,' Julie said as she settled back after drinking Maya's potion which had a strong but sweet flavour. 'I'll try not to be a nuisance to either of you . . .' she whispered but her eyes were closing . . . she was falling asleep.

Maya smiled as she went softly from the room. Julie would sleep through the day, perhaps into the night before she needed more of the healing juices. And that was good because rest was needed, for the spirit as well as the body. She had seen into the girl's heart and felt her loneliness and her pain. But in time she would heal, given the love and care she would receive in this house.

Unless Maya was wrong, her son, who had been lonely for so many years, had given his heart to this girl. Perhaps she was the special one. Maya knew that only a special girl would do for Jago, a girl who could see past the misshapen foot into his heart. There she would find beauty and strength but only if she was the special one Maya had hoped might come.

So she would let the girl stay for as long as she wished and what would be would be. Maya could not heal the hurt her son hid deep inside, though she had done her best to make him strong. Perhaps this girl might. It was a chance worth taking so she smiled and sang as she worked. God worked miracles in His own way. You could pray for what you thought you wanted and never get it, but sometimes you received an entirely different kind of blessing and she had a feeling that the girl in Jago's bed, might be just that.

CHAPTER 23

'You are telling me I can't claim the property?' Furious, Harold Trevors glared at his solicitor. 'He owed me every penny that damned place is worth. It's my right and I want it.'

'I am sorry Mr Trevors,' his lawyer said. 'Where are the documents that secured the loan? It's not that I don't believe you loaned Andy Machin a considerable amount of money, but without a legal agreement and a record of repayments your claim would be thrown out of court. Had you come to me before agreeing to the loan I could have advised you of its legality . . . the courts do not look favourably on large interest payments and the Revenue might investigate your business and want to know more about cash payments. Unless it was paid by cheque and you have all the records and security, made over to you?'

'You know damned well it wasn't on the books,' Harold growled. 'That part of my business is off the record. You told me it could be lucrative, damn it! You must have known I wouldn't declare any interest.'

Arching his hands and looking serious, his lawyer's expression didn't change. 'I was speaking figuratively at the time, since I knew of such arrangements. I would never have advised you to lend money without proper security on the property. Did you not ask for the deeds of the café to hold?'

'He wouldn't give them to me, said he would pay it off quickly but then he got into more trouble and asked for another few hundred.'

'Did you give him more?'

Harold shook his head. 'I doubled his interest and told him I'd make him sorry if he didn't pay.'

'And of course he couldn't so you meant to foreclose on him?' The lawyer nodded. 'Had he lived you might have recovered your money that way. I doubt he would have resisted for long if you threatened him with violence. It's a great pity he was fatally injured in that accident. I fear you can say goodbye to your money. Perhaps it will be a good lesson for the future – and it will hardly break you.'

Harold scowled. 'He cheated me by dying. I told him I wanted the café and made him promise to bring the deeds.'

'His accident – if it was an accident – was inconvenient for you then?' his lawyer said eyeing him speculatively. 'You know the authorities think there was something suspicious about it? It wasn't reported and they say it was either deliberate or a drunk driver that went off and left Andy Machin dying in the road.'

'Tosh!' Harold muttered. 'Why should it have been anything but an accident? He'd been drinking when he came to make a payment. And if someone killed him deliberately it wasn't me – there are others who loan money, you know.'

'So there are,' his lawyer replied sanguinely. 'If I believed you capable of murder, I should have to terminate our association, Mr Trevors. However, I believe you're telling the truth. Let's hope the police don't learn of the loan or they might start to wonder if you were invo—'

'Damn you! Are you blackmailing me?'

'Wouldn't dream of it. I know that some of my clients dabble outside the law, Mr Trevors. I don't interfere and I'd find a good advocate if they came up in court for not declaring their tax – but not murder or drugs. I don't work for criminals.' There was a note of accusation underlying his tone which infuriated Harold.

'I find that damned insulting! I've a good mind to take my business elsewhere.'

'That is your decision to make,' his lawyer replied coolly. 'Now, if there is nothing else today, I do have other appointments.'

Harold swore and left the office, seething inside. He knew for a fact that this particular lawyer wasn't above taking a few backhanders for information given. He'd given him the nod about Vee Bittern's purchase of several small properties in Sackville. Harold had had his eye on those shops along with the café for a while but he'd been otherwise occupied, out of town on personal business when the shops came up for sale. When he discovered who had bought them, he'd cursed, knowing she would never sell to him. He was still seething over the loss of the lumberyard, which he'd had his eye on for years. That damned Jago Marsh would never sell to him – despite the veiled threats.

Harold glared at a passer-by, who was completely innocent and unknown to him. He should have gone himself instead of sending his son – the little so-and-so had messed it up. For once he'd thought he could trust him to put the fright into Jago but it turned out the cripple wasn't easily scared.

'He's six years older than me but I remember watching him in the seniors' playground from before Ma sent me to that boarding school. He used to ignore all the taunts about his foot,' Pete had told him afterwards. 'I admired him for that, Pa, though I never let him see. He's had a real struggle to get where he is. Can't you just leave him be?'

'The way your mother begged me to leave you be – and that turned out well!' Harold had struck his son hard round the head. 'After what you did, I should turn you in and let you rot in prison!'

'It was an accident,' Pete said sullenly. 'I wouldn't have told you if I'd known you would use it to make me do things.'

'You came running because you were scared silly,' Harold grunted. 'I got your truck fixed good as new so no one would know you killed a man.'

'I didn't mean to! It was an accident,' Pete protested, eyes suddenly flaring with anger akin to Harold's own. 'Maybe I should go to the law and tell them what I did, how it happened – and maybe I'll tell them what you made me do with that kid.'

His father sneered. 'They'll put you in prison for killing Andy Machin,' he warned. 'And if they don't,

I'll kill you myself. Your mother isn't around anymore to beg for you. The bitch ran off and left us, remember? She spoiled you – so you'll do what I tell you or I'll thrash you until you beg for mercy.'

Pete had glared at him with fierce eyes but he'd stopped complaining. Harold would keep his son in check. The accident had been a lucky one for him. That night, Andy Machin had refused to pay anything more and wouldn't give up his deeds to the property. He'd defied him, telling him he could do his worst because he no longer cared and then he'd walked off laughing. When Pete came crying to him the next morning, saying that his truck was damaged and he thought he'd killed someone when he was drunk, it all played into Harold's hands. No one would ever know the truth, not even Pete. Harold had been so sure the café was his – and once he'd got it, he would have found a way to get those shops too but he hadn't reckoned on the lawyer being against him . . .

Pete hadn't wanted to deliver his message to Jago Marsh nor had he wanted to take that kid out of school and leave her locked up, but he'd done it because he was scared of his father – and he'd do whatever dirty jobs Harold gave him in future. His little secret made the boy vulnerable and Harold would use him, just as Pete's mother had used him, playing him for the fool with another man.

A grim smile touched his mouth. It was a long road with no turning. He'd got even with the bitch and with Andy Machin – and he would with Vee Bittern one day.

Pete scowled at his friend when they met that evening in Lower Sackville. 'Let's go and get drunk,' Ralph said. But if it weren't for bloody Ralph Cotton, Pete wouldn't be in this mess. They'd been drinking together in Halifax the night of the accident and it was Ralph who had kept pushing him to drink too much so that when he'd left the club he hadn't known what he was doing. He'd driven home in a drunken haze and even now he didn't remember hitting that man or driving off afterwards. All he could remember was waking up the next morning, going down to his truck and seeing the dent on the bumper and the blood. When he'd told his father he'd looked at him oddly for a minute or two and then told him he'd killed someone but not to worry, he'd fix it – but after he had, the demands got worse than they'd been.

It had horrified Pete when his father told him to abduct the adopted daughter of a woman who was respected and well-liked both in Halifax and Sackville.

'That's a serious offence! I could go to prison – it might even be a hanging offence.'

'Killing a man while driving under the influence is a serious offence too,' his father had reminded him. 'You could go to prison for the best years of your life, Pete. You covered up your crime, so no remorse shown – and maybe you did it on purpose and that's a hanging offence.'

'You wouldn't . . . ?' Pete had stared at his father in horror.

'Try me,' his father challenged. 'In future you'll do as I tell you, boy. Your mother made you weak but she's gone now and it's just you and me. So you'll do as I tell you or I'll cast you to the swine!'

Pete had swallowed hard and done his father's

bidding. Prison and a life with no money when he got out was too much for him to face. He'd been indulged while his mother lived with them and he couldn't do without the things he was accustomed to, even if he'd been terrified until he locked the kid in that shed and left her. He'd known there would be a search for her and had left her in a place she was bound to be found quickly. His father had wanted her hidden for longer but too bad, he should have done it himself. To avoid a threatened beating, he'd delivered his father's message to Jago Marsh, though he'd never believed he would be cowed by it for one moment.

Now he looked at Ralph and shook his head. 'I don't want to get drunk again,' he said. 'Let's go and find some girls instead – have a few soft drinks and a bit of fun at the club.'

'What's wrong with you?' Ralph demanded. 'Suit yourself then – I'm off. When you decide to stop being a little saint you can come with me again.'

Pete watched as his friend drove off. Ralph was the instigator of most of their mischief. Yet he liked him and there were not many of his own age that he could call friends. The local lads thought he was a cissy for attending a private school and most of their fathers disliked Pete's father. Harold Trevors was rich and people were wary of upsetting him but he wasn't respected and liked as some folk were.

Pete wondered what his father had done to earn his reputation, what other bad things had he done in the past? He wrinkled his brow in thought. At the moment he was forced to do his father's biding but if he could find something to hold over Harold he might turn the tables. If he could blackmail his father, he might get him to give him enough money so he could go away and start a new life elsewhere.

He would have to do some snooping – but where to start? Would his father keep anything incriminating at home or in his office? Once, he might have hidden it from his wife, but she'd left so he had nothing to fear at home, especially now he had Pete where he wanted him.

A smile touched his mouth. He was pretty sure there would be something – something that would wipe the smile off of Harold Trevors' face and he wouldn't be afraid to use it. His father didn't care about him, so why should Pete give a toss for what happened to him? If there was a way of making his father pay for the slights offered to Pete's mother and himself in the past, it would be sweet revenge.

CHAPTER 24

Jago looked at his mother eagerly as she came out of the bedroom carrying a bowl of used water. He took it from her and poured it into the sink. Maya smiled and nodded at him.

'Yes, she's awake again and feeling better this morning. She asked to see you so you may go in now.'

'Thanks, Ma,' Jago said with his easy smile, dropping a kiss on the top of her head. She laughed and smacked his arm as he passed her, heading towards the room that was usually his but had been happily given up for Julie's sake.

Jago paused at the threshold, immediately aware of the new smell here; it was like his mother's room now and the soft perfume of flowers came from the special soap and oils she made that she used for her skin and hair. The girl was sitting up in bed against a pile of pillows and wearing a long-sleeved nightgown that buttoned right up to her chin. Maya had made certain she was decent before allowing him to visit. He was vaguely aware that it fitted her and so must be something Maya had kept for years, probably for sentimental reasons, but she'd allowed Julie to have it.

'I brought your bag,' he said now, suddenly at a loss for anything better. 'We found it in the wood store. The bear – or whatever it was – was hungry but it found what it was after in your paper sack and left your other bag intact. Though Maya said you were wearing several layers when she put you to bed.'

Julie looked at him in silence for a moment, then, 'Yes, I'd put on as much as I could to help me keep warm. Maya said it was probably that and the hollow tree that saved my life.'

'No, she did that after I got you home,' Jago said. 'I didn't think you would make it for a while back there.' He hesitated, unable to meet her bright gaze. 'I hope you're well now, Julie?'

'Please, Maya says you know I ran away from Miss Cotton. You won't make me go back to her – will you?'

'I don't have the right to make you do anything and nor does she,' Jago replied. 'I know she is a mean old skinflint but what made you run like that?'

'Her nephew,' Julie answered honestly. 'I didn't want to stay with her longer than I had to but it was his behaviour that made me run. He wouldn't let me be and—'

'If he harmed you, I'll see he pays for it,' Jago said grimly. 'He isn't above the law.'

'He didn't hurt me much. He tried t-to . . .' Her voice died away, unable to speak the words. Then she held her head high and said, 'But I fought him off and

221

then I ran away, because he would have tried again and next time I might not have been able to stop him.'

'Do you want me to report it to the authorities?' Jago asked. 'Hank would lock him up for a few nights and if his aunt knew she might send him packing.'

'She dotes on him and wouldn't listen,' Julie said. 'If you see Ralph, you could tell him you know what he did and threaten him – but I don't want to cause trouble for you.'

Jago laughed. 'I might walk with a limp, Julie, but I can thrash a lad like Ralph Cotton if I choose. I just prefer to use the law to keep them in line.'

'I didn't mean you couldn't.' Julie blushed. 'You look big and strong.' She hesitated, then, 'Does your foot hurt you?' It was pointless to pretend and they might as well speak of his disability once and then forget it.

'Not too much these days,' Jago said. 'It used to ache a lot more but the boot helps, you see. It looks ugly but it doesn't hinder me.'

'Good.' She smiled at him and Jago felt the sunshine had just filled the room, even though it was an overcast day. 'I wanted to thank you for what you did.'

'It was one of my men that actually found you,' Jago said. 'At the time we were searching for a young child but Maya says it was meant that we should find you and I'm mighty glad we did.'

'Yes, so am I,' she said and looked serious again. 'Maya says I can stay here but it means you don't have a bed or a room.'

'I can fix up a room over the top of the barn for me,' Jago said. 'I've been meaning to do it for a while because I could do with a man here permanently and

I was going to offer it as accommodation for him, so it will suit me fine for a while.'

'But then you won't have room for your hired man.'

'I can divide it into two. It's only for sleeping – I'll be eating and sitting over here and most of the time I'm at work so I shan't disturb you too much. It will be good for Maya to have company. She doesn't get into town often – except for church on a Sunday, though she can walk or get a lift in if she wants.'

'That's when you go up to the mill and take a walk round to see everything is all right on Sundays.' Julie nodded. 'I saw you at the lake a couple of times when you didn't see me.'

'It's pleasant up there when the weather is nice,' Jago agreed. 'I like the woods and the lake better than the town.'

'I like the town sometimes, but Halifax is big and busy, like a part of London, in a way. I think I prefer it here.'

'You don't miss your home or your family?'

'I don't have anyone,' Julie admitted and he thought how sad and lonely she looked in that moment. 'I didn't like the orphanage they put me in so I went back to London, but my neighbour contacted the council and told them so they sent me out here. They just wanted rid of me, because I was a problem.'

Jago nodded his understanding. No wonder the hurt and pain had shown itself to him. He could feel a deep hurt inside her and knew that it needed time to heal. Maya would know what to do.

'I have to work,' he said abruptly, because the need to take her in his arms and comfort her was strong, but she wouldn't want that from him. 'Rest up for a while. Maya will tell you when you can get up . . .'

'I'll be up when you get home,' Julie said, determination in her voice now. 'I am going to help your mother with cooking and sewing.'

Jago nodded, smiling inwardly as he went out. His mother was more than capable of doing all the cooking and mending but if it made the girl feel useful that was fine by him. He would eat whatever she cooked and look pleased, even if it was terrible.

Jago looked at the pile of cut lumber stacked on the lorry that had come to collect it. It was fine quality and he was proud as he waved goodbye to the driver. As he looked around him, he drew in a deep breath. He loved the peace of the wood with all its creatures and forms of life in the undergrowth.

It had been a good day. His mother's patient was doing well and the lawyer had rung him to let him know that Miss Vee had been in to sign the papers that meant the mill was now his own. He still owed her money but it was arranged for him to pay in easy stages that he could manage and the future looked bright.

He checked the various buildings that were kept locked at night. Because of their bulk, certain logs remained in the open or under a shelter, some even in the water where they'd been floated after being felled on the other side of the lake, because the timber grew on three banks, leaving just one clear for access. Everything was in order and he was about to leave for the night when he saw a car pull into the yard and hesitated. He could simply drive off and ignore his visitor but that wasn't Jago's way.

He stood by his truck and waited for Harold Trevors to approach him but made no attempt to close the gap between them. His visitor looked annoyed because he hadn't gone to speak to him, making him get out of his sleek black car and walk to join him.

'Decent bit of timber you've got here,' Trevors said, his hard eyes surveying the land. 'Looks as if you've been doing some more planting the other side of the lake?'

'If you cut a tree down, you need to plant two more,' Jago told him. 'If everyone simply cuts and clears the land, we'll have no forests and no wilderness left.'

'More interested in real estate myself, big buildings are worth a fortune. Ever think of what this land might be worth if homes for rich folk were built up here? It could be a fine attraction: boats and swimming in the lake and good-quality buildings that folk would be proud to own. You could be a part of that, Jago. It would make you a wealthy man.'

'I'm rich now, Mr Trevors,' Jago said stressing the *Mr*. 'The trees breathe life into this land and the lake is a haven for wildlife as well as being useful to my loggers. I reckon that's worth more than a load of silver in the bank. Can't breathe or eat money, I reckon.'

'You could build log cabins near the lake,' Harold Trevors suggested. He pointed to where some of the trees had been cut and cleared, the land not yet replanted. 'And more substantial houses there, maybe a hotel or a lodge of some kind.'

'We're replanting that area later this year,' Jago told

him firmly. 'I wouldn't mind a cabin by the lake, maybe a couple, but I don't want to turn it into a playground for rich folk, Mr Trevors. As long as I can run this place it will stay as it is.'

'And if you can't?' He looked pointedly at Jago's foot. 'You could maybe have an operation on that, live a life of luxury wherever you wanted.'

'Thank you for the offer,' Jago said but the look he gave Harold Trevors was hard and unyielding. 'However, my answer remains the same. I shall never sell unless I'm old and have no children to come after me.'

Harold Trevors' mouth twisted with wry humour. 'Not likely you will, is it? And kids are a waste of time. Don't put your faith in sons, Jago, or you'll be disappointed.'

With that, he turned and strode away. Jago watched him get in his car and drive off. He hadn't made threats but Jago knew he wasn't done yet. Clearly, he had a plan that involved Jago's land and he wasn't the sort to give up easily. He would come again and again, hoping to wear down Jago's resistance and he might try to sabotage the place if he could. However, it sounded as though his plan depended on the area remaining a beautiful spot and that meant he wouldn't burn the whole of the woodland – not that it would be that easy. Jago had firebreaks all through the area because fire could happen even if it wasn't set deliberately and the breaks gave them a chance to save at least some groups of trees in the event of a wildfire.

He might come in one day and find the mill sabotaged, but that was merely machinery and could be repaired or replaced, even though it would be costly.

It was the trees that mattered to Jago and the wildlife that made their home in them. The air here had a special clean freshness that suited him and he didn't want it to change, to become thick with smoke or polluted like the city.

Frowning, he started his truck and began the drive home. Harold Trevors liked to act the big man and he was undoubtedly a bully, but bullies usually stopped short of doing anything that could cause them ultimate harm and he knew that Jago got on well with the local law officers and too much damage at the sawmill would lead to Harold Trevors being investigated. He would threaten and cajole, even blackmail if he could but he wouldn't step too far over the line.

Putting the man from his mind, Jago began to anticipate his supper after a busy day's work.

The meat pie with mashed potatoes, beans and gravy was filling food for a hard-working man and it tasted delicious. It was followed by a crumble filled with plums that had been bottled the previous year and laced with a creamy custard.

'That was nice,' Jago said and looked from his mother to Julie, who was sitting opposite him at the table and finishing her portion of the crumble. 'Who made it?' He looked at his mother but she shook her head.

'Julie is a good cook,' Maya told him. 'I thought I might need to teach her some things but she has natural talent. She was taught by her mother and grandmother when she was young.'

'Gran was a cook in a big house in the country

227

before she married the butler,' Julie told him with a smile. 'I used to go to her house every day after school and in the holidays and she taught me how to make pastry and custard – and the rest I just picked up myself. Mum was more for the sewing.'

'Is cooking what you've been doing in Halifax?' Jago asked and nodded his thanks as Maya put a cup of coffee in front of him. It was black and strong the way he liked it and he heaped sugar into it before taking a mouthful.

'Yes, for a short while. At first, I just did the washing-up at the café but then Cath died and Andy started to drink too much so I started to help.' She sighed. 'He was knocked down and killed one night. Sally-Anne and me were going to keep the café going for whoever owned it but he was a nasty man so we both left.'

'Is that why you came back here?' Jago asked, his gaze drawn to her face. He'd asked his mother but she'd said Julie would tell him when she was ready.

'Yes. I didn't know where else to go and . . .' She shook her head. 'It was just an impulse. I was lucky your men found me.'

'Yes, you were,' Jago said. He turned his gaze to his mother. 'Mr Trevors came to the mill as I was leaving this evening. He wants to offer me a partnership in a big development up at the lake. He made it sound good but it would destroy the peace and bring too many outsiders.'

'They will come one day,' Maya said stoically. 'Once the land was all my people's and they lived wherever they chose, but the strangers came from across the seas and took it. You can only delay the inevitable, Jago. Miss Vee told me that they plan to build more bridges to access Upper Sackville too, not just yet but one day and then the buildings will spread and it will all be like Halifax.'

'Not on my property. Not while I breathe,' Jago said with a touch of anger. 'Can't they see what they're doing to the land? The beauty they crave will be destroyed once they move into their big houses with their cars and their noise and their boats!' His eyes blazed with passion. 'There are others who feel as I do. If we don't sell, they might give up and go elsewhere.'

Maya laughed. 'I know your answer then, son. Didn't you want to be rich?'

'He offered me wealth, but who do you think would gain most if I'd agreed?' Jago demanded. 'I told him I was already rich with land and my life. I was polite, Ma, the way you told me but he knew I meant it.'

'Good, I'm glad your head wasn't turned,' Maya said and smiled contentedly. 'God made the wilderness and the beasts that live in it – if He hadn't wanted it that way, he'd have done it different.'

'Mr Trevors gave me an idea, though. Talked about log cabins on the lakeside. We might do that, Ma. In time, we could get a man in to look after the farm here and live close to my work.'

'You will need a home of your own one day,' Maya told him. 'When the time comes, I'll stay here, though a willing lad to help with the chores would be welcome.'

'Your home is with me,' Jago said, puzzled. Why

would his mother think he might need his own home? 'Besides, I need you to look after me.'

'So you do,' Maya replied and laughed. 'Your face – it's a picture, Jago Marsh. You'll need to do without me one day, but that won't be for a while yet.'

'You're not ill?' he questioned, heart stopping in sudden fear. Maya never complained. She wouldn't even if she knew she was ill.

'No, foolish one!'

His mother laughed again and turned away to start washing dishes. Julie got up to help her and he left them to it as he went out to walk the farm and check on the animals. The women would have gone to bed for the night when he returned and he could sleep on the old sofa in front of the fire. It was cosy on a cold night but he'd have to fix up the barn because he missed his bed.

The only reason he'd want his own home was if he took a wife – and as Harold Trevors had jibed at him, he wasn't likely to have one of those or sons or daughters to follow him. His mother was right. He could keep back the tide of progress for a time but after that . . . a smile touched his mouth. After that he'd leave it to the National Preservation Society or some such thing. The thought made him laugh and he was smiling as he carried water to the beasts in the barn. Life was good – even better now that Julie had come to stay for a while. She would leave again one day, he knew that. She was too bright and beautiful to stay in this place forever – and if she could cook like that, she could find a husband if she wanted or work in a good hotel.

Jago frowned at those thoughts. He would rather

that Julie stayed with them, at least for a few months. But after that – well, she must be free to go where she pleased and if she needed help to get started, she had only to ask. Yet the idea of her leaving made him sad. He wanted her to stay forever but that was just him being selfish . . .

CHAPTER 25

'Why do you want to sell the café?' Vee asked when the woman returned, not the next day as she'd told Aggie, but more than a week later. 'I am interested in buying but it could be a little goldmine for you. It used to be very busy and I'm sure it could be again.'

'That was my first thought,' Hilda Robinson agreed. 'Andy was a decent cook but I'm better – still, to tell you the truth, I'm nervous. A man told me Andy owed him money and that the café belonged to him but when I asked for proof he went off in a temper. The next day I got an offer of eight hundred dollars from him. I really didn't like him so I refused. He looked fit to murder me, but he muttered something about me regretting my decision. I think if I tried to run it myself, he would make life difficult for me and that's the truth of it.' She looked regretful. 'You probably won't want to buy it now?'

'Was it Harold Trevors who wanted to buy?' Vee inquired.

'Yes, it was – how did you know?'

'Because he used the same tactics on me,' Vee replied with a grim smile. 'How much are you asking for it?'

'Well, I wanted nearer to a thousand dollars, because of the goodwill – I've been asked when it will reopen several times – but I'd take nine hundred and fifty.'

'I'll give you the one thousand. It's worth at least that,' Vee told her truthfully. 'Trevors is a bully but he knows I don't scare easily. I might open all the properties up and make one big store. I'm not sure yet. That's for the future; for the moment I might just find someone to run the café for me.'

'I have a nephew who's a trained chef. He might like the job. I was going to ask if he wanted to come in with me.' She looked a bit regretful, as if she still wanted to hold onto the property. 'He's big and strong and doesn't scare easily. He told me to keep it and let him run it for me.'

'Let me think about it,' Vee said. 'It might be possible for you to sell the property to me but rent it back and let your nephew run it with you. If Harold Trevors knows that I've bought the property and leased it again he'll be annoyed with me and quite possibly leave you and your nephew in peace.'

'Why would you do that for me? You don't know me . . .' Hilda Robinson looked at Vee in puzzlement.

'Let's just say I don't like Harold Trevors any more than you do,' Vee replied with a wry smile. 'Talk to your nephew. Bring him to see me and then we'll discuss the idea further.'

'You're a saint,' Hilda said in wonder. 'That money would give me a nice little bit in the bank, make my life more comfortable and give Jamie a business to run. It's what he really wants and that's why I didn't come back when I said I would. He has been trying to persuade me to keep it but . . .' She took a deep breath. 'I suppose you know that a man like Trevors could cause damage to the property out of spite?'

'Yes, I realise that,' Vee said. 'He could, but I doubt he will. If he does, I have friends who will know where to lay the blame.'

'Well, thank you for the offer,' Hilda Robinson said and smiled. 'I'll talk to Jamie but I already know what he'll say. He will want to get started as soon as possible. He has to give three weeks' notice where he is but it would take that long to get things sorted anyway.'

Vee smiled at her enthusiasm. She was pleased she had been able to help Hilda Robinson and also buy the property she wanted. One day the three properties might be redeveloped but, as she'd told Miss Robinson, that was for the future. It might not be something she would do herself, but Beth would grow up and perhaps marry and have children. Had it not been for the little girl she'd quickly come to love, she might not have bothered with her new ventures, because Malcolm wasn't likely to marry and have children now, even if he were still alive. But surely she would have been informed if his ship had been lost? It was puzzling and a worry but, knowing Malcolm, he would just turn up when he was ready and be baffled when she berated him for not letting her know he was safe.

'You've promised to buy the property and lease it back to her and her nephew?' Aggie stared at Vee as if she were mad. 'After what that man has done? You're asking for trouble, my girl.'

Vee smiled inwardly. She hadn't been a girl for many years but Aggie had always talked to her that way and she accepted the scolding with good grace.

'I can't live my life tiptoeing around Harold Trevors,' she said. 'Yes, I was frightened when Beth was snatched but that makes me certain he won't go too far in his little war against me. And yes, he might do damage to the café and my other shops, send someone to break windows and do physical damage, but I can replace a few windows if I have to and I think him too much of a coward to come after me personally. He knows what would happen if he did.'

'Have it your own way. You always do,' Aggie said with a shake of her head, 'but mark my words, Miss Vee – he will find a way to hurt you if he can.'

'I've always stood up to him and I shall continue to do so,' Vee said in a determined fashion. 'He's a bully, Aggie – and bullies have to be stopped. He has tried to terrify at least two vulnerable women into selling their properties and one sold unwillingly to him but this one came to me. He knows by now that he can't terrify me – or he will do when he learns who bought Miss Robinson's café.'

'You are building a nice portfolio of properties, Mrs Bittern,' Vee's solicitor told her when she rang him the next day to tell him what she wanted to do. 'That real estate is due for redevelopment in the next ten years or so and with Halifax getting so crowded the only way to build is upwards. We need more land and it will be a while before they can build enough bridges to Upper Sackville to make that seem more attractive. We have the ferry but that doesn't always suit, especially commercial traffic. No, it may take a bit longer, because the stone bridge they've recently erected isn't going to solve the problem, though it helps – but when they do, your properties there will shoot up in value. It's a good idea to spread your purchases and not just buy in Halifax so I'd advise you to purchase in Upper Sackville too.'

'Possibly I will, in time,' Vee agreed. He was telling her what she already knew but she had a habit of keeping her cards close to her chest and men liked to tell her things. She'd always had a good eye for business, which was why she'd made the family store a much busier and more prosperous business than it had been in her father's time. Bill had owned property all over the place and most of it had come to her and she'd grown that too.

The property he'd left to his cousin, Paul Miller, had been let to tenants and the income was building up nicely in a special account. Vee frowned as it nagged at her as it did sometimes. What had happened to that family? She'd been in touch with the Red Cross but so far they hadn't had any news for her. Much of the East End of London had been bombed, whole streets lost, hundreds killed and injured, and it was possible the family had left London altogether or had been lost.

That would be sad, Vee thought, but she would keep trying to find Bill's elusive relatives and tell them they had the rent money waiting for them here. If they wanted to sell the property they could – she would buy it and send the money – or they could come out to Canada and start a new life here.

The dog Jago had told Aggie about had given birth to a large litter of puppies some weeks earlier and she and Beth went over on the ferry on Saturday afternoon so he could show them the way to the farm where they'd been reared.

'They're a crossbreed,' he told her, then grinned. 'Well, perhaps mongrels might be a better word. I think there's spaniel, poodle and a bit of who knows what in there too. They should be a nice size and the parents seem friendly animals.'

So now they were standing in a yard and looking at six beautiful healthy puppies. Three were chocolate brown with white bibs, two were black and white and one was pure black with very curly fur. Beth had been down on her knees playing with them but now she was sitting on a bench with the pure black dog on her lap.

'He's the runt of the litter,' Jago's friend told them with a smile. 'He's a bit smaller than the others and I wasn't sure he'd survive but he's got a brave streak in him.'

'I want this one, Mummy,' Beth said looking up at her. 'He likes me – he keeps kissing me.' The dog obligingly licked her face and then her hands over and over again, making her giggle with delight. 'His name is Tickles.'

'That's a fine name,' Jago said and laughed. 'I think she's chosen well, Miss Vee.'

'Yes, if she wants Tickles then Tickles it is,' Vee said indulgently. 'How much do I owe you, Carl?'

'I don't want anything for them,' Carl said. 'I told Jago I needed homes for most of them.'

'I'll be taking that one myself,' Jago said, pointing to a chocolate brown puppy larger than the others. 'He'd be a good guard dog for the farm.'

'You should have one up at the lumberyard as well,' Carl said hopefully. 'The black and white ones are promised to my nephews – if my brother will let them have both – and I'll keep the other one. I just let them run loose round my farmyard at night. It keeps intruders out.' He had half a dozen dogs behind a picket fence, most of them barking and playing a game that looked like tag with a stick.

'No wonder you have a lot of pups to give away,' Vee said shaking her head at him, and yet it was a good idea. The farm was quite isolated and guard dogs helped to keep it safe. The dog Beth had chosen might not be a big fierce animal like some of Carl's, but it would bark and alert the household if anyone tried to get in during the night. In that way, it would be a guardian for Beth and Vee too. Aggie had started to sleep over now too, telling Vee that it was easier than going back home. It was probably going to be a permanent thing once she'd had time to sort out her things. No point in her coming and going or living alone when Vee's house had lots of spare rooms.

'How's your patient now?' Vee asked Jago as they left in his truck. 'Is she recovering from her illness?'

'Yes, she's much better,' Jago told her. 'She's up and she helps Maya with the cooking, sewing and other things too.'

'So will she stay with you?'

'For a time,' Jago said. 'If she wants to move on . . .' He hesitated, then, 'I wondered if you might have work for her, Miss Vee – when she is ready? She's very good at sewing. Not just mending but making clothes, too.'

'Well, if the time comes when she wants to move on, you let me know. I'm sure we could find a place for her in one of the shops, if that was what she wanted.'

'I think she might like to set up for herself as a seamstress,' he said uncertainly. 'She said something to Maya but I'm not sure. She isn't ready yet anyway.'

Vee nodded. She'd read more in Jago's face than he knew. She believed that he was more than a little in love with the girl, but being the man he was, he would probably never tell her.

'What's her full name, by the way?'

'Julie Miller,' he said.

She looked at him, startled. 'Julie *Miller*? And did you say she came from the East End of London?'

'Yes, that's right,' Jago agreed, puzzled at her reaction. 'Her parents were dead or real sick and the council put her in an orphanage but she ran away so they sent her out here. Is something wrong, Miss Vee? You don't think she should be sent back to Miss Cotton? She wasn't happy there.'

'No, certainly not,' Vee assured him. 'It's just I'd like to meet her if she's feeling up to it because I believe Julie came out on the ship with Beth and she might like to see Beth – who loves her – again. Will you bring her to tea one Sunday with you and Maya?'

'Yes, that would be mighty fine,' Jago said, though he looked hesitant. 'When she's ready. She's not quite up to visiting yet.'

'Yes, of course. Well, we'll be going. We have to go to the store and buy some things for Tickles.'

Vee was thoughtful that evening after Beth had finished playing with her puppy and gone up to bed, taking Tickles with her. He had a bed beside her and a block of sand in the back kitchen to use when the need arose, though Vee suspected there would be puddles and whoopsies around the house for some weeks to come. She wasn't too bothered. As a young girl one of her dogs had been a puppy that she'd successfully trained and the dog had followed her to the school gates and collected her each night. Perhaps in time Tickles might do that for Beth . . .

Her thoughts turned from her little girl and the dog to Paul Miller and his wife; she knew they had a daughter, though she'd somehow thought the girl's name was Judy. Paul was Bill's cousin on his mother's side and her husband would have known, but she hadn't taken too much notice until after Bill's death when she'd wanted to contact the family concerning the property Bill had left them.

Was it possible that 'Judy' was actually Julie and that the girl now living with Jago was related to Paul? No, that was too much of a coincidence! It couldn't be that Julie was Paul's daughter and had been living here in Canada for months now, surely? Though stranger things had happened – but if that was the case why hadn't she sought Vee out? Or did she even know of her Canadian second cousin? It was more than likely that she wouldn't. The correspondence had been infrequent even when Bill was alive. Vee frowned. The girl now with Jago and Maya had her sympathy for what she'd suffered either way, but what a wonderful thing it would be if she turned out to be Bill's cousin!

The thought elated her, but then she shook her head. She was letting her enthusiasm run away with her as she so often did but, oh my, it would be nice! She would write to the Red Cross again and ask them about Miss Julie Miller who had been sent to Canada. They should be able to trace her details and show the connection if it was there.

In any case, she had made up her mind to help Julie, because of the kindness she had shown to Beth on the voyage out here. One good turn deserved another but if she *was* Bill's last surviving relative, he would be so pleased she'd been found. Vee hadn't yet told Beth that she knew where Julie was, just in case the girl didn't want to come, but hopefully she would accept the invitation to tea soon and they would be reunited.

Laughing at herself for having rose-tinted glasses, Vee sat down and started to write her letter to the Red Cross, giving all the details she had, down to the name of the ship and dates as well as Julie having run away from an orphanage. Surely they could trace her parents from that, even if they had died?

CHAPTER 26

Pete Trevors watched as Jago parked his truck outside the general stores and got out. He had a young girl with him. She was pretty, so what was a girl like that doing with Jago? He didn't have a sister and he surely couldn't have a girlfriend? Pete noticed that she was a little hesitant, looking over her shoulder as if fearing she was being watched but Jago said something to her and she smiled. Before that he'd thought her pretty but when she smiled Pete saw something more, an inner beauty he felt drawn to without knowing why.

She followed Jago into the store. They were in there a long time but Pete had nothing much to do. He still hadn't found anything he could use to blackmail his father, which meant he was still getting the worst of it at home. Harold Trevors was in a foul mood over something and he'd developed a habit of hitting Pete round the back of the head for no reason at all – either he was late, slow to respond, sullen or rude in his father's eyes and the anger and hatred Pete was feeling was mounting inside him. One day he would get even. He would!

Jago and the girl finally came out of the store, both of them loaded with parcels. Some of them were wrapped in brown paper and looked as if they might be material, flat and oblong and clearly heavy, like a whole bale of cloth. Was she going to make curtains or clothes? Pete thought if she was his girl he would buy her pretty dresses from the best store in Halifax – if he had any money.

He scowled as someone nudged his arm. 'What you staring at?' Ralph Cotton asked and then swore. 'The cunning little bitch!'

Pete looked at him and saw that he was staring at the girl, face twisted in jealousy and spite. 'Do you know who she is?' he asked, struggling to keep his voice flat and disinterested.

'I certainly do. She's the evacuee brat my aunt took in. A charity girl! I fancied her a bit but she ran off after trying to cut me with scissors and poked her fingers in my eyes, too. If I ever get her, I'll make her sorry.'

'You'll be sorry yourself if you harm her,' Pete muttered and his friend glared at him.

'You and whose army?' he taunted. 'If I want her, I'll have her.'

'Why?' Pete demanded, his eyes blazing. 'There are plenty of girls who think you're special – why go after one who doesn't?'

'Who says she doesn't?' Ralph retorted. 'She just doesn't know what's good for her. She wouldn't be with that cripple if she did . . .'

'Don't call him that!' Pete said, reacting instinctively. 'I know he drags his foot a bit but not the way he used to. He has a disability and it isn't his fault.' He wasn't sure why he'd stuck up for Jago but it had just come out.

'You're high and mighty these days,' Ralph jeered. 'When did you get so moral and righteous?'

'I got thrown out of school because of your larks,' Pete said, rounding on him. 'Why don't you grow up? Start acting like a man instead of a child.'

'You can talk,' Ralph retorted. 'Your father treats you like an idiot and if you had any guts you'd do something about it.' He stalked off, muttering beneath his breath.

Pete watched him go, slightly regretful now. He didn't like Ralph sometimes but he had few friends, because of his father. His mother had sent him to boarding school and he'd made friends there, then Ralph's antics got them expelled. He shook his head. If he had enough money to go right away from here, he could make a new life and perhaps make friends. The idea was growing steadily. He hungered for the freedom money would give him.

Sighing, he thought of the girl's smile. She clearly liked and trusted Jago. She wouldn't be interested in a man who had threatened him, even though it was on his father's orders. If he could just find something Harold Trevors had done that was against the law, something that didn't involve Pete, that would stop him treating Pete like some sort of slave. It was as if his father blamed him for his mother's departure.

Pete didn't know why she'd left. It had happened during term time when he was away at school two years previously. She'd written saying she thought she might have to leave his father but then he'd heard nothing more. Pete had asked his father where she'd gone, but he just shook his head and called her a faithless bitch to go off and leave them both. Pete thought that perhaps she'd gone because she was scared of his father. He was scared too, but when he found whatever Harold was hiding, that would all change. Ralph was right, though, his father did treat him as if he were an idiot and he regretted their argument now.

Ralph was simmering with anger as he went back to his aunt's house in Lower Sackville. He'd gone into Halifax to see Pete and he'd been watching that girl – that charity girl. He'd used the words to taunt her and he'd seen how she hated the name. She deserved it! She'd deliberately drawn him on with her looks and her pouts and frowns, flaunting her body. It had served her right when he'd had a go at her – but he'd come off worst and that was a first for Ralph. Girls usually either gave in willingly or after a short struggle. He didn't like losing and his aunt had been angry with him. She'd asked if he'd had anything to do with Julie's flight. Naturally, he'd denied it, but Ralph wasn't sure his aunt believed him. She hadn't been quite as indulgent towards him since then.

It was Julie Miller's fault. She needed to be taught a lesson and Ralph was the one to do it. He licked his lips at the thought of what he would like to do with her. Next time he would make sure she couldn't escape. He needed help and there were a couple of youths in Sackville who liked to please him. They

245

enjoyed having a ride in his truck and getting into mischief. Nothing much yet, but they'd broken a few windows, smeared paint on shop doors and let down the tyres on cars and trucks. They'd thought it great fun but Ralph wanted more. He wanted revenge on that damned charity girl and he would get it one of these days.

At least he now knew where she lived so he could make plans to catch her unawares in the woods near Jago's home. She could scream all she liked there and no one would hear.

A smile touched Ralph's lips. Next time, he would make sure Julie Miller paid the price for her defiance. Maybe he could find a way to make Pete fall in line too. He smiled to himself. Ralph knew something Pete would give a lot to know. If he told him, he would be grateful and go along with his plans . . .

If only he hadn't driven his truck home after he'd drunk too much beer and the whiskey Ralph had persuaded him into having as a chaser. If he hadn't done that his father wouldn't be able to make him do things he thought were wrong. Pete fretted inwardly. If only he could find something incriminating in his father's papers, something bad enough to send him to prison . . .

Pete found the house empty on his return and was glad. He hadn't made up his mind to do what his father had ordered him to do but if he didn't it would earn him a beating – or worse. Harold had threatened to go to the police and tell them about the night his truck had been damaged and he meant it.

The worst thing was he didn't recall a thing about hitting that man. He must have knocked him down without seeing him and driven on, collapsing on his bed and falling instantly asleep. Even when he'd seen the dent on the side bumper, he hadn't realised he'd hit anything more than maybe a deer – until he'd heard about that man getting killed the same night. Like a fool, he'd gone to his father and he'd stood by him, getting the truck fixed quietly by someone who wouldn't blab to the police. Now, Pete was bound to him like a slave.

Pete shivered. This house felt like a morgue to him since his mother had left. His father had always been a bit of a bully but it hadn't been too bad in the holidays with his mother around. Now, though, it was big and empty and lonely. Even the cleaning woman stayed just long enough to do her work, hardly speaking a word. She'd told Pete that the place gave her the shivers without his mother.

Missing her, Pete walked up the wide staircase and made his way to his mother's room. It had been kept locked since she left, not even the cleaning woman allowed in, but Pete had found the key in his father's desk the day before, tucked into a little secret drawer at the back. His father had come home before he could use it but now was his chance.

He hesitated and then fitted the brass key into the lock, turned it and went in. Because it had been shut up all this time, the smell of her perfume hit him immediately, taking his breath; for a moment he paused, half inclined to leave, but then something impelled him to stay. Pete began to look around.

Something wasn't right but he wasn't sure what. Then it struck him – his mother's things were all here, nothing had been touched.

He walked over to the dressing table, its shining surface covered in a thick layer of dust. Puzzled, he picked up her ivory-backed hairbrushes and matching mirror, inlaid with silver. They'd been a gift from his grandfather, a man he'd never met and Pete knew that his mother had loved these things. She might have left behind things her abusive husband had given her, but these? Why would she leave these? Her jewel box was on there too. Pete opened it and saw several pieces he knew to have been gifts to her from before her marriage. Why had she left them when she went?

A chill touched the back of his neck and suddenly Pete knew, with absolute certainty, that she had never left – not of her own free will. Someone had forced her or— The thought was so terrible that he had to rush into the adjoining bathroom to be sick in the toilet.

Here, the scent of his mother was even stronger. He flushed the toilet but could smell his own vomit and looked round for some perfume to spray, not wanting to leave the stink behind when he left. As he reached for an atomiser on the marble surface surrounding the basin, he saw a smear of something in the corner. It was dry and hard to the touch and an indeterminate colour. Hesitating for a moment, he wet his finger and touched it. Uncertain of why he did it, he then put his finger to his mouth, recoiling instantly. It was blood! His mother's blood? Had something terrible and violent happened here?

Suddenly fearful, Pete rushed from the bathroom back to the bedroom. He turned in a circle. His mother had taken none of the things he knew to be important to her, so had she left in such a hurry – or had she left at all?

Hollow with dread and fear, Peter went back out into the hall and locked the door. He closed his eyes for a moment before walking to his own room, locking the door behind him and flinging himself down on the bed. Horror was making his mind race. There was nothing in his mother's room to make anyone believe a murder had been committed, just one little tiny spot of blood that he'd removed with his finger. His only evidence was his intuition and the fact that he knew she wouldn't have gone without that dressing-table set and some of her jewellery – not unless someone forced her or killed her.

Was it a lie that she'd left them? Was Pete's father capable of murder?

The thought was so shocking that he recoiled from it. It was ridiculous, stupid, but . . . possible?

Pete's father had always been a bully but murder was different. Yet if he'd struck out in anger and she'd fallen, hitting her head, it might not have bled much but could have killed her. Head traumas could be fatal. Something similar had happened to a boy at school when he'd been messing about in a tree and fallen on his head. Perhaps his mother had had an accident that his father had covered up?

And if his mother hadn't left, if she'd died in her room, what had his father done with her body?

Pete's thoughts went round and round like flies

around a jamjar. Slowly the thought solidified in his brain. His mother had never left him, that was the reason she hadn't written and told him to join her, as he was sure she would have had she gone of her own volition. No, she was dead.

She was here in this place somewhere. The cleaning woman had sensed something and now Pete understood. His mother was buried here, in the house or the back garden that was so secluded that no one would see where her husband had buried her. Pete's mind worked swiftly. His father had someone in regularly to cut the grass and do the weeding so she wasn't under the borders, too much chance of being discovered . . . Pete frowned, trying to think what was different about the garden. What had been changed two years ago while he was away at school? He knew something had, but obviously he hadn't thought it important when he'd first seen it on his return. What could it be?

For a moment or two he couldn't think and then he nodded. There was a new garden shed, right at the bottom of their land and it was built on thick concrete slabs. If his mother was buried in the garden, he would bet it was there; it was the only place she wouldn't be discovered by accident.

The thought of his mother's body decaying beneath the shed sent Pete rushing for his toilet where he was violently sick once more. His mind was reeling, his body in shock as he tried to come to terms with his thoughts. Surely he was imagining these things and yet the more he tried to deny it, the more he became convinced that his mother was buried under that shed

– a shed that his father never used, because he already had a place for his tools.

So what was he going to do about it? Pete sat and shivered as he went over and over it in his mind. Could he expose his father as more than just a bully and ruthless in business? He'd hoped for some evidence that Harold had fiddled his income tax or stolen something and hadn't found any. Pete would willingly have used that to get his own way – but murder? He ought to report it to the police, have them come and dig up his mother, if she was there, give her a proper burial. But he wasn't sure anyone would believe him.

If he was wrong, his father would thrash him within an inch of his life and then throw him out with nothing and he didn't know how to survive on his own, not without money.

Anger and grief warred inside him, then he felt the wetness of tears on his cheeks. Pete had loved his mother. She'd always protected and stood up for him, never seeming to fear her husband and refusing to be cowed when he'd shouted at her. Had she known something, had a hold of some sort on her husband? Pete wanted Harold to pay for the things he'd done. He wanted it badly, but he hesitated. If he was wrong, if he'd made a foolish mistake, jumped to conclusions, his father would be merciless.

Pete needed more proof, needed to think about his next move, because it would be decisive one way or the other. He would take his time – he couldn't afford not to . . .

CHAPTER 27

Vee saw Harold Trevors watching her as she entered
the café that day but she ignored him. Everything was
sorted legally; she'd bought the property and leased it
to Hilda Robinson, having also agreed to pay for deco-
rating and a new floor covering. Now that it was finally
open she wanted to have a look around and she nodded
approvingly. The tables all had yellow covers and bright-
blue placemats with a small vase containing a single
flower on every other table. They'd done it that way
so folk who didn't like flowers could find one without.
Vee chose a table with a flower and sat down. A pretty
fair-haired girl came to serve her.

'Just coffee,' Vee said and then changed her mind
as she saw the delicious cakes under glass. 'Maybe just
a small slice of that coffee and walnut cake please.'

'Yes, Mrs Bittern,' the girl replied and Vee looked
at her in surprise.

'How do you know my name?'

'Because Miss Robinson saw you coming across the
street and said if you wanted anything I wasn't to
charge.'

Vee laughed. 'Well, that's nice of her. Just this once then, but in future I'll pay like everyone else. If those cakes are as good as they look, I'll be bringing my little girl here sometimes.'

As the girl went off to fetch her order, Vee looked around. The café was spotless and smelled deliciously of baking. She heard the bell go and two ladies entered, looking around them in anticipation before choosing their table. Almost immediately a man entered and then three men together. By the time Vee had drunk her coffee and eaten her cake every table was filled and she didn't doubt that hers would soon have another occupant. The cake and the coffee had been delicious and she would certainly return. She thanked the girl who had served her, leaving a few cents' tip before she left, pleased with her investment. It was what she wanted and it had done Miss Robinson a favour too.

She wandered down to look into the windows of one of the shops she'd purchased just before she bought the café. It was open after the refurbishments and it looked to have good quality gentlemen's outfits for sale. She would tell Malcolm to shop here when he got home . . . The thought was spontaneous and brought a piercing hurt as she wondered if her brother would ever return.

'Don't be dead,' she murmured under her breath. 'I'd miss you, old thing.'

Perhaps because she was caught up by her emotions, Vee wasn't aware of the man until he was right beside her. The prickle at the back of her neck warned her as he grabbed her arm, his fingers digging into her flesh beneath her jacket.

'Thinking how clever you are?' he muttered in a vicious tone.

Vee looked into Harold Trevors' face. 'I have no idea what you mean,' she replied coolly. 'Please let go of my arm, sir.'

'That café should have been mine,' he hissed at her. 'I was owed. Andy Machin didn't finish paying his debt and if you hadn't interfered, I'd have what belongs to me by now.'

'May I ask why you wanted it?' Vee asked, deciding to have it out with him. 'I know you're buying property in Upper Sackville because you believe the price will shoot up once they build more bridges and it's easier to access – but why here in Halifax? Unless you think the price is bound to rise quickly when they rebuild. Folk like this old centre and I can't see this area being redeveloped for a long time.'

'Because the café was mine by right!' he grunted. 'And I don't let go of what belongs to me.'

'If you can prove that by law, you should approach your solicitor,' Vee said and saw her answer in his eyes. The suppressed fury there told her that he could do nothing. 'If you made a loan to Mr Machin without proper security then you were a fool, Mr Trevors. I daresay you won't do it again.' She couldn't conceal her amusement, because he was such a bully and thought himself so clever. He'd probably charged excessive rates of interest, quite illegally, and got his fingers burned. It served him right for treating people like dirt.

As Vee went to move on, he took hold of her arm again. She turned to look at him and saw the bitter hatred in his eyes. 'I can't abide women who think themselves above men. Just be careful, Miss Vee. You might go too far and then you'll be sorry.'

'Are you threatening me?' she asked and met his eyes with a fierce stare of her own. 'Don't imagine you can bully me, Harold Trevors. I've always known you for what you are – a coward who takes his temper out on those he thinks vulnerable. Well, I'm not and I have friends who protect me. Harm me or mine and you're the one who will be sorry. And I am Mrs Bittern to you.'

'High-and-mighty bitch!' he muttered but took his hand from her arm. 'You've been warned, just remember that.'

Vee walked off without a backward glance. She'd stood up to him but the look in his eyes had made her quiver inside. Vee wasn't afraid for herself but now she had Beth and if anything happened to her . . . It wouldn't, she told herself sharply. Beth wouldn't still be alive if that man had meant to kill her. He was just a frustrated snake hissing in anger . . . yet a cornered snake could be dangerous. Perhaps she wouldn't buy any more property for a while, just be a bit careful.

Harold watched her go, her head held proudly, confident of her place and her right to do as she pleased. She'd been just the same as a young girl when her parents owned a big store in Lower Sackville and she'd lived in one of the better houses. His parents had lived in a rundown shack and owned a bit of land that hardly kept them alive. She'd looked at him then as if he were dirt and he'd wanted her to like him so bad that he'd tried to force her, imagining that she would enjoy being kissed. He'd never forgiven her for what happened next. His father had been told and Harold had been thrashed. That was when he'd made up his mind that he would be rich one day, better off than that stuck-up bitch or her family.

He'd worked like crazy to get his first small property and he would never forget how good it felt to collect money that he hadn't had to slave for. Then he'd met Helen and she'd made it clear she was mad for him right from the start. She was another rich kid and her parents gave her a house and money when they married, impressed by Harold's work ethic. He'd owned two shops in Upper Sackville by then and her money bought him the canning factory. It had been barely turning over when he bought it for next to nothing and now it was making huge profits. Harold had a knack for making money.

He'd been fond of Helen in his way and then Pete had come along and she'd turned her attention to the boy, no longer interested in Harold's needs or lusts. When the boy was born, he'd had his suspicions about whether or not he was the father. The boy looked like his mother but there was nothing of Harold in him. He'd become more and more suspicious of her over the years – and then he'd seen her with a man he knew, a businessman with political ambitions and a wealthy wife. Harold had known then that his suspicions were right. His wife was looking at the man in the way she'd looked at Harold before they were married. He'd been played for a sucker by a calculating woman and his anger burned like cold ice.

That evening he'd caught her in her bedroom and demanded the truth. 'How long has it been going on?' he'd grunted as he gripped her wrist until she gasped with pain. 'Is the boy his?'

'What are you talking about?' she'd asked and started to cry, pretending not to understand for more than an hour but then, when he had her on her knees, she'd finally flung the truth at him. 'I don't know if Pete is his or yours!' she'd screamed defiantly. 'We've been lovers since I was eighteen but he was married and she's a Catholic so he couldn't divorce her – but we love each other!'

'So you never loved me?' Harold had been filled with rage. 'I was just the poor dummy you used to cover your affair.'

'Really?' she asked, the sarcasm in her voice stinging him. 'You got what you wanted, Harold Trevors. My father's money and the chance to become rich in your own right. You were so proud of your paltry little shops but I knew you lusted for more. I gave you your chance and you gave me respectability – and I did fancy you a bit at the start, but you're no good at it, not the way he is.'

Harold had hit her several times. He'd wanted to kill her then but her father was still alive and despite what she'd told him – despite what she was – her father would protect her.

'I should tell the world what you are, a dirty little whore,' Harold had said as he'd flung her away from him in disgust.

'But you won't, will you?' Helen's eyes glinted with her triumph. 'You want my money, the money I've got coming to me when my father dies, so you'll accept anything I do and you will never hit me again – ever. If you do, I'll divorce you and strip you of everything.' Her eyes taunted him. 'Don't think I couldn't do it. I know all your little secrets and my lawyers would strip the flesh from your bones by the time they got finished.'

He'd looked into her eyes and known she would do it. She appeared to be the perfect lady, her voice gentle and her laughter sweet. With the boy she was the loving mother and outwardly she was a good wife for a man who wanted to climb. Money alone could never give Harold all that he wanted. Helen was his ticket into the better homes and respectability.

That night he'd made his bargain with the bitch and he'd stuck to it. In public they were good together and Helen helped him get the invitations he needed, giving him the background he'd lacked, gaining him the trust of men he met socially. They'd had separate rooms in their big house and if he needed a woman there were plenty willing enough for a price. It had worked well enough for years, until she told him that her lover's wife had died, leaving him free to marry her and she wanted a divorce.

Harold's mind shied away from that night. He'd lost his temper and struck her hard – too hard. A scowl crossed his once-handsome face. These days he carried too much weight to be truly attractive but he'd been able to get women when he wanted. The trouble was, his anger had made him rough and his wife's betrayal had made him cruel. In truth, the bitch had deserved what she'd got – but even so, he hadn't hated her as much as he did Vee Bittern now – and her death had been an accident . . .

That Bittern bitch deserved to be brought down a peg or two and he would find a way of making her pay. He would take it out on the kid but Pete had refused to harm the girl and Harold didn't want to risk imprisonment himself. If he could push the boy into doing something evil, he would, because he wasn't his son. That had been a bitter blow to swallow; he knew for certain the boy wasn't his because he'd been to a doctor. Harold had always known there was a possibility, because he'd had a bad case of mumps as a lad. He'd assumed that he *was* a father despite that unfortunate occurrence but when he'd found out what a cheating bitch his wife was he'd had the tests done, been told it was highly unlikely he would ever father a child, so Pete's father had to be the rat who'd been having an affair with Helen for so many years.

Well, so be it. Given the chance he would kill Vee Bittern just the way he had his wife but he'd been lucky to get away with that and he couldn't risk it. Some other punishment would have to do. He should have set fires at the lumbermill when it belonged to her. Maybe he would anyway. That would teach that jumped-up Jago Marsh to learn some manners.

Yet he craved that property and burning down good woods was a waste of money. He might still persuade Jago to sell it to him or at least go halves in the project he had in mind.

His anger was cooling now, his business head taking over. He had other fish to fry, more property he wanted to own. There was a nice little block in Lower Sackville that he could purchase for next to nothing. Harold enjoyed being rich. He liked dealing with women who didn't understand business. It gave him pleasure to put one over on them, get what they owned for next to nothing if he could . . . it was just an easy way to score over them – like beating the women who took money from him when he needed to release his pent-up frustration. They cried or stared at him sullenly but took his money just the same. Every time he hurt one of them, he was seeing another woman in his mind.

One day he would take his revenge on her, just as he had the other bitch, but it had to be clever. He couldn't risk getting caught. Back then Harold had wondered if Helen's lover would come looking for her and for months he'd fretted that the man would turn up and demand to see her, but there had been no word; and then Harold had discovered he'd been killed in a car accident soon after that night. It was Harold's good luck. He got away with things and he would go on just as he pleased. There was no one to stop him . . .

CHAPTER 28

'There's a dance on in Upper Sackville this Saturday,' Maya told her son. 'You should take Julie, she'd enjoy it.'

'She wouldn't enjoy dancing with me,' Jago replied frowning at the suggestion.

'You have friends who would be pleased to dance with her and I'll come too if you want. It is just a chance for Julie to meet folk and have a good time. She's well now and she works hard – don't you think she deserves a treat?'

'Yes, of course she does,' Jago said and nodded. 'If you think we should go it will be a treat for you as well.'

For him it would be torture. He would have to stand on the side and watch as other men danced with the girl he now knew he loved – living in the same house with her had let him see that her spirit was as beautiful as her face – but he knew Maya was right. Julie deserved a little fun. All she'd done since she arrived in Canada was work. It was selfish of him not to give her a chance to meet other young folk – and if she

261

found someone who made her happy, then that was the chance he took. If he truly loved her, he would give her that chance.

Julie came into the kitchen at that moment. She was carrying a pile of his work shirts that needed mending, preparing to spend her evening working yet again.

'Do you have a pretty dress, Julie?' he asked and she looked at him in surprise. 'Something you could wear to a dance?'

'A dance?' Her eyes widened. 'Are we all going to a dance?' Her excitement was evident and Jago grinned. His mother had been planning this, probably dropping the odd hint. 'Yes, I have a blue one I made with the material you bought for me a few weeks back.'

'Then we're going on Saturday night,' Jago told her. 'It's a barn dance and there will be young and old – and children too most likely.' The proposed meeting with Beth and her new mother hadn't taken place because the little girl had come down with a bad case of measles and had needed some recovery time. Now Jago said, 'Miss Vee might be there with Beth and I know how much you'd like to see her again.' He thought for a moment. 'What about shoes?'

'Julie has some shoes I gave her,' his mother said quickly and he knew he'd never stood a chance. Maya had made up her mind and Jago gave in to the inevitable. Still, he would enjoy seeing his womenfolk enjoy themselves while he had a drink with some of the men from the sawmill. He would ask the younger ones he trusted most to make sure to ask Julie for a dance.

'Thank you,' Julie was saying. She did a little twirl

around the large kitchen. 'I've never been to a dance but I've always wanted to.'

Jago smiled. It was good to see her laughing – he just wished he was a normal man so he could dance with Julie himself, but there was no use in wishing for the moon. There were times when he knew he had to stand back and watch. He could cut down a tree but dancing was beyond him.

Jago's breath left his body as he saw Julie come into the kitchen on that Saturday night. She was wearing a full-skirted pale-blue cotton dress with a sweetheart neckline, puffed sleeves, a wide sash that buckled at the front and her shoes were white leather. It was her hair that amazed him. She'd washed it and Maya had trimmed it for her and set it into soft waves and she was stunningly beautiful. He knew then that his mother had been right to insist that she had a chance to meet young men. She was so far beyond his reach and she always had been . . . he would be a fool to hope that she could ever love him.

'Well, aren't you going to say anything?' Maya prompted.

Jago looked at his mother and then back at Julie. 'You both look very nice,' he said.

'Nice?' Maya shook her head at him. 'She is *lovely*, Jago. Why don't you say it right out?'

'Julie knows what I mean,' he said and offered a shy smile. He couldn't tell her she was the most beautiful girl in the world and he loved her, because she would be embarrassed. He hoped she knew that he thought a lot of her but Julie needed to be secure and he would do nothing to upset her. 'Come on, let's go. You don't want to miss it.'

Julie looked about the huge barn which had been decorated with paper streamers and flags and balloons. There was a large banner saying that funds were being raised for Our Friends Over the Water. It made her feel welcome. These people here were doing what they could to help the war effort in Britain and she was grateful, even though she no longer lived there.

One of the first people Julie saw was Beth. The little girl was wearing a frilly blue dress and entered with a very smart woman and another older one holding her by the hands. She saw Julie almost at the same moment, gave a cry of joy, broke away from her guardians, and came rushing across the room to her.

'Julie! Julie!'

Julie bent down and swept her up and hugged her. 'Beth, you look so pretty. Are you happy? Jago told me you had a lovely new mummy.'

'She's nice, just like you told me. I miss you, though.'

'I miss you, too, love.'

Julie looked up as the smart lady came towards her smiling. 'Julie Miller, I presume,' she said. 'Beth has told me so much about you, Miss Miller. I do hope you will visit us one day soon.'

'Jago told me you invited us to tea,' Julie said but felt shy. 'And I would like to come one day, if you're sure?'

'Of course I am. Beth told me how kind you were. It's lovely to meet you at last, but you've come here to dance and we're here just for half an hour or so to say hello to friends – this little one still tires easily – but we'll meet soon . . .' She took Beth by the hand and walked away, Beth turning round to wave at Julie.

'That was nice of Miss Vee,' Jago said. 'She's a decent person, Julie. You'll like her when you know her.'

Jago was greeted by friendly faces and voices all round. He was clearly popular with the men who worked with him at the lumberyard and several came over almost immediately. Jago introduced her to five young men who all asked her for a dance. She explained, shyly, that she'd never danced before and they all claimed they could teach her.

'You go on with Kerry, now,' Jago said, nodding at a fair-haired man of perhaps nineteen. 'I'll find Maya a table and get some drinks. Just enjoy yourself, Julie. I'll be watching.'

Julie took him at his word. When Maya had first suggested going to the dance, Julie had objected, because Jago couldn't take part. 'It wouldn't be fair when he has to sit and watch,' she'd said uncertainly.

'It's what he has done all his life,' Maya told her simply. 'He's used to it – and there is plenty he can do. Don't pity him, Julie. He'd rather you mocked him.'

'I wouldn't do either!' Julie exclaimed. 'I just don't want to hurt him.'

'You can't cure him,' Maya said flatly. 'I doubt anyone can, but he can still enjoy life his own way. There are many things you can share with my son, Julie, but that doesn't mean you should never have the pleasure of dancing. He wouldn't want that – don't you know him at all?'

'I know I like him,' Julie defended herself. 'So, if you're sure, Maya . . . ?'

'It has to be this way or he won't move forward,' Maya said. 'It is for his good as much as yours.'

Julie felt there was a deeper meaning to Maya's words but knew there was no point in persisting. Jago's mother would only say as much as she intended and not a word more.

'You're the girl we found,' the young man said as he led her onto the floor. 'I wasn't one of those that found you but I'm glad you're OK.'

'Thank you,' Julie said, glancing up at him. He had a nice smile, friendly and open, but he wasn't Jago. Her eyes sought Jago but he was at the bar, his back turned to her. 'What sort of dance is this?'

She'd noticed that the men and women were forming into two lines as the music started.

'It's a line dance, just sort of stepping, really. We'll watch for a minute and then join the end, if you like?'

Julie agreed and watched as the dancing started. Everyone was laughing and smiling and the music was catchy, making her feet move in time. She soon saw that the steps were simple and repetitive and was ready to join in. A few steps went wrong and she giggled but everyone nodded at her encouragingly and after a few minutes she was keeping up with the others and enjoying every minute.

It was quite a long dance and when it ended the musicians took a breather and Kerry returned her to Jago and Maya. They had cool drinks waiting and Kerry hung around, as if hoping to take her out again, but another of Jago's men turned up and said it was his turn and Julie went with him. This time it was a progressive and she found herself changing partners several times. All the young men were smiling and asking her questions and it seemed no time at all before she was back at the table with Jago and Maya.

She heard her name called and saw that Beth was leaving and waving at her. Smiling, she waved back and blew the little girl a kiss.

'Miss Vee comes just to be neighbourly,' Maya said. 'She never stops long – but we'll visit her soon, Julie, go over one Sunday . . .'

Julie nodded her agreement. She sat down, hoping to talk to Jago for a while, but another partner turned up and she was back in a line dance that went on for ages. It was only when that dance finally ended that Julie became aware of a noisy crowd at one end of the long barn. She looked towards the source of the noise and saw half a dozen young men standing together. They were hooting and calling out to the girls and she thought they'd been drinking – and then her heart caught as she saw that one of them was Ralph Cotton. Her pleasure in the evening drained away, her face freezing as she saw that he had noticed her. He glared at her across the room and mouthed the words, 'Charity girl,' at her.

Julie turned away, determined not to let him hurt her. Jago was talking to a pretty young woman and a man and Maya had got up and wandered off to speak to some older women. For a moment, Julie felt a little sick, wondering if Ralph would approach her and cause trouble, but he had turned away.

267

'May I have this dance, Julie?' Kerry had returned and Julie smiled up at him, relief making her jump up to take his hand. As he led her onto the dance floor, telling her that this one was a waltz and explaining that all she had to do was to follow his lead, she hoped that Ralph wouldn't cause trouble. She didn't look back or she would have seen Jago's eyes watching her, a slightly wistful expression on his face as she went into the young man's arms.

Kerry was talking, telling her how much he enjoyed his work at the mill and how much he admired Jago. 'You'd think he'd just give orders and take it easy because of his problem,' he told her, 'but he never stops. He's as strong as any of us when it comes to hewing trees and his mind is as sharp as a sawblade – just has a bit of trouble moving around at times. He's a good boss and we all like him.'

'I do, too,' Julie said. 'Jago and Maya have been very good to me.'

'I reckon he thinks the world of—' Whatever Kerry had been going to say was rudely interrupted as his arm was caught and Ralph Cotton tried to pull him away from Julie. 'What do you think you're doing?' Kerry demanded.

'I'm claiming her,' Ralph said drunkenly. 'The little bitch can dance with me. She's danced with everyone else.'

'Keep your hands off her,' Kerry said, his expression going hard. 'She doesn't want to dance with you.'

Julie had shrunk away from Ralph. She could smell the strong drink on his breath and knew that if he got hold of her, he would maul her and say disgusting things to her. 'No, I don't,' she said. 'Not ever – and certainly not when you're drunk.'

'Charity bitch!' Ralph muttered. 'She's a thief and a slut, fit only for—'

'Don't you bad-mouth her!' Kerry said, stepping between them. He was young but a big man and far more muscular than Ralph, but Ralph was drunk and he swung a punch at him, yelling obscenely at Julie and her protector.

Julie was so embarrassed she couldn't move, but in another moment, Jago was there and he had Ralph by his arms, holding them from the back as Ralph tried to fling himself at Kerry.

'Behave!' Jago said in a strong, calm voice. 'This is stupid and Miss Cotton would be ashamed of you.'

'What the hell do you know about it?' Ralph demanded. 'Bloody cripple!' He struggled wildly, but Jago held him as two large men approached. 'Let me go, you bastard! I'll see you pay for assaulting me.'

'Leave this to us, Jago,' one of the men said and they took firm hold of Ralph, lifting him off his feet and carrying him from the barn. The youths he'd come in with laughed and jeered but another man ordered them to leave and after a few insults they did.

'Come and sit down, Julie,' Jago said quietly. 'They'll make sure he can't return. Hank will put him in a cell for a couple of hours and that will sort him out.'

Julie nodded but didn't say anything as she let Jago walk her back to the table. Maya was there and she looked at her face, reaching for her hand to touch it in support.

'Ignore him,' she whispered. 'Don't let him spoil the evening, Julie.'

'No, of course I shan't,' Julie replied, but it was too late. It had already been ruined. Even though she did eventually dance with another two partners, once she'd stopped shaking inside, she didn't truly enjoy it, not as she had before the incident.

It was when they got home that Jago looked at her. 'You shouldn't let the things he said to you upset you,' he said. 'He's a foul-mouthed lout and his father should take a whip to him when he gets back from wherever he is. Besides, it's just words. Words can only hurt you if you let them. Rise above them and they mean nothing.'

Julie nodded. It was what he'd done, she knew. She'd heard what Ralph had called him and it was cruel. 'I hate him,' she said. 'I hate him for the selfish things he does and says. He doesn't care who he hurts.'

Jago looked at her and then a smile lit his eyes. 'Don't worry about what he said to me, Julie. I'm used to it; it's like water off a duck's back. I know what I am and I am not a helpless cripple.'

'No, you aren't,' she agreed. 'You're very strong, aren't you?'

'Stronger than most,' he said. 'If need be, I'd have broken the little runt's neck but Hank was right to let the law take over. Ralph's father would thrash him if he was here – not that the little runt would behave like that if he was. Don't be afraid of him, Julie. Believe me, I would kill him rather than let him harm you.'

'Now that's enough, the pair of you,' Maya cut in. 'Hank will give him a warning – it was good he was there. No more talk of killing, Jago and off to bed with you, Julie. Work doesn't stop tomorrow just because it's Sunday. The animals have to be fed and I need my sleep.'

'Thank you for taking me, Maya,' Julie said. 'And thank you for rescuing me, Jago.'

She turned and went to bed without another word. Jago had rescued her but what must he think of her? Ralph had said such horrid things, calling her all kinds of names. If Jago believed that she'd done those things she would be so ashamed.

No, he wouldn't. She blinked away her tears. He was kind and good and . . . Julie didn't know how she truly felt about the man who had rescued her, not once but twice now. She knew she liked him but were her feelings stronger than just liking? After the things that had happened to her in England and then at Miss Cotton's house, Julie hadn't believed she would ever want to be in love or have a man touch her, but sometimes, when Jago brushed against her hand or touched her arm, she felt a tingling inside, a feeling that she wanted more.

Was she a little in love with him? She sighed as she undressed. He'd never shown any sign of feeling that way about her so she'd best keep her muddled emotions to herself.

CHAPTER 29

Ralph awoke with a sore head. He groaned as the light made him wince. What the hell had he been doing the previous night? For a moment he couldn't recall – and then it all came flooding back. He and some friends had been drinking before they arrived at the dance. It had just been meant as a bit of fun and then he'd seen her, the girl from London, the one he couldn't get out of his head. The charity girl had looked so beautiful and so sure of herself that Ralph had lost his temper.

He'd wanted to dance with her but she didn't want to dance with him and he'd tried to make her. The man she'd been dancing with had tried to stop him but Ralph had just carried on pestering her until his arms had been grabbed from behind. Whoever it was had held him firmly by his upper arms and he was very strong. At first Ralph hadn't realised that it was Jago Marsh, the man he'd always jeered at for his disability but it didn't stop him being strong and that had shocked Ralph. However, it was a couple of off-duty police officers who had removed him from the barn and he'd slept in a cell overnight. Looking about him, he shuddered. What his aunt would have to say about this would be unpleasant to say the least and she would tell his father. He might be able to hoodwink his aunt into believing it was just innocent fun, but not his father. When he got home, he would find a way of punishing Ralph that he wouldn't enjoy – but he wasn't back yet and Ralph would make the most of his freedom until then.

A man unlocked the outer door and entered the cell block. It was occupied by only Ralph and he knew the officer who walked towards him with an air of authority. Hank Wrangler, son-in-law to Selmer Connors, who managed the big clothing store. He looked Ralph up and down in a way that made him squirm.

'Give me one good reason why I shouldn't have you in court for your rowdy behaviour last night, Mr Cotton?' he said in a steely voice. 'You spoiled the dance for a lot of people – including me.'

'It was just a bit of fun,' Ralph said, a little whine in his voice. 'I didn't mean any harm. If that girl had just danced with me, it would have been all right.'

'The things you were saying to her were downright filthy and rude,' Hank told him. 'I've warned you about causing a nuisance before, Mr Cotton. This is your last chance. If I have to arrest you again, I'll be charging you with something that carries a punishment you won't like. Being locked up in my cell is nothing to prison. A lad like you wouldn't last five minutes with the hard men – so be warned.'

'Yes, sir.' Ralph had picked up on Hank's words.

He was going to be let off again, but he'd better be careful for a while and act penitent or he would be in real trouble. If he were sent to prison his father would never forgive him. 'It was the drink talking. I shouldn't have done it.'

'If I were you, I'd send that girl some flowers to say sorry,' Hank told him. 'Folk don't like uncouth men and you'll get a bad reputation if you're not careful.'

Ralph just nodded. He felt resentful at being told what to do and he had no intention of sending that girl flowers or any other kind of gift. It was her fault he was here. One of these days he'd get her alone and then he'd make her pay.

Allowed to leave the police station without further punishment, Ralph hesitated about returning to his aunt's house. She would go on at him for ages when he had to explain what had happened and he wasn't ready for that. Maybe he would seek out Pete and see if he could give him something for his headache, spruce himself up a bit before he went home. His truck was miles away and his friend would at least give him a lift to where it had been left the previous night before he'd started his drunken spree.

'No, I'm not doing it!' Pete yelled at his father. They were standing outside the house in the back garden and he was glaring his defiance. 'I've had enough of your dirty work. I told you, I like Jago and I'm not setting fire to his yard or doing any more damage up there.'

'I'm not asking you to burn the place down,' Harold muttered. 'And keep your voice down. I don't want the whole neighbourhood to hear. You'll do as you're told, boy, or I'll hand you over to the cops.'

'No, I won't,' Pete said stubbornly. 'I'd rather go to prison for what I did by accident than keep doing things I hate for you.' He faced his father angrily. 'You're a rotten crook and one of these days I'll prove it!'

The blow his father directed at him was enough to send him sprawling to the ground. 'If you threaten me, boy, you'll wish you hadn't. Killing a man by driving over him is a capital offence and you'll end up on death row if you go against me. Don't think that just being my son will save you. If you'd gone to the cops at the start, they might have believed it was an accident but you came running to me, you snivelling little runt.'

Pete lay where he was and tears stained his cheeks. How he hated this man! He wished he could run away and never hear his bullying voice again. If he had the strength he would kill him, but Pete knew he had neither the physical power nor the guts to do it. He wasn't a killer but this man was. Pete was certain of it and his hatred of him was building.

'Now listen to me and listen good,' Harold said in a tone that brooked no defiance. 'What I want you to do isn't up at the lake this time, though you'll do that as well when I tell you. It's a café and a couple of shops. I want a few windows broken, some damage to the doors; do a paint job on them, anything you like. Just make trouble for the bitch.'

Pete got to his feet. His defiance was broken for the moment but it would return and he'd get even. He listened sullenly to his father's instructions for a vindictive attack on the property in Halifax. Someone had thwarted him once too often and this was his petty revenge. Feeling sick with disgust, but knowing that he didn't have much choice unless he wanted more beatings, Pete nodded, giving in to his father one more time.

'Good,' Harold said, satisfied that Pete's show of defiance had ended. 'Behave and maybe there will be something in it for you.'

Pete didn't answer. His father went into the house and Pete stayed in the garden. He was staring moodily at the shed at the bottom when a sibilant whisper made him look towards the shrubbery and then Ralph Cotton poked his head out.

'Has he gone?'

'He will have by now,' Pete replied. 'How did you get there – and how long have you been there?'

'Just a few minutes,' Ralph said coming out of hiding and sauntering towards him. 'I spent the night in the cells. Have you got anything for a headache? My head is splitting.'

Pete looked at him. 'What did you hear?'

'Just some yelling,' Ralph replied. 'And I saw him knock you down. What have you been up to? He looked mighty angry.'

'He's always angry. I hate him,' Pete said.

'I don't much like my father either, he's a skinflint,' Ralph admitted. 'But he doesn't hit me. He looks at me reproachfully and then makes me do things he knows I hate. When he gets back, I'll probably have to work on a building site, carting bricks for the men or mixing cement to teach me what real work is, but he's never hit me like that. Why do you put up with it?'

'Because I need money,' Pete told him.

'I thought your mother's family was the one with the money? I know you don't know where your mother is or you'd go to her, but aren't there any of her relatives you can go to for help?'

Pete shook his head. 'My grandparents are dead and she didn't have any brothers or sisters.'

'That's rotten luck,' Ralph said. 'At least I've got my aunt. She lectures me if I step out of line, but otherwise she's all right. I hoped you might give me a lift. I left my truck up in Lower Sackville last night and I don't have any money.'

Pete nodded. Ralph was a bit stupid and they didn't always get on, but he was one of the few friends he had. 'Come on, I'll get you something for your head and then I'll drive you up to fetch your truck.'

'Thanks – and I'm sorry about your father. He's a bully and that's rotten for you.'

'Yeah,' Pete agreed. 'I'm going to leave as soon as I get some money.'

'I'd do the same in your shoes,' Ralph said. 'If you come back to my aunt's house with me, I can tell her I was ill and spent the night with you and then she'll make us some lunch.'

'OK,' Pete agreed and grinned. 'We might go up to the lake and swim later if it stays warm. Jago won't be there in the afternoon. He makes his rounds in the morning.'

Ralph grinned. 'We could maybe find something to have a lark with too. That would please your old man.'

'What do you mean?' Pete asked, his spine prickling. If Ralph had heard everything his father had said, he might suspect what Pete had done that night and use it against him one day.

'Nothing. Just, you told me he doesn't like Jago because he won't sell.'

Beth was playing with her puppy which was a lively, pretty little thing with shining black fur and curiously light eyes that always looked a little sad. It had rolled onto its back and Beth was tickling its tummy. She'd named the dog well because it seemed to delight in tickling and scratching behind its long ears.

'Shall we take Tickles for a walk later?' Vee suggested and the child looked up with a smile.

'Yes, please,' she said. 'He loves to go for walks. We could walk up to the lake.'

'Yes, though we might go in the car for part of the way and then park it and walk,' Vee agreed. 'We could take a picnic. Do you think Aggie would make us a picnic if we asked her?'

'Oh yes!' Beth clapped her hands in pleasure at the idea. The weather had been warmer of late and they spent as much time as they could outdoors, either in the garden or walking in the countryside that lay beyond Vee's house.

They didn't often go as far as the lakes but the beautiful weather was tempting.

When asked to provide the picnic, Aggie was happy to oblige and said she would come too. 'You'll be able to rest and enjoy yourself if I'm there,' she told Vee firmly. 'Otherwise, you'll be up and down after the dog or the child. Besides, I feel like a little holiday.'

'We're only going for a few hours,' Vee reminded her with a smile. 'But you're more than welcome to come.'

'You know I like a picnic,' Aggie told her. 'I remember when I was young, we had lots of picnics round here and the young men and women made it a special holiday. I packed baskets and shared them with a nice young fellow a few times.'

'I didn't know you had a beau,' Vee said. Even after all the years of knowing her, Aggie could still surprise her.

'He went off to war in 1914 and didn't come back,' Aggie said. 'Don't look like that – I learned to get over it. I had you and Mr Malcom to look after.'

Vee blinked back tears and nodded. Aggie had been a second mother to them, but she wished she'd known about her friend's loss before.

'You still have,' she said, because she couldn't think of anything better. 'You have Beth as well now.'

'That I know,' Aggie said with satisfaction. 'I'll pack us a nice basket, Miss Vee, don't you worry.'

It was pleasant up by the lake as they ate their picnic lunch. The sun was warm and they sat on a blanket and relaxed, enjoying the peace until an hour or two later when the near-silence was broken by the sound of a noisy truck driving up at speed. It spun round in a circle and then two youths got out and raced across the dry earth to the lakeside yelling and shouting at one another. They stripped off and jumped in, splashing and calling out as they swam in the cold waters.

Vee and Beth had paddled at the edge so she knew that even on this sunny day the water was cold. It slightly irritated her that the peace of the afternoon had been shattered but there had never been any bar to folk swimming here if they wished. The woodland and the sawmill were privately owned but the lake was just there for others to use if they wished and sometimes in summer folk swam or took a canoe out on the water.

Jago said not many people came but a few did and Vee's irritation was slight. If this area was opened up to a wider public the way Harold Trevors wanted, then it would constantly be in use. It was only its remoteness and lack of facilities that prevented more using it now.

The boys had quietened now anyway and were lying on the opposite shore in the sun. She and Beth got up and went to paddle again and then she heard another engine and saw Jago's truck enter the lumberyard. He was accompanied by Julie and they got out and went into his office, then after a few minutes they came out and walked towards where she and Beth were paddling in the shallows.

'Lovely afternoon,' Jago said smiling at her. 'Don't often see you up here?'

'We came for a picnic. It is so peaceful most of the time.' Vee looked at Julie, who had sat down next to Beth and was playing a hand game with her. They were laughing and had clearly played the game before; it was probably a favourite from their voyage out.

'Why don't you join us for our picnic? Aggie packed enough for six people.'

'We'd love to another time,' Jago said, 'but Maya is expecting—'

A loud shout of laughter disturbed the peace. Jago's hand went up to his brow and he shadowed his gaze to look across the lake to where the young men had clambered up on a wooden landing stage. They were too far away for him to make their faces out.

'I hope they haven't been annoying you?'

'No, just a bit noisy for a while but they were only having fun. I'm just glad it hasn't been made a commercial area yet.'

'It won't be while I hold the gateway,' Jago promised. 'The lads are welcome to swim providing they do no damage.'

'Well, we're going soon and I haven't seen any attempt at sabotage. Have you had any trouble, Jago?'

'A couple of small things,' he replied with a frown, 'but nothing really bad. I daresay I know who might have caused it, that's why I come up and check twice on a Sunday now. I might have a swim myself later.'

'Well, it's certainly a lovely day for it,' Vee said. She looked at Julie. 'Did you enjoy the dance, Julie?'

Julie nodded but looked to Jago and he replied for her.

'Most of it,' Jago replied. 'There was a bit of bother. There were some rowdy lads and one of them upset her. Hank probably told you?'

'No, I haven't spoken to him, but Selmer rings me most evenings with any news he happens to have.'

'Ah,' Jago said, 'he's a good friend, Miss Vee.'

'Yes, he is,' she replied and smiled. 'Well, Tickles looks as if he's worn out so we'll wend our way home.'

'Glad the dog is working out,' he said and turned away as she called to Beth and walked to join Aggie, who had begun to pack up their things. As she and Aggie stowed everything in the car, she saw the youths had returned to their clothes and were dressing. They got in their truck and drove off. If they'd intended mischief her presence and the arrival of Jago had changed their minds . . .

'No sense in risking anything now,' Pete said as he drove Ralph back to his aunt's house. 'We were seen and they'd blame us for any damage.'

'I thought you said that bloody Jago never came up there in the afternoon?' Ralph muttered his discontent. He was in the mood for causing damage but Pete had insisted it was too dangerous.

'He never used to. Maybe it was because it was warm and he fancied a swim. I'm not risking it anyway. I don't want to go to prison.'

'No . . .' Ralph recalled the warning he'd had from Hank earlier. Another false step and he could find himself in court. Damage to property was a serious offence but he was still seething inside, angry that he'd been made a fool of at the dance, hustled away while that girl stood and gloated and there she was this afternoon, sitting on the grass playing with that kid. Flaunting herself again. 'I don't either, but one of these days . . .' He left the threat open.

Whatever he did to get even, it had to be when he had a chance of getting off scot-free.

CHAPTER 30

'This is good,' Jago said that evening as he ate the beef pie that Julie had cooked for him. 'It's almost as good as Ma's.'

Julie turned to look at him, a question in her eyes. 'Didn't I put enough salt in? What isn't right?' she asked, clearly anxious.

Jago burst into laughter. He saw his mother shake her head at him. 'It's perfect,' he said. 'I just wanted to see your reaction if I criticised. The pie is delicious, Julie. You're a wonderful cook.'

She laughed and threw a dishcloth at him. It was wet and hit him square in the face, making him gasp in surprise. He grabbed it and aimed it back at her but missed. It landed in the sink with a splashing noise.

'Children, children,' Maya scolded. 'If you want to play games go outside before you break something.'

'That's a good idea,' Jago said and stood up. 'Want to go for a walk round the place with me, Julie?'

She hesitated for a moment and then smiled. 'Yes, I'll come. I'll finish the chores later, Maya, if that's all right with you?'

'Why not?' Maya asked with her lazy smile, so like Jago's. 'It's a beautiful night. Enjoy this weather while it lasts.' She waved them away.

Julie dried her hands and went to join Jago. It wasn't the first time they'd walked round the farm just before dusk at night, checking the fields and the animals, the puppy Jago had brought home following at their heels. Sometimes it ran off to explore, snuffling down holes in the ground made by some wild creature and then chased after them, desperate to catch up. The dog – called Goldie, because of its colour – adored Jago and always strained to go with him to work in the mornings but was made to stay on the farm.

'He's to guard you two,' Jago had told them when Julie said he should take the puppy with him. 'He can't do much yet, but he can bark.'

'He certainly knows how to do that,' Julie laughed as Goldie shot off after some birds that had settled on the corn field.

'He's doing his job,' Jago told her. 'Those pesky things will eat their weight in corn if you let them. If I had my way I'd shoot the geese – they make good eating – but Maya won't let me. She says they could be the spirits of my ancestors.'

Julie nodded. Maya believed that spirits of those long dead lived in other creatures and she hated Jago to shoot birds or small animals, unless it was really necessary.

'If we were hungry, I would cook them for you,' she said, 'but I'll not eat them myself. We have the farm animals and the crops . . . it's enough to feed us. We do not need more.'

'They are rather beautiful in flight,' Julie said,

looking up as the geese circled above them once before flying off to find another feeding patch.

'You are beautiful,' Jago said and she looked at him in surprise.

'Don't be daft,' she said, a flush in her cheeks. 'I know I'm not.'

'Have you looked in a mirror lately?'

'To do my hair,' she said and put up a hand defensively to her cheek. Her hair was caught back from her face, scraped into a tight bun, but the profile of her cheek needed no embellishment in his eyes. 'You shouldn't tease me. You're always teasing me . . .'

Suddenly, tears welled in her eyes and she turned away and ran back to the house. Jago stared after her. What had he said? In his opinion she was lovely beyond compare. He was in love with her, had been, he reckoned since the first time he saw her and the more he got to know her, the more he knew she was the only girl for him. But he also knew he couldn't expect her to love him.

Did she think he wanted to harm her, to do things she didn't want without her permission? She was in a difficult position, he knew, his guest and living under his roof. Surely, she couldn't think he was the kind of man who would demand a shameful payment that Jago would never dream of asking. If she loved him he would only wish her to be his wife and lover and he knew that could never be. He'd spoken out of turn, struck suddenly by how beautiful she looked as she watched the wild geese fly.

Should he apologise, try to explain? Perhaps it was just better if he let her go for now. Someone had hurt her in the past – that Ralph Cotton for one, but he thought there was more. Jago would have comforted her if she'd confided in him, told her she was safe with him, but until she learned to trust him, he could say nothing . . .

Julie went straight up to her room. She didn't want to look at Maya or speak to her, because she would see the uncertainty that was pulling at her heart and Julie was afraid to let anyone see that. She didn't know much about love. Yes, Julie had loved her father but he'd been away so often and then he'd died before she could talk to him about the things that troubled her – about her fears. And her mother had been too ill to talk to her daughter about such things when the time came, leaving Julie alone with no one to love her.

How she longed to be loved! Julie dashed away the foolish tears. Her feelings for Jago were so mixed that she didn't know how to handle them or what they meant. Sometimes, she just wanted to fling herself into his arms when he came home at night and tell him how much she'd missed him, but he was always teasing her now. She thought he treated her as a child, a girl he was fond of but that's all. And how could he love her? She was just an evacuee girl who was bad inside. Julie knew she must be bad, because otherwise why would men want to do bad things to her? Her uncle had told her it was her own fault for being so pretty, the man at the orphanage had said the same, and Ralph had told her she begged for it with her eyes.

The memory of her public humiliation by Ralph, who had called her all kinds of filthy names in his drunken rage, had stung and hurt her. She'd felt that everyone would think he was telling the truth and that she was a slut and a whore. But it wasn't true. It wasn't true! She hadn't asked her uncle to touch her and she certainly hadn't invited Ralph Cotton's advances – but perhaps it was because she really was bad, even if she didn't know why.

Now Jago had told her she was beautiful. Julie had deliberately dragged her hair back so that she wouldn't look pretty. She didn't want to make Jago think she was easy and lose his respect and affection. He and Maya had been so kind to her but if she let her hair down and tried to look nice the way she had for the dance, it might give them the wrong idea. And it would break her heart to leave this place of safety. Julie felt settled here with Jago and his mother. She loved them both . . .

A little jolt of something that might have been surprise or fear went through her as she realised the depth of her feelings toward the people who had taken her in. She loved them both – but in very different ways. Maya was like a mother or perhaps a sister, because she never told her what to do, just left her to do what she thought needed doing. It was a good relationship and Julie's spirit had begun to heal in the warmth of her kindness.

But her feelings for Jago . . . Julie felt hot all over as she examined her reaction to his compliment. She'd wanted . . . oh, if he'd asked, she knew she would have gone into his arms, done anything he asked of her. She *was* a wicked girl! Surely it was wrong to have such feelings for a man who surely thought of her as just a child he'd rescued from certain death?

Jago was a good man, not like those others who had wanted to use her. She was wrong to think bad things of him, so it must be because she was bad herself.

Julie cuffed away her tears, washed her face in cold water and went back downstairs. Maya would have done all the chores and that wasn't fair because there was more than enough to keep them both busy – and besides, she'd promised to make Maya a new dress.

Maya had found an old sewing machine in the shed and Jago had oiled the parts and made the treadle work. Now Julie could sew anything she wanted with the lovely cottons that Jago had purchased in town for them. She smiled as she remembered hand-sewing the dresses Miss Cotton had given her to make over – and suddenly her heart stilled. Would Ralph Cotton tell his aunt that she was back? Would she come looking for Julie and make her leave this place where she had found happiness and love?

She couldn't bear it if she was made to return to Miss Cotton now. She didn't mind working at the school but to live in that cold house without the laughter and warmth she'd found here would destroy her. Perhaps she ought to leave and go right away? She had a little money, some she had earned and some Jago had given her to spend in the store. She'd bought some chocolate for Maya and some humbugs for him, but she'd kept the rest. If she got on a train or a bus and went miles away Miss Cotton and her despicable nephew wouldn't ever find her. And yet . . . And yet, she wanted to stay here with Jago and Maya, even if he didn't love her the way she loved him. He couldn't, could he? If he did, he would surely have told her. Julie had been living here for months now. The cold weather had gone and the trees were garlanded with green and wild flowers bloomed in the wilderness that surrounded the farmed land.

Gorgeous birds flitted in and out of the trees that bordered Jago's farm and little furry animals popped out of burrows deep in the ground – he called them groundhogs and said they were good to eat.

'We don't eat them, because they're wild and Maya won't,' he'd told Julie, 'but most folk do around here. Maya would never forgive me if I killed a creature for no reason.'

'She truly believes the spirits of her ancestors are in living creatures, doesn't she?'

'Yes,' he'd said and smiled at her. 'I'm not sure where that comes from – perhaps her people on her mother's side, the people who were here before the outsiders came.'

'Yes, I know,' Julie had nodded her understanding. 'Most of the people who live here are outsiders to your mother, aren't they?'

'My father was but she fell in love so she married him and her mother's folk refused to speak to her again. Many of them died a while back of a disease that went through their village like wildfire, killing young and old. Maya would probably have died if she hadn't been on the farm. She still reveres their spirits and I think she takes gifts to her special place for them.'

'I've seen her go into the woods carrying things.' Julie had been wide-eyed with wonder. 'Do you believe in the spirits, Jago, or are you a Christian?'

'I was brought up as one, my father saw to that, and Maya goes to church. She doesn't worship old gods, just remembers and respects her spirits.' He'd grinned at her then. 'I rarely go to church but I believe in being decent and honest and helping folk where I can. I find solace in the woods, but I'm not sure I believe in God or gods, just life and living it well.'

'I'm not sure either,' Julie had told him. If there was a God, why hadn't He helped her? Yet, when she thought about it, she realised that someone *had* been looking out for her. She'd been brought to this beautiful country and though at first her life hadn't been good, she had discovered the lake and found peace there – and Jago. Julie thought now that from the first she'd known instinctively that he was different to most men she'd ever met, that his spirit was at peace. Now where had that come from?

Julie shook her head. There was an inner peace and strength to Jago, which was surprising given all that he'd had to put up with – the pain and nuisance of his foot that brought him jeering and cruel taunts from others at school. Somehow he'd overcome that and become a strong man, still affected by his foot but perhaps stronger because of it.

She had admired him but over the weeks and months her feelings had changed, becoming this tumultuous uncertainty inside her. She loved and yet she feared to love all at the same time.

A sigh left her lips as she went back into the kitchen. It was foolish to torment herself. Jago and Maya were her friends and she could ask for nothing more, but perhaps when Maya's dress was made she would think about going away . . . it might be best rather than letting Jago discover the truth about her wickedness.

CHAPTER 31

Ralph watched the little scene unfold between that damned Jago Marsh and the girl he wanted to punish from the shadow of the forest. It wasn't the first time he'd spied on them. The little bitch was flaunting herself as usual, flirting with Jago with every movement of her head and her body. The thought of that slender body lying pale and naked beneath him made his groins ache with his need. He would have her – oh, how he would have her before he beat her lifeless!

Licking his lips, he imagined all that he would do as he held her down and then he frowned. She would struggle and fight and she was strong – stronger than he'd first thought looking at her. If she fought too hard, he might not get his way with her. He could hit her and punch her in the stomach and she would go down, but he wanted her conscious as he took her. He wanted to hear her cries of protest turn to moans as he ploughed her and hoped that she would beg him . . . No, he needed help to make sure he got his way.

Turning aside when she ran back to the house, Ralph scowled. Who would he ask to hold her down for him? The lads he'd once suggested something to had laughed and said they would help as long as they got their turn and that had made him hold back because he didn't want to share her. He was certain Jago hadn't had her – what girl would willingly lie with him? And he hadn't forced her or she wouldn't be looking at him so invitingly.

There was only one friend he could really trust, Ralph realised. Pete would have helped him once upon a time – not that he'd ever attempted rape before – but he'd helped him seduce girls who were too innocent to know what was happening until it was over. The girl at school, the girl who was the reason he and Pete had been expelled, had got frightened at the last moment and cried to him to stop, but he hadn't, of course.

Ralph shrugged the memory of his dismissal from school from his mind. He had to get Pete to help him, and although they'd fallen out again after their swim Ralph knew something that would help Pete blackmail his father. He knew that his friend hated his father and he understood his need to get away and that he needed money to do so. Well, Ralph knew something that would make Harold Trevors pay good money.

He'd heard a lot of what they were saying as he hid in their garden. He'd already known Harold Trevors' secret but hadn't realised that Pete didn't know the real story and was accepting the blame for something that bastard his father had done.

Even Ralph was shocked at the depth to which Harold Trevors could sink. He'd been blackmailing his son for a crime he'd committed, forcing him to do things he didn't want to do. Ralph smiled unpleasantly. No matter the arguments he had with Pete, he liked him all right and he didn't like Harold Trevors. He wouldn't hesitate to turn the tables on him and make him pay. Oh, he'd pay all right when Ralph told Pete the truth.

Pay enough for them both to go off and have a good time. And they could make him do it again and again. He gave a high-pitched giggle at the thought. It was easy money and his good luck that he'd seen Harold Trevors driving his son's truck at that man – the man he'd left dying in the gutter. That had been no accident and Ralph had felt shocked at the time, but not shocked enough to report it to the authorities. Oh no. He'd hugged his secret to himself, certain that it would come in useful one day.

Should he tell Pete and make him grateful to him or should he keep it as a bribe to force him to help subdue the girl? Or should he go back to the louts who had demanded a share of the spoils?

At the back of his mind the warning from Hank Wrangler still lingered. Ralph had to make certain he wouldn't get caught or he might be the one going to prison rather than Harold Trevors. But it rankled that the charity girl smiled at Jago Marsh the way Ralph wanted her to smile at him.

What could she see in a man like that? He scowled and all softer thoughts fled. She was just a little charity girl and he'd get even, if it was the last thing he did . . .

Jago stood looking at the sky as the light began to fade. He hadn't followed Julie or apologised for upsetting her, although he'd wanted to. He longed to take her in his arms, tell her he was sorry and would never hurt her, but of course he didn't have the right to love her or to expect her to love him.

All these weeks, he'd hoped she would learn to trust him. No, face the truth! He'd hoped she would learn to love him, though he'd known that was a foolish dream, but the way she'd cried and run away had stung him. Was he so repulsive to her that she couldn't bear even a compliment from him?

He must apologise! Even as Jago was about to go back and ask his mother how best to restore the good atmosphere that had existed earlier, he caught sight of a flash of white in the woods. What was that? Not a bird or an animal. Perhaps a man's shirt – but who would be out there at this hour?

'Someone there?' Jago called, the back of his neck prickling. He set off towards the woods, determined to discover who was watching them, but even without seeing him, Jago had a good idea of who it might be . . . yet what could he want?

Jago was certain of only one thing. If Ralph Cotton was lingering in the woods he was up to no good. If he could catch him, he would put fear into the lad, but it was unlikely he would be able to; despite all the things he'd trained himself to do, building his strength by exercise and determination, he still couldn't run or walk fast, so whoever had been watching them was almost certain to get away. If Jago'd had his gun, he would have fired in the air as a warning, but he seldom used or carried it.

Realising he wasn't going to catch up, Jago stopped.

'I know who you are,' he called out. 'If you want to speak to me, come to the house. But if you cause harm to my family – and that includes Julie – you'll regret it. So be warned!'

Jago couldn't know for sure that it had been Ralph or even that he'd really seen a man's shirt, just that flash of white, but it was the best he could do and with luck any intruder would have been frightened away.

CHAPTER 32

It was late when Jago got back and both Maya and Julie had gone to bed. The fire had been banked for the night, which had grown colder now that the sun had gone. Maya had heated several kettles of water and brought in the tin bath from its place on the lean-to wall out back. He smiled and began to strip off his things. Having a bath in front of the warm range was a pleasure he indulged in less these days, because it was normally late when the women went to bed.

Easing the boot from his misshapen foot, he cursed it for aching and making him too slow to catch up with whoever had been watching in the woods.

Absent-mindedly rubbing his foot to ease the ache that came whenever he pushed himself too hard, Jago sat for a few moments, half-dressed, pouring kettles of hot water into the bath and tempering it with a jug of cold water. The cold water was faintly scented with the herbs Maya had put into it. They helped to ease his aching, though he had no idea why they should, but his mother understood them and used them in many ways.

The water just right, Jago eased himself into the bath and relaxed. It was pleasant just to lie and let the warmth surround him, allowing it to take away the strain and make him feel good. In water he was whole. When he swam in the lake, as he did when no one else was around to see, he was as swift as any man, his foot no longer dragging him back.

His eyes were closed as he relaxed, drifting away in the pleasant warmth, when he became aware that someone had entered the kitchen softly, smelling of a sweet herby scent he associated with his mother. Hands touched the back of his neck and he sat forward as she began to wash it for him with the soap that lay on the stool beside the bath together with flannel and towel. She'd done it so often in the past, never saying much, just her soothing touch helping him. Yet there was something different . . . Jerking his head round, eyes wide open now, Jago muttered a startled oath as he saw that it was Julie who had begun to softly massage the back of his neck. His oath made her draw back uncertainly.

'I didn't mean to startle you,' she said looking nervous. 'I used to wash my father's back and I wanted to do something nice for you, to make up for being foolish earlier.'

'You didn't startle me – at least, only for a moment. I thought it was Maya and I didn't mean to swear. Please forgive me.'

'Of course I do,' she said and smiled in a way that made Jago's heart stop and then race on. 'I would forgive you most things, Jago. I-I think you are my friend.' Her eyes looked into his steadily. 'I'm sorry I ran away earlier. For a moment I thought . . .'

'You thought I might try what that rotten devil Ralph Cotton tried?' Jago felt hurt that she could think it of him but understood. 'You've been hurt and abused and I can't blame you if you don't trust anyone, but I hoped you knew that *I* would never hurt you.'

She hesitated a moment, then, 'I do know. That isn't why I was upset.'

'Why then?' He was bewildered.

'It was partly because of him, the things he said and did, but he wasn't the only one who did things . . . h-horrible things,' Julie confessed. She was kneeling by the bath now, her eyes never leaving his face. 'I want to tell you, Jago. I couldn't ever tell anyone before but I will tell you. When I was thirteen, my uncle started creeping into my room at night. At first it was a game and I didn't understand when he touched me and said all uncles did it, but then he wanted me to do more and I couldn't. He frightened me and I said I would scream for my father . . .' Julie's eyes filled with tears. 'He said that he was paying for my mother's doctors and if I didn't let him do what he wanted he wouldn't do so anymore. I started to sob and he touched me again and – I bit him, I couldn't help it, and he went away then but he said if I didn't let him do what he wanted the next time, I'd be sorry . . .' She gulped back a sob. 'I didn't know what to do and then my mother became much worse and was taken into a hospital, and my uncle stopped coming, because I went to live with a neighbour for a while. And I didn't see my father much and then he went to war and was killed and I was sent to an orphanage. A-and there was a man there who looked at me and

said things that frightened me so I ran back home . . .'
She bent her head, covering her face. 'It must be me,
Jago, I must be bad or men wouldn't do things like
that to me!'

'No, Julie. You're not bad. Your uncle was evil and
Ralph Cotton is a spiteful idiot, but you – you're
lovely, inside and out.'

Julie swallowed back her tears, her eyes beseeching.
'Do you really think so? You don't think it was my
fault, that I'm w-wanton and all those nasty names
Ralph called me?'

'I know you're not,' Jago told her. 'You're innocent
and sweet and – oh God, I could thrash all the people
who hurt you. *They* are the evil ones, not you.'

The tears were trickling down Julie's face as Jago
reached out and put his hands about her face, holding
her gently and looking into her eyes. He kissed her
softly on the lips just once and then sat back.

'I love you,' he said, his gaze linked to hers. 'I would
never want to hurt you, Julie. If I was a normal man,
I would ask you to wed me and be my wife, but I
know you couldn't love a man like me. I will always
be your friend and look out for you, protect you until
you find someone you can love and trust . . .'

Julie hesitated and then reached towards him, kissing
him firmly on the lips. 'I don't care that you walk with
a limp,' she told him. 'I've seen your foot and it doesn't
scare me – I'm just sad that you've been made to feel
it's so bad that you think no one would wish to marry
you. Because I will if you ask me. I think I love you,
Jago, though I don't know much about love except what
I've learned in this house. I know I am happy here.'

'You've seen my foot?' he asked, looking at her. 'Tonight, when I was sitting here?' His eyes were intent on her face.

'No, when you swam in the lake last year. I saw you dive in and swim across it and back and I watched you get out and dress.' She raised her eyes to his. 'I saw you several times at the lake when you didn't see me.'

'Why did you never speak to me until the day I gave you a lift?' he asked in wonder.

'Because I didn't know you and men frighten me. I thought you looked nice and I liked the way you went round checking on things on a Sunday when no one else was there – but I didn't *know* you. It was only when I knew you that I was able to trust you.'

'And you trust me now?' he asked.

'I wouldn't have come to wash your back if I didn't,' she replied and her smile was a little wicked. 'I thought and thought, Jago, and I realised that I had to stop being afraid if I wanted to be with you – and I do. I want that more than I can tell you.' She gave him a shy smile.

Jago laughed. His heart was bursting with love for her and it was taking all his strength of will not to leap out of the bath and embrace her but he was damned if he was going to propose to the girl he loved, naked and slippery with soap.

'I'm not sure I trust myself right now,' he said and chuckled as his body reacted to the touch of her hands as she resumed her washing of his back and shoulders, her fingers working the skin in a way that made him think of things he'd like to do in return. But he wouldn't, not until his ring was safely on her finger and she was ready to be his wife. 'I think I'm clean enough now. Hand me the towel and turn your back, I'm going to get out.'

'I've seen you get out of the lake,' Julie reminded him impishly but turned her back as he asked. Jago rose and wrapped it about his waist, before stepping out onto the peg rug before the fire. Julie turned towards him with another towel in her hands. 'Sit down and let me dry your feet . . .'

Jago hesitated and then did as she asked. She wanted to show him that she had no feelings of revulsion as she softly dried first his misshapen foot and then the other and sat back on her heels looking up at him.

'I want you to be my wife,' he told her softly. 'But this isn't the time or the place to ask, dearest girl. You are still very young so we need to wait a while anyway, but I'm glad we've talked. Thank you for coming to me – and for telling me your story. I knew something had hurt you deeply but I didn't know what. I know I'm not like other men—'

'You are different to most others I've met – in a good way,' Julie told him, gazing up at him with sweet innocence. 'You are worth ten of men like Ralph Cotton and a hundred times more than my uncle. Be proud, Jago. You are beautiful – your body is beautiful, like that of a young Greek god that I saw in a book once.'

Jago threw back his head and laughed long and loudly. Sheer joy coursed through him. She was the beautiful one but she didn't know it. He would show her how lovely she was, this wonderful girl who had given him the precious gift of her love. He would teach her to love softly and gently, coaxing her like a frightened wild animal. Nothing should harm her. Although Jago was not a rich man, he believed that he would do well and he would give anything he had to this girl he loved so much it hurt.

'Go back to bed now, Julie,' he said softly. 'We have lots of time to fall in love, for courtship. We'll spend the summer really getting to know each other and enjoying ourselves.'

'Yes, I'll go,' she agreed. 'I'll leave you to sleep. You have to be up early for work.'

'I intend to work for us now,' he said. 'I'll build us a splendid cabin by the lake and make it a palace for you. It will be for us when we marry.'

'What of Maya?'

'She wants to stay here. She'll have a girl to help her as well as a man to do the heavy chores. I'll see to that.'

Julie nodded. 'You don't have to build something special for me,' she told him. 'I love it here and I love Maya too.' She smiled up at him. 'I know I'm young but Maya told me she was only sixteen when she married your father and she will teach me all I need to know about being a good wife.'

'Good. Maya is a wise woman and loyal. I'll teach you to drive and you can visit with her as often as you like, but she would expect us to have our own home. I've already found the right place and started to clear it . . .'

CHAPTER 33

'You've been avoiding me,' Ralph accused as he caught Pete's arm a few days later when they passed each other in the street. 'Why?'

'I've been busy,' Pete told him. 'It wasn't deliberate. Do you want some coffee? Come back to mine. There's no one around. He's gone off on business and won't be back until late. I've got plenty of food.'

'All right,' Ralph agreed, pleased. 'I've got something I might tell you if you help me.'

'That's blackmail,' Pete protested, laughing. 'My truck's over there – where's yours?'

'Parked down the street. We'll take yours if you like.'

They climbed into Pete's truck and Ralph offered him a cigarette. Both of them lit up and then Pete drew away from the kerb, checking carefully in his mirrors and double-checking.

'Why do you check three times?' Ralph asked. 'Not afraid you'll hit someone, are you?'

'No, of course not. Why would I be?' Pete said but looked uncomfortable. Ralph knew in that moment that he was right. He weighed it over in his mind and then decided he would tell his friend the truth. He would try to make him promise to help him, but even if he didn't, Pete ought to know what his father had done. Ralph didn't have many friends and Pete was definitely the best of them.

When they were in the Trevorses' house, Ralph looked around. It was a big house but didn't feel like a real home and something about it made Ralph's flesh creep.

'Have you got a radio?' he asked and Pete nodded, indicating the Bakelite set on the kitchen dresser. 'Let's liven things up a bit!'

He switched on and the lively sounds of the Glen Miller orchestra came over the airwaves. 'That's better – it's a bit spooky in here.'

'Yeah, I know,' Pete said, looking in the big refrigerator. 'I could grill some steaks if you want and fries?'

'Haven't you got any cake or chocolate?'

'Sure, if you prefer that.'

'We can eat proper food out, why work for it?' Ralph said. 'Is there any beer?'

'You can have beer. I'll stick to coffee.'

'Afraid of getting drunk?' Ralph looked at him and laughed in triumph, forgetting that he'd meant to use his knowledge to make Pete help him. 'You didn't kill that man, you know,' he said. 'Your father did. I saw him!'

'What are you talking about?' Pete's face had gone chalk white.

'Your father was driving your truck, must have taken it after you got home for some reason, and he drove straight at him, Pete. Yeah, I'd had a lot to drink myself but I slept it off on a bench and woke in the early hours. I was sitting there with a splitting head when I saw it happen. This guy was walking along the pavement, staggering a bit. Your father drove up onto the pavement and knocked him into the gutter – and then he backed over him before he drove off. He let you think it was you so he could make you do what he wants.'

For several seconds Pete looked horrified and then he nodded. 'You're not making it up, are you? *He* did it and all the time he let me believe . . . The bastard! How could he let me think I'd done it?' Pete turned away hurriedly and vomited in the kitchen sink. He leaned over it weakly for a few minutes before turning on the tap to clear away the brown liquid he'd brought up. 'The rotten devil,' he said, quieter now.

'Now I've told you, you've got to do something for me.'

Raising his gaze to Ralph, Pete looked him in the eyes. 'What do you want from me?'

'I want you to help me teach that bitch Julie Miller a lesson,' Ralph said. 'Just help me get her down and hold her. You don't have to do anything. I'll do what's necessary.' He laughed. 'I know she's living with that Jago Marsh, the little tramp. A bloody cripple! I'll show her what a real man can do.'

Pete looked at him in silence for a few minutes and then nodded. 'When?' he asked and Ralph explained his plan. 'OK,' Pete said, 'now let's get drunk. I know where he keeps the best whiskey . . .'

After Ralph had gone, Pete took a cold bath to sober himself up. They'd drunk a bottle of Harold's whiskey between them and then Ralph had been sick and gone off to catch the bus. He'd said his aunt would be angry if he didn't turn up. Pete had been glad to see him go. He'd agreed to Ralph's plan just to get rid of him, but he had no intention of helping him rape that girl. He was finished with Ralph, finished with his father, finished with this place. There was a new life somewhere and he meant to find it.

Ralph had known about his father's actions all this time so why wait until now? Because he wanted Pete to help him do something he didn't have the guts to do alone. Well, he wouldn't and he was sick of them all. He just needed to get away and he'd made up his mind how to obtain what he needed.

When he'd managed to clear his head with a pot of strong coffee, Pete began to think. He wanted to run as far away from his father as he could, but he needed money. Pete hadn't found anything to blackmail his father with; sure, he felt that his mother's body was under the concrete floor in that shed, but though his first wild thoughts had been to take a pickaxe and break up the floor, he'd realised he couldn't face finding her there.

Now that he knew that his father had taken his truck and deliberately knocked down and killed a man, Pete was certain that he had also killed Pete's mother. His f— No, he wouldn't call him father anymore. He was Harold, a man he despised. The thought of what Harold had done made him want to vomit again but there was nothing left in his stomach to bring up. His guts still twisted with pain, grief and disgust. He had to leave and he needed money for that, and he knew there were some valuable items lying around in his mother's room which he hadn't dared take before.

She would want him to have them, wouldn't she? He didn't like the idea of stealing her things and tried to think what else he could take. There were still some drawers he hadn't searched in his father's desk because they were locked and he hadn't been able to find the key, had been afraid to smash the wood because of his father's anger, but now it no longer mattered.

He found a strong screwdriver and a hammer and marched into his father's study with what had been one of his mother's shopping bags. Into it he placed a silver cigarette box and a silver paper knife from the desktop, also a little bronze statue of a naked lady with long hair. They would be worth a few dollars but not enough for what he needed. In one of the open drawers he found a gold cigarette lighter and a pair of gold cufflinks, also a gold and diamond tiepin.

The third drawer down was locked. Pete took the screwdriver and hammer and attacked the lock. It took some strength and several minutes but eventually the wood splintered and he was able to pull the drawer open. He saw a little black notebook that was well worn. Opening it, he discovered page after page of figures . . . money loaned and repaid, part of Harold's dirty little business. He would look at that closely later, Pete thought as he slipped it into the bag with the other things he was stealing from his father. No, *Harold*. He didn't have a father.

There were other papers in the desk and a leather jewel case. When he lifted the lid, he saw what he thought must be a diamond necklace. He wondered briefly what it was doing in the drawer but placed it with the rest of his loot and broke the lock on the bottom drawer. Inside he saw a large black cashbox and pounced on it with glee. To his surprise it wasn't locked and he opened it eagerly. The contents made him gasp.

There were piles of money in the box; rings with huge diamonds and other precious jewels; and heavy gold chains lay side by side with ropes of pearls and yet more diamonds.

Why would Harold hoard such things? Surely, he had no use for them? Was he handling stolen goods? No, these must be items lodged with him for surety against the repayment of a loan. Pete had no time to stop and count the money but it was mostly in big bills and must run into thousands.

Tipping it all into his bag, he raced upstairs to his mother's bedroom; fumbling with the key he let himself in and began to help himself to the precious things she'd left behind. Some of them he might sell if he needed to, but others he would keep. They were surely his by right and she would have wanted Pete to have them rather than her murderer.

After he'd taken everything that he could reasonably carry, Pete went to his own room and packed the clothes he needed and a few items his mother had given him. He carried them down to his truck, glancing at the clock. Had he got time to get more? Harold could be back at any time now. No, he had enough, more than enough to get himself to somewhere Harold would never find him.

As he started the truck and drove off, he began to

smile. There was one place he might go that he was sure Harold didn't know of, a place his mother had told him about but it might be difficult to get there because it was in England.

Suddenly, it came to him. He would get to England and join the forces fighting the war that was raging right now. He could put what he had safely in a bank in England and join the army. He wouldn't be the first Canadian to do that and Harold would never think of looking for him there. Pete knew he had relatives on his mother's side in a place called Cambridge. He would find them and, if he liked them, make a home near them. No one need ever know what he'd done here in Canada.

As he drove away, he felt a weight lift from his shoulders. He was free of Harold's domination at last, free to begin another life. His one regret was that Harold had got away with murder. Yet there might be a way to make sure he was punished . . . Pete smiled. There was no guarantee it would work but it might . . .

Harold saw his son's truck had gone when he got back late that night, tired and angry. He'd been given a valuable diamond and ruby necklace as surety against a loan three years ago by a woman he'd believed respectable and honest. She'd told him she needed money but didn't want her husband to know and Harold had made the loan in good faith, expecting her to repay at a reasonable rate of interest. But she hadn't paid him a penny! Scowling, he went into his study. He'd taken the necklace to his usual buyer only to learn that it was a fake. He'd been played for a sucker because he'd thought the woman honest. By God, she'd be sorry by the time he'd finished with her!

Then, as Harold saw the ruin of his beautiful antique desk, his jaw dropped. Two locks had been splintered and, as he rushed to check, he knew that everything of value had gone. He'd had nearly twelve thousand dollars in the bottom drawer along with a fortune in gems lodged with him against loans by various clients and some of them were regular payers and would want their property. He'd been robbed – and he couldn't go to the law and tell them of his loss because his loan business was unofficial and fell short of the law in many ways, so he'd never paid a cent in tax on any of his profits from it. The last thing Harold wanted was a nosy cop poking around in his affairs. Yes, he had lost a small fortune but he could lose a lot more because he'd never fully declared his income, which was why he didn't flaunt his personal wealth. His car was a modest sedan and a lot of the property he owned hadn't been declared.

Cursing, Harold went upstairs. The door of Helen's room was wide open, the key still in the lock. That made him frown. Where had that come from? He'd thought he had the only key. Entering, a shudder went through him. He didn't like to think of that night. Harold hadn't meant to kill his wife, just to teach her who was the master. He shook his head. The bitch deserved it!

A quick glance told him all he needed to know. Everything of value had gone. A grim expression settled on his harsh face as he went down the hall to Pete's

310

bedroom. Someone had been in a hurry here too and the drawers and wardrobe had been left open. A few things he knew Pete prized had gone so he had his answer: the little runt had robbed him of everything he could lay his hands on and scarpered.

He'd kill him when he found him! Pete would wish he'd never been born when Harold was done with him.

It was only when he returned to the study that he realised the black book had gone too. Of all that he'd lost, that scared him the most. In it was a record of all the loans he'd made over the years, to whom, how much, interest, balances – the lot! Without it, he had no idea who owed him what; worse than that, it would cause him a lot of trouble if it fell into the wrong hands.

Pete wouldn't do that! He'd taken what he could and run but surely he wouldn't send that book to the law?

Harold could imagine what Hank Wrangler would do if he got his hands on it. He'd warned Harold off from upsetting Vee Bittern. If it were not for his inter-ference, she would have had a few frights in the night before this and the slight damage he'd forced Pete to carry out at her café was nowhere near enough to satisfy him . . . he was still planning his revenge on her. However, for the moment he was too sickened by what had happened to think about revenge.

Swearing, Harold knew he should have killed him as well as the bitch or had him locked up for knocking that café owner down. Pete would have confessed to it like the fool he was if he hadn't interfered but it had seemed like a good idea at the time to avoid having cops snooping around.

He'd been afraid of what was buried under the foundations of that shed. Was there a smell that trained dogs could pick up? Harold had fancied he could smell rotting flesh a few times and he'd seen flies buzzing around the place on hot days though he'd buried her deep and covered her with concrete. No one could know his wife's body lay there. No one would ever find it unless they dug it up – but why would anyone think of doing so? Everyone believed she'd left him.

Harold went into the kitchen. It smelled of whiskey and vomit and he opened the back door in disgust, looking across the garden to the shed he'd erected with his own hands.

'I'll bet you're laughing now,' he muttered, remembering the mockery in her eyes just before he'd struck her the blow that had sent her crashing against the marble surround in her bathroom. A shudder went through him, as it always did when he thought of that night and the terror that had possessed him as he hid her body until he could dig the foundations of the shed and bury her. It was one of the reasons he didn't employ much help these days. People were nosey and he could never quite believe he'd got away with murder – twice now. Once by accident and the second, well, that had given him pleasure after Andy had told him he wouldn't be paying another cent.

'You're a bloodsucker,' he'd yelled at Harold, no longer afraid. 'You're not getting my café and I've more than repaid the loan. You won't get another cent from me.'

Harold had let him go, but he'd known Andy was half-drunk and would head for his favourite bar so knowing the boy was in bed upstairs, drunk, he'd tracked him in Pete's truck and then killed him, letting Pete think he'd done it by accident. How was he to know the boy would turn on him and do this? He'd always been so easy to subdue with a look or a cuff of the ear, but maybe Harold had pushed him too far when he made him lock that child in a deserted shed . . . or it might have been when he'd knocked him down?

Shrugging, he returned to the study and found a full bottle of whiskey. Tonight, he would drink and forget his problems but tomorrow he would start the search for Helen's son. Harold hadn't squashed him like the insect he was, because he'd been useful, but no longer. If he got his hands on the little runt, he would break his neck.

CHAPTER 34

Vee opened the letter eagerly. It had come from the Red Cross and might have the news she'd been searching for all this time. Scanning the first few lines, she gasped in a mixture of shock and pleasure. It seemed that the girl that Jago had rescued from freezing to death might indeed be the daughter of her husband's cousin. Checking the details over at least three times, Vee nodded her satisfaction. Julie's parents were both dead, though her uncle on her mother's side was still living but in prison.

The letter didn't give details of the uncle's crime, but she frowned. What kind of people had Julie's family been? Bill had always spoken of his cousin as being decent but – no, she mustn't judge. It hardly mattered to her. She liked Julie and wanted to know her better, but even if she hadn't liked her, Vee's duty was clear. Julie owned the property in Upper Sackville that had been left to her father by Vee's husband. She had to tell the girl of her good fortune. There was also money from the rent, which had accumulated to several thousand dollars over the years: for a girl sent out from England as an evacuee it was a fortune. With the money and the property she was a wealthy young woman in her own right.

Smiling to herself, Vee thought that she might visit the family that afternoon to give them the news. Now, Julie could choose what she wanted to do with her life. She would be independent. It was a wonderful gift to give her and Vee was feeling pleased with herself as she got ready.

'I'm not sure what time I'll be home,' she told Aggie as she put on her favourite red jacket and a straw hat over her white linen dress. The afternoon was bright, the sun warm outside. 'You'll collect Beth from school for me, won't you?'

'Of course I will,' Aggie told her. 'Get off and give the young lady the good news, Miss Vee. You won't rest until you've done what's right.'

'You know me too well,' Vee replied with a smile. 'I feel quite excited. It isn't every day you can tell a young girl she is rich. I'm just not sure she will know how to handle the money.'

'Well, you can do that for her until she's older if she wants, but you were perfectly capable of looking after the store when you were not much older than her. If she's been through as much as you think, then it will have made her harder and stronger.'

'I'm not sure,' Vee replied. 'Jago told me her spirit needs to heal.'

'Well, having a bit of money can't hurt, can it?' Aggie said. 'It's in the bank. She doesn't have to spend it all at once.'

Vee shook her head at her. Aggie had no qualms it

seemed, but Vee knew that it would be a big thing for a girl who had previously had nothing to inherit a small fortune. She could help Julie invest wisely if she chose but she wouldn't push her advice on her.

Vee's thoughts were mixed as she headed out to wilder areas of Lower Sackville and the land Jago worked. One day the peaceful atmosphere of both Upper and Lower Sackville would vanish. Tall buildings would fill the skyline as they did in Halifax and the population would double and treble. In a way it was a shame but Bill would say it was progress. He wouldn't have let his woods be decimated, though. She smiled, because she knew Jago felt the same about replanting, keeping the new growth going in perpetuity. It was the reason she'd sold to him. He was like Bill in many ways, with the same honest smile and clear eyes. They could have been related but weren't. It was character more than looks that made them seem similar in her eyes.

She smiled when she saw Jago waiting as she drew up outside the sawmill. She'd rung his office and let him know she was on the way. He would be very surprised when she told them why she'd come but she wouldn't do so until they were all together at the farm . . .

'You can't mean it?' Julie stared at Miss Vee in bewilderment. When Jago told her she wanted to speak to her she'd been apprehensive, and her first thought was of Beth. Was she ill or something? She hadn't even known that she had relations in Canada but Miss Vee said they were related by marriage. 'You're my father's cousin?'

'By marriage. Your father was the son of my husband's mother's sister. They wrote to each other occasionally and Bill left him a property in his will. I did write to him when my husband died and he wrote back once but never said what he wanted to do with the property so I just let it and put the money in the bank. There's nearly two thousand dollars and the property's worth around another thousand, perhaps more if you keep it for a while. You could sell it once the lease ends, relet it or use it yourself.'

Julie caught her breath. It was scary. She didn't know how to take it in or what to think. 'Are you sure it belongs to me now?' she asked, feeling stunned. She looked at Jago for reassurance and he nodded and smiled.

'You're independent now,' he told her. 'You could set up that business you spoke of if you wanted.'

'What kind of business is that?' Vee asked.

'I want to make lovely clothes,' Julie said. 'I'm good at sewing and I thought I might do a bit of dress-making but now I could have sewing machines and employ other girls to help me and . . .' She shook her head in wonder. She could do all kinds of things if she wanted.

'If you made beautiful clothes I could sell them in my store,' Vee told her with a smile. 'You've been left a little fortune, Julie, but if you wanted to work hard, you could turn it into much more. Upper Sackville, where the property is situated, is a quiet area now but it will grow and prosper and you can too. I could help you to get started. There's a bigger market in Halifax – and why not the whole of Canada if your clothes are really beautiful?'

317

'I can't imagine it!' Julie told her. She put a hand to her face. Her heart was racing so hard that she felt it might burst. 'Why are you so kind to me? You hardly know me.'

'You are my family,' Vee said simply. 'Besides, you helped my Beth on the ship and I would like to help you.'

'I loved Beth from the beginning. She was like the little sister I never had.'

'And she loves you,' Vee said. 'She talks of you often . . .' She hesitated, then, 'If you wanted, you could live with me, too, although I know you are well looked after where you are. Beth and I would both like you to visit often, Julie. Come whenever you have time and don't wait for an invitation, please – that applies to you, too.' She smiled at Maya and Jago.

'Thank you, Cousin Vee,' Julie said, using the name the smart lady had told her to use when she arrived. 'It is kind of you to ask me to live with you, but I'd rather stay here, thank you. I *will* visit soon, though.' She looked at Jago shyly and then a smile of pure joy lit her eyes. 'We are to be married – at least . . .' Julie felt herself blushing, because he hadn't actually asked her yet, though he'd promised to.

Vee looked at him, her smile lighting up the angles of her face in delight. 'Now that is wonderful news! I am so pleased for you both. Jago, congratulations. I hope you will both be very happy.'

'I *am* happy,' Julie said and her eyes fixed on Jago. He smiled and nodded but said nothing and she sensed something, a doubt that hadn't been there earlier.

'Well, that was good news for you, child,' Maya spoke for the first time. 'Will you stay for tea, Miss Vee?'

'I'd like to but I must get home for tea with Beth. What I should like is to give a little party for Jago and Julie – and you, Maya. It will only be a small affair but we'll ask Selmer and Hank and a few others. We should celebrate. It isn't every day friends get engaged or married. When is the wedding to be?'

'Not for a bit.' Jago spoke for the first time in a while. 'Julie is still young – and she needs to get used to all this, to make up her mind what she really wants to do. Besides, it will be a few months before I finish building the cabin up near the lake.'

'Ah yes,' Vee nodded at him. 'I'd like to talk to you privately, Jago. I want to discuss something with you. Perhaps on the way back to the sawmill to collect my car . . . ?'

'As you wish,' Jago said. He looked to Julie but she saw reserve in his eyes and wanted to beg him not to go. She had to tell him that she loved him, make him see that the money meant little to her, other than that it would help them as a family and for the future, for their children.

'We'll talk when I get back, Julie,' he said. 'I shan't be long – I need to finish some work, but I'll be home earlier than usual.'

Julie watched him leave. Something was wrong. She could see that Maya felt it too. Rushing to the window Julie waved as he drove off but she wasn't sure that he'd seen her.

'It's a bit of pride, that's all.' Maya's voice from

behind her made Julie look round. 'He thought himself not good enough for you and now you're rich while he still owes a lot to Miss Vee. So he'll feel he's standing in your way unless you take all the opportunities this money gives you.'

'But that's silly and wrong!' Julie cried. 'I didn't ask for it. I don't need much for my business – not the one I want to start. Cousin Vee has more ambition than I have. I don't want to sell my clothes all over the country, just to a few people locally.'

'You don't know what you want until you start,' Maya told her. 'Money has a funny way of changing folk – the more they have the more they want.'

'Then I'll give it away!' Julie said vehemently. 'I love Jago. I want the life he promised.'

Maya smiled. 'You're a good girl, Julie. Don't let my son's foolish pride spoil your pleasure in your gift. I'll talk to him and, in time, his own good sense will realise that it doesn't change anything.'

Julie nodded. 'Do you mind if I go for a walk, Maya? I'd like to be on my own to think for a while.'

'Do whatever you want,' Maya said, 'but be back before Jago gets home. He'll need to talk and it's best he doesn't think you've changed towards him.'

Julie nodded and left, taking her jacket from behind the door. It was still warm out but the evenings could become chilly very quickly. She would walk in the woods for a while where it was so peaceful and quiet and she enjoyed the song of birds she still didn't recognise, though Maya was teaching her. She needed a little time to think things through, but she already knew that what she wanted most was to be with Jago and nothing else really mattered.

Jago drew to a stop close to the sawmill and turned to look at Miss Vee. She had outlined her proposal to him as they drove and he was frowning.

'I can't accept such a gift,' he said firmly. 'We made a bargain, Miss Vee, and I'll pay what I owe just as soon as I'm able, like we agreed. I can't take it for nothing.'

'You're too proud, Jago,' Miss Vee said shaking her head at him but she was smiling. 'In your shoes Bill would have said just the same but I'd really like to forget the loan and just let you have everything. You will be married to my husband's second cousin – and it's likely that Malcolm won't be coming back so she may be my closest blood relative now.'

He glanced at her, sympathy and concern for her in his face. 'You would have heard if his ship had sunk and he'd been lost,' Jago said. 'Don't give up on him, Miss Vee. I thank you deeply for all the kindness you've shown us, but I must refuse your offer.'

'Even if I make it a wedding present?' she said.

'Even then,' he said firmly. 'A nice tea set for Julie will be welcome but I'll stick to my bargain.'

'You have my respect, though I wish you weren't so stubborn,' she replied and then laughed. 'I suppose I should have known better than to offer.'

'You did it because you're you,' he said. 'Are we still friends, Miss Vee?'

'Yes, we are,' she said instantly. 'Always, Jago – and

I am so happy for you and Julie. She is lovely and I don't just mean to look at.'

'She is beautiful,' he agreed. 'I believe she loves me and I'd hoped we could marry in August, after her birthday – but it is only fair to her that we wait a bit longer for the wedding now. She's rich and she could be much richer so she needs to be free to make up her mind.'

Vee looked at him doubtfully. 'Don't cut off your nose to spite your face, Jago. Pride is all very well, but Julie loves you. Don't hurt her by withdrawing just because she has a little money now.'

'It is a great deal of money,' Jago told her, 'and could be much more if she takes your offer of help.'

'I doubt she will,' Vee replied. 'Go home and talk to her, Jago. Take your happiness and never let a little thing like money get in the way.'

He grinned at her then, so much the man she liked and trusted. 'I surely will, Miss Vee. You take care now.'

Vee waved to him and drove away smiling. She was half sorry she'd rushed to tell Julie of her good fortune. It would be sad if it caused Jago to draw back out of pride. Had she made it worse for him by offering to give him the sawmill – or the bit of it he hadn't yet paid for? He was a proud man. She'd known that but she'd wanted him to be on an equal footing with his wife-to-be and without the debt he would have been able to do so much more.

Vee felt tired when she reached the street she lived in, parking and locking her car, too weary to bother with opening her garage. The car wouldn't hurt left in the street for once. She missed Malcolm far more than she'd ever realised she could and her worry for him was constant. She prayed that he was safe and would come home so that she could tell him how grateful she was that he'd brought her Beth. Her life had been empty after Bill's death, but now she had the child and it was so much better. She wanted her brother to share that happiness. Perhaps, when the war was over, she would be able to persuade him to stay home and help her with her little property empire. Together, they could build it up for Beth – and perhaps Julie too.

Her head filled with hopes and dreams for the future, she glanced at the house, noticing that a part of the roof looked as if it needed repair. Vee made a note to ring someone in the morning. She sighed; she would be glad to be in and sitting down with a nice pot of tea – yes, she fancied a cup of tea this evening, though normally she preferred coffee. It would be good to see Beth's little face and hear what she'd been doing at school today.

Busy with thoughts of her daughter and still looking at the damage to the roof, at first, she didn't see the car speeding towards her. When her instincts warned her of danger, she looked round and saw the lights of a car just before it caught her on its bonnet and tossed her high in the air. She was aware of sharp pain as she fell and then everything went black.

Beth had cried for Vee and taken a lot of comforting when she heard that she would have to stay in hospital. It had taken Aggie a long time to comfort her and reassure her that her mother would come back.

'Hank says she has concussion – that means she's in a sort of sleep – and she has some bruises and a broken arm but she was very lucky,' Aggie told the sobbing child. 'It means that your mother will be in hospital for perhaps a week or two and then she'll come home.'

'Promise?' Beth demanded, looking at Aggie in such a way that her heart caught. Knowing that Beth's birth mother had died in a similar accident and that there was a possibility of brain damage and she couldn't be certain, Aggie promised. She had to believe it for her own sake, because the idea of a world that didn't have Miss Vee in it was too awful to contemplate, and for the child's sake, because she would never stop crying otherwise.

'Promise,' she said solemnly, her fingers crossed behind her back. 'You go up to bed like a good girl and say your prayers and I'll bring up a glass of hot cocoa and a chocolate biscuit.'

'Thank you,' Beth said and rushed at her to hug her. 'She's the best mummy in the world. I don't want her to die like my other mummy . . .'

Aggie's eyes filled with tears as she watched Beth run off to say her prayers before climbing into bed. She would do her best for little Beth if the worst happened but she knew she was too old to replace the woman who had taught the child to be happy again.

She sighed as she set about making the cocoa. If only Mr Malcolm was home! He would know what to do. She'd known, of course, that the driver of the car hadn't stopped and Hank had told her that witnesses seemed to believe it might have been deliberate.

'We know who that was then,' Aggie had said. 'He hates Miss Vee, always has and I believe it was him that had Beth taken off. The broken windows at the café were down to him, too, even if he did have proof that he was at a business dinner. I know it and so does Miss Vee.'

Hank had agreed. 'I couldn't prove any of it so I couldn't arrest him – but if he is the one who deliberately knocked Miss Vee down, he has gone too far and I'll get him this time. I give you my word – he won't get away from me.'

Aggie had managed a chuckle. 'Like the Mounties – they always get their man.'

'Something like that,' Hank agreed. 'And I had an interesting letter this morning so Mr Harold Trevors would have been getting a little visit later this evening anyway. Meantime, you take good care to lock up tonight, Aggie, and I'll let you know if there's any news.'

Sighing, Aggie carried the tray up to Beth's room. The little girl was still on her knees and praying hard. A smile touched the old woman's face. If the prayers of an innocent child could help, Miss Vee was certain to recover.

CHAPTER 35

Julie was back home before dusk, arriving just as Jago drew up in his truck. He smiled at her and she waited for him to get out and come to her. When he did, she moved towards him and kissed him on the lips.

'I love you,' she said. 'I don't care about the money, Jago. I want to get married as soon as we possibly can after my birthday. I know you think I'm too young but I don't want to wait.'

'I haven't asked you yet!' he said and then laughed. 'It looks as if you just asked me and my answer is yes. I'd be a fool to let pride get in the way, Julie. For a few minutes I felt it would be wrong to take advantage because you are young, beautiful and rich – but then Miss Vee made me an offer that I turned down . . . She's a wise woman, though, and I got to thinking. I reckon love is more important than anything. I'd marry you tomorrow if we could but we'll wait until the cabin is built, so maybe next spring and it will give you time to decide what you want to do with all that money.'

'I'll start a little business the way I told you,' Julie

replied and hugged his strong arm. He looked down at her, eyebrows raised. 'No, I don't want to be a famous designer and earn thousands of dollars. I just want to be happy and make dresses for my friends and folk I like for a few dollars.'

'Don't decide yet,' he told her. 'I want you to have a good life, Julie. I want you to have pretty clothes and maybe a few diamonds for your finger.'

'A plain gold band like Maya's is what I'd like,' she said. 'One day, perhaps an eternity ring. I saw one once and it was pretty but I don't need lots of gifts, Jago. You and Maya have given me love and I think that is the greatest gift of all, don't you?'

'Surely right,' he agreed. 'Julie, you are as lovely on the inside as outside. I don't know why you want to marry me when you could have almost any man you chose but I'm not going to throw away my luck by being a fool over a bit of money.'

'If you do, I'll hate you,' she declared but there was love in her eyes and he stopped, drawing her in and kissing her in a way that took her breath.

'If you do that often we'll have to get married the day after my birthday!' Julie said, tipping her head to tease him as she gazed up into his face. 'I wasn't sure what love was all about, Jago, but I know now.'

'And I know I'd die if anything happened to you,' Jago murmured huskily. 'I'm going to get you a keeper ring to wear until we're wed – to show the world you're mine, just a plain band with a knot and made of gold or silver. No big diamonds, nothing shiny, just a promise between lovers.'

'That sounds nice,' she said and leaned into him as

he put his arm around her. 'I like my Cousin Vee, Jago. She's a lovely lady – very smart and rich but with a good heart.'

'Yes, she is a good person,' he said. 'She'll give us a party like she said and a nice porcelain tea set for your wedding gift. You'll like using that.'

Julie looked up at him and smiled. She'd had a funny feeling someone had followed her back to the farm that evening. When Jago arrived, she'd felt relieved he was there and had been going to tell him, but she hadn't wanted to spoil things when he'd smiled at her so she'd just kissed him. It was probably her imagination anyway. After all, who would just follow her and not speak? A sudden suspicion crossed her mind, sending a shiver down her spine, but she refused to live her life in fear of Ralph Cotton.

As they went into the warm kitchen that always smelled so fresh, filled with the sweetness of herbs and baking, Maya looked at them, nodded and smiled.

'That's it,' she said. 'Sit down and eat your supper, you two. Julie made that delicious beef stew yesterday and I've added a few bits and pieces to make it tasty for tonight. What did Miss Vee have to say to you, Jago? She doesn't want her money sooner?'

'The opposite,' he replied, washing his hands at the deep sink and then drying them on a clean soft towel. 'She wanted to forgo the debt for the sawmill, offered it as a wedding gift.'

'You refused, of course.' Maya looked approving as he inclined his head. 'I hope you didn't offend her?'

'Of course I didn't. I wouldn't upset Miss Vee for the world,' he said and grinned. 'That looks good,

Maya.' His mother had turned the remains of the previous day's stew into a pie with a golden crust. 'Oh, I'm hungry!' Just as he sat down to eat, he heard the sound of a vehicle draw up in the yard and got up, walking to the window to investigate. 'It's a friend of Hank's . . .'

Jago opened the door to the young officer. 'Have you come on business, Rusty?'

The red-haired man walked in. He looked serious and glanced from Jago to Maya. 'Sort of. Hank didn't want you to learn of it from someone else. We know you how much respect Miss Vee . . .'

Jago's spine prickled. 'Something happened to Miss Vee?'

'She was knocked down by a speeding car this evening. We're pretty sure it was deliberate.'

Maya gave a little gasp and so did Julie. Jago's fists clenched at his sides, his brow darkening. 'She was just here this afternoon,' Maya said. 'She came to tell us some good news for Julie – it seems she is distantly related.'

The officer nodded. 'Yes, she was seen leaving the sawmill this afternoon by some of your men. And a neighbour saw her leave the car parked in the street near her house half an hour or so later. As she got out, she stood looking at something for a second or two and the car drove straight at her and sent her flying. She was lucky not to be killed but they say that she'll be all right, providing that there's no damage to her brain. At the moment she's still unconscious.'

Jago swore and his mother looked at him in surprise. It had seldom happened in her hearing before or in Julie's.

'It has to be him – Harold Trevors – if it was deliberate!' Jago said. He moved towards the door and took down his jacket but Rusty moved smartly in front of him.

'Hank knew you might try to go after him if you heard it was deliberate. He told me to restrain you, if necessary, Jago. You don't have to do anything. Hank has taken some other officers with him and will take Mr Trevors into custody for questioning.' He hesitated, then, 'And not just over that – some other interesting facts have come to our attention . . .'

For a moment Jago hesitated, wanting to thrust the officer aside and go after the man he suspected of harming Miss Vee himself, but the moment passed as he gazed into Rusty's eyes and he hung his jacket back where it had been.

'I hope he resists and you kill him like the rat he is,' Jago muttered but returned to the table. 'We're about to eat – join us if you wish.'

'I'd like to but I have to get back,' Rusty replied. 'Now, don't go doing anything daft the moment my back is turned. We'll make sure he gets what is coming to him this time.' He hesitated, then, 'I shouldn't tell you, but I know you folk won't talk: we received information about him and if what the letter says is true, Harold Trevors will be tried for murder and if the evidence is there he'll be executed for his crimes.'

Jago nodded. 'Your words go no further,' he promised. 'I hope you find what you're looking for.'

'I'll let you know,' Rusty promised. 'See you, Jago – Maya, Miss Julie . . .' He nodded and went out, closing the door behind him.

Jago sat at the table but made no attempt to eat his meal and Maya gave him a sharp look.

'Eat,' she instructed. 'You too, Julie. Then we will all pray together for Miss Vee – but no sense in wasting good food because it won't help her. She's in God's hands.'

Jago looked at his mother. 'If they don't get Harold Trevors for this – and I know he's guilty – I surely will.'

'You just hush,' Maya told him. 'Miss Vee wouldn't want that and you know it. Let the law take its course, Jago.'

'Yes, you must,' Julie added her voice to his mother's plea. 'I know how much you think of her and we must give thanks that she is still alive. Isn't that so, Maya?'

'It is what we will do – but eat your supper first.'

Jago looked at her hard and then inclined his head. She was right and he knew it, but he had never felt this angry in his life.

Jago's mood did not lighten when he heard the next day that Harold Trevors was missing.

'Hank says his place looked as if it had been burgled, drawers were broken open and stuff was taken from his wife's bedroom apparently.'

'So he *has* got away with it!' Jago seethed and Rusty frowned.

'Now, don't go getting foolish ideas. Hank isn't that easily fooled; we're doing a bit of digging and I mean that literally, though I can't tell you the whole story yet.'

'I just want to know you've got him,' Jago muttered.

'The thing is, if his car was stolen along with the other things, we might not be able to pin the deliberate attempt on Miss Vee as being his fault.'

'You mean it could have been someone else driving?' Jago frowned. 'Pete, maybe?'

'His son is also missing but we don't think he had anything to do with this.' Rusty shook his head. 'Hank thinks the anonymous letter he got was from Pete Trevors, which is why he's taking it seriously. Pete was seen leaving Halifax on a ship and his truck was parked at the waterfront, hidden behind a warehouse, and the keys left in. Wherever he's bound he's gone for good and Hank thinks it might have been him that robbed his father. We've got an alert out for Harold Trevors and we're looking for his car.'

Jago looked at him thoughtfully. 'You know he'll wriggle out of this if he can?'

'Surely do,' Rusty replied. 'But we'll get him for something. The evidence is piling up against him and even if it's tax evasion, we'll have him locked up for a long time.'

'He deserves more than that,' Jago said grimly. 'I always thought him too cowardly to actually murder anyone but maybe I was wrong.'

'I should say you underestimated him, as many have before you, and he certainly is a bully – but even a cowardly bully can turn if he's cornered. You just remember that, Jago. If he should come your way, call us and let us capture him. Don't attempt it yourself.'

Jago looked at him fiercely. 'Give me a badge and I'll shoot him down the instant I see him!'

'Can't do that, though I'd surely like to,' Rusty said with a grin. 'Don't lose faith in us, Jago. We'll get him, I give you my word.'

Jago nodded. 'Good luck – and I appreciate you keeping me in touch.'

'Hank thinks a lot of you,' Rusty confirmed with a smile. 'Oh, I should have told you: there's one bit of good news. Miss Vee has woken up and is making progress. Hank will visit her later today if the doctors allow it.'

'Thank the Lord,' Jago said and meant it. 'Maya will be happy that she's recovering and I certainly am.'

'Hank was relieved, I can tell you, but he isn't letting up. Whoever drove right at her meant her to die and we have to get him, alive or dead.' He touched the gun at his hip. 'Between you and me, I'm with you: unless he surrenders immediately, I'll shoot him where he stands – and I do have a badge. But I have to take him in if he comes quietly.' He grinned at Jago. 'Let's hope he puts up a fight, eh?'

As he waved goodbye to the young officer, Jago was thoughtful. It was surprising that Harold's car hadn't been found yet. Maybe he'd made a run for it and was in another province by now.

Harold's car bore the marks from where he'd hit her. It hadn't been planned but he'd been drinking heavily ever since he'd discovered what Pete had done and his mind had been fuzzy with it. When he saw that damned woman standing by her car in the road he'd just acted on impulse, driving straight into her and then speeding off. Afterwards, he'd been terrified by what he'd done.

When he'd finally stopped, he'd sat shaking for ages, unable to think clearly what to do.

Finally, he'd realised that the police would probably be looking for him. His car might have been recognised and that nosey Hank was gunning for him anyway. He'd been warned about making threats towards Vee Bittern and the first person they would come looking for would be him.

As his head cleared, Harold knew where he would hide his car. He had an empty warehouse on the docks that he'd bought ready for the future when they started to build bigger bridges over to the Upper Sackville area and they'd need it for storage – or maybe the warehouse would have to be knocked down if a bridge was situated where he hoped – but that meant he owned the land and that meant more money.

He scowled as he thought of all the cash he'd had stashed away in case he ever had to make a run for it. For a long time he'd carried the fear that someone would come looking for Helen and discover that she was buried under the shed in his garden. That money was to have been a new start in another country if he had to run but Pete had taken it, every last dollar.

He could hide the car but where could he hide himself? There wasn't much left in the house of portable value, not real money, the kind he needed now. Damn that son of Helen's! He would kill him if he ever got his hands on the brat!

Harold's money was mostly tied up in property and other businesses. He had a few hundred dollars in his personal bank account, but even if he'd had thousands, he couldn't access it. The minute he stepped inside the bank they would be on him and once they got him . . . And what had Pete done with his little black book? Had he realised its significance? Had he handed it in to the police?

Cursing, he drove to the docks, unlocked the warehouse and stored the car inside. He looked around as he pocketed the padlock key. With any luck they would waste days searching for his car and by then he could be far away – yet he probably had just fifty dollars in his wallet. Harold knew a deep cold fear inside. He was a wealthy man but he couldn't touch what was owed him and he didn't know where to go.

His head had begun to ache and he longed for the comfort of his own bed. He saw a bus draw up at a stop close by and started towards it and then stopped in his tracks. They would search the buses and his description would be everywhere. Hank only had to pick up the phone to contact colleagues all over the country.

He might be safer close by, somewhere he could hide out and stand a good chance of not being caught. A smile came to his face as he thought of somewhere. He knew the ferry was due soon. If he could cross over to the Upper Sackville area without being recognised, he had a small empty cottage there he'd been going to spruce up and rent out. If he gave himself a chance to think, he might be able to come up with a way to get enough money to give him a start somewhere else, all he needed was a hundred dollars or so. Now, who kept that kind of money on the premises? It would have to be someone who employed several men – and he knew someone like that. Maybe there wouldn't be as much as a hundred but he would take whatever he could and maybe settle an old score at the same time but he needed to hide out for a few days and hope the search had died down by then.

Blast Pete for taking his money and all those jewels! He wondered briefly where his wife's son had gone but then forgot him. He had to save his own skin now and Pete could go to the devil for all he cared.

Pete stood looking out to sea. He'd managed to get a berth on a ship headed for England and by signing on as crew no one would suspect that he was carrying a fortune in cash and jewels. When he got to England he would sign up for the Royal Air Force, train as a pilot if he could. If not, he would do whatever job they gave him. At last, he would be free of his overbearing father. It would be the start of a new life and one he believed he would enjoy.

He smiled as he thought of the revenge he'd taken before he left Halifax. A large brown envelope was on its way to Hank, the inquisitive officer of the law who had arrested Pete and then let him go a couple of times. Pete knew he wouldn't just ignore the black book he'd sent together with the cryptic message that they should look under the shed if they wanted to catch a murderer by the name of Harold Trevors. That black book was proof of tax evasion and illegal practice at the very least, enough to cause Harold serious trouble, even if they didn't find the body under the shed in the back garden.

Pete wasn't sure how he felt about that. Part of him hoped his mother had got away, but another part of him knew she was there and the thought sickened him. Maybe if he'd been the tough man Harold had wanted him to be he'd have just gone ahead and killed him in revenge, but he wasn't. Pete would rather fly planes over enemy territory than stand up to that bully. He didn't know what he'd find in England, but one thing he knew for sure. He would never return to the land of his birth.

CHAPTER 36

Ralph's aunt had been shocked by the news that Pete had done a bunk and the authorities were looking for his father.

'If the son hadn't gone off, I should have forbidden you to see him, Ralph,' she told her nephew when she heard the news some days after Pete's disappearance. 'He was always a bad influence on you. Well, your father is coming home soon and I want you to promise me you will behave yourself, otherwise I shall have to tell him that I can't manage you and he will be angry. Your father is a busy man, doing important work for the Government now. We cannot let you be associated with people like Pete Trevors and his father. They are saying he is a murderer!'

'Do they know for certain he knocked that woman down?'

'Miss Vee is a lady,' his aunt rebuked. 'I like her and I'm very upset over it. I hope that man goes to prison for a very long time – and he will if the rumours are true.'

'What rumours?' Ralph asked, intrigued.

'Well, someone whispered to me that the police believe he killed his wife and hid her body in the garden somewhere. I've been told they are digging for it now, but don't talk about it, Ralph. We can't be certain.'

Ralph felt hollow inside, his feelings a mixture of anger and regret. Had he told the authorities what he'd witnessed that night he'd seen Harold Trevors knock down and kill a man, Pete might not have run off. Ralph didn't care that a woman had been knocked down and hurt, he cared that his only real friend had gone off. It meant he had no one to help him teach that charity girl a lesson.

'Well, I always thought he was a nasty man,' Miss Cotton said, looking pleased with herself. 'Well, I have to go to work now, what will you do with yourself all day? If I were you, I'd look for a job. Something you might enjoy. If not, your father will find one for you.'

'Thanks for the advice,' Ralph said, deciding to act contrite, though he was still simmering with anger inside. 'You've been good to me, auntie. If I upset you, I'm sorry.'

'That's all right,' she said. 'I think a lot of you, Ralph. I'm just sorry I let you go around with that Trevors boy.'

Ralph thanked her again and after she left he went outside and saw that a pile of wood needed chopping. It was one job he didn't mind doing. He frowned. He would have to work once his father was home, his days of slouching about as he pleased were almost over.

Ralph chopped the logs and replaced the axe in the shed then went out and started his truck. He was bored, angry and defiant. All he could think about was getting even with that girl . . .

Julie decided to go for a walk. She would take her time and go up to the lake, walking through the woods that she now knew so well. This warm spell might not last much longer and then would come autumn when the leaves would change to a kaleidoscope of colours, bright orange, red, dark purple and yellow, before they fell.

'I'll walk up and meet Jago,' she told Maya.

'Yes, do,' Maya agreed. 'This weather will change in a couple of days. I feel it in my bones.'

Julie nodded. She didn't doubt that Maya knew when the weather would change. She was a wise woman and knew many things and Julie truly loved her. Maya had become the mother she'd lost so many years before she actually died, because of her debilitating illness and the bond between them grew stronger every day. Maya talked about her people, the way they'd once lived and their customs and beliefs and Julie was fascinated. Listening to Maya, she was learning so much about the country she now lived in. She gave her a hug before she left and Maya looked into her eyes.

'You are a blessing on us,' she told her. 'Keep safe, my child. Don't linger too long in the woods alone. They haven't caught that man yet.'

'If I see him, I'll run,' Julie said. 'But I'll take one of Jago's walking sticks with me just in case.'

Jago had a variety of walking sticks, though he seldom used one, preferring to make himself walk without their aid, except on very bad days when the pain in his foot troubled him. Choosing a thick, knobbly one, she looked at it in satisfaction. It would hurt if she hit someone with it, enough to make him think twice about attacking her.

She left the house and Maya watched her go. Looking back, Julie saw Jago's mother looked anxious, but surely she wasn't truly worried? Julie walked almost every day alone and no one was ever around and the men who worked in the woods for Jago would protect her, not harm her, she knew that – if she met any, they always touched their foreheads to her and smiled. Everyone knew she lived with Jago and his mother and she'd learned that most folk liked him, liked his honesty and his kindness and his reputation for being a fair man.

Julie walked, alone with her thoughts that were now happier than she had ever thought they could be. She loved and was loved. It was so much more than she'd expected to find when she was sent out to a new life as Miss Cotton's charity girl.

When she first heard the rustling sound behind her, Julie startled and looked over her shoulder. Was she being followed? And if so, by whom? The back of her neck prickled as she recalled Maya's anxiety. She knew Jago's mother had sensed something but had not wanted to speak her fear or place it into Julie's mind.

Was there someone there or was she imagining things?

'I don't know who you are,' she said loudly, clutching Jago's walking stick tightly. 'But I have a weapon to defend myself and there are men working nearby. They'll come if I scream.'

For a moment there was silence and then a man emerged from the shadows. He looked wild and unkempt and it took a while before she realised that she had seen him before. It was Harold Trevors who'd told her to keep the café open for him – and he was wanted for murder. They'd heard the previous evening that a body had been found in his garden under a shed; it was the body of his missing wife, or so everyone was saying. Tests would have to be done and no one could say for certain Trevors had killed her, but why else would she be there? Besides, he had almost killed Miss Vee and he wouldn't be forgiven for that.

'I know you,' she said, trying not to tremble or show fear. 'Come near me and I'll scream.'

He stood for a moment looking at her and she knew that he had been drinking heavily because his eyes looked glazed and dull. As he lurched towards her, she smelled the stink of whiskey on his breath and though he tried to grab her arm she moved back out of reach, brandishing her weapon. If he thought he could bully her, he was mistaken.

'Come here, you bitch!' he muttered thickly. 'I need money and if I've got you that stubborn bugger you're shacking up with will give it to me.'

'I am going to marry Jago,' Julie said proudly, stung by the ugly accusation. 'I'm warning you. Try that again and I'll—'

She didn't have time to finish what she was saying, because he lunged at her, grabbing her around the throat and squeezing so hard that she couldn't breathe. She struggled and tried to hit him with the stick but he held her with one hand on her throat and wrenched the stick from her with the other. Julie could hardly breathe. She felt herself falling into blackness and thought she would die . . . life was so wonderful but it was going to end here. He was going to kill her and she wasn't strong enough to stop him. Her strength was ebbing and she knew he would win. Then, just as suddenly, she was released from his stranglehold and fell to the ground.

Her glazed eyes saw a figure behind Harold Trevors who raised his arm which was holding the stick she'd dropped and he brought it down with such force on the back of Trevors' head that the man crashed to the ground. Julie's terrified gaze flicked to Harold's face and saw his staring eyes.

'Jago . . .' she whispered hoarsely. And then, 'You've killed him.'

'Remember I did it for you. I saved you. You've got to remember and tell them I did it for you!'

Julie couldn't answer. She was lost in a bottomless pit, floating down and down into the blackness. All she could think of was that she needed Jago to find her again or she would die here.

Jago found her later that night. She was still unconscious and he'd returned to the woods to search after Maya came looking for him, worried and fearful because Julie had been gone so long.

'I shouldn't have let her go alone,' she told him, tears on her cheeks. 'I had a feeling but I didn't want to make her afraid of the woods, of her home. She has to live here and so I hesitated. Forgive me, Jago. If she dies it will be my fault.'

'No!' he'd growled harshly. 'Not yours. She wants to live here. She needs to be able to walk alone in these woods and she ought to be safe here. You could not have known.'

Jago had called his men out to search the woods. This time it was his party that found her almost halfway to the sawmill and he carried her back to his home, refusing all offers of help, even though he limped and his foot hurt like hell, his face set like stone. Maya had Julie's bed warmed and ready and her eyes lit with relief as she saw the girl.

'She's been attacked,' she said, as her son laid the girl he loved down. 'But she will live . . .'

'Someone else had been attacked, too,' Jago told her. 'Harold Trevors was lying close by, his head cut open by my walking stick.'

'Julie took it with her, just in case.'

'But it belongs to me.' His voice carried meaning. 'She couldn't have struck the blow that killed him, it would take a man's force – and who is most likely to have done it?'

'No! You were with your men all day,' Maya said, understanding him. 'No one would think—'

'Wouldn't they?' Jago said looking at her bleakly. 'Rusty heard me say I'd kill that devil if I saw him and if he attacked Julie they will all believe I did it. Had I seen him, I might have.'

'You didn't,' his mother said instantly. 'You wouldn't have left her lying there, Jago. You might kill in anger to defend her but you would have brought her home to me at once. I know you would have knocked him down but you wouldn't kill – not that way.'

'You know that and I know that but will the police believe it?'

'They have to,' Maya said, looking at him steadily. 'Otherwise, they would have to hang you for murder.' She shook her head. 'Hank wouldn't allow that, Jago. He knows you.'

'If Julie dies they might as well hang me!'

'She won't,' Maya promised. 'So just don't do anything stupid. Wait here and let them come looking for you and then tell them the truth.'

'What else would I do?' he asked. 'I'm glad that man is dead, Maya, but I wish it hadn't been in my woods and I wish he hadn't harmed Julie – if it *was* him.'

'His is the face I saw in my vision,' Maya told him. 'I think someone saved Julie's life but then got frightened and ran away. Would one of your men have done it?'

'They would have beaten him but not killed him,' Jago said with certainty. 'I don't know who did this but I'm pretty sure it wasn't one of my crew. Something would have been said and I'd have been told she was hurt sooner.'

'Then until the mystery is solved the law will suspect you,' his mother said as she began to bathe and soothe Julie's throat with healing ointments. 'When Julie wakes up, she will tell us the truth.'

'I pray she does,' Jago said grimly. 'And not just for my sake. She's had a rotten life, Maya. It is time she had peace and happiness.'

'And you will give it to her,' Maya confirmed. 'It was why I hesitated over the vision, because I have seen another of you and Julie and your children living happily by the lake.'

'Then I hope that is the one that rings true,' he said and closed his eyes briefly. 'I'm going back to the yard, Maya, and then I'm going to ring Hank and tell him what we found although he probably already knows.'

Ralph crouched in the woods, cowering in fear and shaking. He'd killed a man and he was terrified of the consequences. Yet, when he'd seen Harold Trevors attacking the girl he loved – yes, he loved Julie Miller – the anger that had been simmering in him since he'd heard Pete had gone off had erupted. He'd seen the heavy stick lying on the ground, swooped on it and struck home with all the force of his youth and power.

Vomiting into the ground, now, Ralph tried to bring his shaking limbs under control. Julie had seen his face before she lost consciousness. She knew he had struck the fatal blow, but would she tell the police that?

Why shouldn't she? Ralph knew he had been vile to her, venting his feelings of frustration on her from the start, but he hadn't understood where those feelings came from until he saw that evil man attacking her. Then, in a blinding flash it had come to him.

He loved Julie, wanted her for himself, but he'd been too immature, too stupid to court her. He hadn't understood what his feelings meant, only that he wanted her, was angry when she ignored him and jealous when he saw that she loved Jago.

'Please let her be all right,' Ralph said aloud. It was perhaps the first unselfish thought he'd ever had in his life, but he prayed that she would be well and happy again.

Even if he couldn't have her, he wanted her to live.

CHAPTER 37

Vee opened her eyes and looked around her. Her head still ached slightly but it was good to be alive and she might so easily be dead. She knew exactly who had knocked her down, because she'd seen his wild, staring eyes and the hatred on his face. A little shudder went through her as she thought about that awful moment just before the car struck and her head banged so hard on something that everything went black. She'd thought she was going to die and she had to thank those who called an ambulance and got her to hospital quickly for her life.

Vee sighed. She hadn't been able to remember it all when Hank first came to see her, but she could now. She would have to ring him and tell him that she'd seen Harold Trevors' face as he drove straight at her.

A nurse, seeing she was awake, came to her, smiling. 'Are you feeling a little better, Mrs Bittern?'

'Please, call me Vee,' she told her. 'My head aches still but I'm thinking more clearly now and I need to make a call to the police. I need to speak to—'

'There's an officer sitting outside your room,' the

nurse told her. 'You've been under police protection since you were brought in, so if you feel up to it, I'll ask him to come in.'

'Yes, please do,' Vee said. She put up a hand to her head, which was bandaged. It felt tender and she knew her face would be bruised, but it didn't matter what she looked like. She was alive. She would be able to return to Beth and Aggie soon. Aggie had been in to see her earlier, bringing her a picture the child had drawn for her and telling her that Beth was frightened and missing her.

'Good afternoon,' the young officer standing just inside the door said, bringing Vee's thoughts back to the present. 'You wanted to speak to me, ma'am?'

'Yes. I saw the face of the driver that hit me and can identify him positively as Harold Trevors. I am in no doubt as to who knocked me down – and he did it deliberately.'

He smiled broadly at her. 'That's mighty fine news, ma'am. It will help to convict him. We've already found his car where he hid it and we've been looking for him and he's been found. I can assure you, he won't be a bother to you in future, ma'am. We kept the guard on your room just in case it wasn't him but I reckon we can stop that now you've confirmed it was him knocked you down.'

'Thank you,' Vee said, and relaxed. 'I was a little anxious in case he should try anything further. He meant to kill me and I was afraid for my daughter.'

'We've had a guard on your house too, ma'am. No need to worry anymore. I'm not sure if I should say, but Mr Trevors is dead.'

'Really?' She felt relief and then anxiety. 'What happened to him? Can you tell me?'

The officer looked uncomfortable. 'Now, don't you go worrying your head over things. It will all be sorted out, ma'am.'

'Yes, I'm sure it will be . . . and thank you . . .' Vee sighed and leaned back against the pillows, closing her eyes. She could relax now and concentrate on getting better because the hospital would never allow a young child to visit so she had to convince them she was well enough to go home to Beth.

Her thoughts turned to other things. Jago had refused her gift of the money she had loaned him but she would certainly add Julie to her will. She smiled as she remembered the young girl's lovely smile. Julie would make Jago a good wife and Vee wished them all the happiness in the world. Clearly, she had suffered, before she came out to Canada and for a while it hadn't been much better here, but it would be now. Jago would make certain of that and Vee would help them in any way she could.

Julie had more money than she might ever have expected and there was no reason why she shouldn't have a long and happy life here. Vee was pleased that she had been able to give the girl such news and looked forward to giving them the party she'd promised.

It would be a lovely surprise for her little girl when they met again to learn that the girl she loved like a sister was related to Vee. She would ask Aggie to arrange the party just as soon as she got out of here. In the meantime, she would write Julie a letter telling her how happy she was to have her here in Canada and how much she hoped they would be friends.

Julie received her letter three days later, frowning over it as she handed it to Maya to read. 'Miss Vee's home now and she's invited us to a party to celebrate our coming marriage – do you think she doesn't know about Jago?'

'I doubt they've told her,' Maya said, looking at her sadly. 'Her friends would know she would worry for him if she heard he'd been arrested for murder.'

'It's so unfair!' Julie burst out, her eyes filled with anxious tears. When she'd come to herself the morning after Harold Trevors' attack the first thing she'd asked Maya for was Jago but he wasn't there. The evidence was damning. Harold Trevors had been attacked from behind and the weapon used to kill him was Jago's stick. 'I've told Hank what happened. He came here to take my statement when you rang him. Why doesn't he believe me?'

'I think he does,' Maya told her, 'but he has superior officers who are insisting that Jago goes to trial because everyone knows that Jago had vowed to kill the man after he knocked Miss Vee down – and you are his wife-to-be. Had he arrived and seen that devil attacking you, he would have fought him any way he could. He might have killed him without meaning to go that far.'

'He didn't! Besides, why would I lie about what happened?' Julie asked, tears starting to run down her cheeks. 'I can't lose him, Maya. I just can't! I think I should want to die if they blamed him in court and took him away from us! I can't let this happen. I have to make Ralph Cotton confess to what he did!'

'He can't be found,' Maya told her. 'The law has men out looking for him and they'll find him eventually, no matter where he runs.'

'I know he attacked that man to save me,' Julie said, 'but he didn't mean to kill him so he was terrified and ran. Why can't Hank accept that and let Jago go?'

'We need a good lawyer to speak up for him,' Maya said and nodded her head. 'Get your coat, Julie. We're going to see Miss Vee. She'll know what to do. I'll drive Jago's truck and we'll go there right now.'

'Can you drive?' Julie was surprised.

'I learned years ago but I don't like it so I never do, but we have to get there and I'm not waiting for a bus that might not turn up for hours!'

Vee was sitting quietly with a book when Aggie showed them in. She looked up, immediately aware that something was wrong to bring her visitors here without a phone call or a specific invitation, because Maya never just called round, welcome though she'd have been.

'Is Jago all right?' she asked, her instincts alert.

'He's in prison!' Julie blurted out without even asking how Vee was in her anxiety. 'They think he killed Harold Trevors but he didn't. Ralph Cotton did that when that horrible man was trying to strangle me. He attacked him from behind but used Jago's walking stick, which I had taken with me just in case I needed it.' She paused to take a deep breath.

'Jago's been accused of murder? That's ridiculous,'

351

Vee said, outraged. 'Surely Hank knows him better than that? He must do!'

Julie had her breath back. 'He apologised, but the evidence pointed to Jago and I wasn't conscious. When I woke up I told Maya and then I told Hank. He said he believed me but his superiors say Jago has to stand trial unless they have sufficient evidence otherwise. They think I might lie to save Jago.' She stared at Vee miserably. 'He was working alone in the woods for a time so no one can say for sure what he did.'

'Have they spoken to Ralph Cotton about this? Surely what he did wasn't murder? He simply saved your life.' Vee frowned. 'This sounds like a bit of official stupidity to me.' She tapped her fingernails on the table beside her. 'I'll ring my lawyers immediately and we'll get Jago out on bail – and then we'll find Ralph and persuade him that the best course of action is to tell the truth with a good lawyer to defend him.'

'But if he won't confess or can't be found, they could still make Jago stand trial for something he didn't do,' Julie said through her tears.

Vee shook her head, a look of determination on her face. 'Not if I can help it. I know Hank's superior officers and I imagine I know who has been such a bloody-minded fool. I'll have a word or two.' She smiled at Julie. 'Everyone knows that Jago isn't a murderer. No one in the area would convict him. And if anyone tries, they will have me to contend with.'

This was said so fiercely that Julie gave a choked laugh. 'Thank you, thank you so much,' she said. 'I've been terrified that I might lose him and I love him so very much.'

Vee stood up and gathered her into her arms, stroking her hair. 'You and I are family,' she told her. 'I'll get the best lawyers to defend Jago if it should come to a trial but it won't. Once I've spoken to a few folk, Jago will be home and then we'll sort this mess out.'

'And you can just sit down and rest for a bit,' Aggie said coming in with a tray of coffee and her homemade biscuits. 'I'm not having you back in the hospital.'

'I'm as fit as a fiddle now,' Vee retorted. 'This was exactly what I needed to get me thinking and going again. It shook me the way that man came straight at me in his car, but now I have something more to fight for and I shall.'

'I'm sorry I had to do this,' Hank apologised as he let Jago out of the cell later that day. 'Miss Vee's lawyer told my boss the evidence is all circumstantial and with Miss Miller's solid testimony – and the fact that Ralph Cotton has done a bunk – we don't have enough proof to hold you. So they've allowed you out on bail.'

'That means I could still stand trial,' Jago said and frowned. 'Do you think I'm guilty, Hank?'

'No, my friend, but I had to do my duty and arrest you,' Hank admitted. 'You'd been heard to say you would shoot Harold Trevors on sight and he was attacking the woman you loved. The fact that it was your walking stick that killed him seemed cast-iron proof to some around here.'

Jago smiled oddly. 'Had I arrived when he was hurting her, I might well have killed him,' he said. 'I'm grateful to Ralph Cotton, Hank. If he stands trial for this, I'll use the lawyers Miss Vee sent to help me get him off.'

'Well, in my opinion, he was a bit of a hero and did us all a service – and I never thought I'd say that of that young man,' Hank stated wryly. 'I doubt he'll stand trial for more than manslaughter at most and should get a lenient sentence. If it were up to me, I'd give him a medal. Harold Trevors would have been executed for murder, and I wish it had happened that way.'

'Well, at least you know the truth,' Jago said. 'If you want me back here you know where I am. I shan't be running.'

'Never thought you would,' Hank said and offered his hand. 'Are we still friends?'

'Surely,' Jago replied and smiled, taking his hand in a firm grip that made Hank wince. 'Just glad we got that clear.'

He left the station but sat for a moment at the wheel of his truck before driving off. Miss Vee had got him out and his friends believed in his innocence, but unless Ralph Cotton was found and admitted the truth, he could still face trial for murder.

CHAPTER 38

Ralph had run away because he was scared of what he'd done, though in striking that man from behind he had undoubtedly saved Julie's life. Had he tried to fight him, Harold Trevors would probably have killed them both. Then he'd panicked and run, but now, after a few days of being cold, tired and hungry, Ralph decided he had no choice but to return to his aunt's house and throw himself on her mercy. Surely, she would help him out of this mess?

When he walked into the kitchen, he discovered that both his aunt and father were sitting there, and she looked as if she had been crying. Seeing Ralph walk in, looking dishevelled, she burst into tears.

'I thought you were dead!' she cried. 'Is it true? Did you kill that man?'

'I didn't mean to,' Ralph said, feeling sick with fear. 'I saw him trying to strangle Julie Miller and I just picked up a stick I saw lying on the ground and hit him. I thought it would just stun him but then I realised I'd killed him and I ran because I was scared. But I can't run forever. I'll have to turn myself in.'

'No, you can't run,' Ralph's father said and fixed him with a straight look. 'Is that the truth – no lies? Tell me now so that I can best help you.'

'It's the truth, Dad,' Ralph said. 'I just hit him to stop him killing her. I only meant to stop him, not kill him.'

'Then you're a hero not a villain and we'll get you the best lawyers available,' his father said. 'You're my son, Ralph, and no matter the foolish things you've done in the past, I love you. I'll stand by you and I promise they won't try you for murder.'

Ralph felt the tears well up inside him. He'd been a childish, arrogant fool to resent his father and aunt when all they wanted was the best for him. He'd thought his father mean for not giving him more but now he was offering to spend money to save him. In that moment, Ralph grew up. Standing with tears running down his cheeks, he felt his aunt and then his father embrace him. And understood how lucky he was – so much luckier than Pete, his friend, who had run off, goodness knows where, because his father was a murderous bully who had beaten him and lied to him.

'With the evidence they've found against Harold Trevors, it should be an open and shut case,' his father told him. 'That man would have stood trial for at least one murder and he'd have been executed. Who is going to convict you of murder? All you did was act instinctively to save a life.'

'You don't hate me for bringing shame on you?' Ralph said and couldn't believe it when his father smiled.

'You've done some bad things, Ralph, and I was angry when I heard about them, but I think you've learned your lesson. I want you to understand clearly that I will not tolerate such behaviour in future. However, what you did to save that girl was a brave act and I'm proud of you for owning up to it. If your blow hadn't felled him, Harold Trevors could have killed you, too.' He looked his son up and down. 'I think you should get cleaned up and then we'll take a ride into Halifax. We'll tell your story and, if they arrest you, I'll have you out of there by tomorrow.'

'Thanks, Dad,' Ralph said feeling a warmth inside that he hadn't known for a very long time. 'And you, Aunt Phyllis, for believing in me. I promise I won't let you down again.'

His father nodded. 'I don't think you will, Ralph. You've had a hard lesson and it isn't over. You may well have to stand trial for manslaughter and it could carry a prison sentence but we'll face that when we come to it.'

Ralph nodded. He was frightened, but he knew there was nothing else he could do. If he continued to run away, his life was in ruins. Now he had a chance that things would go well for him. One day, perhaps, he would love another girl and next time he would know the difference between love and lust. In the meantime, he had to trust his father and hope that a judge would believe him and spare him a prison sentence, because he wasn't sure he could take it.

Jago couldn't quite believe it when Hank came over in his official car later that evening to tell him that Ralph had told the police the exact same story as Julie.

'So your superior officers believed him but not her?'

'Love can sometimes make folk do foolish things,' Hank told him with a shrug, 'and the evidence did point at you. Besides, the boy's father has influential friends.'

'And he's in prison?' Jago asked. Hank looked embarrassed but shook his head.

'He was sent home with his father and told his case would be looked at, but it's likely he won't stand trial for much more than assault – and I expect him to get off with a community service. After all, he saved Julie's life.' He shuffled his feet. 'Don't be bitter that you got different treatment, Jago. You had a motive for murder and he didn't.'

'I'm not bitter,' Jago said and grinned. 'I'm glad. Ralph has caused problems in the past but I'm willing to forgive them, as is Julie, because he saved her life and that's all we really care about. I hope they dismiss the case. Harold Trevors only got what he deserved.'

'You don't know the half of it,' Hank agreed. 'That man got away with a lot of crimes and caused a lot of misery. I think you'll find folk round here will be behind Ralph all the way when the story gets out.'

Jago nodded. 'Trevors was a rich man but he was a greedy one – a selfish, evil man.'

'We might never have been able to prove any of it if we hadn't been told where to find his wife's body and given a little black book,' Hank said. 'I believe his son sent us the evidence. Ralph told us that he saw Harold beat him and he made Pete believe he'd killed a man while driving under the influence of alcohol – a killing he did himself. The pieces fit and we have more than one witness to his attempt to kill Miss Vee.'

'It's a pity he didn't get to suffer the consequences of his actions in law,' Jago said, 'but justice has been served.'

'Surely has,' Hank agreed. 'I just wanted to tell you that you're in the clear and to apologise again.'

'You were only doing your job,' Jago said, and hesitated. 'Would you stand up with me at my wedding? I was going to wait until the cabin was built, but Julie wants to get married on her birthday. She's asked Miss Vee, as her closest relative, to sign the consent forms and it's done.'

Hank's face was wreathed with smiles. 'I'd like that fine,' he told Jago. 'It's the best news I've heard in an age.'

'So it's next month,' Jago told him. 'Miss Vee is giving us the reception – she wouldn't take no for an answer and Maya agreed with her. She'll be giving Julie away, too.'

'Yes, she would want to do that,' Hank said and looked rueful. 'She gave me a right dressing down and the chief, too. I reckon he told me to let Ralph go because he thought she might go after him again if he didn't.'

'Miss Vee knows how to strike when she wants,' Jago replied. 'I wouldn't like to have been your chief.'

Hank laughed. 'I'll be on my way, then. Give my regards to your mother and Julie. I have to go arrest a few drunks to lock up for the night – keep the big chief happy the law still works round here.'

Hank went off chuckling. Jago had gone outside when he arrived, in case he was about to be rearrested, but at last he could put the sorry business behind him and as he went into the house, he saw that his mother and Julie were smiling.

'It is over,' Maya said and it wasn't a question. 'Now we can plan for the wedding.'

'Oh, Jago!' Julie cried and ran to him, putting her arms around him and resting her head against his strong body. She looked up at him, love and anxiety mingled in equal parts. 'Is Maya right? Is it truly over?'

'Yes. Ralph confessed. Apparently, he was coming here to apologise for his behaviour to you in the past, Julie. When he saw Harold Trevors attacking you, he just did what came instinctively. To many he will be a hero.'

'I told them what he did but they didn't believe me,' Julie said indignantly.

Jago gave a wry grin. 'Apparently, they thought you might lie to save my skin, though of course that was nonsense.'

'Well, I might, had it been necessary,' she said, 'but it wasn't.'

'No, it wasn't, because Ralph confessed. I never thought he had it in him, but it seems there's hope for him yet.'

'Yes, of course there is,' Julie agreed. 'I hated and feared him because he was nasty to me but now I've forgiven him. He saved my life – and perhaps yours too, Jago.'

'Yes, that may be the case and I'm grateful to him . . .' He hesitated, then, 'Shall we ask the family to the wedding?'

Julie looked at him for a moment. 'I suppose;

after all, if Miss Cotton hadn't paid for me to come out here, we would never have met.'

'Then we shall,' he said and looked at his mother. 'Do you agree, Maya?'

'It would be the right thing to do,' she said, 'though they may not wish to come. You must make a list of your guests for Miss Vee so she knows how many to expect.'

'I don't know anyone except the people you know,' Julie said. 'There was another little boy on the ship, and Davey, who disappeared, and Beth. I've told Miss Vee I'd like Beth to be my bridesmaid and she said Beth was so excited she couldn't sleep.'

'What was the other child's name?' Jago asked. 'We might be able to trace him and his new family.'

'He was called Arthur Gibbs but his new name was Henderson. A nice couple and they said they have a candy store in Halifax.'

'I'll ask Hank or Miss Vee,' Jago promised. 'One of them will know. We can ask them to the wedding too if we can trace them. I'll ask the men from the sawmill and their families – that way you'll begin to make friends, Julie – and of course, Selmer and Hank and his wife.' He looked at his mother. 'Is there anyone you'd like Maya?'

'Only one or two of my friends from church,' she said. 'They have families and some of them are Julie's age. Yes, let's ask them. It will be a good number and a happy time that we should share.'

'Yes, we must give thanks,' Jago said. 'We'll come to church with you next Sunday, Maya, and hear the banns read.'

CHAPTER 39

It was a beautiful August day, Julie's wedding day. She'd made her own dress, a simple gown of white silk with long sleeves and a round neck that made her look as sweet and virginial as she truly was . . . a young girl who shone with happiness. The reception had grown to include a lot of Miss Vee's friends too and was being held in the large barn that Jago had taken Julie to on the night of the dance.

'We may as well celebrate in style,' Vee had told them when they questioned the need for such a big venue. 'Let's show everyone the bond between us, Jago. It will help to clear any last rumours or reserve on the part of the community and it's time we had something wonderful to enjoy around here.'

Jago had given in gracefully. Beth was Julie's number one bridesmaid but two of the young girls she had taught sewing to had come forward and asked if they could be as well and she'd agreed.

Two days before the wedding, Miss Cotton arrived with a large box tied with pretty ribbons. 'This is from my brother and Ralph and me,' she told Julie.

'I am sorry I didn't believe you when you complained of his behaviour. If I had, he might not be in trouble now.'

'It doesn't matter to me,' Julie said, 'but I'm sorry Ralph is still in trouble. I'd hoped that my testimony would see him exonerated.'

'Well, the lawyers say they are hopeful that he won't get a custodial sentence. He may be let off with a caution and the proviso that he could be brought before the courts again if he's involved in any trouble or acts of violence. He may also have to do some kind of work for the community in his spare time.'

'That doesn't seem fair,' Julie said and Miss Cotton gave a little sniff.

'Life is seldom fair, Miss Miller. You had nothing when I brought you out to Canada and now you have a whole new life. Whereas Ralph's is in ruins . . .' She coloured as she realised how that sounded, and Julie knew she was still the same person as before, even though she had come to apologise.

'Yes, I was lucky, but Miss Vee was looking for me so I should probably have come one day anyway,' she said, deciding to ignore the slight accusation in Miss Cotton's voice. She probably didn't mean it the way it sounded.

'I wanted to say thank you for the invitation but we shan't come – it might not be appropriate at the moment. Please apologise to Mrs Bittern for me.'

'Yes, of course I will,' Julie agreed.

After Miss Cotton had gone, Julie shrugged. Sometimes you couldn't help other folk, even if you tried. Miss Cotton had let pride get in the way, but that was her affair. Ralph hadn't been as reticent. He'd been to see Jago at the sawmill and asked him for a job.

'If they let me off with a warning, would you take me on, Mr Marsh?' he'd asked. 'I'd rather work for you than my father, even though we're getting on better these days.'

'Yes, I'll give you a job,' Jago told him. 'Come to me when you're able and we'll see how you like it.' He'd looked intently at Julie when he'd told her. 'You don't mind that I said he could have a job?'

'No, I don't mind,' she told him and hugged him. 'He wasn't like my uncle, who is truly bad, just a silly lad, showing off. Oh, Jago, I'm so happy I don't mind anything as long as I have you and Maya and Miss Vee – and Beth. She really is like my sister and is looking forward to the wedding so much.'

'That's good,' he said and held her, gazing down into her face. 'We're all happy, my dearest girl.'

Now it was the day of the wedding. Julie had gone to stay with Vee the previous night, because it was unlucky to see the groom on the morning of the wedding. Maya had looked regretful, because she'd wanted to help her dress but she couldn't leave Jago.

'He wouldn't be able to knot his tie if I wasn't here,' she'd said with a loving smile. 'I can't recall him ever wearing one before.'

'Poor Jago. He'll be so uncomfortable in a suit and tie,' Julie had giggled and then the smile left her face. 'I keep thinking how nice it would have been if Cousin Vee's brother had been here. She hasn't said much but I know she's worried sick. Nothing official has come but nor have any letters or postcards from him.'

'I know she's worried,' Maya had said, then smiled. 'But Julie, I have a feeling all will be well.'

'Do you really see things in the future?'

'Yes, sometimes. Sometimes it's just flashes of people or happenings but at others it's just a feeling. Of late I have sensed that Mr Malcolm is close. For some reason he is hesitating but I do not know why . . .'

Julie had hugged her and kissed her cheek. 'You are wonderful! I think it's where Jago gets his kindness from.'

The older woman had shaken her head. 'That is all his own, Julie. I am not always as kind in my thoughts as Jago. He may have learned patience from me but he is himself and that is all any of us can be.'

Maya was so wise, Julie thought now on the morning of her wedding. Jago was himself. He had been hurt many times but he had never become bitter. He was gentle and kind, honest, true and brave – and that was why she loved him so much.

She made her way downstairs, Vee following behind. Aggie and Beth and the other two girls were standing there, watching her descend and they both cried out in delight as they saw her.

'You look beautiful,' Aggie told her. 'Doesn't she look beautiful today, Beth?'

'Julie is always beautiful,' Beth said in her innocent fashion and darted forwards to receive a kiss and give her a bouquet of beautiful flowers. There were scented lilies, roses and some other sweet flower that Julie did not know the name of and she smiled as she held them to her nose.

365

'You are beautiful too, Beth,' Julie said and kissed her. 'Do you like my lovely flowers?'

'Jago sent them,' Aggie told her as Beth nodded. 'He sent flowers for the bridesmaids and us too – wasn't that thoughtful of him?'

'Jago *is* thoughtful,' Vee said, smiling her approval. 'Is that the car I can hear?' she asked and looked towards the door as it opened. She gave a little scream of delight as she saw who it was. 'Malcolm! Oh, thank God! I thought you'd been killed.'

'Vee, I'm so sorry,' he said and came towards her immediately. 'I was wounded again after we left Malta and then in hospital for a very long time. Someone wrote to you for me but you obviously didn't get the letter . . .'

'I would forgive you anything,' Vee began, her face alight with relief at seeing him. Then her eyes went beyond him to a young woman standing half in and half out of the room. 'Perhaps you should introduce us, Malcolm – who is this young lady?'

Malcolm looked slightly uncomfortable as he beckoned the girl forward. She wasn't a young girl, perhaps in her early thirties and attractive but not beautiful. 'This is Sheila – the nurse who brought me back to life, Vee. She's my wife . . .'

'Your wife?' Vee stared at him and then went to embrace Sheila. 'Welcome, my dear. You are so very welcome to our family. I never thought it would happen for my brother but I am so glad it did!'

A look of relief flashed over Malcolm's face as he held out his hand to his wife. 'There, I told you so. Sheila was afraid you wouldn't approve of her.'

'If she makes you happy, I love her,' Vee said. 'I want to hear all about it, Malcolm, but it will have to wait until later – we have a wedding to go to. You two won't make it to the church but you must come to the reception afterwards and I'll tell you all my news.'

'A wedding?' Malcolm looked at her incredulously and then saw Julie. He laughed. 'For a moment I thought you'd decided to make poor old Selmer a happy man.'

'No, I haven't and I shan't,' Vee said, raising her eyebrows. 'I like him and I trust him – but there was only ever one man for me. I have a family now and it is growing. That is more than enough for me!'

CHAPTER 40

Jago looked at his bride as she began her walk down the aisle towards him. She was so beautiful, so serene and innocent and lovely in the simple dress she had made herself. After today she would have many young girls asking her to make theirs for them, he was sure. Never in his life had Jago expected to marry and his bride's beauty took his breath. How could a man like him deserve her? Yet he knew that she truly loved him, that she wanted this marriage as much as he did and Maya had told him that theirs would be a long and happy life with several children.

'That is the future I saw for you by the lake,' she'd told him that morning. 'I knew there was some darkness to come – and it did – but that is past now. You have the future to make yourself and I know you will make it well.'

'If I do, it is because you taught me the true meaning of life,' he'd said and embraced her. 'I am lucky to have you as my mother.'

'I have been lucky to have you. And now you will have Julie and you must love and protect her always, just as your father did me until his death. He would have been so proud of you, Jago, of all you have achieved. It could have been otherwise . . .'

'No, it could not. As a child I was stubborn like you, Maya, and I refused to give in to the bullies and their taunts. As I grew older and stronger, I knew they no longer mattered. Those born with a disability have no choice but to live with it – but how they live is their choice and I chose to be happy despite it.'

'You always will be, my dearest son,' Maya told him. 'You will make Julie happy – and do not fear, your sons will be whole.'

'How did you know I wondered about that?' he asked and then he'd smiled. 'But of course you knew. I know that my disability does not have to be reflected in my children. I asked the specialist about it, years ago, and he said it was unlikely to be something that was passed on. He couldn't tell me why it happened to me, but he reassured me that I would most likely have healthy children.'

'I know that you will. I think God gave you the mark you carry because He knew that you could bear it. God seldom gives us more than we can bear – and if He does, He carries it for us.'

'You are a special woman,' Jago told her then. 'I never thought I could find a woman as special as you, Maya, but in Julie I believe I have.'

Maya had smiled. 'Perhaps she is even more special than I,' she said and kissed his forehead. 'Now we must leave. It's the bride's privilege to be late but not ours . . .'

Now, as Julie walked down the aisle towards him

and stood by his side their eyes met and held in a look of shared love and joy in their wedding day. The church was filled with friends, with people who had come to wish them happiness and, when they emerged as man and wife at the end of a beautiful service, others were waiting to shower them with rose petals and give small gifts to the bride for good luck.

Julie smiled the whole time, holding on to Jago's arm and slowing her steps to match his. Her happiness was there for everyone to see and everyone was laughing and talking, excitement in the air as they gathered for the reception.

'You have made me very proud,' Jago whispered to her as they received their guests. 'I am very lucky to have found you, my love.'

'I just want to be with you all my life,' she whispered back and saw the answering glow in his eyes.

Her heart was full. She had never believed life could be this good for her and she still felt that she was dreaming sometimes. It was after they had cut the cake, which Aggie had cooked and Miss Vee had iced with delicate artistry, that her friend came up to her, looking into her face searchingly.

'Is everything as you wanted it, dearest?'

'It is more than I could have ever asked for,' Julie replied and kissed her. 'I haven't seen Arthur, though. Did Hank manage to find him?'

'Halifax is a big place,' Vee said vaguely. 'He hasn't yet but no doubt he will.'

Julie nodded. It was just a small request she'd made, wanting to know that the child who had travelled out with her was well and happy, as loved as she and Beth were, but the thought disappeared from her mind as she and Jago circulated, thanking and talking to their guests. They had been given many gifts, some small and some much more valuable, including a porcelain tea and dinner service and some silver cutlery from Miss Vee and towels and tablecloths from the families of Jago's crew. Julie was delighted with every gift. She had never owned very much and to have so many things for her new home was almost overwhelming.

Jago's cabin was nowhere near built yet, so for the time being they would continue to live with Maya, though Jago was taking Julie away for a few days. He wanted to show her more of the country that was now her home and explore parts that he'd never seen himself.

It was all new and exciting and she could hardly contain the feelings that bubbled inside her, just as the French champagne Miss Vee had provided bubbled up her nose.

First of all, they were going to stay in a little house in Upper Sackville that Miss Vee had loaned them for the night and then they would travel on, but as yet Julie didn't know where they were going. It hardly mattered. She was Jago's wife, no longer a homeless charity girl and life could not have been better.

Later that evening, as she lay in her husband's arms and touched his face, her cheeks wet with tears of gratitude and joy, she understood how lucky she was to have married a man who was sensitive to her every response, a man who gave far more than he took and was generous with his love so that she had known a wonderfully gentle pleasure.

Julie had wondered how she would respond to the physical side of marriage for her memories of being touched had filled her with revulsion, but Jago had made her forget her fears and brought the woman inside her to glowing life.

'Are you all right?' he asked after their loving and touched her damp cheek. 'Did I hurt you?'

'Not at all,' she said. 'My tears are of joy, Jago, my love, nothing more. I am content and happy.' She was happy and believed that happiness would last as long as she had the man she loved, beside her.

EPILOGUE

'You didn't tell her about the boy, Arthur?' Aggie said that evening when they were sitting in Vee's parlour enjoying a last cup of coffee before retiring. 'What Hank told you?'

'She asked and I said Hank hadn't found him yet.' Vee frowned. 'If you mean, did I tell her that the shop his adoptive parents used to run was closed and no one seemed to know where the family had gone, no I didn't. I didn't want her to worry on her wedding day. Hank hasn't given up on his inquiries. He wants to know now for his own peace of mind. Folk don't just disappear like that for nothing. It was a thriving business until a short time ago. What could have made them give it up and just go without telling anyone?'

'They probably just decided to move elsewhere,' Malcolm said and his wife nodded. 'I can't see where the mystery is, Vee. I met them when they collected the boy and they seemed a decent couple, anxious for a child to love and raise.' He was thoughtful and then, 'Perhaps because of the war and Halifax being an

373

important military area they thought it safer to move inland.'

'Yes, well, I hope that is all it is,' Vee replied, 'but Hank has got a bee in his bonnet over it and he'll keep searching now he's started.' She gave a little sigh and changed the subject. 'Why don't you tell me more about how you two met and fell in love?'

Sheila blushed and looked shy, but Malcolm reached for her hand. 'Sheila nursed me – and I was in quite a bad way, Vee. It happened on the way back from our trip to Malta. The ship was hit and several of us were injured, though it didn't sink – that's why you didn't get an official notice. I had a letter sent when we limped into a British port but then I collapsed and it was touch and go for a while. The ship needed a lot of repairs, and when she sailed it was without me, because I was in a British hospital. I think it was bound for Malta again.'

'I've been sick with worry,' Vee said, 'thinking you lost at sea or dead, but it doesn't matter now that you are home.'

'Good.' He smiled at her. 'Before I left England, I went to see our distant relatives. They're managing at the moment but I offered to pay their fares if they wanted to come out. They thanked me but seem set on staying put so we'll send them as much as we can in food and clothing.' His gaze went to Sheila. 'It was then I discovered Sheila was a friend of our Great-Aunt Annie. She'd been staying with her and helping her now that she's living alone and our distant cousins are all serving in the forces.'

'Well, that was nice,' Vee approved thoughtfully. 'Have you two considered where you will live?'

'We can manage in the rooms above the shop for now,' he said. 'I'll sort something out, don't worry.'

'You must buy a nice house not too far away from me,' she said. 'In fact, I've had my eye on a good property only a few blocks away. If you like it, I'll give it to you as a wedding gift.'

Malcolm nodded and smiled. 'Always the same Vee, wanting to look after me. It seems you're becoming a property tycoon. What got into you?'

'You bringing me Beth,' she replied smartly. 'Life was dull before that but it has been anything but since. So I owe you a nice gift for giving me such a wonderful one, brother.'

'Then I'll give you one,' he replied, eyes gleaming. 'Sheila is going to have our baby and I'm giving up the sea. I'll look around for a job and see what takes my fancy. I can do some volunteer work for the war effort but I'm too old to be conscripted, even if they bring it in, which I doubt they will.'

'You could help me or run the store,' she suggested but he shook his head.

'Selmer and you manage quite nicely. No, I'll start a business of some kind. I have money put by and a few ideas. I think I might like either a bookshop or an antique shop.'

'Well, I have an empty shop just waiting for someone to take it on,' Vee said. 'I think it would be big enough to sell both antiques and books . . . a lovely combination.'

Her brother laughed. 'You're determined to look after me whatever I do,' he said and gave in with good grace. 'I'll look at your shop, Vee, and if it suits me, I'll rent it from you for a start but then I might want to buy it.'

'Whatever you want,' she said, yawned and stood up. 'I'm going to bed. I understand you want a home of your own, Sheila, but until you find it, please consider this house yours.'

She kissed them both and left them to do as they pleased. Going softly into Beth's room, she saw her child sleeping peacefully. Beth was tired out after her exciting day. People had made a fuss of her, telling her how pretty she looked in her pale pink silk frock, which was hanging outside the wardrobe so that she could look at it before she went to sleep.

Vee was tired too, though pleasantly so. It had been a successful and busy day and wonderful to see the young couple so happy and so much in love. It was funny how love could change lives. She'd been so happy with Bill for all those years and for a moment she felt a pang of regret that he wasn't here to share her pleasure in the child and Malcolm's return.

His marriage had been such a surprise, but a marvellous one. The news that Sheila was to have a child was overwhelming. So much to look forward to for the future. Times had been troubled of late and she hoped that now they were going to improve.

Across the water in Britain, the people were still struggling, short of food and suffering in many, many ways so Vee would continue to raise funds to send food parcels to them; it was a small token but it helped and she felt closer ties to that country now that she'd found Julie.

Once again, she smiled at the happiness of the young couple. It was so nice to see and Julie deserved her good fortune.

As she undressed in her own room and got into bed, Vee thought once again of the little boy Julie had asked her to find. Despite Malcolm's reassuring words it seemed strange that Arthur and his adoptive parents should simply disappear like that. She hoped that Hank would be able to find them and that she could give Julie good news of the boy or, better still, arrange for him to visit his friends from the ship.

'Oh, blow it!' she muttered as the desire for sleep left her. She knew she wouldn't be able to stop thinking about Arthur, and she would need to find a way to reconcile her thoughts. As she lay restless, she made up her mind that if Hank couldn't find the family – or his official work took him from the search – she would find a way herself.

Having decided that, she felt herself relax and was soon drifting off into a peaceful sleep, dreaming of all her plans for the future.

Read more about Cathy Sharp's orphans whose compelling stories will tug at your heartstrings.

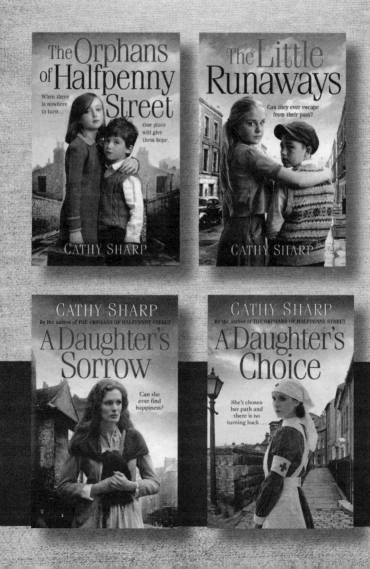

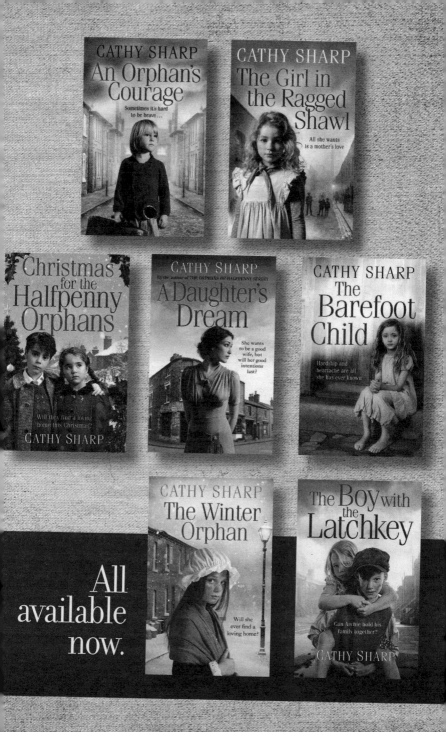

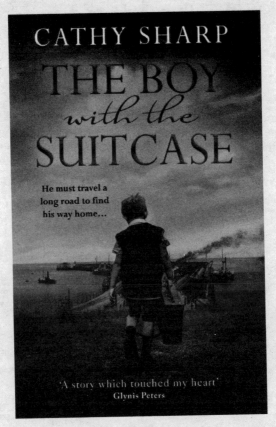